The Beta

Kirsten Erickson

Copyright © 2018 Kirsten Erickson

All rights reserved.
ISBN: 9798678795403

The Beta

June 17th
2018

Molly Wood interviewing Melinda Gates in the "Make me Smart" Podcast on NPR's Marketplace:

Q. Molly Wood: And of course, everyone knows that you worked in tech yourself. You were at Microsoft in the '80s and '90s, you have a degree in computer science, an MBA, but to your point about what's happening in the United States, there were more female computer science grads back then than there are now. What do you think has happened?

A. Melinda Gates: Nobody actually knows. Again, I've gone back to look at the data, what has been collected, on why we've lost so many women getting computer science degrees at the undergraduate level and nobody truly knows the answer. But the belief is from when you look at when that peak happened, which was about at the time I was in computer science, the industry became a few years after that very gamified. The big thing being sold on personal computers at the time were these games. And a lot of them were sort of shoot-em-up games, war kinds of things. And when you used to have Pac-Man or the adventure kinds of games, girls were interested in those things, women were interested in those things. The more, sort of, social or neutral games. But as soon as the gaming industry became very male-dominated, very male-focused, girls sort of started to leave the field in droves, saying, "I'm just not interested in that."

Me: "Yeah, like Melinda said. I'm just not interested in that."

Dear Google Earth,

As a young gi I always loved maps, and I still remember the shiver that went down my spine the first time I accessed Google Earth. Seriously—the whole world at my fingertips!

Concerning Google Earth History, please be aware that I will sign any necessary paperwork that whets the legal appetites of your vast array of lawyers to establish I have no claim to such a futuristic project—as long as you promise to get to work and make this dream come true. I need a decent VR history curriculum for my child which means you have ten years to roll out Google Earth History for School.

Last note—hire a few teachers, will ya?

Dear Microsoft,

I am a Microsoft kid and have always been impressed with the philanthropic efforts of The Bill and Melinda Gates Foundation. As a Washington State teacher, I watched first hand as the Foundation struggled to find a way to impact education. I'm not surprised, as educating kids is harder than eradicating disease, which often has a more straightforward fix. The Bill and Melinda Gates Foundation will make a future impact in education. Learn from your mistakes and don't give up!

Dear Amazon,

You are my Washington State peeps and the only company for which I have been willing to share my credit card info with—drastically limiting my online shopping opportunities. I love you and I hate you. With power comes great responsibility. Use it wisely. The way you physically connect our world may someday pave the way for advances in education.

Dear Facebook,

Much relieved to hear that education would be a major focus of the Chan Zuckerburg Foundation I was pleasantly surprised to see education at the top of the list. I predict Facebook's contribution to education will be sometime in the near future and have something to do with all the data ya' gathered. Data, data, data.

Dear all other Tech and Gaming Companies,

Make more games for girls. Or better yet, simply focus on better games with less violence. It's that easy. Make a choice. Make the right choice.

The Beta

Dear Tencent,

I think you are going to save the world from Global Warming and so I want to extend my thanks ahead of time. Maybe the solution will include gamifying the environment? Thank You!

The Author

June 5th
2008

J.K. Rowling in an address to Harvard graduating class:

"Imagination is not only the uniquely human capacity to envision that which is not, and therefore the fount of all invention and innovation. In its arguably most transformative and revelatory capacity, it is the power that enables us to empathise with humans whose experiences we have never shared…

…Unlike any other creature on this planet, humans can learn and understand, without having experienced. They can think themselves into other people's places.

Of course, this is a power, like my brand of fictional magic, that is morally neutral. One might use such an ability to manipulate, or control, just as much as to understand or sympathise…"

Very Good Lives: Copyright © J.K. Rowling 2008

-No apartments or futuristic skyrise trailers were exploded in the making of this book.

Prologue

Johanna opened the door to get out of the car then reached back inside to pull out her hardhat. It was sleek, black, and sexy. Or at least that is what she told herself whenever she cringed at the thought of having to wear the sweaty accessory all day long. After all, she wasn't the brawn on the jobsite. She was the brains.

But she did follow the rules. OSHA rules, company rules, and blueprint rules all in addition to the rules she made up herself. While she wasn't technically in charge of any employees at the Umatilla site, as lead engineer she could overrule almost any decision or action unilaterally.

Her car had been toasty warm with the bright January sun heating up the interior on the drive in, but as soon as she stood up a chilling wind pulled out wisps of hair along her neck. She knew better than to try and fight them until she reached the interior of the worksite.

The infrastructure layer was nearly complete and that would quickly be followed by the perimeter layer and finally the data layer, the layer for which she was wholly responsible. In order to get out of the wind she headed to the section of the building that would eventually serve as a secure entry to the facility. She waved to a few colleagues from afar and headed into the building.

A vibration on her leg indicated her husband was calling. Still in the wind she picked up her phone while shielding the microphone. "Hey babe?" She answered in a mix of greeting and question.

"Morning sweetie, how was the drive down?" her husband asked. Johanna could hear the baby and three-year-old in the background.

"Smooth. How are my little guys?"

The Beta

"Ahhh . . ." the pause was accompanied by some shuffling and a plaintive cry. ". . .We're fine. Just fine. But do you remember seeing George?"

George was their three-year-old's stuffed bunny. No wonder her husband was calling her this early. A day without George would be a long one and she wasn't due back to the house for a week. "Did you check the backseat of the Jeep?"

"No. That must be it." Johanna could now hear more shuffling. He was probably heading straight out to the garage.

Johanna waited patiently until she heard more heavy breathing, a few doors opening, and then her son calling out for the toy.

"We got him. You are a life saver."

"I love you."

"Love you too."

Johanna was surrounded by boys at work and boys at home, and one perk was that she often had the women's bathroom all to herself.

She tidied up her hair under her hardhat and was leaving the bathroom when she ran smack into her direct superior, which caused her to jump in surprise.

This was a direct superior who was never on-site without notifying her ahead of time. Alarm bells began to ring. Had something gone wrong? Was she in trouble? Johanna was not used to feeling like this and she didn't like surprises.

"Did I startle you?" he asked calmly.

"Yes, a little." Johanna replied with a tactically even voice. "What brings you here?"

"Well . . ." He held up a thin manila envelope. "I want to show you what's in here." He motioned for her to go ahead of him. "Let's talk in the secure room."

Johanna took a deep but undetectable breath and used the short walk to calm her sympathetic nervous system. She didn't think this was how a firing would begin, but then, she had never been fired before.

They sat down together and it was his constant smile that belayed her fear of firing but made her altogether more curious

The Beta

and irritated at the same time. What information would he bring all this way in an envelope instead of their normal phone call or email communication? Manilla envelopes were quite old school.

But he didn't waste any time. "I have your next project here." He handed over the envelope and waited expectantly.

She opened it to discover a simple three-page memo. There was a security notice across the top, but unlike Amazon's government contracts, this clearance was internal company business.

Johanna was able to scan the memo quickly. It outlined the familiar process of building a data center. Over the last ten years Johanna had overseen the building of five separate data centers, as they were her expertise, and this project looked no different. It was slated to be built on the Columbia River in Washington State, near copious amounts of clean energy and a tech-ready workforce. Amazon's data centers around the world were tightly secured and the specs on this center looked normal. Why in the world would he treat these plans so differently?

Between scanning paragraphs Johanna kept looking up at him with a quizzical face. His eyes were dancing, waiting for her to figure out the surprise.

It was there, on the very last line. "What the. . .?" Johanna asked out loud. "Why in the. . .? This makes no sense?" She was confused, befuddled, and a bit offended all at the same time.

"It's Amazon's contribution. This is your next project Johanna."

She read the last line to herself over and over again in disbelief. As an AWS lead engineer she was in charge of building an entire data center that would be used exclusively by Google.

"What's the catch? What do we get in return? How can they use our servers without our software, they're inseparable!"

He smiled again. "What will we get in return? Think deep."

One year later.

The data center had been fast tracked and was to-date the quickest build ever completed in Amazon's history. Johanna stood in the middle of the data center ready to "flip the switch," which

The Beta

essentially meant after all systems were finally in operation she would personally call corporate and share the good news.

"Well, here we go." She was surrounded by her co-workers for this last celebratory step. A bright spring sunshine shown down on them and half the crew was already wearing summer clothes.

None besides herself actually knew that all these servers, rows and rows of data and the computing power, would be used by their rival Google. But it was all for a good cause.

Johanna flipped the switch.

In the Mainframe, over 800 miles south of Johanna's data center, a crowd was waiting patiently. They were all busy, some on computers, some in Virtual Reality and others milling about in conversational collaboration. They had everything to do and nothing to do. This brief moment of silence was like the nothingness before the Big Bang, both figuratively and literally.

Mark looked over at Doug who was breathing in coffee mug fumes in nervous anticipation. Doug looked up.

"Ever thought we'd be working together again?" Doug mused. "Especially on something like this?"

Mark nodded, and that was when he noticed the coffee mug Doug was holding. It was covered in images of Christmas, with the jolly old elf himself sitting front and center next to a fireplace.

In fact, the whole room was mutely festooned in odd Christmas paraphernalia. An odd stocking here, a picture of Santa Claus there, and more than a few hanging bits of real holly someone brought from home were hanging above the doorways.

Mark's thoughts were interrupted by Doug, who jumped half-a-mile when his phone vibrated.

The co-workers surrounding Doug hushed as he answered his phone. There were no details to be gleaned as Doug simply nodded to himself and said, "yes, yes," to various prompts. But his smile grew and so did the excitement of those around him.

Finally Doug hung up the phone, reached his arms out wide and said in a booming voice, "Let Operation North Pole begin!"

The Beta

There were a few minutes of outright whooping and hollering as the news spread across the expansive space. No sooner did each set of ears hear the news than everyone began rushing to specific workstations much like the Star Trek crew heading to their battle stations.

"Can you really believe we're doing this?" Doug asked Mark.

"At least I get to watch history in the making."

"Then here we go." Doug hit the button.

The Mainframe was an old school tech term repurposed to accurately describe a huge room covered in multiple workstations, each with a large screen and various peripherals.

Suddenly the screens all went black. This quieted the room of any leftover sound and a stillness settled over the hive.

Deep in the ground a connection 800 miles away was being formed between two of the greatest tech companies of the modern age. Information was flowing, processors began to process, all actions necessary to launch a partnership never seen before.

Above the ground in the quiet and dark Mainframe something began to appear on the empty black screens. A tiny light shown at the center of each and then suddenly exploded in light.

Doug smiled over at Mark as if to say, 'Did you get that?' They had known each other long enough to understand the unspoken message.

The light coalesced into the sun and spinning frantically through billions of years, the Earth formed right before their eyes.

Mark took in a deep breath. Much of what was done and would be done to this digital planet relied heavily on the work he did at Deep Mind. But the particulars, the details, the controls, those would all be the exclusive province of Doug and his crew at Google Earth History.

Slowly, after everyone had a chance to marvel at the replica of Earth in front of them, the twirling subsided and a slow zoom took the viewers down over the Northern Hemisphere and into the frosty polar region. An icon popped up that read, 'The North Pole.'

Doug's voice now echoed over a loudspeaker to the entire Mainframe. "This is the North Pole!"

The Beta

    Cheers broke out and suddenly the controls for each screen splintered as crews jumped into VR gear and entered the simulation. Inside of the North Pole icon was a smaller icon of a little house. Each screen showed the participants clicking on the house and entering a winter wonderland scene.

    Mark could hear exclamations of awe as engineers, coders, and UX designers got their first glimpse of the virtual town that would control all of this digital Earth.

    Doug had one last thing to say. "Welcome to Santa's Workshop."

The Beta

Part One
The Beginning

She didn't want to do it.
She didn't want to do it.
She didn't want to do it.

Before Kira decided to go through with it, she only had a passing awareness of the security cameras at her school. But in the weeks leading up to the day she painstakingly located every security camera; those in the parking lot, above all the entrances, the hallways and cafeteria.

The only places that seemed to escape their prying eyes were classrooms, bathrooms, and locker rooms.

Totally compulsive, Kira planned her route for weeks. She didn't want to deviate too far from her normal routine, because even if a camera couldn't watch what she was doing inside a locker room, the hallway cameras were sure to capture when she entered and exited.

So far, she hadn't opened her backpack. But her conscience could feel the weight of the four items inside as easily as . . .

She took a deep breath. She didn't want to do it. But she would.

The first step was easy. Her second period class was PE and the weather was warm. Dressing down in the locker room as normal she made sure to take a little longer. When her friend Emma yelled at her from the door to hurry up she replied, "I have to use the bathroom! Tell Mrs. Wilson I will be a minute."

The Beta

"Gross!" Emma yelled back as she held her nose and ran out the door laughing.

Kira was alone in the locker room. Instead of heading to the bathroom stalls she reopened her locker and pulled out her back pack. It was now or never.

She slowly unzipped it, holding her breath without thinking. Inside was a large plastic bag and next to it were three small plastic bags containing plastic gloves. Boy, was she paranoid.

It felt awkward. This certainly didn't come naturally to her. She didn't know exactly what to do next. Did she pull out the plastic bags and walk over to the other side of the locker room? Or did she walk her backpack over to the other side of the room and then pull out the plastic bags? From where she was standing now, no one entering the locker room could see her. But as soon as she arrived at her destination she would be in full view of the door.

Just do it, just do it real fast.

She didn't want to do it.

But she would.

She opened the small plastic bag and yanked on the plastic gloves. Then, gingerly, she opened the big bag and pulled out a thin manila envelope. When she packed in the morning she carefully laid out four unmarked envelopes, oriented from front to back so she knew exactly which was which.

Practically running and at the same time holding the envelope like it was a bomb, Kira made it across the room to locker 787. It was a sports locker. She wasn't sure who it belonged to, maybe a volleyball or softball player. Kira had no idea how athletic lockers were organized, but the important thing was that it was a big locker. She shoved the envelope into one of the air vents at the top. It made it about an inch up before getting stuck and crinkling up.

"Uggh," she muttered quietly. "Just go you!" She tried the next vent and the next vent but the envelope wouldn't fit. What the heck was she going to do?

The Beta

Kira jiggled the lock but it held tightly. Thankful for her plastic gloves, she felt along the locker groping for an idea. When her fingers hit the bottom, she gave the locker a little lift and squeezed the envelope inside an inch at a time. About halfway through it got stuck again, so she tried to pull it out but it wouldn't budge. What had she gotten herself into?

Feeling frantic now she repeatedly lifted, pushed and alternately pulled trying to get the envelope either in or out; she didn't care which. On her hands and knees, she got eye level with the crack at the bottom of the locker, as if peering inside the dark locker could give her a clue.

But it did! Something inside was blocking the envelope and if she tried a little to the left...ta da! Pushing with the tip of her plastic covered fingertips, she squished all but a tiny fraction of the envelope inside the locker. Unless you really looked closely, you could never tell it was there.

She ran back to her backpack and then paused with her gloved hands halfway inside. Kira carefully stripped off both gloves and moved them to a back pocket she had specifically labeled in her mind as the "used" pocket.

Three envelopes and two pairs of gloves to go.

The second drop off was both easier and harder. She had to go to a part of her high school she had never been to before, through the band room and into equipment storage. Luckily, the teacher wasn't around and all she had to do was mumble about looking for an extension cord to one of the clarinet players and she found herself all alone in a room with a lock. Working quickly, she locked the door, pulled out her gloves and placed the envelope on a shelf crowded with old music and marching band straps. There was no one to see her exit the band room.

The third drop off almost made her puke. First off, it was the room of one of her nicest teachers, and it made her feel terrible that she was doing such an atrocious thing right under his nose, but it couldn't be helped. Secondly, it was going to be almost impossible to be in the room alone. How the heck was she going to use plastic gloves? Maybe she should give up trying to use the gloves.

But determined to keep her fingerprints and skin cells off the envelope, Kira put the plastic glove on her left hand in the bathroom before class and then casually kept it in her hoodie pocket.

Halfway to class she cursed out loud. The inside of her hoodie was probably crawling with her own skin cells and now they were covering her sterile glove. She was so stupid. Oh well, at least they would have fewer skin cells. And it was all a numbers game.

She sat in her regular seat in the back. Normally she placed her backpack to the front right of her seat but today she tried the back-left corner and unzipped the main pocket so she could see the third envelope through the crack. Kira leaned back casually with her left hand in her hoodie and her right hand clutching a pencil.

She glanced briefly around the room.

Kira could feel her stomach start to churn. But she had to do it.

Class took forever and she spent almost the whole time growing antsier as her teacher lectured on and on. History was her least favorite subject, it was so boring and completely useless. She kept glancing over at the bookshelf where she was supposed to leave the third envelope right between two binders. How was she ever going to get the envelope there without anyone noticing?

Finally, with ten minutes to go they broke out into their groups to resume working on posters. She could either find a way to do it now or after school. But if she waited until after school it would ruin all her other plans. The entire reason she was doing this in the first place was for that last envelope—her three o'clock appointment.

Giving up all hope of keeping her skin cells off the goods she reached in her backpack and pulled out both a folder and the envelope in one swift motion. From her current angle in the back of the room no one could see the envelope. Her final destination was only six feet away and no one was blocking her path. Slowly, nonchalantly she acted like she was going toward the side of the room to join her group and then let her attention wander to the bookshelf. Placing her body so it would block her movements she slipped the folder and envelope in between the two binders and smoothly pulled out the folder. She was getting good at this.

"Are you thinking of joining the Geography Bee?" asked a voice behind her. While it took a second for her consciousness to register the words, her body jumped half a foot.

She turned to see her history teacher smiling at her and an "um yeah" slipped out before she could think of anything else to say. She would rather die before entering any geography bee.

He reached over and pulled out the Geography Bee binder and she lost all hope. He was going to find her out and she was going to be in so much trouble!

But in a last bid she flipped her demeanor to that of a confident and excited potential Geography Bee participant. "What do I need to do to enter?" she asked as she tried to block the view of the empty space in the bookshelf between them.

Her teacher opened the notebook and was flipping through carefully organized papers. "Here are the entry forms from the last two years. It looks like school registration happens in about a month."

"A month?" Kira gulped. What was she getting herself into? She didn't know anything about geography.

"Good thing you brought this up or I may have forgotten to get this rolling. It's been a busy year so far." He was still flipping through the binder. Moving to the back to a section labeled study materials he opened the binder clips and pulled out a thick section. It was like an inch thick.

"I'm not really sure . . ." was all Kira could say. It was working, her teacher wasn't looking at the shelf.

"I'll make some copies of these and get the signup sheet ready. You can find them online if you want to start studying." He smiled at her once again. "Now get to work, you only have a few minutes left in class."

"Yes, thanks." She said and unwillingly walked away. Keeping watch out of the corner of her eye and simultaneously trying to take off the glove in her hoodie with one hand Kira could see her teacher replace the binder and walk away. Taking a closer look, she could see that the envelope was sticking out now by about two

The Beta

inches. A big conspicuous manila envelope. Ah well, if her teacher hadn't noticed it now he probably wouldn't notice later.

Trying to put it out of her head Kira turned her focus on her group project. But her stomach wouldn't relax and she spent the time trying not to look in the direction of the envelope.

"Where you going?" Aliayah shouted across the parking lot in Kira's direction. Darn it. Kira paused for a moment gathering her wits. Her high school was big enough she hadn't expected to run into her friends on the way out of the parking lot. And now that she was obviously heading to the crosswalk instead of to her car she would have to tell Aliayah something.

"I forgot my parking pass so I had to park in the neighborhood!" Kira gestured vaguely past the park and baseball fields hoping that would satisfy Aliayah.

"Wanna ride to your car?" Aliayah offered.

"Nah, I wanna walk." Kira gave the fastest shrug of her life and then turned and walked toward the busy street. A loud truck rumbled by at just the right moment covering any possiblity of her hearing Aliayah's protests.

Kira felt bad as she crossed the street and began walking past the baseball fields and into the park. Aliayah was probably wondering why she ignored her and turned down a free ride. Kira couldn't wait for this part of the day to be over, and even more Kira couldn't wait for what lay ahead of her down the park path.

She stopped a minute on the curb of the baseball field parking lot and sat down. It was early spring and the weather was still chilly and wet, leaving both the baseball field and the parking lot deserted. Pulling her backpack around she reached inside and gathered up the used plastic gloves into one fist. Adding the last one from her hoodie pocket she scrunched them as tightly as possible then glanced down at the grate that covered a drain in the parking lot.

Why was this so hard for her? Well, she supposed it was because honestly, she had never purposely littered in her life. Recycling and composting were so prevalent in her household and city that her actual use of garbage cans was quite minimal.

The Beta

She also had to get her conscience past the little blue circle glued to the cement with a picture of a frog. It read 'No Dumping, Drains to Creek'. Hopefully she would forgive herself someday.

But she had to do what she had to do. So, with one last look for witnesses and cameras she took a deep breath and squished the ball of plastic through a grate and into the sewer system.

It was done. The hard part was done. Right before zipping up her backpack she reached out with both hands and caressed the fourth envelope, almost trying to spread her skin cells along the paper edges. This is what she had sacrificed her dignity for. Today, four would be her lucky number—no matter her entire life had been spent thinking the opposite.

Raindrops began to splash down on the envelope and she quickly tried to brush them off but the wet drops looked like mini tear stains.

Kira stood up and entered the dark canopy of trees.

Her car was parked on the other side of the Hartman Park but her parking pass was only tucked inside her glove compartment, not lost.

The walk wasn't long but it only took minutes before she pulled her hood up and tucked her hands into her warm hoodie pocket. Kira walked past the tennis courts and along a trail that eventually led to another called "Owl Hollow". Her heart was racing as she approached the intersection. It was quiet and dark but she was not alone.

Kevin was right where he said he would be, right on time. The little part of her heart that doubted him flipped into rightness. He was true, he was honest, he was here. She had never felt so safe and so loved. They both smiled at each other as she approached.

"Hello lovely," he said quietly but without hesitation as he pulled their rain-soaked bodies together. He just stared at her. Stared into her eyes, stared along her jawline, keeping her totally confused about where she was supposed to direct her gaze, and then ever so gently kissed her forehead.

"You are so beautiful." he said, For the next few minutes he just held her as he used his finger to trace along her cheeks and eyebrows and ears.

The Beta

"Ahhh," he sighed, disentangling himself and then adjusting her to his side as he began to lead them down the trail toward her car. "I wish I didn't have to work so soon. Thanks for the ride."

When they got to her car they both hopped in as she stripped out of her hoodie and turned up the heat to dry out.

"Did you have any luck?" he asked stretching casually in the passenger seat as his long legs attempted to make room in her tiny car.

She just smiled at him and flipped around to retrieve her backpack. Pulling out the fourth envelope she let it crinkle and pressed the last of her skin cells along the paper edges as she passed it over to him.

He paused before accepting it and leaned over to give her a very sensuous kiss on the mouth. "Thank you," he said, "I mean it."

She could have sat there forever, kissed him forever, but the car clock said 3:48 and he had to be to work by four. She let out her own sigh as she pulled out of park. Kevin's workplace wasn't far but she didn't want to be responsible for his being late.

She could hear him pull the papers out of the envelope and give a low whistle. "Where do you get this stuff?" he asked in awe. "You know this is going to save my life, don't you?"

She only smiled mischievously. "My little secret."

"Boy aren't you mysterious?" Kevin replied as he slipped the papers back into the envelope and then into his own backpack.

"Remember, you have to destroy them once you are done. If copies get out, eventually the school will shut this down. These aren't for just everyone." she admonished him.

"Promise" he replied and then stared out the window quietly. "Besides, why would I want to mess with the curve when I am on top of it?"

Kira wasn't exactly sure what to make of his quiet reply, but she didn't have much time to think as they pulled up into the parking lot. She parked on the far end of the lot hoping they had enough privacy for one more kiss. She didn't turn off the car but she did turn toward him as he opened the passenger door. He was halfway out before he turned back, "Oh I almost forgot."

She smiled and leaned his way as he reached his long torso inside and gave her a kiss.

"How much do I owe you?" Kevin asked, completely upending the moment. Kira didn't actually need any money but if she didn't ask for something he would probably be suspicious. He would probably figure it out.

"No . . ." she started.

But he had already thrown a fifty-dollar bill on the car seat.

"Thanks," he said and closed the door. The rain drops on the car door window simultaneously slammed to the ground.

Kira didn't know how to feel. She picked up the bill and felt along the creases. Somewhere in there were his skin cells. At least she knew how she felt about those.

First History Lesson

He was exactly as tall as the Earth.

It was spread out before him like a large floating marble. James reached out and gave it a gentle flick and the globe slowly began to rotate. He felt like a giant astronaut and the heavy equipment on his head only added to the effect.

Impatient in most things, James felt oddly reticent to begin this journey.

He was a person who always threw out the instructions and skipped the introductions. Today however, with utmost reverence, he clicked through the menu and chose the introduction with patience and purpose.

At an almost nauseating speed he could feel the Earth shrink below him as he was cast back into outer space. A smooth rich voice which might have been female or male began to narrate:

"Welcome to Google Earth History for School."

Then like a planetarium show, but one with astonishing reality, James was tossed even further back all the way to the edge of the universe. The androgynous voice resumed and led him through a brief history of space and time.

Then he was flying past the edge of the Milky Way, past Pluto, through the asteroid belt and once again to the exactly same spot where he began.

Standing toe to toe and nose to nose with planet Earth. His home.

The controls were easy to use and became almost instinctual for James within the first hour. He had used Google Earth VR but this was light years beyond that experience.

The hard part was choosing where to start. James had always loved everything about history and geography. Almost every time period or location interested him. Now he had the chance actually to explore any period of history. How would he ever begin?

Remembering a game from his childhood, James spun the globe, closed his eyes, and then with a prayer to the heavens clicked a location at random. When he opened his eyes he saw the pointer had landed on the East Coast of the United States. Ok, so not the most romantic location. To be honest, U.S. History had been his least favorite subject in middle school. Still something was drawing him in that direction.

He clicked on New York City and instantly zoomed in until his view hovered just to the south of Central Park. Next was the tricky part. He opened the timeline function and a huge chronological bar expanded at the top of the screen.

Starting the cursor at the present date he slowly ticked back the years a few at a time; for the moment there was little change within his current view. Remembering the events of 9/11, he pivoted to the left so he could see the World Trade Center Towers as he continued clicking backwards on the timeline. Slowly he saw the new construction melt down piece by piece until he hit the year 2001. There was a pile of rubble in the ground which suddenly was replaced by the original World Trade Center Towers.

He pulled off the timeline and an interaction menu to his right was suddenly apparent and full of options, both verbal and visual. "Would you like to take a pre-assessment at this point?" the voice

The Beta

from the introduction asked in a surprisingly relaxed voice. Since when did a teacher asking if you wanted to take a test end up being a soothing experience he wondered?

What the heck. He might as well.

"Yes please," he said tentatively. A typewritten option was in front of him as well, but he wanted to test out the voice activation controls.

"General New York Geography or History of 9/11?" the voice responded.

James smiled. "Both please," he challenged the voice.

"Beginning Pre-Assessments."

No way. Most artificial intelligence assistants were much more limited. This program could actually respond to his request for both assessments?

While his view of New York didn't waver, the timeline and side menu disappeared while an airborne keyboard popped up at waist level. James's gloved hands glowed green as he sat, his hands on the floating home row keys.

The questions came fast.

He could both read and hear the question. "Who masterminded the attacks against the World Trade Center in 2001?"

Since he could read much faster than the voice could speak he blurted out "Osama Bin Laden?" in a questioning voice.

"Incorrect"

Huh?

A multiple-choice form of the question replaced the original and after glancing at the names he wasn't any closer to knowing. He randomly clicked on choice B instead of answering with his voice.

"Correct" said the voice. He didn't know whether to address the voice as a computer, a program, or a teacher. He supposed if this were school he might as well begin to think of the voice as his teacher.

Faster and faster the questions kept coming. The computer used maps, images, graphs, and even videos to quiz his basic knowledge of both topics.

It took five minutes and he was exhausted.

The Beta

"Pre-Assessment complete" the teacher stated. As if by magic, all of the quiz questions were laid out before him in miniature with little green and red markings to indicate his scores.

"Learning modules calculated. Would you like to dive into any of these specific questions before returning to Earth?" the voice asked.

Despite his exhaustion, James was curious about the mastermind behind 9/11. He had been a bit embarrassed that he thought Bin Laden was the man. After all he clearly remembered hearing about President Obama ordering his assassination with a drone when he was in the fourth grade.

"Um, tell me more about the mastermind behind 9/11?"

"Khalid Sheikh Mohammed was named mastermind of the 9/11 attacks by the 9/11 Commission, but the trial has yet to commence." The narrator paused as a new set of learning options popped up on the screen in front of him. "Would you like to review Khalid Sheikh Mohammed's Early Life, Terrorists Attacks, Capture, or Current Legal Situation? Subcategories are available in each section."

Whoa, James thought. This is an overwhelming amount of information. Where to start? Well, he was always curious about how people's childhoods shaped their adulthood. So what the heck. He clicked on the Early Life option.

He was flung out into space once again; the globe spun as the Middle East came into focus and the narrator's voice began. "Khalid Sheikh Mohammed was born in either 1964 or 1965 in either Kuwait or Pakistan."

Huh? James thought. How could it be that no one knew when or where he was born? Was he like one of those hippie home birth kids? But then he realized life in the '60s in the Middle East was much different than his life in the early 2000s.

"Which is most likely to be true?" he asked interrupting the teacher. Surprisingly, the teacher paused, oblivious to his rude intrusion. Even more surprisingly, the teacher responded to his exact question with an exact answer.

"A source comparison is indefinite. The reference to a Kuwaiti birth comes from a BBC report that did not link a specific source." An image of the BBC report and internet link appeared on his left.

The Beta

"The Pakistani claim comes from a *New York Times* article, *Human Rights Watch*, and *Who2.com* - none of which identify the source of their information; they could easily be referring to one another." More images appeared on his right. He clicked on the *New York Times* article and the internet link expanded into a readable format.

"When a fact cannot be confirmed with additional evidence or narrowed down to a verified first-person account, a light red glow will emanate from around the simulation items. Green back glow is applied to highly verified items and yellow to those that fall somewhat in between. Any items can be accessed to dive deeper into sources," the narrator explained. Why hadn't this been part of the introduction? James wondered.

But presently he was utterly overwhelmed with the possibilities. History was obviously going to be his favorite subject this year.

"Return to previous location? New York?" James inquired.

It only took a few seconds as he once again flew back to New York City and was standing before the original Twin Towers.

"Would you like to observe the 9/11 re-creation?" asked the teacher. "The module is six minutes long with multiple opportunities for enrichment and exploration."

"Um, yes I suppose." James replied.

A slew of preference settings appeared in front of him. He noticed one labeled *graphic violence 18 years or older* was set to the "on" position. This rankled him a bit, not because he couldn't handle seeing something violent, but because now that he was 18 he was constantly reminded of how his parents red shirted him in kindergarten. It was so embarrassing. They, like many parents their age, made the decision to enroll him in kindergarten one year late so he would be taller and more mature than his peers. Instead, he always felt awkward and the taller thing hadn't worked out had it now? You'd think 5ft. 5in. Asian parents would have been more realistic about that one.

Now, while most guys his age were heading off to college he was signing up for the draft and anticipating one long senior year of high school. At least he was allowed to be part of *The Beta*.

His viewing angle in VR changed, and now the sun was only beginning to peak over the horizon of the Atlantic Ocean. A different voice began narrating this time as the model of New York

The Beta

altered almost imperceptibly. "The year is 2001. Recorded events begin to unfold at 6:00 a.m. in Portland, Maine, where Mohammed Atta and Abdulaziz al-Omari board a flight destined for Logan International Airport in Boston, Massachusetts."

The Earth in front of him shrunk a bit as his view expanded from New York to encompass the whole of New England. It took him a minute to focus on the East Coast, but then he could see the thin line of an airplane trajectory make its way swiftly across the continent and drop down on what he thought must be Massachusetts.

Then the Earth zoomed in again so he could see both Boston and New York. "Next, at 6:52 a.m. Marwan al-Shehi calls Atta from another wing in the Logan airport and confirms the attacks are set. Atta and Omari board Flight 11 headed for Los Angeles at 7:35 a.m."

There is a pause and James sees a small plane begin to rise on the horizon. The narrator continues "At 8:14 a.m. Flight 11 is hijacked. Two flight attendants are stabbed and Atta quickly takes over controls in the cockpit."

Next, a misty image of a woman came into focus to the right of the slowly moving airplane. "Flight attendant Betty Ong is able to contact American Airlines using an in-flight phone."

His ears filled with static as the voice of Betty Ong filled the air around the plane, which was still making steady progress across Massachusetts. "The cockpit is not answering, somebody's stabbed in business class—and I think there's mace—that we can't breathe—I don't know, I think we're getting hijacked." It gave him shivers to hear the real voice of a real person who would die in the very near future.

"At 8:26:30 a.m. Flight 11 makes a 100 degree turn south heading toward New York City." said the narrator with chilling calm. "And at 8:21 the flight's transponder is disconnected."

Another face faded in where Betty Ong's had disappeared and a breathy voice spoke out. "Eh... We have some planes. Just stay quiet, and you'll be okay. We are returning to the airport." James heard the terrorist while looking at his disembodied image.

The simulation kept slightly altering his angle and height. The Atlantic was now directly in front of him, the rising sun apparently muted so he could see the land and plane better. A second airplane entered his view.

"At 8:37 a.m. Flight 175 confirms visual contact of Flight 11 with air traffic controllers," the narrator continued. "Little does Flight 175 know that hijackers, led by Marwan al-Shehhi, overtake their cockpit not five minutes after sighting Flight 11. Soon thereafter, Flight 175 crashes into the South Trade Center Tower."

Still as tall as the Twin Towers, James saw a life-size replica of Flight 11 slowly make its way past his face as it headed toward its final destination. He could see each individual window and the clear markings of the two A's, one red and one blue, on the tail. With dread he moved his face a few inches closer, but gave a sigh of relief when he verified that he could not see inside the doomed airplane. That much realism would be too much. He shivered, but then began to slowly circle around the plane as he followed its course.

This was simply amazing. Even though he was in a well-engineered re-creation within Google Earth History, he could still move around at will and see the event from almost any angle.

He crouched down and dipped his head so that he could see the underbelly of the plane: the engines, the slight bulges in the middle, and even the creases where the aluminum sections were joined together. Too busy being awed by the minute details of the plane, he didn't realize they were at the Twin Towers until his nose was just inches away.

He instinctively whipped his head back to avoid collision with the towers and his eyes opened wide in shock. There was nothing he could do but watch Flight 11 plunge into the building. A billowing plume of flames erupted, enveloping his face and obscuring his view so that he could almost feel the heat on his face. He yanked his head back even further, just in time to see the tail end of the jet enter the building.

All of those people, dead in an instant. Tilting up, he could just imagine all the people in the floors above the plane. Did many of them make it out? How many were there?

"How many people were in the floors above Flight 11?" he asked, not expecting an answer (all his experiences with Siri,

Cortana, and Alexa taught him not to expect much), but the teacher voice replied without a hitch. "According to the 9/11 commission 1,402 people died in the North Tower who were at or above the impact."

James just stared, frozen to one spot now. It seemed like forever, but the simulation was only six minutes long. That's what the narrator said, right?

The simulation was obviously sped up; he watched as the smoke spread throughout the tower, pouring out from various floors. There were tiny motions in the upper left-hand corner of the tower. Squinting his eyes to better see he realized there were people hanging out the window waving their hands.

Something flitted past his face and he could actually feel it brush his cheek.

It was a small human figure flying through the air. It landed on the sidewalk near where his giant feet would be if he could see them in the simulation.

James reached up under his headset to where the tiny human brushed his cheek. His finger traced the saline path where a tear had made its trail.

His vision blurred as water vapor condensed inside his headset. Slowly, he took off the contraption, backed up a few paces, and sat down.

This was only his first history lesson.

English

It was the end of English and Kira's teacher was distracted by some obnoxious suck up, giving her the perfect opportunity to pull out her phone. The school's app was lame so it took forever to scroll through the ill-formatted grading screen to find her most recent scores.

The Beta

She still had a solid C in Chemistry. Kira had neglected her studies as of late and barely managed to keep that C grade. There was just so much in life outside of school that competed for her attention and time. She scrolled down to the next class but sure enough her math teacher was still two weeks behind in entering grades. What a pain in the butt it could be to have a lazy teacher like that, but at least her parents couldn't complain yet, she had evidence that every assignment was turned in on time and waiting to be graded. Next, Kira scrolled down to her history grade.

"Oh," Kira said softly. No one heard what she said but her eyes began to water immediately. The 65% was listed in an automatic red font and was enough to drop her overall grade down to a D. The very worst part was that she had really tried on this test. That's what hurt, to know this was the result of her very best effort.

To keep herself from crying she sucked in her breath and pretended none of it had happened. Something inside turned cold and hard but it dried up all the tears.

None of the earlier denial helped once she hit the driveway. Her parents were going to kill her. She pulled up in her parking spot next to the house and her emotions turned to an angry resentment by the time she reached the front door and entered the security code.

But she could ignore it all until her parents chose to check her grades online, which they did like clockwork every Tuesday and Friday night.

"Mom?" she called out, hoping any evidence of tears or anger was wiped out with an innocent overlay.

No answer. Kira threw her backpack on the kitchen counter and habitually rooted through the pantry for a snack.

"Mom!" she yelled out loudly this time. If her mom was anywhere inside the house this volume should do the trick.

Still nothing. Kira munched on a handful of chips and began going room to room looking for evidence of her mom, or sister, or even her dad who rarely arrived home before seven in the evening.

The Beta

"Mooom!" This time she used a causal singsong tone not expecting any response. She checked the garage but it was empty.

"Hmph . . ." she said to herself, stumped, but kind of excited that she would be alone for a while. Freedom!

Kira walked back down a long hallway, saw a trail of chip crumbs she must have scattered on the way out, then shrugged and grabbed a bowl of ice cream. If she was going to be in trouble soon enough she might as well break every rule and be as slothful as possible.

A half-hour into her TV and ice cream binge Kira's phone rang. It was her mom. She almost didn't answer it but Kira was curious about how much longer she might have until the guillotine dropped.

"Hey mom." Kira answered. "Where are you guys?" Kira's mom and little sister were usually home early on Friday afternoons.

"Hey honey, we're at the hospital sweetie. Lauren had another reaction." Her mom's voice conveyed her worry with an uncharacteristic tremble.

"Is she ok?" Kira asked, the empty ice cream bowl fell to the floor, drips of chocolate left behind on the sofa.

"She's ok. After what happened last time the doctor wants to keep her overnight for observation."

"Thank goodness."

"Can you get a few things together for me? Dad will be by to pick stuff up before he joins me at the hospital."

"Of course, mom." Kira ran into the kitchen and opened the junk drawer to look for something to write on. "I'm ready, what do you need?"

After the list was complete her mom asked, "Will you be alright tonight?"

"Yeah . . ." Kira took a calculated risk. "Do you mind if I go to Annie's?"

There was a pause on the end of the phone. Friday night was usually when Kira's grades would hold her hostage from doing anything else but moping around the house avoiding her homework. Kira held her breath.

"Sure honey. Thanks for getting those things together for us."

"No problem Mom."

The Beta

Kira hung up the phone and gave a shout of joy. She couldn't have better luck! Her sister stuck in the hospital overnight was exactly the break she needed. They would be so busy taking care of her sister all weekend they wouldn't be checking her grades anytime soon.

Then her conscience kicked-in and Kira felt dreadful. Was she really celebrating her sister almost dying? Was she so selfish she would rather her family be stuck at the hospital just so she could have a fun weekend?

Feeling icky but thankful all at the same time Kira sent her sister a silent prayer to get better soon, then pushed away any bad feelings and ran up the stairs to pack her mom's bag.

Child of the Woods

He was a child of the Woods and Wetlands. Literally. In more ways than one.

His morning routine was pretty predictable.

Groggy eyes and long stares out across the trees. Sometimes he would look out the window from his bed for a half-hour before moving a muscle, just thinking, daydreaming, or falling in or out of sleep. It was a rare day he had to be anywhere or online before eight a.m.

Walking down the stairs into the kitchen he found his mom crouched in concentration over her laptop with a cup of coffee in her right hand. She must have been doing something pretty intense because she generally looked more composed and she didn't even notice him walk in the room. Normally, she was the type of mom that could hear him coughing from half a mile away. He tested her with an honest morning cough.

"Good morning sweetie," she said without moving her eyes from the screen. Whatever she was doing must be really important. He walked around to peer over her shoulder curiously but wasn't daring enough to actually read the words. Nothing from this far

The Beta

away tipped him off to what she was working on, although sometimes it was pretty sensitive stuff. James was getting an espresso when his dad walked into the room.

"Morning," he said to James's mother Eve, kissing her on the head.

"Morning Dad," James said.

"I'm glad you're up." His dad began as he joined him at the espresso machine. "I have something for you."

Unsure if the something was a cool present or some euphemism for a chore James kept his mouth shut by sipping his drink and waited to hear more.

There were no forthcoming details as his dad made a coffee but James could see twinkling in his eyes. Unable to wait he began pestering his dad. "So, what is it?"

"Well, you're technically eighteen now, right?"

His dad knew this was a sore spot with James so he didn't know how to respond. He glared at his dad but nodded.

"I got you a job."

Huh? This stumped James and now he was wary again. It was August and the official school year was about to start, even though he had technically been earning credit through his early access to *The Beta*. There were tons of perks when both of your parents worked at Google. But why in the world would he need a job? James had never worked in his entire life unless you counted the chores his parents and grandparents foisted upon him for supposed character building.

"Check your headset," was all his dad said.

Huh? James's internal vocabulary was reduced to rubble, but now he was intrigued.

"My headset?" he asked his dad, nodding his head to the basement door.

"Yup. Check your beta messages," his dad smiled, "and you'll need to come into work with me next week for orientation."

James ran down the stairs two at a time and hooked up. Even though his view was already blocked by the headset he could hear his dad following him down and sitting on the desk stool to watch.

26

The Beta

James opened his messages and saw a new entry from The Dev Team at Google Earth History. Why would the Dev team be messaging him? And how would this be related to a job?

"Have you opened it yet?"

"No . . ." James opened the message but there was no message inside. "All I see is an attachment."

"Open it!" His dad sounded uncharacteristically eager.

James clicked on the attachment.

A long intricately carved golden key spun in all its three-dimensional glory before him.

All Together Now

They entered the 520 Bridge going west that morning. Kira looked over at her Mom's speedometer and her body tensed just a bit—her mom was a savvy driver but she was always going fast. She couldn't actually remember exactly how many times the cops had pulled over her mom—maybe five or six times. Although the result of those stops had mostly resulted in warnings, with only one or two tickets.

Flicking her eyes back to the road she saw the "Good to Go" signs advertising the bridge's automatic tolling system. She didn't know if it was the uncanny combination of G's and O's that made her repeat the phrase, or a silent prayer that her mom's fast driving not turn into a tailspin, but either way she couldn't help but chant "Good to Go" over and over until they hit the part of the bridge floating on water.

Her body finally relaxed as they cruised out over Lake Washington. The 520 bridge was the world's longest floating

The Beta

bridge and when Kira looked out over the water she almost felt like she was in a speedboat. Tapping the controls slightly she rolled the window down and edged her nose to the fresh air.

Within seconds a sharp voice from the backseat shouted out "It's cold back here! Close your window!"

"Fine," she replied and closed the window without even looking at her mother, who ignored both of her children, as if to save her energy for another fight.

Kira shot a dirty glance back at her sister sitting in the middle back seat but didn't wait for the return glare. Today both of their schools were closed and mom was dragging them to work at the Doppler Tower.

Neither of them really minded as mom liked having them with her at work and after her sister's last allergy scare last week it felt good to have her sister where they could keep a close eye in case anything happened.

And there was plenty for the kids to explore at the Doppler Tower, but the subtext was that Kira would be responsible for her sister all day, so no need to start picking fights this early in the day. She, like her mother, would save her energy, and reserve it for a good match with her sister if needed later on.

Knowing she only had so much dedicated alone time before they arrived, Kira scrolled through her iPad. They had every Amazon device known to man, but her parents hadn't fought her when she asked for an iPad even though it was tantamount to being a traitor.

Scrolling a bit mindlessly she was drawn to the news section. A CNN article titled "Tech Giants Collaborate on Unprecedented Educational Gaming Partnership" was accompanied by a picture of eight people standing in front of a blank white background.

Tech Giants huh? Which tech giants she wondered? The word gaming drew her attention just as much as the word educational made her hesitate. But the article was being pushed Apple News so it must be significant. Kira tapped on the item.

A video loaded at the top, and too lazy to scroll down and read, Kira decided to pop in her earbuds and listen as her mom focused on driving across the bridge.

The Beta

Kira watched as the screen showed several cars leaving what appeared to be the Googleplex in MountainView, California and then Apple's headquarters. An anchor's voice piped up, "We have just learned that employees from several rival corporations have been secretly meeting for over a week here at Facebook's headquarters in Menlo Park, California. How they kept this under wraps is anyone's best guess." The anchor paused to gather more information in his earpiece. "The helicopters are arriving at Facebook's headquarters outside of San Francisco where the official announcement will be made within the next few minutes."

What did these guys have up their sleeves? Kira wondered.

Their house may be full of Amazon products, and she loved her iPad, but the phone in her pocket was a third generation Google Pixel. She always figured there would be some kind of benefit from using devices from different companies and her loyalty lay with no one, except perhaps her mom's Amazon paycheck.

Several figures walked calmly out onto the stage. A hush fell over the room and across the cable lines.

This was like seeing the top world leaders in one place at one time, but these were leaders of technology. This was way more exciting than seeing presidents. The security at this event must be crazy. No wonder they didn't announce it ahead of time!

Even the CNN ticker paused, then slowly reacted by reading out the names of all the participants. Ma Huateng of Tencent, Tim Cook of Apple, Mark Zuckerberg of Facebook, Sundar Pichai from Google, Satya Nadella from Microsoft, Bil Gates from The Bill and Melinda Gates Foundation, Jim Ryan from PlayStation and Yves Maitre from HTC. There wasn't one single female on stage. It was also fascinating to her that the companies represented some of the best Asian and American minds in tech.

Tim Cook stepped to the forefront and once again the world held its breath.

"This all began with a logical, innocent question," started Tim, but then right on cue Jim Ryan jumped in.

"I was visiting a school in Los Angeles when a student asked me, 'How come you have all these great games for home like Grand Theft Auto and Fortnite but you can't make a decent game for school?' I almost responded with an automatic reply about how

The Beta

PlayStation's educational games were the best, but I realized the student was right. So I made a few phone calls."

This was where Bill Gates stepped in. "Jim wasn't the only one thinking along these lines. We all were. All of our companies and nonprofit organizations have strong initiatives and connections in the education world, but none of us were making the impact we wanted. And the student was right. We have the technology and skill to give students around the world a better education, and we can give it to them right now."

Then up stepped Sundar Pichai, "So we knew we had the skills, the drive, and the hardware, but what we did not have was the determination or focus. Working together over the past week we have discussed how we might make a significant, permanent, change in the educational world by working together. There were tough decisions to be made. For example, if we spent the same resources looking for a cure for AIDS, would a cure be discovered in the next twelve months?" Sundar and Bill exchanged solemn looks. "But then we realized, if we start by educating our children the best we possibly can, a cure for AIDS and other advances will be that much closer."

Finally, Yves Maitre was front and center, "There were many of us at HTC, Google, and Facebook who were making investments in Virtual Reality. And it was then that we realized we needed to make a compromise. If we worked together for a short time at the right moment it will be possible to provide cutting edge virtual reality experiences to students around the world."

Mark Zuckerberg was next to speak "And so it is with great pleasure we announce our intent to radically change the face of education within the next year. The first step will be to designing a piece of virtual reality hardware and educational operating system that is both inexpensive and cutting edge. This is the core of our alliance."

Mark continued, "Then, taking advantage of our collective obsession with competition, we will independently launch efforts to produce the highest-quality learning software this world has ever seen. Students, get ready to learn history, math, science, and language in one of the most captivating online platforms you have ever experienced. We are going to bet that you . . ." Pointing emphatically at the screen Mark continued, ". . . the student of tomorrow, will choose to 'play' your school work just as much if not more than Fortnite or GTA."

"We are placing our bets on you and we expect much," Yves added.

"The real work will begin this fall as we collaborate with schools across the nation and across the world to launch a massive beta test," said Satya Nadella. "By launching such an enormous beta test over a nine-month period we will be able to refine and release the product you as students have been waiting for all of your lives exactly twelve months from now."

"Thank you for your time," Bill Gates added in conclusion, "As we prepare to meet with world leaders we expect you, the student of tomorrow, to prepare for our coming. Be ready. At the end of next summer we will be ready for you!"

The figures on the screen drew away from the podium and looked out at the crowd briefly before filing off the stage.

Chills ran down Kira's spine. This had to be a hoax. A really good CNN hoax. She started searching up everything that came to mind. Joke, hoax, trick. But instead of a quick Snopes debunking she was faced with a long list of news sources echoing the same headlines. NBC, Fox, CBS and even the BBC.

"Uh Mom . . . ," she started pulling out one ear bud at a time. But when she looked up at her she could see that her mom's eyebrows were furrowed tightly in concentration. By this point they were nearing the end of the 520 bridge.

She could see her mom's jawline relax as they crossed on to solid ground before she responded. "What hon?" She was probably thinking about work. Her mom always thought about work.

"You are not going to believe this!" Kira now sputtered without dignity. There was no way to hide her awe and enthusiasm now. "Apple, Google, Microsoft, Tencent, HTC Vive, PlayStation and a bunch of others are going to work together to make a gaming system! The best gaming system in the world."

It didn't take long for her mom's face to scrunch up in incredulity. "Yeah right, what are you reading, fake news?"

Ignoring her flippant reply, Kira pressed on. "I told you that you were not going to believe it. But it's true! Unless all the major news outlets are spreading the same lie."

"Well that wouldn't be the first time would it?" her Mom replied.

She looked down at the iPad in her lap and scrolled through all the timestamps on the news releases. All of them read as being 9 minutes old, no make that 10.

"I'm telling you, let me read the transcript. I seriously saw Bill Gates, Sundar Pichai, Tim Cook and a bunch of other people on the same stage!"

"They would never be so stupid as to be in the same place at the same time. And besides, Bill Gates isn't in charge of Microsoft anymore."

"But seriously mom. They're doing it for the kids!"

"What?" she asked.

"For school, for education." Kira was not being as articulate as she normally would be. In fact she realized she was not making any sense. "Just let me read this."

And so, as they made their way to the Doppler Building—winding under tunnels and through busy streets—Kira read, her sister napped, and her mom began to tap her fingers nervously.

Orientation

James walked into the Mainframe and almost tripped over his own feet. The building was gigantic. He was used to the enormous size and scope of Google as a company, but this place overloaded his senses.

It almost reminded him of a sports stadium, except here the viewers watched hundreds of people dressed in black gear make strange movements in the air with their arms. At a football game one might vacillate between watching the action on the field and the huge Jumbotron. It was much the same here as James's head moved back and forth from the people using the VR and the multiple screens showing them in Google Earth.

He followed his dad closely as they made their way to a cluster of desks on the east end.

"Hey Mark, James." Doug greeted them and clapped them both on the back. "Good to see you guys." Then he turned to James and got straight to business. "Did you fill out the online application?"

James nodded. "About three days ago."

"Autumn?" Doug called out to a woman behind one of the desks. "Can you check to see if James Chiu's application paperwork made it through HR? I tabbed it for rush status last week when I opened the position."

Autumn smiled at the three of them before replying, "On it."

Doug turned back to James and his father. "If Autumn gives me the green light it means I can officially assign you to a work group today."

"What type of work did you have in mind for us, Doug?" Mark asked.

"There are two main objectives we are focusing on for the first version of Google Earth History. First, we want to tackle all the basics, those popular places, people, and events that you might traditionally find in any given history textbook." Doug pointed to a shelf behind him that was stacked with old fashioned history textbooks.

"Second, and this is what I am really excited about, is that we want to make sure and capture the history and essence of those places in the world that are unique to the human story. Many of them are UNESCO World Heritage sites or places that have a special religious significance." This time Doug's eyes wandered across the room to the multitude of screens and without saying a word James quickly realized that many of the personnel suited up in VR were working on just those types of places.

They were interrupted by Autumn's voice. "He's through the system. What type of clearance do you want me to initiate?"

Doug walked over and grabbed a tablet from her, dragged and tapped his fingers across the screen for a while, and then handed it back.

The Beta

A few seconds later Autumn spoke up again, "You forgot your signature Doug, I do need your signature."

Doug took the tablet back and scrawled his signature across the pad. He then turned back to James and said, "You ready to get to work kid?"

Assignment #1

This was his space, his workshop, his domain. There was probably nothing quite like it in the world. When James was little, the room was filled with his toys and random home gym equipment and then as he got older the toy corner was replaced with a home theater set.

Now it was all business, although a stranger off the street would be hard pressed to identify what type of business.

He had to share his space with his dad which could be a bummer at times. Like any growing boy he tried to passively dominate the whole room, constantly monopolizing the playlists, reorganizing the computer desktop, and leaving his leftover dishes on the desk. He drove his dad nuts. Anywhere else in the house he was as neat nicky as his parents but not in this space.

Except for the floor. The floor was completely clear of debris and the only furniture in the room was evenly spaced along the walls leaving the middle completely open.

There was a desk, chair, and computer to his right, a large two door wardrobe to his left, and on the ceiling a large overhead monitor that projected on the flat wall in front of him. There were also a series of wall mounted black cubes surrounding the space.

He was in his element. Using voice activation, he turned on the room speakers to start his morning playlist and then flung open the doors of the ancient wardrobe. Inside it looked like the closet of some gothic astronaut. A messy gothic astronaut.

Technically the left side of the cupboard was his dad's and the right side was his, but since they were nearly the same height and build at the moment he could probably get away with using either set. Picking through the options he decided the headset, gloves, and one controller would suffice for what he had to do this morning.

His VR headset was wireless, but in order to provide the cutting-edge tracking that made this type of VR the best in the world it still relied on a combination of outside-in and inside-out tracking. The outside-in tracking used base stations or what some called lighthouses to follow his movements throughout the room, which was why his space needed to be both large and free of objects that could obstruct the view. However, every piece of equipment he strapped to his body also used markerless inside-out tracking. The camera on his headset would constantly scan his environment for objects and then the accelerometers and gyroscopes were the final pieces of data that made VR work so seamlessly.

Technically, he could use his equipment anywhere in the world. Yet outside-in tracking still wasn't very accurate and the latency could be bothersome. The few times he took his equipment into his backyard to experiment he was always frustrated with the results.

Most of the equipment in the room was voice activated and so he was able to turn down the lights, turn on the computer, and activate his program without flipping a switch. It had taken a while to get the controls working smoothly but now that he had it down he couldn't help but to rely on voice commands.

In a manner of seconds, he was there. Floating precisely above the familiar North American continent—using the built-in developer menu gave him access no minor child in the world had at this moment. Technically he could tweak any portion of Google Earth History although he tended to keep to his pre-approved list of projects.

His current project was partially his idea and partially his dad's idea. As of late his father showed some belated enthusiasm to share his Buddhist roots with James which coincided nicely with James's own interest in the history of religion. So as the Google Earth History project groups began to divide and form his dad secured a key position on those work groups focusing on religious history. James had taken it upon himself to explore historical artifacts related to many of the world's major religions of his own accord.

With a practiced flip James turned the globe 180 degrees and zoomed into the Arabian Peninsula. As he approached the Earth he could easily pick out Makkah and the white tent city of Mina, but it was a lonely hill to the northeast that was his current destination.

Doppler

It was obvious Kira's mom did not share any of her present enthusiasm for the major news announcement at this point, but she was sure to come around eventually. It wasn't cool that Amazon was not invited into the partnership.

She knew her mom would get over it—and besides, Amazon, J.P. Morgan, and Berkshire Hathaway recently kicked everyone's ass conquering health care. Nobody had seen that coming and they had started a revolution; never mind the fact that bringing down health care costs may have also saved the American economy through the early 21st century. Every modern technology company simply couldn't solve every world problem. They had to divide the successes.

They walked into the Doppler Building and through the security checkpoint. She and her sister visited often enough they were already cleared for entry and even happened to know a few of the first-floor security guards that day.

Kira's mom awoke her sister without fanfare, handed her a backpack, and hustled them both from parking lot to front door. But Kira couldn't feel bad about anything anymore. All she knew was that finally, I mean FINALLY, the world was going to put money where they should, where it mattered.

Ever since she was a kid, like any other kid with access to devices and the internet, Kira was put through the torture of playing stupid educational games. She did have fond memories of playing **PBS** games and Starfall while her parents nodded appropriately in the background, and while those were kind of cool she also knew almost immediately that they were nothing compared to fun games such as Lego City. The distinctions had been clear in her then. The difference in quality was noticeable to most four-year-old kids. Four-year-olds were smarter than most people gave them credit for.

Of course, she had been much older when she realized that it wasn't that educational games were dumb on account of them being educational. It was that nobody ever put the money necessary into developing good games for school.

Thinking deeply Kira wasn't paying much attention to her surroundings when she noticed that her mom stopped the hurried pace. It took a second for her to slow her roll and dive back into reality. They were on the third floor right next to the Expressions Lab but her mom was looking somewhere else, toward the game room that Kira and her sister would probably settle into later in the day when boredom drove them down to the haven of couches and screens.

The game room was crowded for so early in the morning. Most people wouldn't dare take a break for video games until at least mid-morning, but a small crowd of employees gathered round the screen that was broadcasting something. The game controllers were left unattended on the coffee table so it must not be a game Kira thought.

Her mom walked closer and Kira and her sister followed, both quietly and attentively. There was still an active hum to the building that kept Kira from hearing what was going on, but it wasn't but a minute or two before Kira's mom looked down at her. "Honey, you were right." Her mom's forehead wrinkled and hands tightened before she visibly made a move to relax. Her mom was going to have a rough day.

Kira could be empathetic to her mom, after all her job description included something to do with **PR**. But even with the hushed adults who were just beginning to understand what this announcement meant for their jobs and their company, Kira knew exactly what it meant. What it meant for all the young people around the world.

Feeling confident, feeling taller, feeling cared for, Kira understood that the most powerful people in the world finally made the right decision at the right time and for the right reasons.

It was a little like being the first person to land on the moon or winning the Civil War. Sometimes you just have to be crazy and do the right thing. And this working together to make educational VR . . . it was the right thing at the right time.

A final thought kept nagging her. How was she going to get her hands on one?

The Cave of Hira

Near the top of the high hill was a quiet cave, but as he approached an icon reminiscent of a grandiose Pokemon gym grew and churned as it came alive. These icons were only visible in the developer view and indicated the location of a major Google Earth History subdivision worksite. No passwords were needed as his biometrics were automatically checked and visually represented by the long elegant key his dad and the Dev Team gave him. It slowly slid into place and caused the icon to unfold into an up-to-date view of his current work and progress.

James's particular task today started with an unassuming 360-degree photo. The image had been taken by someone standing at the top of the mountain. It was a selfie filled with the bodies of tourists and some of the rocks were painted with messages. He would need a translator to read the writing.

This place was called the Cave of Hira, the place where Muhammad prayed and passages from the Quran were first revealed to him by the Angel Gabriel.

Collaborating and coding historical topics connected with religion was trickier than all get out. Considering that every attempt was made to keep the project private while still reaching out to experts and leaders across the world, James supposed the project was going pretty smoothly. The other Google employees working on this project were struggling to decide how to narrate the story of Muhammad's first experience with the angel Gabriel,

The Beta

because there were two fairly different historical accounts, one attributed to Ibn Hisham and the other to Al-Bukhari.

And there was the rub. The Google team working on Mount Hira had a limited number of resources to complete the project in a month, and since narrating three dimensional experiences took significant time, only one version of Muhammad's experience at Mount Hira could be included in the first release. If they choose the version recounted by Al-Bukhari they would be favoring the one revered by the Sunnis' and if not, well this was where Google Earth History was quickly discovering that everything was political.

Luckily, James's job was pretty simple. He was preparing the three-dimensional physical historical setting for the short re-creation by identifying all pertinent photos and videos and then slowly editing and stitching them together. Basically, he was the hill and trail guy.

It was hard to explain, but one of his friends who loved photography and used Adobe Photoshop all the time was able to extrapolate how his job was a bit like using Photoshop in a three-dimensional setting.

When he was done with his part he will have prepared a fairly accurate historical re-creation of the 100-yard path that went over Mt. Hira and dipped down into a small cave that couldn't fit more than one standing person at a time. A cave revered by Islamists from around the world.

He used his controller to highlight a modern pilgrim and after deleting him from the image he checked the computer's work at filling in the background. The more input he gave the computer about desired and undesired images, the quicker the computer was able to properly fill in the blanks. And the more input of pictures and videos he could feed into the computer properly fitted together, the more realistic an end product would emerge. The first few hours of his work had been incredibly slow-going.

For example, once he accidentally forgot to indicate to the computer that a concrete slab installed by modern pilgrims was an undesired characteristic in his historical view, and much later in his work he was surprised when the AI started throwing in straight line concrete slabs as background from time to time.

The Beta

Luckily he didn't have much trouble going back in time to locate his mistake, and once corrected he could zoom forward in his project without all the modern concrete mucking up his desert mountainside. James was kind of surprised at how quickly he became attached to his projects.

At least he wasn't the one who had to determine what form the Angel Gabriel should look like.

Strange

Kira pulled her hoodie tightly around her, and then moodily ripped it off and fished around in her backpack for a warm shirt, put that on and then the hoodie again. Warming her hands in her hoodie pocket she then proceeded to jump up and down, trying desperately to raise her body temperature.
There was five minutes before the bell and she just didn't feel like going to class till the last minute. The fluorescent lights had an odd cast to them and every face she looked at seemed gaunt.
Her leggings felt too tight today and her stomach was empty.
The four minutes she gave herself did nothing to warm her body so at the sound of the bell she turned reluctantly to head for class. Right before she turned down the hall she saw Kevin—or at least she saw his back. He was tucked in the middle of a large group of people. Her body responded to "that group" of people with a mild ripple of revulsion, but before she could verify what she thought she saw, they moved into the south hall and she turned north, late for class.
He told her he had broken up with that girl, but if that was true why was he always still with her?
Everything at school bummed her out.
Ever since she had dropped those manila envelopes at the school Kira couldn't shake that icky feeling every time she changed in the girls' locker room or went to history class. Her conscious would not let her live it down—but her fear would never let her

come clean—so she was stuck in this self-inflicted molasstic morass of purgatory.

That thickness directly contrasted with the electric thrill that ran through her every time she heard a rumor or mention of the virtual reality initiative.

The collaborative projects technically had no permanent name but it had been quietly but emphatically dubbed *The Beta* after the press conference two weeks ago, even after the companies shared their own name for the hardware.

She still wasn't sure how she was going to get her hands on *The Beta*, but it was all she could think about. Almost.

The Day

High school was a little brighter for Kira the next day. Some of the sepia tones were lightening as the possibility of hearing *The Beta* announcement lurked around every corner.

And it didn't take long—by second period the kids were mysteriously lining up for an all school assembly.

Stuck with her English class in the second tier of bleachers, Kira felt herself getting overwhelmed, claustrophobic, and anxious all at the same time. If the dangling carrot of *The Beta* wasn't hanging so precariously in front of her she would have been heading to the bathroom five minutes ago. But here she was . . . waiting.

And there they were. While there were still no official signs of what was going on and the hum of whispers around her belied no clues, Kira could see the people responsible for the announcement mingling with the superintendent and principal toward the right corner of the gymnasium, the only venue big enough to fit the entire student population.

She didn't have long to wait.

The Beta

Assignment #2

James grabbed a clean towel and switched out the foam face pad on his headset before putting it on again. This time he picked out a thinner pair of gloves before restarting the Developer.

He zoomed out a little way out from his previous location on the Arabian Peninsula. His next destination was both popular and hotly contested. A little south of Jerusalem and a little north of Bethlehem was a shrine and mosque that was purported to be the gravesite of Rachel, wife of Jacob from the Bible.

Once again, he found his worksite symbol and it blew up in front of his eyes. His key automatically connected and he heard the all too familiar voice say "access granted" before entering the main platform.

This time he paused a bit before entering further. Looking around he saw the items you might see in an employee break room of sorts. While the Google Earth History geographic location they were working on loomed faintly around him in greyscale, he was also firmly in the middle of a very solid room. It almost reminded him of a construction work trailer without any walls or ceiling.

He walked over to the bulletin board and tapped on an icon labeled "work log" to open a separate screen. With a quick flick of his fingers he was able to scroll through the most recent entries. Rosenthal recently updated the simulation settings for 1945-60 and Al-Mazur had put in more hours than anyone establishing the interior mosque graphics for the entire timeline.

James moved over to the cartoonish "help wanted" sign that was a humorous twist on what jobs needed to be accomplished next.

Sometimes he had almost unlimited choices and other times pressing jobs were highlighted if they needed to be accomplished in order to move on to the next step. He appreciated all the color coding and prioritizing the Development Artificial Intelligence, or AI, did for him and his coworkers. It made working on such incredibly large projects fairly easy.

The Beta

The majority of the job options on the current list were coded red indicating research. James sighed a little bit inside. It wasn't that he wasn't interested in learning the details and history behind what was sure to be a fascinating dive into Rachel's Tomb, but that most of what he would be doing involved endless reading and fact checking and sometimes what he discovered contradicted the work already completed by his coworkers.

So with a bit of reluctance he clicked on a random red job not even paying attention to the title, but then straightened his back a little and did some fast arm circles as a way of tricking his brain into getting excited for the job—after all, this was his school work and school wasn't always fun.

The timeline stretched out before him as the present-day Rachel's Tomb slowly melted back in time. It only took about ten seconds to move one hundred and fifty years back in time and the physical structures in front of and around him shifted quickly. Walls melted away and buildings disappeared. The tomb itself crumbled and was rebuilt several times although no matter what the current structure consisted of, the edifice always faced in the same direction toward the Muslim Sakhrah or Dome of the Rock.

James's basement was huge, about nine meters by ten meters, so the space he could move within freely was awesome. Walking over to a corner of his real-world room he jumped virtually to the tomb's main gates and positioned himself right outside to set-up camp. His camp looked almost like a programmer's cubicle but completely customized to his tastes. James's hands began to fly in all directions as he bulit his custom workspace. He usually utilized about nine large screens hanging in the air around his head and waist, but also a virtual desktop at a 45-degree angle where he could temporarily toss documents and lists. His objectives as assigned by the AI were always front and center in a large font he had programmed as a preset. This particular job was titled "Hole in the Wall."

The directions were relatively simple, his job was to examine the 1843 account of Ridley Haim Herschell who described being "obliged to remain outside the tomb, and prayed at a hole in the wall, so that their voices enter into the tomb." This was at a time the tomb was primarily used as a mosque and so Christians and

The Beta

Jews were denied entrance. In addition to examining Ridley's account he was to look for any contradicting, or supporting evidence in documents and pictures and then determine if a scene depicting Ridley and his party praying through the hole should be included within the Google Earth History re-creation, and most importantly exactly where the hole should be located.

James pulled Ridley's account from Google Books, conducted a quick search of images to get as many as possible related to mid the 1800s, and then finally tweaked one of his screens before moving out of his workspace to get to the tomb's entrance.

Before conducting any research James wanted to get a feel for the land at this time. Al-Mazur had spent the most time on the historical physical set up of the tomb area and like other researchers doing their best he had very little actual historical evidence to base his decisions upon. Looking around, James saw a barren landscape whose flora and fauna were based upon modern Israeli environments, and even the curvature of the land was based upon present day topography and it was likely that not much had changed in five hundred years at this particular location—but it wasn't certain.

Mommy May I?

Mom?

Kira texted in the midst of the chaos. For twenty minutes the suits in the middle of the gym used videos and loud music to blaringly pump up the student population about their decision to make her high school a site of *The Beta* test.

If *The Beta* wasn't actually as cool as the hype, Kira would have been completely put-off by the presentation with its loud music and videos. How could advertisers and business people think teenagers like this kind of crap?

But it only took a quick look around the room to realize not everyone was as critical as she. Barely perceptible, but undeniable, heads and legs bounced around to the thumping music in an odd sort of hypnotism. OK, Kira got it. Their methods worked on the majority.

Yeah sweetie? her mom texted back. That was fast.

we're in the gym and they just announced the beta test

She paused for a minute to make sure she wasn't missing anything important from the stage, but the rep was still going on about what the commitments were if your application was chosen for *The Beta*.

do you mind if I apply for the beta? I know you already said sure but I wanted to check again, she finished texting.

of course you can baby

Her mom's reply was short but Kira let out a breath she didn't realize she had been holding. Opening her phone's browser, she navigated to the application website and started typing in her information. No time like the present.

Rachel's Tomb

For some odd reason one of the programmers must have set introductory controls to a partly-cloudy full moon night and James only noticed it now. Often Google Earth History would sync any location's weather with your real-life weather if appropriate, as a way of keeping your internal clocks in working order, but Rachel's Tomb always started at night.
A bit frustrated at the control some unseen person had exerted over his surroundings, James pointed at the moon and spun it across the horizon to be promptly replaced with the sun at mid-morning. Everything now in proper order, he walked around the site slowly.

The Beta

Rachel's Tomb was adjacent to an ancient graveyard with mounds and rectangular rock linings. The main tomb was a white dome on top of what appeared to be four original pillars that had been filled in with plaster. Attached to the main building was another rectangular structure with a long low unfilled arch. He reached out to touch the stone wall and his haptic gloves provided a barely perceptible movement that caused his hand to hesitate. This sort of feedback was just enough to trick his mind into thinking of the wall as real, even though he quickly followed up with a determined swipe right through the stone, proving that he was a ghost in this land.

He shivered, although real ghosts shouldn't shiver, and continued around and into the main tomb. There, directly under the white plastered dome, was a ten-foot-long pyramid of 11 large rocks also plastered like the dome above. Supposedly the 11 rocks were meant to represent Rachel's 11 children—excluding the twelfth, Benjamin, for whom she died giving birth.

James toyed with the idea of the story being literally true and then imagined his own brothers and sisters having to move such heavy stones to commemorate the death of one of his parents. What an honor it would be to conduct such a difficult physical feat as a way to respect one's parents, and an option modern families were left without when businesses charged for every part of the grieving process.

All of a sudden, he felt at peace with his role in this simulation. No one really knew if this was Rachel's grave—a matriarch beloved of Jews, Christians, and Muslims—no one was sure exactly what the tomb looked like throughout its half a millennial history, and even though there were hundreds of accounts throughout the past five hundred years it was impossible to tell which parts were true. But if visiting this sacred place throughout time could connect him with reflections of his life, his family, and their place in the world; the work he was doing for Google Earth History for school was more than valuable.

With one last glance at the Hebrew inscriptions on the inside of the tomb, remembering one source talking about how they were interspersed with Muslim symbols throughout the years, he returned to his virtual workstation and began combing through the documents and pictures. Reading, rereading, and comparing from different angles.

He had little luck in trying to figure out where hole in the tomb should be, the hole where Jews would have to whisper their prayers. Beyond Ridley's short paragraph describing his visit, there was not a single piece of visual evidence to indicate where the hole would have been. He grabbed one last picture from the 1930s and teleported himself in the direction of where the picture was taken. Holding up the old photo to compare it with his current 1843 location he searched carefully. The buildings in the background and what must be an old Model-T parked next to the tomb distracted him, but he thought he finally had his best guess. He logged his photo comparison viewpoint as having no obvious contradictions and then teleported to the far side of the tomb.

At the time of Ridley's visit, Muslims had been using the building to conduct burial ceremonies and Ridley's traveling party would have probably skirted around the cemetery and approached the tomb from the back. Choosing a place just above waist height James used his forefinger to scribble with thick blue pen in the air "Put hole here" and added an arrow to indicate the best spot slightly above waist height.

Lastly, he typed out a short paragraph summarizing his research, highlighting the uncertain results, and reasoning for picking that location for the hole. After marking his beginning and end times he attached a log of all his movements and research to his account so his dad, or any employee for that matter, could check his work. When he first started working months ago his dad asked other employees to painstakingly trace his son's steps. It had resulted in endless criticism, but it had been necessary to gain their confidence so he could keep his job/school work access. Thank goodness that period of his life was mostly over.

Finished with the project he tapped the office space icon and the world ghosted out around him as the job board reappeared. There was enough time for him to take one more job before switching locations. He was startled by a woman materializing right in front of him. She had long dark hair and a brown colored outfit, that although not tight fitting, still gave the impression of a beautiful body.

The Beta

Uncomfortable and embarrassed he stepped back several feet quickly. He wasn't used to running into other employees in these virtual workrooms very often and not many employees took the time to enable a realistic looking avatar like she had done. In fact, James's appearance was a simple comic floating head with glasses and a baseball cap. He wasn't sure how his disembodied figure was supposed to interact with her realistic one, but he was being so quiet she hadn't even noticed him yet.

Curious, he just stood still and watched trying hard not to breathe too loud. She was scrolling through the job postings. But curiously she was looking at those far down at the bottom. The ones plainly marked non-essential.

Gathering his non-existing courage in this lack of consequences virtual world, he returned to his position right behind her shoulder so he could see what she was reading. He was totally stalking her but he couldn't help himself. What would she be doing with the tasks down at the bottom of the list? That wasn't helping the team complete the simulation.

She finally slowed down and was clicking and scrutinizing the details of each task. The titles he could see over her shoulder included "Stones and Labor", "Keys and Childbirth," "Lady Montefiore," and "Modern Red String for Fertility."

Suddenly she disappeared and a small icon indicating her work location appeared on "Keys and Childbirth."

James stood puzzled for just a moment and then everything clicked into place. There was a whole history, a whole emphasis, a whole narrative about what Rachel's Tomb meant to the women of the world and the AI had prioritized that work as a non-essential add on at the bottom of the list.

He was about to extract himself from his headset when his eye caught a bit of floating color to his right. There, scrawled in the middle of the work trailer like graffiti on a train car were the words "Bilal bin Rabah Mosque."

James shrugged. If there was anything he had learned so far was that the world was a complicated place, full of conflicts.

He couldn't fix everything in the world, not even with Photoshop.

The Beta

The Twins

 The twins' house was creepy although Kira supposed you could say that about almost any block in Seattle during the right type of drizzly day. The ground was damp and plants grew one on top of another so that even the best gardener couldn't make heads or tails of any untailored patch of growth. And that is exactly what Seattle was and will always be . . . swaths of living breathing rainforest mixed with temporary efforts to tame the space with cement and wood. Regardless, the moss will creep across the porch almost instantaneously after the last nail is hammered, then up the side of the house behind some ivy, and into the cracks around the window pane.
 Breathing in Seattle is much the same. Either you get a fresh lungful of windswept ocean breeze mingled with straight O_2 coming off the copious amount of plants, or you get a lungful of moss threatening to kill you like the nefarious black mold known for gutting houses.
 Kira hitched up her leggings which had inched down her thighs during the long walk and prepared to enter the twins' haunted house.
 Not sure whether or not she would be getting a fresh or moldy lungful Kira nevertheless went all in and took a deep breath. Almost choking, she exhaled the unexpected smokiness when she recognized the smell. Someone had been smoking marijuana in the neighborhood. Actually, when the twins' parents went out for the night they would sneak out and smoke in the backyard. But Kira couldn't tell if it was them because half the neighborhood smoked pot from time to time. You never really saw anyone just doing it on their front porch, but walking through town it wasn't uncommon to catch a whiff leaking out of some half-opened garage door or drifting along an alleyway.
 The smell mellowed her out without having to take a single hit, and the formerly creepy house quickly transformed into her dear

The Beta

friends' house. Kira had been friends with Annie since she was eight and if you are friends with Annie you enter into some type of weird honorary twinsie relationship with her brother Lahn, who was only three minutes younger than her but born on a separate day. Imagine that, having a birth twin that had a different birthday. Maybe that's why they were so darn close to one another and always trying to prove to a world that gave them different day birth certificates that they were in fact twins, which didn't take much effort on their part as they dressed alike and looked so similar.

Kira pressed the doorbell and proceeded to stick her tongue out and cross her eyes at the camera, never mind the fact that both of the twins' parents were probably looking at her on their phones right now. If she ever wanted to be President of the United States she would have to bribe the Zhao family to keep their ever-growing collection of web doorbell videos under wraps. They were so embarrassing. Of course if she was POTUS Kira would be sure to have the twins on her payroll—legally or otherwise.

Mrs. Zhao opened the door and once again Kira's senses were knocked down by an unexpected yet wholly welcome smell of braised meat. Her taste buds lost control and she inhaled deeply. Mrs. Zhao gave her a welcoming hug as she pulled Kira inside and closed the door.

Kira slipped off her shoes and tucked them under the entryway bench but kept her back pack on as she followed Mrs. Zhao to the kitchen. Unabashedly Kira walked all the way up to the stove and let the smell of caramelized sugar and pork belly engulf her senses. When she pulled back to smile at Mrs. Zhao, the scent cloud was replaced by the equally exhilarating smell of fresh cooked rice coming from the rice cooker on the counter.

"Will you stay for dinner?" Mrs. Zhao asked.

"Do you have to ask?" Kira replied casually followed by a more formal, "I would love to, thank you."

"The kids are upstairs," said Mrs. Zhao pointing upstairs with her wooden spoon.

Kira suppressed the desire to grab the spoon and lick it, the delayed gratification of eating at the Zhao's tonight tonight would have to overrule her baser instincts.

The Beta

Climbing the steps two at a time Kira unslung her backpack before knocking on Annie's door and waited patiently for her friend to answer. The Zhao's house was relatively new construction and the upper floor included a large elegant arched doorway for the master bedroom on the south end, and opposing it two identical but smaller arched doorways to the east and west for the twins.

Annie opened the door but didn't even make eye contact with Kira as she twirled around and plopped herself back down in front of her workstation. They had been friends forever but Annie often failed at basic friendly overtures.

Kira threw her back pack down on Annie's perfectly made bed and walked over to stand behind her friend to see what she was up to. It had to be pretty important for her to have so blatantly ignored Kira.

Annie's set-up was pretty impressive with three large screens forming a semicircle on her desk. She had told her parents she was learning to code and needed all of the equipment. Since they were more than willing to encourage their young daughter in any STEM field she desired, it had taken Annie little effort to get her parents to purchase the technology surrounding her. And technically Annie did do some coding from time to time.

Annie was furiously copy/pasting physics answers so Kira plunked herself down on the bed and reached over to her own backpack. Yanking on a side cord she freed her water bottle and took a deep drag, not realizing just how thirsty she was, the nerve-wracking day causing her to forget to eat or drink. Following up with some lip balm she unconsciously chewed on her slightly sweet lips as her hand trailed over the books and papers in the big section of her backpack.

Kira didn't want to do any of her homework, but with her grades still so low she needed to at least try or she would be grounded forever. She was dreading history the most, as she couldn't wrap her head around why she should care about a bunch of dead white guys. Chemistry was also beginning to kick her butt as the stoichiometry got more complicated.

The Beta

But her thoughts were rudely interrupted when Annie pounced on the bed beside her and flipped over onto her stomach putting her eyes right next to Kira's elbow.

"Ow," Kira replied, not actually having been hurt.

Annie crossed her eyes and flipped over again stretching long across the bed. She spent so much time at that desk.

Knowing she wouldn't get to start her history until she got home tonight, Kira tossed her books aside and tickled Annie in retaliation, who promptly unstretched and screamed like the girl she was. They both started laughing and then paused to catch their breath.

"So . . . how did it go?" Annie asked her, looking very curiously at her friend. It had been a week since Kira dropped off the envelopes and this was the first time they had the chance to talk in person.

"Oh, my goodness I was so scared. The first envelope got stuck halfway in the locker and I thought for sure someone was going to walk in, but then it finally made it through. The band dropoff was way easy but the last one in history class was tough, the teacher almost caught me. I had to agree to sign up for a geography bee. Like that's ever going to happen!" Her heart rate spiked as she remembered the day. Kira had never done anything like that before. It was exhilarating and kind of disgusting. "Never again, Annie!"

Annie was obviously enjoying her out of character struggles. "I didn't make you do it Kira, you were the one that came to me." she reminded her friend.

"I know," Kira blushed. She could never tell Annie that the fourth envelope wasn't only for her. The fourth envelope was also for Kevin. But Kira could never tell Annie that. Yet Annie never would have sold her the answers if she knew Kira was giving them to *him*. If only Annie had the answers for her history class, but he was the one teacher that never used the same tests over and over.

Now Kira felt bad about everything—lying to Annie, participating in a cheating ring, lying to the world about Kevin.

Luckily Annie changed subjects but before she could get too distracted. Kira pulled out the fifty-dollar bill he had given her and handed it over to Annie.

"What's this for?" Annie asked, truly taken aback.

"You know, for the chemistry answers," Kira replied.

"Oh no silly. Not only are you my friend, but you helped deliver those other three envelopes. You will never know how helpful that was!" Annie replied with a mischievous smile.

"Well, thanks." Kira said, and she pulled back her arm with the bill inside. The bill that contained some of Kevin's skill cells. She was so loopy in love Kira couldn't even admit it to herself except in these endorphic moments.

"C'mon," Annie said jumping up. "Do you really think I'm going to let my brother beat us to the thit kho?

They proceeded to race down the stairs like twelve-year-old's hell bent on pork sautéed in caramelized sugar with quail eggs, not to mention the rice.

The Lottery

The high school students were given two weeks to enter their applications. The results would be announced three weeks after that, and since Kira applied so early this left her with thirty days of agony. While Kira had heard all sorts of official and unofficial details about the application process it sounded as though there would be some type of lottery system for applications that were equal in all other regards, but the process was as transparent as Christmas wrapping so all she could do was wait.

She wanted to be part of *The Beta* so bad, but it seemed almost everyone else did too. She heard of a few kids too cool to try, and a handful that may have missed the deadline, but even Kevin submitted his application.

She mentally crossed her fingers in her heart and prayed both of their names would be chosen.

Not by coincidence she saw his text just minutes later. It was a sign! They were destined to be in *The Beta* together.

can you give me a ride after school? Same place?

Is that all he ever wanted? Well, at this point she would take what she could get.

Favors

She was back in Owl Hollow again but this time Kevin was late, was nowhere to be found and her phone was as silent as a mouse. Not wanting to appear needy she only checked it periodically and instead decided to explore around a bit. In the back of her mind she reasoned he was somewhere nearby.

A few meters away were some well-worn bike trails with carefully cultivated jumps all in a row. They almost reminded her of the mounds in the Southeast United States. Great longs mounds one shaped like a snake and others including pyramids and an amphitheater.

But there were no bikers to be seen so she set herself up as queen of the hill on one that would give her a good view of their aforementioned meeting place. She was quiet, stalking a prey she hoped would soon appear.

The leaves didn't have to whisper long before she heard some scuffling footsteps and watched him appear into view. He wasn't looking in her direction, nor did he look around before pulling out his phone and tilting his neck down. Would her generation have some type of neck complaint when they all grew old?

Suddenly conscious of her own posture she rose like a swan and pulled out her phone to receive his text.

hey where are you? I'm late did you already leave?

well sort of... ;)

She could see his face frowning in frustration. Wait a minute, she was the one doing the favor. What could he be upset about? Pausing just a moment she continued her text.

The Beta

look up

And he did. Only a brief flash of irritation flashed across his face before he quickly schooled his features. And once their eyes met it was all Kira could do to stop herself from running into his embrace.

Instead, she *walked* straight into his arms forgetting her frustration. He nuzzled his nose against her with closed eyes and warmed her chilled body with his. All too soon he pulled her to his side as they began walking to her car.

"How did you do on the chemistry test?" he asked her.

"Um . . . great," she replied with feigned enthusiasm. She dreaded what he might ask next.

"Sooo . . . can you get me the next one?" he asked predictably.

"I will try. I think so . . ." she was half thrilled with his request and the attention it brought to her, but also half cranky that she would have to keep asking the twins for more answers. They were getting a little suspicious as it was, and participating in the whole cheating ring make her feel icky. It was just not her thing.

"Well if you can't get them make sure to let me know. I would have to start studying you know." He tightened his grip around her waist and kissed her on the head. "With so much work I don't know how I could ever fit it in. Speaking of work, I'm late!"

She unlocked the car and they jumped in at the same time. Kira spoke her mind. "They are announcing *The Beta* winners tomorrow."

"Huh?" he replied as he buckled his seatbelt. "Oh yeah, I think they're announcing it sometime sixth period."

Kira was once again frustrated with his lack of enthusiasm. What was it about him today, it was like everything he said irritated her.

"You don't think you'll be picked?" she asked.

"Well, nah it's all about the numbers and how many people applied? Maybe fifteen hundred?" He was so pragmatic.

"You never know," she responded mysteriously.

You were meant to be mine Kira thought to herself. Even though she knew he was right, and she knew the chances of both of

The Beta

them being picked was practically impossible, it didn't stop her from dreaming. If they were both chosen he would be exclusively hers. All hers.

The next day the high school was a roiling mess by sixth period. Kira couldn't decide if the person in charge of the PR was either a genius or an absolute idiot. While not every kid was dying to be picked for *The Beta*, high school students didn't need much of an excuse to go crazy at the end of the day.

Sixth period attendance verified, one piece of paper homework turned in, and they were released to the gymnasium for a repeat of the pep style rally introduction.

Kira vacillated between feeling absolutely sure that she was destined to be chosen and repeating the odds over and over. 1 in 100 chance, 1 in 100 chance. It was something like that.

While the assembly was as flashy as before it didn't take them long to get down to business and begin announcing the winners.

A booming voice announced the first lucky student. "Makayla Johnson!" The resulting cheers were so loud Kira placed her headphones over her ears as she watched the lucky girl pick her way carefully down the bleachers and up to the front of the gymnasium.

"Nathaniel Nugyen!" boomed the voice and a boy who used to tease her unmercifully in fifth grade made his way to the front with confident gestures and high fives.

Each name rolled across the screen and across her eyes; every name she could hear faintly through her earphones; and with every name she used her sharp thumbnail to embed a slash mark on the skin of her hand. Nine slash marks, thirteen slash marks, fifteen slash marks, and then . . .

"Angelique Nelson!" and with that last name Kira's eyes teared up, her ears became hot, her hand hurt, and her heart stopped. It took a few seconds to make sure she wouldn't cry and then she left the auditorium, headphones still on her ears acting like a shield from the noise and her feelings.

The Beta

Assignment #3

James grabbed a clean towel and tried to blot out as much of the dampness as he could before putting the headset on again. This time he picked out a thinner and significantly more expensive pair of gloves before restarting the Developer.

After exploring Islam, Christianity—and Judaism to a certain extent—he was ready to learn about the Buddhism of his father's family and would plan to devote significantly more time to this project.

Turning the globe around to East Asia he zoomed into Henan Province in Dengfeng China. The work space here was a complete opposite of Rachel's Tomb. In Israel he was shocked to have run into any employees, but the Shaolin Temple was a popular worksite and about six employees were in the work room either choosing their daily tasks or reviewing work. While all Google Earth History employees could be identified with their real names and specific employee numbers, they were still allowed to choose their own avatar.

A quick glance revealed six male avatars, two dressed up in detailed martial arts clothing and the four others with names written in Chinese characters. James pulled up the real mugshots of the two dressed up employees to reveal the images of a scruffy looking white guy and an overweight old man. He tried not to be too overly judgmental, James was drawn to the power and mystique of martial arts films as much as the next guy, but he certainly would never be caught dead dressing up an avatar in cheesy Kungfu clothing if he was a white guy.

Part of him was frustrated with the cavalier attitude of those who were only drawn to this historical site because of their 1980s obsession with westernized martial arts films. This site which included some of the most sacrosanct locations in China meant much more than martial arts. He hoped there were enough level-headed Chinese employees to make sure those white dudes didn't get their grubby, unclean western fingerprints all over their history.

The Beta

The job board here was so immense James started with a search instead of a scroll. He typed in his query and was rewarded with a short list of tasks. He signed up, but disabled the automatic start, because before he began his work today he wanted to take a tour of the location.

This was his third time at the site in as many days. He always started his work day here next to a small arching rock bridge that crossed a meandering stream. This was by far one of the most beautiful places in the entire world and he was developing plans to persuade his parents to make the trip in real life. They always talked about going to China and he wasn't entirely sure why the plans hadn't yet come to fruition.

After jumping down the long path he found himself looking at the Shuce Cliff of Zhong Yue Mountain, the birthplace of Chinese Zen Buddhism. He stood on a walkway built right into the middle of the mountain. It looked rickety from far away, and despite his knowledge that he was safe in VR, his ordinary fear of heights put him on edge. Taking some deep breaths, he slowly relaxed and looked far above his head. This was the middle of the Five Mountains of China. The slivered edges of greyish rock rose gracefully into the sky punctuated by greenery in the summer and light browns in autumn. James could almost inhale the fresh air to match the scenery.

His final destination and task this afternoon was at little-known place called the Pagoda Forest. James settled himself in the middle of the forest and did a leisurely 360. He was surrounded by tall pagodas which were actually the grave markers for accomplished Shaolin Monks. So far, he learned that each pagoda was constructed with 1-7 levels—always an odd number—with each level representing an accomplishment or stage of enlightenment. Some of the pagodas were round and some were square, but simply walking through the forest gave one a feeling of grandeur, so different from his experience in American graveyards. Of course this was no ordinary graveyard.

Getting to work he turned on both his audio and visual translators for today's session. While most of the employees were working down the valley at the actual Shaolin Monastery building, a few people seemed to take an interest in the pagodas like he did.

The Beta

In fact, several older Chinese professors wandered through recently and both reviewed his work, one even making a suggestion.

To James it was very important that all of his sources for this project be reliable, authentic local Chinese sources. It proved more difficult than he initially thought, not necessarily to find the sources but to fully understand which were the most reliable. While he had some notion of which university and news sources were worth using in the U.S.—learning about an entire other continent of people and places would require years of work. And even though the Google translator was fairly accurate, there was a whole other study on the meaning and etymology of names that added another fairly significant layer to this task.

Yet he plugged away knowing that he might learn slowly, but this was his culture, no matter how distantly removed. Did it matter that he was third generation American but still 75% Chinese? Would it be different if he was second generation but part white? Sometimes he felt bad that his work was not perfect. Maybe a Chinese American kid shouldn't even try to take part in reconstructing Chinese culture. At least he wasn't one of those white dudes.

Sometimes he felt like he was participating in a large three-dimensional Wikipedia of the visual universe.

The graphics for the modern-day pagoda forest were already in place and the interior was pretty high-quality inferring that a decent camera crew covered the grid. But when James moved off thirty feet in from the pagoda forest, the image, though high resolution, was still dependent upon AI algorithms to fill out the vegetation. James suspected AI would never quite make the leap from machine to organic.

He set up his workspace inside a low brick wall near the Yugong Pagoda. It reminded him of the walled off gravesites where his great-grandmother was buried in Hollywood Hills California.

That's when it hit him. The Pagoda Forest held some kind of grip on James that he could not quite figure out. It wasn't like Mt. Sinaii, Makkah, or the Kashi Vishwanath Temple. It wasn't where a religion was born but instead where the religious came after death. None of those were the connections that compelled him.

What drew him to this place was how each grave stone was a true detailed monument that gave significance to life.

James knew that most modern Buddhists choose cremation, and many older traditions used to expose the corpse by leaving it in the forest, but it wasn't the type of burial he considered significant here in the Pagoda Forest. It was the pagodas themselves, the story they told, the way they immortalized and honored each monk's life.

He knew that millions of people in large metropolises across the world were dying each year resulting in crowded graveyards, recycled cemetery plots, and bodies buried one on top of another in the same spot.

James shook with revulsion, as he imagined being forgotten so soon.

But that is what the pagoda in front of him meant, that is what the virtual world around him signified. Not everyone was lucky enough to be buried under a pagoda that told a story, but eventually everyone could choose to leave their story in VR. VR had the potential to make sure no one was forgotten.

Again

"Chemistry again huh?" Annie looked sidelong at her. Kira was once again sitting on Annie's bed after school, homework spread before her, with Annie waiting patiently by her as the laser printer spit out a slew of papers. It seemed like the printer would never stop.

"Yeah," Kira puffed air out of her cheeks in what she hoped was realistic exasperation as she pointed meaningfully to all the books and papers spread before her. There was something inside her that felt terrible about not saying anything to Annie about Kevin and therefore she ended up lying about the Chemistry answers he needed as well.

Kira leaned back to scroll through her phone, completely ignoring the homework she had purposely emphasized but angled

The Beta

so she could catch any wayward expression on Annie's face. The main reason Kira refused to tell Annie about Kevin is that she was sure to chew her out. Far from keeping her opinions to herself Annie would go even further by detailing exactly what Kira should do about "him" and in the end she would probably do everything Annie ordered her to do. So therefore, Kira was not telling Annie and it formed a weird wall between them only visible to Kira.

The printer finally quit and Annie pulled out the sheaf of papers and joined Kira on the bed. Kira gathered in most of her homework to give Annie more room and then she watched her friend sort and pull out smaller groups of papers and put them into those same manila envelopes that now automatically gave Kira a pit in her stomach.

"So . . ." Annie looked at her with an odd look, "I don't want to ask but would you mind dropping off another two like you did last time?" Annie was holding two of the envelopes with some measure of expectation, but her odd expression must have been the result of her guilt.

A little delighted that maybe Annie's guilt in asking her to help drop off papers matched her own guilt at lying to Annie about Kevin, Kira quickly nodded.

"Do you mind giving me the answers to the next chemistry test too?"

"Sure," Annie's response was automatic, but Kira saw her look over suspiciously, "I didn't know you would so easily become a cheater. What's really going on Kira?"

She decided to go into full theatrical mode to slip this one past Annie by rattling off a million ideas like they were little distracting missiles, "Well, I'm really stressed out about the PSAT and not only that but mom is stressed out about her work and then they keep giving me grief about my grades and college, and for some reason chemistry isn't sticking. Maybe I'm getting distracted," Kira took one last inhalation before she finished off her diatribe, "And my mom almost took the car away last weekend, I'm in love with half the boys at school, and I didn't get into *The Beta*."

"Aiyee . . . that's enough, of course I will help you." Annie finished filling the last envelope and handed three over to Kira, putting her arm around her shoulders in the process. "And you're going to be just fine girl!"

"I hope! It doesn't feel like it right now," then to add in another diversion, "by the way, what has your brother been up to lately? I don't see him around as much as I used to."

"Oh, he's like you, taking the easy route," Annie profoundly disapproved of them actually using the cheat sheets even if she didn't mind selling them. "And goofing off more than usual. He's going to regret all this someday."

Kira swore she could actually see and hear a hint of worry in Annie's demeanor, so she offered her support in return, "He's going to be fine."

"He better be!"

Drop Off

This was her second time making a drop off in the band room but it didn't change how she felt. No matter how many times she dropped off another envelope her heart still raced, her face turned red, and she felt sick to her stomach. Kira wasn't sure whether it was slightly more comforting to drop off in a familiar place or more nerve-wracking as the chances of getting caught increased with repetition.

In fact, Kira was pretty shocked that the twins hadn't been caught by this point. If they were telling her the truth their "side business" of selling answers was a little over four years old, starting back in jr. high when they were eighth graders. Supposedly, one of the twin's best friends inherited an old binder on Pacific Northwest History and the test answers contained within still matched the tests being used in class.

Their friend made a habit of copying all the answers and distributing them freely and widely to all eighth graders. It became such a habit that a group of them would gather at their half lockers and memorize the multiple-choice answers only minutes before the

The Beta

test. Kira could remember chanting "a, d, c, b, a, a" to the common tune of *Jingle Bells* one Christmas.

This gave Annie and her brother the idea of gathering test questions and selling the answers to make a little money. At first, they did it more for the challenge than the money, but as time went on their little business was too profitable to give up so easily. Annie eventually leaked the basics to Kira, but she never let on how they advertised and communicated with their customers.

Kira ignored the handful of band members that were eating lunch in the main room under the pretenses of practicing, and walked straight back to the storage rooms. Thankfully the room was empty and looked much like her previous visit. The third shelf was so high she stood on tippy toes and ran her hand along the shelf as she felt for an envelope, because this time she was instructed to pick up cash as well as drop off answers and that's what was causing her such apprehension. If anyone caught her now she might be accused of running the whole show.

Unable to feel anything, Kira looked around for a way to boost herself higher so she could actually look along the shelf. It didn't take long to find an old metal folding chair that creaked as she opened and positioned it beneath the shelving.

Kira jumped on top of the chair and looked around the shelf. It was dusty, dirty, and full of old unused musical equipment. She gingerly shuffled the items around trying to figure out where an envelope could be hidden when she saw a bit of white poking out of the back of a black case. Reaching out as far as she possibly could stretch, Kira nabbed the corner and pulled it out successfully. Whew, already feeling better she checked inside the unsealed envelope to confirm there were two twenty-dollar bills when the sound of the door opening made her jump.

"Excuse me, what are you doing in the storage room?" an adult voice asked.

Kira froze, trying to see who it was but the bright light of the hallway behind the speaker blocked her view. Oh crap, she was caught red handed. "I . . ." but nothing else came out of her mouth and the adult came forward swiftly revealing his identity. It was the band instructor, Mr. Moore.

The Beta

His body language and demeanor all indicated a very suspicious nature as he walked quickly towards her. He was tall enough to peer into the third shelf without the help of an old metal folding chair. This gave Kira enough time to drop the envelope and move her hands to a black music case in a last-minute ditch of distraction.

"What are you doing here?" he asked again.

Kira almost started crying and why was he so accusatory unless he knew all about the cheating ring and the envelopes?

Yet infinity hung in the air as he waited for her answer. Somehow, no matter how clumsily, her brain remembered the name of one of the trumpet players she knew back in sixth grade.

"I was meeting Riya to have lunch." Kira replied, only narrowly avoiding the ingrained vocal tic of raising her voice at the end of any sentence that caused everything to sound like a question. It was such a natural part of her generations' way of speaking that it often made conversing with older people confusing, for the older people at least.

"Meeting Riya back here?" he asked, the overriding tone being doubt. He kept switching between looking at her guilty face and scanning the shelf between them.

Kira felt silly standing on the folding chair so she got down and at the same time replied, "Not meeting here, I was looking for . . ." she doubted an extension cord would pass the test so she threw out something while implausible for a band storage closet at least not unlikely in general, ". . . a charging cord for my phone."

Mr. Moore kept rummaging through the shelf and he looked over his shoulder to address her as she began to inch out of the room, her backpack not fully zipped and three guilt ridden envelopes in plain view.

"Students are not allowed back here without my permission, and unless you are part of the band you do not have permission to eat lunch in the main room," he said crossly. "Riya should have known that."

"Yes, sir," she replied hoping the military honorific would appease him. She walked out into the band room with him at her heels. Turning the corner to get out of there as soon as possible, the mission obviously aborted, she ran smack into another student.

The Beta

It was Riya. Of all the luck.

Mr. Moore interrogated her immediately. "Riya you know non-band students are not allowed to eat lunch with those who are practicing right?"

Riya nodded her head obediently. Kira couldn't move even though she felt like running.

Mr. Moore continued, looking like he was almost ready to grab Kira by the shirt collar. "Then why did . . . what is your name?"

Oh goodness she was doomed, she was positive she was doomed, but her legs wouldn't follow her desire to run so the only option was to succumb to fate. "Kira, sir."

". . . invite Kira here to eat lunch?" Mr. Moore used a threatening voice which certainly had the desired effect upon Riya.

It only took half a second for Riya to look confused and blurt out, "I didn't invite anyone to eat lunch here, I haven't even talked to Kira since elementary school."

Both Mr. Moore and Riya turned to look at Kira, whose face was infused with guilt and crimson with anxiety. What had she got herself into?

"I . . ." Kira began but before she could continue Mr. Moore interrupted her.

"You are going to come with me young lady." He said motioning her to follow him out of the band room and into the hallway. They didn't have far to go before she realized he was leading her directly to the vice principal's office.

Kira had never been in trouble at school in her entire life. Her heart sank.

It didn't take long before they were both seated across from Vice Principal Martinez. Mr. Moore was explaining the circumstances in excruciating detail when she heard him ask to search her backpack.

Both of the men looked directly at her. She knew there was no expectation of privacy on school property—well perhaps they couldn't search her cell phone—but other than that they were going to find the answers to three different tests in her backpack and she was going to be in big trouble. Kira could see it on their faces—she was screwed.

The Beta

Not wanting to look them in the eye anymore Kira pulled her heavy backpack up off the floor and hauled it onto the desk. She did not utter a word as the vice principal opened each pocket starting with the small ones and working his way back to the largest where the envelopes were hidden.

As he approached the final pocket Kira considered speaking out and fessing up. Things always went better when the criminal cooperated, right? But another baser instinct held her to silence as he reached his long arm into the pocket and felt around before zipping it up again.

Not realizing she was holding her breath Kira coughed as she began to breathe again. If they weren't looking for the envelopes what the heck did they search her bag for?

"Kira, would you please turn out all of the items in your pockets?" Curious, but holding a ray of hope in her heart Kira obeyed with an obvious acquiescence as she clearly dumped out each coat pocket with a shake and dug out the minor change and phone from her leggings' back pocket.

"She must have left her vaporizer in the band storage room. I thought I checked it out but I'll look again." replied Mr. Moore.

So that was it! Kira almost laughed and her open book face looked immediately relieved. Who cared if they thought she looked pleased because they couldn't find any contraband vapor cartridges on her, after all she didn't vape. But they weren't looking for her cheat sheets!

Elated, Kira was able to honestly answer all of the vice principal's questions to his satisfaction except the one about why she was in the band closet in the first place.

Taking some time to distress her features, Kira spoke about being lonely and sad, trying to give every hint at being depressed without forcing him to take some kind of mandatory action based on that information. She rambled on a bit about how finding a quiet place to text her good friend from another school raised her spirits and no one had noticed or bothered her in the band room closet. Then her phone was about to die so she was looking around for a phone charger. The excuse was a little flimsy but not unwholly impossible.

The Beta

Mr. Martinez seemed to believe her and asked her to wait for Mr. Moore's return before leaving. The bell startled Kira and she looked up at Mr. Martinez. He worked on his laptop as she watched students fill the halls through the office window.

Of all the coincidences she saw Annie's brother walk by and a brief shadow of horror flick across his face before he turned away, missing Kira's friendly wave of reassurance. Oh crap, he would think she was caught.

Confident Mr. Moore wouldn't find any evidence of vaping, but still a little unsure if he would find the envelope of money, Kira knew she wasn't in the clear yet. She didn't yet dare open her phone to text Annie to let her know everything was O.K.

Mr. Moore returned looking frustrated, "There was no vaping equipment in the room," he reported and seemed ready to say more but Vice Principal Martinez interrupted him.

"Was this the same storage closet in which you found the others?" Mr. Martinez asked. Mr. Moore's suspicion made more sense now that Kira realized he was hunting vapers in his storage closets.

"No," Mr. Moore replied.

"Well then I think you are cleared of any wrongdoing Kira, sorry for the trouble." He looked pointedly at Mr. Moore, "After talking with Kira I think it is safe to say she clearly understands no students are allowed in the storage room ever or in the band room for lunch without your explicit permission and supervision."

Kira realized there was an undercurrent to that statement as band students were currently in the band room all alone with no teachers. Ha! Mr. Moore was the one who was in trouble! Served him right for being so suspicious, although she did have a bit of sympathy for the difficult cat and mouse game of catching vapers. Because of vaping equipment's small size, minimal smoke, and disguising scents, vaping on school grounds was rampant. It was common in the girls' restroom to have one stall smell like mint the next like cherry; it was a bit like walking into a soap shop.

Mr. Moore got up to leave for class and Kira followed suit when she heard the vice principal call out behind her. "Can you wait a minute Kira?" he asked. Dang, she thought. Maybe her talk of being sad went too far and now he was going to make her talk with a school counselor about depression.

"Give me a second Kira, I need to get Maura." he instructed.

Kira groaned inside, she was pretty sure Maura was one of the school's counselors. First she is accused of vaping and now she would have to discuss depression. Could the day get any more frustrating?

Sure enough, he returned to the office with Maura who sat down next to Kira. "How are you doing Kira?" asked the counselor.

"I'm good." Kira replied, trying to look calm, confident, and happy—the complete opposite of her emotions the last hour.

"Good, well we have some exciting news to tell you." Maura began and Kira couldn't hide her confusion.

"News?" she asked, taking a keener interest in Maura. The vice principal's demeanor changed as well. There was positive tension in the air now.

"After our talk today Kira, I think you may find this news will brighten your day," added the vice principal.

Well, get to the point thought Kira. Not getting caught was enough to raise her spirits the rest of the week.

"Kira, I know this isn't as impressive as a big announcement in front of the whole school, but one of our chosen few was unable to make the commitment." Maura paused here and both of them looked at Kira expecting her to have caught on by now.

Logically Kira knew exactly what they were referencing, but her fragile ego didn't dare hope until they were forced to utter the words out loud with unquestionable clarity. So once again she held her breath and her silence.

"Kira," Mr. Martinez's smile widened, "You have been chosen to join *The Beta*!"

"Seriously?" Kira responded. It was all she hoped for and for some reason she couldn't believe them.

"Yes Kira, I'm serious. You will make a fine representative." He looked pointedly at her, "That is, if you are still interested?"

"Yes, yes!," Kira replied a little too hastily. "I really want to." She looked at both of them. "What else do I need to do?"

The Beta

"Nothing on your part. Representatives from *The Beta* will reach out to you and your parents very soon. Congratulations!" Mr. Martinez replied. "You are excused."

Kira thanked Mr. Martinez and Maura, promising to reach out if she had any further questions. She did, indeed, have a million questions but didn't feel like this was the right time to ask. Her sympathetic nervous system was in overdrive. Walking in here thirty minutes ago she expected to be expelled and instead her dreams were coming true. It was a little too much to process.

She needed to find Annie or Lahn right away and let them know everything was alright. That's when it hit her. Once she joined *The Beta* she would no longer go to the high school and she would no longer have a regular excuse to see Kevin.

Kira scanned the crowded hallway for any sign of her friends. Wanting a better view, she jumped up on a pedestal tucked into a corner overlooking the main entryway. The perch allowed her to see wide and far while remaining mostly hidden.

She pulled out her phone and texted Annie.

I've got good news where are you?

Annie was never a prompt responder so Kira went back to looking, not wanting to miss either of them.

It was then that she saw him across the room. Kevin. Her heart always sped up when she thought of him and jumped when she first saw him. It was no different now. He was running his hand through his hair when suddenly a girl crashed into his arms. She was laughing so loud Kira could recognize her voice immediately. The girl wrapped her arms around his neck and he kissed her softly on the forehead.

Kira dropped down so they wouldn't see her, and her heart dropped too. This day had been one hell of a rollercoaster.

The Beta

Part Two
History

Biometrics

"May I please have your hand?" The woman in uniform asked her with indifference. Kira hesitantly extended her left hand and the women practically yanked it a foot closer in her firm grip. "Now relax."

Kira associated fingerprinting with criminals in all the shows she watched, so it felt a little creepy as the attendant skillfully rolled each finger across an electronic pad and then reviewed for any rejected prints and rerolled the offending scans.

She smiled a little weakly at her dad who smiled back. Each accepted student had to have one designated parent willing to go through the process. She thought that was a little strange but at least her dad was willing to do it—her mom probably would have flatly refused if dad hadn't volunteered so readily.

The walk and shuttle ride into the Microsoft campus was gorgeous. It was September and fall had made an early appearance in Western Washington. A unusual cold snap from the arctic triggered something in the deciduous trees causing them all to be frosted with autumn colors, yet the leaves were still stuck stubbornly to their branches.

They were with a small group of sixteen people, eight kids and eight adults, led by a smiling "tour" guide. Although they were not really on a tour, it was more like a cross between a pre-employment screening and job orientation.

Once everyone finished submitting their fingerprints they were led down the hall to a room that looked like an optometrist's office. Here they were going to have their retinas scanned.

The Beta

It was also kind of weird to have all these strangers in the room with her as her body parts were intimately recorded and measured.

She supposed it was not that big of a deal. If everything went smoothly she would be spending the next year or two with these kids both online and in-person every Friday. She couldn't believe that of all the days of the week they would choose Friday as the one day she would actually have to get up early and go somewhere. What a drag! Oh well.

She sat in the optometrist chair and answered a series of questions about her eyesight that were verified as she answered questions about what she could see on what row.

But the very last part of the exam was different. The clinician pulled over a tripod on a swivel that held a huge camera. He asked her to bring her chin and forehead as close to the straps as possible and then proceeded to take picture after picture of her irises.

She knew this because the scans appeared on a large screen behind him. Her eye was blown up as big as the 50-inch screen so she could see every little minute detail.

The eyes, her eyes, she thought to be as unremarkable as a cheap chocolate bar, as common as a tree bark, as boring as a brown grocery bag.

Instead the scan showed the most gorgeous panoramic view of a complicated, multi-faceted, rainbow brown eye. Like a tiger's eye, her iris was layer upon layer of gold, black, bronze, orange, yellow, brown, tan, ivory, and jet. There could be no eye in the world that replicated the beauty she saw before her on the screen.

Kira had been looking so closely at the image of her iris both the clinician and her dad caught her with her head out of the straps peering over the man's shoulder.

The man coughed politely and smiled, waiting for her to return her head to the proper position before commencing with additional iris scans.

When the exam was finished she got up clumsily, feeling a little embarrassed, to make room for her dad. Glancing around sheepishly she was glad no one was staring at her, or at least they were kind enough to pretend not to.

The Beta

She watched her dad's iris scan with fascination. He was 100% Chinese while her mom was a fourth German, an eighth Polish, an eighth French and half Native American from the Sinixt Lakes Tribe. If only her mom was here to get the iris scan she could compare her parents iris's to her own.

Finished, they followed their guide out of the room and into the hallway. Kira felt a squeeze on her elbow. She looked up at her dad, surprised.

"I'll be right back," he whispered to her and swiftly returned back down the hallway and into the optometrist room before she could ask any questions. Weird.

Alone, she followed the pack slowly, nervous that he would lose them. Yet the white hallway was long and before they turned the corner she looked back and saw her dad come back out. He caught up with them right before they took the next turn.

"What was that all about?" she whispered.

He smiled as he tucked a large white envelope under his arm. "A surprise," was his only reply.

The next to last set of biometrics were not much different from a visit to the doctor. Blood pressure, heart rate, and weight. She wasn't exactly sure how her weight fit into the picture but she didn't have the guts to ask. And thankfully the doctors were discreet and didn't weigh them in a manner that shared the results with the group. When she was back in the car she would ask her dad if he considered recording their weights creepy.

Finally, they began to take measurements for which she could clearly understand the purpose. The last room they entered looked more like one of NASA's storage rooms. Suits, gloves, headsets, and all manner of VR paraphernalia hung on the walls. This is what she was waiting for!

The person taking her measurements was a woman who looked like an elegant seamstress with her hair pulled up into a bun, thick black glasses, and deeply painted red lips. Kira held perfectly still as the woman used a tape measure on her arms and torso, asking her to place the measuring tape along her belly button and nipple line. It was more than a little awkward, but more than a little worth

The Beta

it for what she would get in return. The final result would be personalized VR gear that was molded to her body!

Curious, Kira asked the woman a question. "Do you actually make the VR suits here?"

Frowning, the woman paused in irritation as she was tightening the measuring tape around Kira's right palm. "Partially, most of the parts are manufactured offsite and we have to assemble them and do some alterations."

She squeezed a little tighter on her palm for no reason and then loosened the tape to take the measurement. Sucking in her pride Kira kept her mouth shut as the measuring tape made its way across and around all sorts of body parts.

After the last measurement she watched the seamstress enter in the final data points on her laptop, print out the results and hand her a copy on a clipboard. It was weird looking at a professional and technical readout of her body metrics. She spent the next twenty minutes flipping her gaze between reading her measurement report and watching her father squirm under the woman's blunt gaze as he was subjected to all the same pulls and prodding's.

Kira always read everything and so in her boredom she combed through the technical paragraphs at the end of her printout. She wasn't really sure why they were given the printout as it seemed mostly written for the employees that would be building their customs suits, but the third paragraph from the bottom caught her eye.

Because of the precise measurements and close fit of the personal VR suit, new equipment may need to be procured in the event that the subject has either grown 1.5 inches in height or an increase/decrease of 10 lbs. in weight.

Whoa . . . that didn't give any of them much wiggle room! She glanced up at some of the teenage boys in the room who she knew were still growing like weeds since they were all sophomores in high school. They would need new suits by winter.

Either way they were not paying a dime of this project other than their time and feedback. She was sooooo lucky!

"I'm done kiddo!" Her dad's voice snapped her attention back to the room.

The Beta

Thankfully they were finished with the red lipped woman, who was replaced with an incredibly handsome young man. Kira was now as quiet as before but for different reasons.

"Can I have your printouts please?" he asked, speaking to her dad. His mouth twitched in a slight smile. Dude, he was cute and she was getting custom VR equipment. Life was good. But why did he ask her dad for her printout instead of her directly?

She handed him her clipboard, bypassing any notion that her father would speak for her.

"There are a few pieces of equipment, such as gloves, that we may be able to try for a true fit today." He led them deeper into the labyrinth of equipment.

They were in a large high-ceilinged workshop that was split into informal niches dedicated to different parts of the VR suit. They walked past the head sets, torso suits, and leggings to a glove counter. Walking behind the counter he motioned for them to take a look as he read down their printouts, scanning with his hand and eyes.

Once he found what he needed he turned to the wall behind him which was filled with rows of small boxes. Pulling one out he looked closer, frowned and returned it, then climbed a small step ladder in search of another box. Only a minute later she knew what this situation reminded her of—the scene in Harry Potter where he received his first wizarding wand from Ollivander.

The association made Kira light up even more inside, and she couldn't tell how much of that excitement was slipping through her normally calm facade.

He pulled three boxes, placed them on the counter and then turned his eyes and attention directly on her—making up for his earlier sexism. "Let's give these a try first." He opened the box on the left and pulled out a slim pair of tight-fitting black gloves, one of which he handed to her.

She expected them to be bulky and thick, but they were like nothing she had ever seen associated with VR. Pulling the glove on in one sophisticated motion she turned her hand from side to side.

He reached out his hand with the palm face up and looked inquiringly her way, "May I adjust them?" he asked.

She put her hand forward slowly and tried not to provide any resistance as he stretched the glove back and forth, pulled and reset each finger, and then tugged in different directions on the palm fabric. My goodness, he was practically caressing her hand in every direction. She had died and gone to heaven.

But heaven was fleeting.

"That is a perfect fit if I ever saw one," he said with honest surprise. "So these gloves are for those programs that require a deft and specific fingertip touch. They can type on floating keyboards, trace finger width patterns, and also provide visible grip to objects. However, these gloves will not provide any feedback or sensation." He finally looked a little closer at Kira, as if sizing up whether she was worthy enough to hear what he was going to say. "Here at the shop we call these gloves 'Slick' and they are seriously the next level in VR interactions. You can give the computer more input with these babies than any handset or glove developed so far. They are the best of the best." He looked closely at her face, "How do they feel?"

"Like magic," was all she could come up with, yet it was an honest reply as the gloves did feel silky and light on her hands.

Her wand had found its match.

Eye Pictures

Kira was laying on her bed at home and staring out the window when she heard a knock on her door. Sitting up a bit she didn't hesitate to call out immediately. "Come in!"

It was her mom and dad, and they were holding a brown paper wrapped package.

Her dad handed her the gift not saying a word but with a nod indicating she should open. He looked happy. He looked mischievous. Her mom looked kind of smug. Kira's parents had no humility.

The Beta

Not one to turn down a free gift Kira yanked at the raffia and the thick paper wrapping kind of unfolded itself.

Inside was a black frame facing backwards so she slowly turned it over to see what it contained. Kira was speechless.

It was a picture of a supernova, a large pool of glistening gems and fire.

It was huge colorful picture of her iris.

She looked up at her parents with those same eyes and their gazes met. She set the picture down and hugged them fiercely.

The Goods

Kira still remembered the day her gear arrived. It was one of those rare sunny days that makes living in Seattle more than worth it. Her house was surrounded by lush green plants. The sun was burning off the last of the thick dew off the grass causing the air to carry the perfect amount of moisture, scent, and distant sea air. It was nearly impossible not to breathe deeply all afternoon on a day like that. Simply intoxicating.

But then all of a sudden she couldn't breathe at all. The delivery truck pulled up stopping precariously close to her dad's old Subaru. The driver walked up carrying box after box.

Kira's mom signed for the packages and shut the door. Heaven must have approved because her gear boxes were surrounded by a large halo of liquid sunshine streaming through the dining room windows.

She still wasn't breathing. Frantic, dying for air like the living room was a fishbowl, she ran across the room and cranked open two of the windows to let the outside air flood inside—over her—over the gear boxes.

Kira's mom was watching her take a deep breath. She smiled at her daughter. "Well, I think I'll leave you and your boxes alone."

"No, no, you can stay mom. Don't you want to see?" she asked, slightly quirked at her joke.

The Beta

"Of course, but I want to finish getting dinner ready. Why don't you start unpacking and I will join you in a bit," she replied, giving her a quick hug before retreating to the kitchen.

Kira's mom knew her only too well. While she really wouldn't have minded if her mom stayed and helped pull the gear out of the boxes, it was nice to do it by herself. Kind of like a birthday or Christmas present, it's really annoying when someone wants to 'help' you open it up. It goes too quickly like that.

Although after opening a few boxes she kinda wished her mom had stayed to help. Thank goodness her toddler sister was gone because she ended up needing several knives and a large pair of scissors from the kitchen to help her cut through all sorts of tape, strings, and wires—not to mention oodles of packing peanuts and bubble wrap.

Kira understood the equipment still cost a pretty penny despite the program's intention of making the gear affordable for both schools and homes. But geesh! Wading through all this packaging made her feel gross. It probably represented a cut tree, several gallons of oil, and a full garbage can of non-recyclable material. Not to mention the hazards for those who manufactured and disposed of the toxic chemicals in the process. But she sighed in resignation. Kira couldn't solve all those problems—at least yet. First she needed to make it through high school. That was the first step.

Most of the equipment belonged to the program and was already tagged with outward signs of ownership and barcodes. Without having to look closer or read any policies, she was reasonably sure there were also codes and chips inside the equipment to prevent theft from becoming a profitable business.

The largest box contained the four main components of the program. One 40-inch screen, one 27 inch screen, a console, and a large slate. The console looked a little like a cross between the Playstation 5, Xbox 2, and an old school Atari. This came as little surprise as it represented the two main companies working together, with a nod to the original gaming system that started it all. As far as Kira knew, the similarities were cosmetic, an attempt by the companies to appeal to the younger gaming crowd. Inside the console was original hardware designed to be cost effective,

The Beta

compatible, as well as cutting edge. So they jokingly named it "Opensource Hardware" because it was so basic and easy to modify.

Kira shook her head a little. The strategy behind *The Beta* was to make money on separate software, private consoles, and their traditional gaming systems but everyone was dubious. Kira was maybe one of those skeptics, but she was also among the thankful. Finally, technology companies were truly putting aside their differences, working together, and for the greater good.

The second box was large and square. When she opened it up there was a little note that read: Assignment. Before your first Friday meeting complete 30 hours of work in any class of your choice. Well, that was kind of nice. Getting to choose what she completed the first week of school was a welcome change. Underneath the note she could see several software packages.

The smallest box on top looked like a video game. Dark metallic colors and fantastic cover art with the words 'High School Credit Machine' along the front. It really did look like a videogame in all respects. She flipped over the box to read the back. "Ready to earn high school credit? Simply have your current high school send all transcripts to our parent company H.S.C.M. Once current progress is entered any credit earned through approved games will be added to your transcript and will be sent to your home high school. Getting high school credit was never so easy."

Huh? High school credit easy? Kira wasn't sure about this slick advertisement. What about honors, International Baccalaureate and Running Start? Were the credits accredited and fully transferable? What if the data was lost? But since she couldn't answer any of those questions and she needed to trust *The Beta*, Kira opened the package. Instead of a DVD the "High School Credit Machine" looked more like an external hard drive with a USB cord.

She began to pull the other classes out of the box, each packaged like a video game. First was Algebra 2 and despite some designer's fancy attempt to make numbers look enticing, Kira could still feel the dread associated with math. The physics box couldn't trick her any more than the math despite its fancy

The Beta

packaging and the health class looked particularly ridiculous with its mix of food and body images.

There was still one more box. The box was taller than the others, completely black and free of text. The only image was a glowing Earth that could be seen on all six sides of the box.

She picked it up and turned it over in her hands, curious. Each of the six sides was a different view of the globe. There was China, where her father's family came from. One quick turn and she saw Europe where half her maternal ancestors originated. And lastly North America, her current home and the home of her maternal grandmother. It always felt strange to feel so interconnected. The Earth was truly her home and it was precious to her.

Not sure what she would find inside, Kira peeled off the sticky seals to open the box. Instead of Styrofoam or plastic she pulled out an interior paper box that was split in two with more seals. Once the seals were cut she pulled the top section off to discover a miniature globe nestled in satin fabric.

It looked like a snow globe. There was a thick heavy base below the globe which was attached by a small short stick. One side of the base included a winding device just like a music box as well as places for a power cord, USB port and HDMI cable.

Kira plugged in the box and an ethereal light began to emanate from the intricate Earth. Wanting to see the lighting effects in all their glory Kira ran around the room to close all the blinds and turn off the lights. Her efforts were well rewarded as the dark room allowed her to see all the details perfectly. It literally felt like she was holding a miniaturized replica of the Earth. She turned the winding device and although it played no music, the Earth itself began to spin and pale wisps of clouds made their way across the Pacific right in front of her eyes.

"Mom?" Kira yelled, but when she received no response she unplugged and carried the globe into the kitchen.

"Hey mom?" Kira repeated as she entered the kitchen. Her mom had the TV up way too loud but could obviously hear her now.

"Yeah babe?" came the response. Her mom gave her a quick glance over her shoulder.

Her mom was too busy cooking and newsing to check out the globe right now so Kira switched subjects. "Did you and Dad decide where I can set up the system?" she asked.

"Oh," her mom's face crinkled with the bad news, "I know it wasn't your first choice but I think to begin with you're going to have to use the third bay in the garage."

"Awwww mom!" the garage smelled and could get cold in the winter.

"It's just for now sweetie until we can get the downstairs rec room cleared out. Besides, it gives you the most room to move around in VR and it's safe and dry."

"Mommmm," Kira tried one more whine, this one of the ten-year old variety.

"Nope, we've decided. Besides, I think you should wait for your dad to come home before you really start setting up. He's is almost as excited as you are."

"Fine!" Kira replied. If only her mom took a second to look at Kira's face she would really see her. Parents could be so self-absorbed.

Kira left the room with her precious mini-Earth. She plugged it back into the wall socket and sat herself down to watch it twirl in the dark room as she waited for her father to get home.

Day #1 Nancy Hart

The room was huge and futuristic looking. The walls and ceiling were white but everything else in the room was black and sleek.

"Welcome to the classroom," said the woman leading Kira's group. She pointed to the room behind her but none of the students were looking at her anymore and she knew it.

Kira was as awed as the other students. The teacher stopped talking and the students took it as a cue to explore on their own.

They still hadn't had the time to properly size one another up, but Kira automatically noted that they must be some carefully crafted mix of socioeconomic backgrounds, cultures, and all those other categories. Or at least there were exactly four girls and four boys.

The girls and boys automatically gravitated toward one another as they explored the room. The boys leaped ahead touching anything they could get their hands on while the girls started forward with quiet purpose.

Kira could tell there were eight pods set aside for each students' VR area. While there was nothing physical separating the large spaces the slight color change in floor color indicated play areas about eight meters by six meters; much, much larger than her VR space at home. The floor was soft and squishy and reminded her of a rubber tire high school track surface that was painted an interior grey.

The group of girls circled toward the closest unit with only a few glances back to their teacher to make sure this was what they were allowed to do. Once given tacit approval through another brief nod they began to act as boldly as the boys.

While each individual unit was open on three sides, the back wall was smooth and black with a slight interior curve. A small hutch space was carved out on the left and included a modern one-legged chair and an adjustable desk space with a laptop. There was a charging station and upon closer inspection all sorts of doors opened up to divulge VR gear, empty storage, and even traditional school supplies like paper and pencils.

One of the girls opened the Mac-book sitting at the desk and pressed a button. "Hey," said the girl, Kira couldn't remember her name, "Look!"

Peering over her shoulder Kira watched as the screen lit up with two simple words. "Welcome Kira."

This computer was hers which probably meant this station was hers. Sweet. This meant she was technically at the back of the class furthest away from what she assumed would be the teaching station. Although now she was tempted to change her favored seating position. No longer would she need to hide in the back. Now, things were going to be different. School was going to be different.

The Beta

Upon this discovery the girls spread out rather quickly in search of their individual stations. The boys were still down at the other end of the room having passed too quickly through their station exploration and missing what the girls had discovered about the computers. The boys were just nowstarting to explore and mess with the teaching station.

"Welcome to the lab." said a loud voice, clear and distinct throughout the room. It took a second for Kira to realize it was their teacher's voice which was amplified through some type of hidden microphone, although she couldn't see any kind of device on the woman's collar, shirt, or hair.

"I am Professor McKenzie and at this point you may call me either 'teacher' or 'Professor McKenzie.' She looked calmly around the room and slowly began to make her way down the long and informal middle corridor of the room to the boys at the teaching station, speaking as she went and pointing ahead of her, "You have found my teaching station there." The boys backed up from the computer they were about to fiddle with.

The control station looked like a kick ass modern version of a Star Trek command deck. A curved counter ringed the dais and was elevated significantly above their VR spaces. It was complete with buttons and levelers that looked like they belonged to NASA. As the teacher passed by Kira and the other girls, she crooked a finger indicating that they should follow her across the room. Kira quickly obeyed the silent command.

Professor McKenzie was quiet for the last twenty paces of her walk across the room and the boys were inching perceptibly backwards in response to her approach. Although Kira couldn't see Professor McKenzie's face she could almost feel the amusement hovering under the surface.

Kira was glad their teacher was a woman. While she wanted to be completely androgynous in this respect, and not care either way if her teacher was a male or female something deep down inside her felt relieved. Of course she didn't really even know if she liked their teacher yet, it always seemed that you either really got along with other women or you didn't.

The teacher was now making her way around the curved console and as she did she paused and reached out her hand. "Like all machines, this one has an 'on' button." Smiling, Professor McKenzie pressed a button. Kira could see the look of awe on the boys' faces from across the room.

The whole place lit up with a muted light as screens behind every single VR space including the teachers were activated. Each screen was huge stretching meters across and floor to ceiling.

Kira didn't entirely buy the fact that the teacher had showed them a true 'on' button because the screens behind the teacher's station looked like it had multiple desktops already running all sorts of programs and windows.

In one swoop the screens behind each of the student spaces suddenly were occupied by eight perfect copies of an evening woodland scene complete with fireflies and a log cabin. The mood it set was one of serene curiosity.

"You will be spending every Friday here with me, and the rest of the week on your VR sets at home. While you will be logging into the same account with the same progress both here and at home, the equipment we will use here is undoubtedly more sophisticated. Part of what we hope to do here with this beta trial is compare which cutting edge technologies we can incorporate in our less expensive home sets that truly make a difference in your education. During debriefing sessions you will help us understand the differences between the two set-ups as we compare your progress data. Currently 80% of our Google Earth History participants are college students using the software to either gain credit or to access our job training modules. You are the remaining 20%. You won't run into college students within the simulation." She paused and looked around at all her students before jumping right in. "Did you all complete your Google Earth History homework?"

Kira smiled inside, like any of them wouldn't have spent hours using their home VR equipment, not to mention playing around inside the amazing Google Earth History. This teacher had a bit to learn.

There were a few tentative nods but no one had the courage to speak.

"Well if you won't tell me . . ." Professor McKenzie must have somehow communicated with the consoles because all of a sudden

The Beta

there were reports everywhere. Reports on the teacher's console, individual reports on each students' space, and their names were attached to everything! At first Kira felt a wave of mortification and then nervousness, but after thinking about it for a minute she just felt curious. In regular school the teacher never shared students' scores publicly like this.

Kira made her way up to the teacher's console, as the professor didn't seem to mind the boys being up on the dais she figured she could too.

There was so much space up there and the screen was so big. Kira walked past the boys so she could see everything. All eight students progress in Google Earth History was laid out before her. She could see the dates they logged in, time spent on lessons, scores on assessments, and then most importantly she could see how their skills were assessed and credit assigned. She looked closer at her high school credit and saw that not only had she already received significant credit in World, U.S. History, Civics and Geography but she also earned a bit of credit in Biology, Botany, Chinese, and met multiple English Language Arts standards that placed her at a college level in most skills. That must be why a separate Language Arts curriculum wasn't included in the box, at this point they didn't need "4" years of English anymore, they only needed to show that they could master the skills.

Even with all the details the words in front of her were huge. She reached out to touch one line and it was suddenly replaced with a pie chart. No frickin way! This giant screen was also a touch screen!

Surprised, she stepped back and then used the opportunity to inconspicuously look at the other students' progress.

The results were interesting and telling. From a quick glance she could see that everyone technically had completed their homework, which included logging into Google Earth Lessons for a total of 20 hours before their meeting today. In fact not a single student finished less than thirty-five hours which was pretty impressive.

"Dude, I got over 25% of my U.S. History Semester A completed!" one of the boys shouted right next to her. Kira rubbed her ear painfully but she couldn't help but to smile and share his enthusiasm. Kira took it as an invitation to look closely at his scores. Smiling at him as she peered over his shoulder, "What did you see?" she asked.

"Well, my great-grandfathers were both in WWII so I spent a bunch of time following their paths through the war." He said. The boy looked somber, so Kira didn't pry but he continued anyway. "One of them was so badly injured in the war he had to spend a year at a hospital in Hawaii before transferring back to the Pentagon where he originally met my grandmother."

"She worked at the Pentagon during WWII?" Kira asked. She twisted her head around to look at him briefly before returning to his scores.

"Yeah," he replied and then pointed to a bar graph in front of him. "Check this out. So I spent a lot of my time going through WWII re-creations from the Pacific Theater and Florida but before I did either of those I had to pass some tests on geography." He touched the geography graph and up popped a more detailed account. "See, I was right."

Kira could see what he was talking about. In the Geographic breakdown it showed a mastery of West Pacific geography and the Eastern United States.

He kept talking as if she wasn't really there, almost to himself. "It was a two-hour re-creation and I went through the whole thing. The end was the most terrible part. Thirty-five thousand soldiers died on both sides and one sources say 22,000 of them were civilians. All on this little island in the Pacific. One of the last parts of the re-creation showed me an entire Japanese family jumping off a cliff." The boy's brow furrowed and his hands clenched. He almost looked like he was fighting with himself. "It's not like my grandpa was in the simulation, there was no way they could choreographic down to individual soldiers with that many people . . . but I knew he was in the Second Marine Division and I stood on the same beach he was at when he was injured."

Kira and the still nameless boy were startled out of the moment by Professor McKenzie's strident voice. Wait, he didn't have to remain nameless. Before Kira returned her attention to their teacher she looked on the screen above American History A. His name was Ryan.

The Beta

"No doubt you have many questions and we will have lots of time to debrief and discuss Friday afternoons, but today I will be introducing you to group history simulations." the professor began. "Ryan" she called out. It was half a command and half a question.

"Yes professor." The formerly nameless boy replied in an almost military fashion. Kira smiled, maybe his World War II re-creation had rubbed off on him in more ways than one.

"I believe that you completed the Battle of Saipan re-creation and focused on World War II for the majority of your hours?" she asked.

"Yes ma'am," he quipped and then noting her raised eyebrows retracted, "I mean yes, professor." Nobody in this day and age liked to be called ma'am. When Professor McKenzie did not continue immediately he hesitantly added. "My grandfather fought in that battle."

Kira could tell this was of no surprise to Professor McKenzie. Where were they getting their information? Did they know everything about their students? Kira shivered a little. She knew it was a bunch of technology companies working together, but she had not a clue as to what extent they were mining their data from outside sources.

"So, the Battle of Saipan re-creation held a particular connection for you, did it not?" the professor asked.

Duh thought Kira.

"Yes," Ryan kept his answer short.

Kira was curious about how far the professor was going to take this interrogation. She didn't think anyone else could tell, but after their brief conversation Kira could feel the raw emotion emanating from Ryan. Was he the type of guy that would share his thoughts or keep them tightly controlled? She couldn't quite tell yet.

"Within Google Earth History you will have access to many re-creations of historical events. Opportunities to watch events unfold before your eyes, immersing you in the same shoes as those figures that wrote the Declaration of Independence or first walked on the moon. But not only will you have the chance to watch re-creations engineered for you there will also be opportunities to act out historical events yourself."

The Beta

The professor made her way to one of the many teacher consoles and was manipulating controls to change the main screen. Up popped the largest digital screen view of Earth Kira had ever seen. As she and Ryan were closest to the screen she could estimate the size of the digital Earth. Maybe 12 feet tall?

"Beyond exploring Google Earth History as you would the traditional Google Earth there are three main types of experiences." Here Professor McKenzie zoomed in to the East Pacific to the island of Saipan where a glowing blue ring icon floated above the island. "These are called 're-creations' and have been available to you thus far. The re-creations can be brief, as short as a few minutes, or quite long—such as in the case of Saipan which lasts over two hours. The re-creations limit you to the role of a spectator." Here the professor paused and smiled. "Technically you could sit passively through a two-hour re-creation daydreaming of something else and still log your hours. However," and here she again paused with a meaningful glance. "Your answers on a post-assessment would be a dead giveaway."

"Wait a minute," Ryan blurted out, obviously thinking of something else besides his time spent on Saipan. "My reports say I have completed over 25% of U.S. History Semester A? Does that mean I could only complete WWII re-creations for a semester of credit?"

"You nailed our problem on the head and it is your time in *The Beta* that will help us answer that question, but first let me ask you this. How do you get U.S. History Semester A credit in your current high school?" She opened the question to the group with the turn of her head.

"Well . . ." a blonde girl in the back both raised her hand and started talking at the same time. "We go to school all semester, read a textbook, complete the assignments, take tests and at least do C work?" her upswing tone indicating the statement was really a question.

Professor McKenzie nodded. "And do you know how many hours you attend that one class in a semester?"

Kira could almost see the math each teenage brain was calculating. Shout outs of 100 and 90 rang through the room before she could place an answer with a person.

"Ninety hours is the correct answer for here in Washington State. Next question, how do the skills and knowledge of any class of students—let's say all the students that receive an A—compare and contrast by the end of the semester?"

It was quiet for a bit, but this group of students was thawing out fast.

"Well, if they all got A's then they probably answered 90% of the test questions correctly." said the blonde. Kira wished the scores were still on the board so she could start matching names to faces to scores. She couldn't believe the class hadn't been properly introduced to one another so far.

"And if they completed all the same homework they would be learning the same things from the book," this time the answer was from a girl with long dark hair. Kira smiled to herself. Why did she always categorize people by their hair color and length. Maybe it was a genetic trait? Easy identification?

Being careful not to snort in derision at herself, Kira added, "That is unless they cheat!" Oops, she hadn't meant to say that out loud. But seriously, with the ridiculous rote assignments and assessments teachers churned out—even their 'complex tasks' designed to encourage critical thinking were often meaningless busywork—cheating on homework and tests was more rampant than her teachers realized.

As Professor McKenzie's gaze narrowed in on her for a brief extra second it took everything in Kira's power not to shrink away. Counting and breathing slowly Kira focused on telepathically sending the professor innocent thoughts. She was sure the twins were going to be breathing down her neck trying to figure out if there was a way to cheat this system, after all it might turn into a full-time business for them after high school. Kira, not wanting to betray her opportunity to be part of *The Beta* or disappoint the twins, was simply praying that the hardware's biometrics and software were cheater proof so she wouldn't have to choose sides.

"Addressing cheating is a large part of our beta test as well, but back to grading. High scoring students who attend class for 90 hours of seat time know mostly the same information and get the same credit. There are some differences of course. Some cheat," she nodded her head to Kira, "some spend more time reading the chapter on World War II because it interests them," with a hand flourish she indicated Ryan as her example. "But in the end they all end up knowing at least the basic outline of U.S. History. Although speaking philosophically it is like we have traded general common knowledge by sacrificing personal interest."

It was then that Professor McKenzie's tone changed significantly, "On one side we have the sensibilities of traditional teaching and grading to satisfy. In order to get you your accredited high school diplomas we need to meet a basic minimum in any given class. For U.S. History you will need to have a good working knowledge of our country's geography, history, and culture to get your required two semesters of credit." Then she used her hand to indicate the other side. "But on the other hand you now have school software that can assess and give credit not only for your prior knowledge of a subject, but also your current skill level. For example, Kira did you note the Language Arts skills assessed during your time using Google Earth History?"

Startled out of deep-thinking, Kira jumped a little at hearing her name. It took a second for her head to catch up with what her ears had absentmindedly taken in. "Um . . . a little," she managed to stammer in reply. Only seconds later Professor McKenzie pulled up a window highlighting Kira's reports in huge font on the big screen. Not again! Was she going to have to get used to her grades being shared with everyone all the time?

"Do you know how these skills were assessed?" the professor asked.

Kira looked closer at the list of skills. Reading comprehension, fluency, paragraph structure, and using evidence from text to support an answer.

"Well, I had to type out several paragraph answers in an assessment of one re-creation which would make sense for the paragraph structure and use of evidence." She kept thinking. "And I suppose I was asked to read a few passages out loud as part of one exercise which would be fluency. But I am not exactly sure about the Reading Comprehension skill," Kira replied, glad to be done talking.

Professor McKenzie smiled at Kira and reclaimed the groups' attention. "You are on the right track Kira, and if you notice your scores, each of those standards have been assessed at a post high school level." She paused a moment to let that sink in. Other students had similar scores but the professor was taking them in a different direction with this one.

"What would a Junior English teacher do with a student like Kira? A student who has already demonstrated high school mastery of many of the skills taught in English classes?" Her pause here was short. "Should a student like Kira be required to sit through two more full years of English classes? Another 340 hours of seat time? What if Kira was able to fulfill both her English and History requirements by reading American Literature because that is what she is interested in learning? Or what if she was able to earn credit for Chinese History, a class that her current high school cannot offer?" Professor McKenzie practically winked at Kira without winking. Had she followed Kira's explorations of China last week?

The wheels in everyone's heads were beginning to turn.

"Anything is possible. To satisfy traditional educational structures your skills, knowledge and seat time across all applicable high school subjects will be regularly monitored through these simple bar graphs." She pulled up a screen with all of the semester credit classes Kira needed to complete for graduation. Because they had only had one week of school her bars were quite low, but they were all there. All the possibilities were open to her. "When you have met a desired minimum of skill levels and content combined with a certain amount of seat time you will see your bar graph fill to the top and high school credit awarded."

"The system is not perfect, but as a beta testing group you will have the support of a cadre of talented teachers and counselors to make sure credit is awarded where it is deserved. And I have no doubt universities will be keen to accept you, if only to compare you to traditionally schooled students."

Although it looked like the room around her was about to burst with more questions, Professor McKenzie quickly quelled that option. "We digress, I did not plan on discussing grading this morning and we are quite behind schedule." with a flick of her wrist she turned back to the console and the Earth once again took up their view on the main monitor.

The Beta

"In review the glowing blue ring indicates a historical re-creation. Created by other people with specific viewpoints and timelines to teach specific standards, you are a passive observer in these." She then moved their view to the Mediterranean and pinpointed the City of Athens. Above the city stood a three-dimensional gold gem. It hovered and sparkled above the city. "This icon represents an experience you do not yet have access to that we like to call '*Simulations*.' This particular location is the City of Athens in the year 400 B.C. during the time of Plato. These settings are like an online multiplayer role-playing game. You choose a character, home and job, and then you can explore the historical simulation at your own pace in a game-like manner. There are embedded missions you can opt into or you can simply observe. Credit can be earned just like re-creations but we will get into that in more detail when we release this option to you."

Next Professor McKenzie moved back to North America somewhere on the East Coast. The switch was so fast that Kira couldn't tell which state they were in, although she knew they were somewhere south of Washington D.C. Here Kira could see a green icon of six small people connected by their feet. The professor clicked on the icon and the same idyllic cabin on the student screen appeared behind her.

"Today we will introduce you to an option that is partially like a re-creation but allows you to role play living history with a specific group for a short time frame. These are called *Living History* within the platform and are differentiated from *re-creations* where you are only an observer. And without further ado or instruction I would like you to suit up and begin. Let's see what you can do."

It didn't take but a millisecond for everyone to jump into action but seconds later they heard the Professor's voice again, this time amplified by a microphone. "Wait, I forgot. This next segment will take approximately ninety minutes online. Make sure to use the restroom and eat or drink if you need to. That will reduce the chances of you needing a break mid-simulation. We will start in 10 minutes. Go!"

Thankful she didn't need to use the bathroom, Kira walked straight to her station. She was simply awed by how much room she had to move. It took quite a few steps to make it to her hutch.

The Beta

The interior was sleek, black and it took more than a few looks over her shoulder at other students to discover how to open the hidden panels and find her VR suit. Glancing at her open laptop she could see large font text instructing her to wear the full suit, gloves, and controllers.

She and all of the other students had been advised to wear minimal tight-fitting clothes that would work well with the full body VR suits. Kira took off her hoodie and shoes then tucked them back in the corner of her gear box. It took her much less time than she thought to put on all the pieces. They were kind of like the set that was made for her at home but this headset was slightly heavier.

A faint change of color in her play area designated the middle of her space. Making her way to that spot she set her controllers and gloves on the ground before looking around. No one else had suited up as quickly as she had, but even from far away she could see Professor McKenzie looking at her and giving her a telepathic nudge.

Taking a deep breath like a scuba diver, Kira put on her headset. Even though the headset did not cover her nose or mouth the analogy with diving was quite apt. Scuba divers took a moment to adjust to the water temperature and lighting, and VR explorers did much the same. The first glance inside her headset was always a little unnerving, but then within a few moments she began to acclimate.

The forest cabin was in front of her and the shadowy forms of her disembodied hands and controllers lay amongst a pile of fall leaves at her feet. Kira crouched down and pulled on both gloves. In the simulation they looked like real hands that were the size, color, and shape of her own, yet they were attached to no visible arms until she picked them up.

Properly equipped she could look around. What she thought was mid-morning sun filtered through the forest and cast a warm yet unearthly glow on the cabin before her. A gentle wind stirred the trees in alternating waves, first to her left and then far past the cabin. All of a sudden she saw something move and heard a chirp. Looking closely, she saw a chipmunk tail flick behind a tree and then all was silent.

The Beta

On Kira's right she saw green floating text that read "Nancy Hart Mini Group Simulation." She clicked on the text and the words were replaced with eight miniature figures. There were six red coated soldiers, one woman and one child. Each figure made small imperceptible movements as they floated for her inspection. Walking closer she could see their chests lower and raise with each breath, and some of the soldiers would absentmindedly scratch themselves. The young girl child suddenly placed her hands behind her back and shifted from side to side as though bored.

That was when things got really spooky. Now that Kira was close to the doll-size floating characters she realized that not only their eyes, but their heads were all looking at her, a detail she hadn't noticed upon earlier observation.

Professor McKenzie's voice filled her headset and Kira breathed a sigh of relief. "Most of you are now suited up and in the simulation. Please choose your character. You will have approximately ten minutes of assessment and preparations before the group simulation commences."

In scrawled black letters below each character Kira found an option for the "history" of the character. Suddenly two of the soldiers disappeared. Not wanting to be left out of a choice she clicked on the woman character and confirmed her decision without a second thought, even though she hadn't read any of their bios.

It was then and there that Kira decided she would almost always choose to be a woman in her studies. The voice of women had for so long been ignored, erased, or diminished throughout history. She knew that the intent of the simulation's choices would be to give students the opportunity to walk in others' shoes. People of different races, religions, socioeconomic status etc. But Kira would choose to be a woman. To look through the eyes of a woman whenever the chance presented itself. And the only woman besides the child available in this simulation was the main character, Nancy Hart.

A life-size image of her character appeared next to the cabin surrounded by multitudes of icons. At first, Kira just walked around the woman observing the character she would play. Nancy Hart was much taller than Kira with fierce red hair and a pock marked face. Clicking on an icon labeled "Stats" Kira read about how smallpox was responsible for the marks on her face and according to the Georgia Encyclopedia, "She was also cross-eyed." One early account pointed out that Hart had no "share of beauty - a fact she herself would have readily acknowledged, had she ever enjoyed an opportunity of looking into a mirror."

Kira smiled and looked up into Nancy Hart's eyes. Nancy Hart looked right back at her and she could see how her left eye was looking a tad bit up while the right eye focused on Kira. Nancy Hart smiled back and Kira's eyebrows shot up. This was getting too darn realistic for her!

Another voice spoke up but this time it was familiar. "Welcome Kira, are you ready for your Revolutionary War pre-assessment?" said the soothing voice of her AI teacher from back home.

"Oh God yes," Kira groaned thankfully and a little too loudly, feeling bad about involuntarily taking the Lord's name in vain. What would the other kids in the room think of that? The room was huge but not huge enough to keep them from hearing her despite their headsets.

Back home she was mostly alone in her garage and she may have gotten in the habit of joking with and berating her AI teacher a little too often and a little too loudly. It felt like a double-edged sword that her artificial teacher's voice was such a comforting factor on her first Friday with the other students.

After taking a seven-minute pre-assessment on the Revolutionary War, Kira heard her AI teacher voice indicate that her "learning modules were being calculated." She was glad Miss McKenzie had a doctorate and liked being called Professor McKenzie. That way Kira could keep her two mentors straight in her head - the flesh and blood McKenzie would be her Professor and her AI would be her Teacher.

She spent the rest of her prep time reading a more detailed overview of the events in Georgia and then detailing what was known of Nancy Hart's life leading up to the incident at the log cabin. At the end of the session she took a quick test to gauge her comprehension and then was instructed to take off her headset.

Her cheeks were flushed and red, but so were the faces of all her classmates. Two of the boys closest to Professor McKenzie were still working inside their headsets but the rest of them were taking a break.

She walked back to her station, grabbed her water bottle and took a drink. The other students were sticking close to their individual stations and Professor McKenzie was doing something within her headset as well.

Looking over at the two boys still in simulation she could see a replica of what they were seeing on the display behind each of them. While it was too far for her to read the text, she could tell that both of them were finishing up pre-assessments.

Professor McKenzie took off her headset and gave her hair a shake as the two boys did the same. While the curly brown-haired boy was obviously sweaty from the experience, Professor McKenzie looked perfectly polished despite taking off the headset. Kira felt a pang of jealousy as she was not one of those people who looked great after exercising or doing VR. Every time she took off her headset, she had a temporary red streak across her forehead and her hair was a mess. Even her little sister sometimes made fun of her disheveled appearance after working hard on the VR set all afternoon.

Professor McKenzie spoke up, "One last thought before we begin our group simulation. Each of you has been presented with background information about your character and are about to be given a set of defined actions you must take in the simulation. These defined actions must be accomplished within a timely manner as instructed or you will be taken out of the simulation and replaced with an NPC otherwise known as a Non-Player automated Character."

She looked directly at one of the boys and continued, "Much like a mystery, you have only been told what your character needs to know and do within the simulation. There will be surprises from other characters that will teach you about the different perspectives of this Revolutionary War event. Also there is minor violence contained within this simulation. All of your parents signed waivers allowing you access to the more graphic pieces of the curriculum contained within Google Earth History. While I doubt you will be too distraught over today's experience, it is important to remember that if you ever need to stop during a simulation or need to process

The Beta

what you have seen do not hesitate to stop and ask for help. I am here for you and we have counselors at our disposal."

Kira's listened more intently. What type of violence might they see? She wasn't much for first person shooting games or horror flicks so this put her on edge. It also made her curious. What exactly had Ryan seen during the Saipan War re-creation?

"Please return to your stations and let the simulation begin." instructed the professor.

They rushed back to their assigned locations and Kira decided to pull her loose hair into a ponytail at the back of her neck for this session. Gloves and headset on she found herself back in front of the log cabin with the eerie red headed Nancy Hart miniature floating next to her.

Now there was a new option to click that read Simulation Instructions. Kira opened it and a long list of bulleted text unraveled before her in the air. As the main character in this particular simulation Kira had quite a few required actions. She read down each bullet trying to memorize every action, and was relieved when she could hear Professor McKenzie's voice in her headset informing them that these required action steps could be pulled up mid-simulation if they forgot what to do next. Kira was curious to see if all eight of the students could work together to make the simulation run smoothly.

When Kira got to the last two bullet points she sucked in her breath involuntarily. Now she knew why the professor had mentioned violence. Kira wasn't shaking, but she wasn't entirely sure she could do this.

The professor's voice cut in one last time, "Thirty seconds to start unless someone indicates that they need more time?"

No one made a sound. Suddenly both the image of Nancy Hart and the bullet points faded away in front of Kira. The cabin and the woods around her came into greater focus and the morning light filtering through the trees seemed more real.

Looking down Kira could see the long skirt that was on Nancy Hart now swirled around her figure, and when she brought her gloves and controllers in front of her face she could see Nancy Hart's hands. She was now officially Nancy Hart.

The Beta

Unsure of when the next part of the simulation would take place Kira began to explore around the cabin. She knew her VR space was quite large but she wasn't sure when the blue chaperone wall would pop up so she tried to walk around the entire cabin. She made it about halfway before the chaperone wall came into view and necessitated the use of her controllers to "hop" forward so she could continue around the opposite side of the cabin.

A sudden bird sound startled her and she literally jumped. Out of the forest came three large turkeys talking loudly and running up to her. She laughed as her brain began to recognize their gobbles. It was obvious they were tame, so she knelt down to get a closer look at one as it bobbed its head around looking at her. The detail on the animal was exquisite. Kira had never seen a real turkey up close and while the bumpy head totally repulsed her the feathers were breathtaking. Spots of sunlight glinted off the colorful highlights of each feather.

"Mother?" came a loud voice from behind and sent the turkeys scattering. Kira turned around toward the sound of the voice and saw a young girl of about ten approach her.

What was Nancy Harts daughter's name again? Kira thought frantically. It took her a second to pull up the cheat sheet of bullet points and when she did figure it out the list popped up right where the little girl was standing. The girl walked through the floating letters completely oblivious. Nancy Hart's daughter could be played by any of her classmates, but the voice was girlish and that made Kira wonder if the simulation shared their actual voice or somehow changed it in the simulation. Then she shook her head, there is no way the simulation could be that advanced. Kira didn't know her fellow classmates enough to recognize their REAL LIFE voices yet.

Sukey, that was the name of the daughter. She quickly flipped off the cheat sheet to make the words disappear and turned toward the little girl who was twirling to make her skirt float around like a top. Yeah, the little girl was probably played by one of her female classmates. Was that sexist to assume?

Kira decided to jump right into character, "Sukey, did you finish all of your chores?" she asked the little girl.

The Beta

It took one more twirl before the little girl stopped and gravity pulled down her skirts. "Ummmm," she smiled. "Yes?" It was more of a question than an answer.

Kira thought quickly, "Go inside and find something to feed the turkeys." Kira was always obsessed with testing Google Earth History to see if they had been able to program in something as simple as food within the cabin and the ability of the food to act like food and attract the possibly tame animals. Of course, she really had no clue what wild or tame turkeys liked to eat. In her Google Earth Simulation back home, she could open a small internet browser and look for the answer in any given place but when she tried to do the same thing here nothing happened. The developers restricted the ability to access the internet in the game to make the simulation more lifelike and harder to play.

Kira shrugged and watched the little girl Sukey follow her directions. One thing she wanted to do before the action started was find the hole in the wall. She was supposed to use the hole to pass rifles to Sukey. Kira continued to study the cabin wall from the outside but all she could find was a door at waist level right next to the stone chimney.

She used her controller to lift the latch and open the door. Stacked logs filled the space and that was when she realized people used to pass firewood through this opening to make replenishing the wood supply much easier. As she looked closer she could see a nice large hole between two logs so she bent down to take a closer look. She could see Sukey rummaging through shelves on the opposite wall. "Did you find anything Sukey?" she called out. She wanted to make sure Sukey knew where the hole in the wall was too.

"Whoa dude!" the still girlish voice called out while the character named Sukey turned around and spotted her face through the hole. "The acoustics in this headset are dead on. It sounds exactly like you are talking through a hole in that direction. I can't get over the reality of this place!"

Kira laughed at the truth of the statement and the incongruity of a ten-year-old during the Revolutionary War saying 'Whoa dude.'

"You're right, this is amazing." She responded and then closed the latch.

As she headed to the front of the cabin to meet up with Sukey she was startled by a dirty man who jumped out of the woods and ran straight up to her.

"They're after me!" he called out in a rushed panic. Kira was unnerved by him even though her simulation instructions called for her to help the Whig escape. He bolted inside the cabin and Kira followed. Trying to get into character, she thought about Nancy Hart and took a deep breath.

Sukey look startled too and Kira was surprised to find how protective she was of this simulated ten-year-old daughter.

"How far behind are the Torry soldiers?" she demanded of the man who paced back and forth. She wasn't even going to ask his name, it wasn't mentioned on the simulated instructions as there must be no historical account of that particular detail.

"I don't know," he replied and kept pacing.

"Well, you can't stay here. But we can give you some food and water." She motioned for Sukey to hand over whatever was in her hands that she had been preparing for the turkeys. "Then we can divert them if they come looking for you."

Kira was tired of his pacing so she put her hands on her hips and motioned him to go out the door.

He took the chunk of break from Sukey and awkwardly made his way past her. He paused at the door and spoke. "What about the water ma'am?"

Kira told Sukey to follow and headed outside where she remembered seeing an empty bucket. She picked up the bucket, accidentally dropped it because her thumb let off the trigger button of her VR controller, and then picked it up again. She was feeling clumsy because she was feeling nervous.

"Sukey, grab some water from the spring." she ordered and then pointed to the man to follow Sukey. She used the controllers to lift her skirts on the sides as she followed the two characters into the woods. How did the Sukey character know which trail led to the spring Kira wondered? The Nancy Hart character had been provided with no map of any sort.

The Beta

It was a question she would have to ask later, but Sukey headed straight down the path and it only took two VR 'jumps' to make it through the woods south of the cabin's chimney and to the spring hidden in the brush. If Kira were to make a quick estimate she would guess that the spring was several hundred actual feet from the cabin.

She paused to watch Sukey dip the bucket in the pool of water and the unnamed Whig character stood, openly gaping at the world around him. Kira understood where he was coming from. It was like a person's first visit to Disneyland. There was so much to see you had to stop and take it all in slowly.

But the simulation wasn't giving them that sort of time. Once Sukey lifted the bucket and the Whig unceremoniously poured a significant amount on his face and clothes Kira spoke up, although she struggled through laughter. The simulation was impressive in the fact that the Whig's clothes were now wet looking, but the coding for water entering a mouth still had much to be desired. "Do not fret Whig. Your secret is safe with us. Travel safely—but go now!"

He smiled, saluted, and without a word bounded in the opposite direction. Kira watched him go and his running was smooth as far as she could see.

How did the simulation seamlessly stitch together his movement when Kira knew he must have needed to stop walking and 'jump' to the next area? She had so many questions.

"Well, Sukey, are you ready to return to the cabin?" Kira asked her simulated daughter.

"Yes Mother, but look at this!" Sukey was standing next to a tree stump holding a large conch shell. The girl put the shell near her lips and gave a good blow. The sound was deep and reverberating, for some reason it reminded Kira of something she would expect to hear on a tropical island.

"Help is only a call away with that conch shell, aye?" Kira asked the girl.

"Yes, Mother." Sukey replied as she carefully replaced the shell on the stump. Without further ado Sukey began skipping toward the trail toward the cabin. Kira had to admit that whoever was playing the character of Sukey was doing a fine job.

The Beta

Kira kept trying to figure out what made the simulation so smooth. She knew Sukey must be 'jumping' forward with her controllers as she skipped. Kira was doing the same to travel quickly down the trail, but every time Kira looked at Sukey the girl was skipping seamlessly along ahead of her. If Sukey looked at Kira's character would she see Nancy holding stock-still like Kira was irl, or would she see Nancy walking leisurely behind her? She would be sure to ask Professor McKenzie.

They returned to the cabin and Sukey obediently procured more food from the cupboard. She found cheese and corn and so they entertained themselves by breaking off pieces of cheese and throwing it to the turkeys.

All of a sudden, the turkeys ran gobbling back in the woods and the forest sounds went completely quiet. Kira looked up to see six Tory soldiers on horseback slowly entering the clearing. Too far away to dive into the safety of the cabin, Kira could see Sukey move to hide behind her dress.

"Good evening captain," Kira said in a firm voice. She had no clue if there were captains in the Revolutionary War. If only they had more time to prepare for this time period she would have studied. She was determined to play her part the best that she could. Her next directions instructed her to deny seeing the Whig and then do what they told her to do.

"We are in pursuit of a Whig who came this way. Where is he?" Here the soldier paused searching for the right word. ". . . Ma'am." but the honorific was no honor at all. The way he said ma'am implied that he doubted her to be worthy of even that simple title.

"No one has stopped at the cabin for days. We can't help you." Kira lied through her teeth. Not a proficient liar in real life Kira found it just as difficult in a directed educational simulation.

Two of the Tory soldiers hopped down from their horses and began looking around the perimeter of the cabin, peering at the ground like experienced trackers. Kira couldn't believe her real heart was beginning to pound. One of the soldiers peered cautiously through the partially opened cabin door and then yanked it open and ran inside. Kira sucked in her breath.

The Beta

The other soldiers continued to surround her and Sukey as they looked for clues. One of the Tory soldiers studied the path leading to the spring and Kira was once again distracted by another curious thought about the simulation. Had they actually left real tracks in the simulated ground? With nothing better to do Kira looked down at the ground and casually pressed her boot firmly into soil and grass in front of her. When she lifted her foot she saw a clearly defined print that had not been there seconds before. "No effing way!" she whispered loudly.

Oh crap, she thought in her head. Everyone must have heard that and looking up only confirmed her suspicion—as the Tory in charge of watching her and Sukey now had a wide grin on his face. Kira did not want to give Professor McKenzie a bad impression of her on their first day of simulations. She wondered in what way Professor McKenzie was viewing the simulation, in a headset or at her desk on a monitor?

"What did you say . . . Ma'am?" he asked loudly.

"Oh nothing," Kira replied feebly as she unconsciously rubbed the print out with the toe of her foot.

The Tory looking at the path to the spring was now returning with a determined look on his face. "Ma'am," he began with little fanfare, "I will only ask you one more time, where is the Whig traitor?"

She didn't pause before replying through truly gritted teeth, "We have seen no one, good sir," and like anyone with decent mothering instincts she reached behind her to where she figured Sukey would still be clutching at her skirts. Of course, her gloved hands couldn't really feel anyone behind her so she turned her head to confirm the girl was still there.

Sure enough, Sukey was right there but her face didn't look as scared as a young girl surrounded by soldiers would most likely be in this situation. Turning back to look at the Tory, Kira literally jumped when she came face to face with the end of a musket.

Panicked, Kira thought back to all the simulation instructions. Nothing in that list of bullet points indicated that she was going to get shot! She still had like ten more bullet points of actions to complete! What the heck was happening?

The Beta

"I think you are lying." It was all he said before he smiled and pulled the trigger.

She gulped but nothing physically happened as she knew it wouldn't and it took a moment for her brain to register that whatever he had shot was actually behind her shoulder not actually her.

"Mama?" Came a small voice behind her. She turned her head to see but not feel Sukey tugging on her skirts and pointing to the bushes ten feet away. There lay the biggest and most beautiful turkey that only moments ago had been feasting on bits of corn from their hands.

Surprised by the shooting and overwhelmed by the unexpected emotion rising up in her throat, Nancy turned with a righteous fury that unleashed itself on the soldier. "You evil man!" she spat wishing she had the appropriate 1700 swear terms at her disposal. "You rip through the countryside killing and taking whatever you want. You aren't King's Men you are highwaymen!"

"Watch what you say wench!" the same soldier replied retraining his musket on her person.

Nancy was confused. Were they allowed to use such profanity in their simulations? Was he told to call her a wench? Wasn't that a little different than her accidental non-period semi-curse of no effing way? The whole sexist slam made her even angrier whether the simulation instructed him to say such a thing or not. She felt like she was tied in a knot.

Glaring back at him and hoping her simulated face showed as much fury, Nancy held her ground with pride. The Tory soldier in charge cleared his throat loudly to get the attention of the musket wielding fiend, who immediately glanced up at his superior. With a simple nod the man pointed the end of his musket down and glared back at her.

Clearing his throat once again, the first soldier addressed her in a commanding voice. "Be that as it may ma'am, while you deny seeing any Whig soldier you will not withhold hospitality for the King's Men. That cooked turkey will do nicely for our dinner and any drink you have." He ordered his soldier to pick up the now very dead turkey and then motioned to Nancy and Sukey to enter the cabin ahead of him.

The Beta

Legs now tense from the encounter, Nancy limped over to the door and into the cabin, but not without giving the Tory a baleful glare. Once inside she and Sukey moved to the opposite side of the one room cabin as far from the door as possible which put them back in the kitchen cupboard area next to a hearth that was almost large enough to walk inside.

Nancy wanted to say something but words were eluding her as she tried to remember what was next on the list of her bullet pointed tasks. Then she realized Nancy and Sukey were now required to serve the soldiers roast turkey and lots of wine.

"Um, set the table please Sukey." was her first command. She needed to find the wine and then figure out how to cook a turkey. She couldn't really cook a turkey, that took like hours right?

Only the head soldier was in the cabin thus far and he was wavering between watching them and glancing outside. She could see past him through the door where the other Tories were surrounding the one who shot the turkey. She was still mad about that.

Glancing around she began to tackle the problem of finding the wine. It wouldn't be in a wine bottle but maybe some kind of keg or ceramic thing? There weren't many places to look in the cabin but a small cloth toward the back corner caught her eye. Lifting the semi dirty cloth she found a cache of six ceramic containers with real corks. This must be the alcohol.

She pulled one up and it lifted slower than her real hand motion. That must be a coded nod toward how heavy the bottle would be in real life. As the simulated bottle made its way following her real hand motion she put the container on the wooden dinner table with an inflated bang. It was satisfying to hear her simulated bang followed by a clearly audible and real sound.

The soldier smiled and yelled outside, "Come on in, there will be something to drink while the turkey is cooking."

The soldiers filed in one by one and the last Tory held up the defeathered turkey carcass in his hand. He appeared to be totally repulsed by the dead turkey. She couldn't blame him as she had never cooked a dead animal in her life. She laughed inside as she imagined him plucking the feathers outside of the cabin. Served him right.

The Beta

The soldiers stacked up their muskets near the wood pile on the opposite side of the cabin while the evil Tory handed her the turkey. Was she supposed to roast it or boil it? Since the beginning of the simulation a roaring fire occupied the hearth. She saw a large metal spit with a handle built into the side. While boiling it in a big kettle might be easier it seemed more authentic to roast it over the flames. So without further ado or any washing Nancy hefted the prize turkey up and proceeded to impale it on a long metal spit.

She was disgusted with herself. She knew this was only a simulation but she could still remember the turkey's bright eyes, brilliant feathers, and the realistic way it bobbed its head. How could the Tory have killed such an innocent animal? And now she had to burn it over a fire. Gross.

The bird's legs and head flopped down from the main body and Nancy knew this was nothing like the way her mom tied the legs together at Thanksgiving dinner, but then again this wasn't cooking class. Moving the spitted bird over the main flame she turned her attention back to the soldiers and her job.

She knew how this was going to end even if nobody else did, which was the crazy part about these simulations. Somebody—some teacher or developer had decided which facts each player needed to know in order to play out the simulation and come away with a deep-seated understanding of history. This understanding would be a much deeper understanding than just reading a paragraph, watching a documentary, or having a class discussion. When Nancy was done with these Tories they were going to understand exactly how she, an American Patriot, felt about what they were doing to her and her family. They were never going to forget.

The soldiers began pouring from the ceramic bottle but she unceremoniously ripped it out of one fellow's hands and began filling their tin cups herself. Sloshing the wine and filling each vessel liberally, their conversation quieted a moment as she finished. Realizing that they needed to be simulated drunk before completing her next action, Nancy made a mental note to keep their cups full. She had five more bottles tucked in the corner.

The Beta

After they finished their first round of wine Sukey put cheese and bread on the table and Nancy spoke rather loudly to her daughter. "Sukey, we need water from the spring. Go fetch a bucket."

Sukey paused at the doorway and looked back at her before asking. "Where is the bucket mother?"

Not seeing a bucket nearby, she yanked the black kettle from the hearth and walked it over to Sukey. As she set the kettle down she whispered into Sukey's ear "Go past the spring and blow the conch shell. Help will come! Then wait by the pass-through woodpile door."

Sukey nodded and dragged the kettle behind her. Nancy was glad Sukey had her own set of instructions to follow so she didn't have to whisper more details. Nancy then turned to face the Tories. Once they completed their third round of wine she was going to make her move.

Returning to the hearth she turned the spit. Sure enough, the cooking time in this simulation must have been programmed to run quickly. The turkey was sizzling golden brown on three sides and only needed a quick turn before finishing. One thing she didn't seem to need in this simulation was hot pads.

After she poured the third round of drinks, she pulled the turkey off the spit on to a large fry pan. Kira plopped the roasted bird it in front of the lead Tory and rummaged around for a carving knife which she handed directly to the man.

Now was the time. As the crowd of 21st century teenagers tried to carve a simulated turkey from the 1700s with much laughing and general joking, Nancy quietly began to push each of their five-foot-long muskets out the small hole in the wood pile. The first one slid through cleanly which meant Sukey had opened the door from the outside and was waiting to grab each musket so they wouldn't make a clunking sound on the ground outside. Two muskets, three muskets, four muskets through the wall.

As Nancy was reaching for the fifth musket she heard a "Hey, she has our guns!" There ensued a bunch of scuffling as they tried to stand at once from the bench seats.

Flipping the musket on to her shoulder in her best impression of a bad ass 1700s patriot woman, Nancy gripped the large trigger

The Beta

with two fingers and set her feet as she shouted. "Stay right where you are. Don't move!"

One of the soldiers ignored her command and began rushing her "You aren't going t--"

It was the soldier who shot her turkey. He didn't finish his sentence because she pulled the trigger. A light smoke engulfed her end of the cabin and every teenage Tory stood stock still as they saw blood begin to slowly ooze on the white portion of his uniform where the musket ball entered his torso.

"I said don't move," she repeated quietly, but seriously. She shot a man. Kira had never even considered shooting anyone in her entire real or simulated life, but shooting him had been the very last bullet on her to-do list.

Shooting him is what Nancy Hart did in real life. Shooting him felt like a historical necessity and she deeply understood why Nancy Hart did shoot because of the simulation. It didn't make it feel good but it did make it make sense.

Only a few seconds passed but it seemed like forever before neighbor patriots alerted by Sukey with the conch shell streamed in the cabin door and took over her vigil. Her simulated husband wanted to shoot them on the spot but she insisted they be hung properly.

Nancy was done. And so was Kira.

She took off her headset and the dimly lit room left her dizzy and confused. The modern trappings seemed out of place. She was exhausted. She felt this weird sort of pride in having completed her set of tasks properly. Kira felt as though the bastards who killed her turkey and repressed her fellow patriots learned a lesson. She felt totally disgusted that she had just spit a turkey and shot a man. They were very different things but both left a vile taste in her mouth.

She felt awe. Never before in her life had she understood history more than she did now. Kira would never look at another American Revolutionary picture without feeling a kinship to the cause—and for a short period of time a small part of her would answer to the name "Nancy" without skipping a beat.

The Beta

Sinixt

Kettle Falls, Washington State 1800s

After a few months of haphazardly following her every whim, whisking from country to culture and time period to time period with no real goal in mind beyond enjoying herself, Kira began to slowly hone in on some parts of the world she wanted to savor deeply. And so began a habit, every day she spent some time in each of those worlds.

It was a brilliant day at her home in Redmond, one of those few sunny days that the Seattle area enjoyed. Very few places in the world can compare with a sunny day in Seattle. There is something that happens when the unfamiliar solar rays hit miles of well hydrated greenery that had been saving up energy for months. If you have ever imagined what it would be like if plants photosynthesis and ATP generation could triple within a matter of minutes that's what happens in Seattle on a sunny day. The plants literally grow two inches and the vegetation breathes deeply like a sprinter catching their breath.

And so Kira felt a little like she was betraying the great outdoors as she headed into the dark garage and started all systems. Putting the equipment on took a while and she was already pretty sweaty in this sunny fall heat. Her garage did not have an air conditioner.

Recently her VR equipment began to fit perfectly. At first the suit had been stiff and new with a faint plastic stink. Although she couldn't wash most parts because of the electronics, they now smelled more like her deodorant than a plastics factory. That was a good change.

There was always one place she went first every morning in Google Earth History. Honing in on Washington State she slowly zoomed in—not to her home on the west side where Seattle creeped along the Sound, but to her ancestors' home on the east side.

Her eyes always traced the great Columbia River that flowed into the Pacific. First bordering Oregon, then slithering through the Tri-Cities as if trying to avoid the historic traces of radiation secretly seeping out of the Hanford reach and the ghosts of WWII, whipping through the windswept gorge north where a few brave salmon managed to reach the impenetrable energy producing coffin that was Grand Coulee Dam, slowing into the sluggish man made reservoir that was Lake Roosevelt, making a final turn north at a junction called Two Rivers where the Spokane River joined the Columbia, narrowly missing the Columbia Princess Ferry, and finally passing over a bridge to settle on a large peninsula at Sx̌ʷnitkʷ.

There was a rock here in her time and here in her headset. She had visited in real life and it was a touch point of sorts for her in virtual reality. It had probably been hauled up the cliff by some repentant white person who foresaw the need to save something as they decimated her ancestral land, or maybe an ancestor saved it? How would Kira ever know what really happened?

While the one-fourth of her who was Sinixt cursed at the desecration of the original falls by Grand Coulee Dam, the one-fourth of her that was a variety of European ancestries apologized, and the two quickly made up. It was much easier for her who was mixed to forgive and move on. Those without that built in peacemaking mechanism had a harder road to follow. Her Asian half looked on from afar and laughed a little without smiling on the outside.

The rock was only a little higher than her waist. During her visits in real life she walked around the small wooden fence and jumped right up to sit on it, using her hands to trace the hundreds of smooth grooves built up over thousands of years of sharpening. Had her great-great-great-great-great grandfather sharpened a point here? or here? her hands would wonder. Either way, the groves were soft and silky and sensuous to the touch.

In virtual reality the rock was blurry and insubstantial. As the rock was not very important to most people or near an important place no one had taken the time to add detail to the image. She could not touch it. Her high tech advanced gloves only gave the

The Beta

briefest of warm vibrations as her virtual hand passed through the edge of the rock and then through the rest like butter. Despite the incredible realism of this simulation her brain could never quite get over the ability to move through solid objects she had touched in real life. She felt like a ghost. It was a little easier to believe in places she had never visited before.

Switching on the icons layer for her school work the landscape in front of her was suddenly filled with cartoonish pins indicating lesson opportunities.

But she had only one place in mind. Not far from the modern Sx̌ʷnitkʷ bridge that spanned the shortest distance between the shores, a diamond shaped icon floated with unassuming grandeur above the west bank. In a way, it reminded her of the green floating icons from an early version of The Sims back on her parents' old PS4. But really, it hovered and twinkled with more promise than any icon in her past or present.

This light gem represented her past and her future. Within Google Earth History there were several opportunities to live in the past via re-created historical settlements. She wasn't really sure who decided what historic places were worthy of such initial investment, but she did know she was lucky. The Sinixt were her ancestors and someone was taking the time to recreate a Sinixt village from early 1800s and she was one of the first people to visit. It was like winning the genetic lottery.

There were multiple nagging mysteries she was determined to solve. Was the information for this re-creation coming from reliable sources? Were actual Sinixt descendants taking part in the creation of this ancient village or was it a bunch of random strangers? She knew she could begin asking these questions at their Friday sessions on the Microsoft campus but right now she just wanted to look and learn. She just wanted to be.

And so with a swish to the floating golden gem icon and a flick of her wrist, Kira pressed the trigger button and the current virtual world around her vanished.

The transitions in Google Earth History were considerably more seamless and modern than many of the VR transitions she experienced when the technology was new. Some of the earliest games either ignored transitions altogether and flashed white light suddenly in your headset as they loaded, or tried to wow you with stomach churning effects that reminded her of the introduction to Dr. Who shows, hurtling you through some crazy time warp tunnel.

But the distinction here was subtle, soft and purposeful. As the program downloaded a recreated Sinixt village at Sx̌ʷnitkʷ circa 1800 the dark void around her was populated with her learning goals, achievements and opportunities.

Everything she did in Google Earth History was likely to gain her some type of high school credit. Within the Sinixt village simulation she could earn U.S. History credit, World Language credit, Biology credit, English credit, and Fine Art credit. And her progress was clearly laid out for her both before, during and after each visit to the simulation. She was still getting the hang of what sorts of actions in the simulation yielded the most credit, but so far it had been so enjoyable she hardly had to pay attention to how her learning was adding up to real world benefits. She closed her eyes to the information and waited for the virtual morning sunlight to brighten her face before opening them again.

She could choose to re-enter the simulation at the current time of day and weather in the real world or the exact time she had last visited. So far, she kept the setting to match the Seattle time and weather, so when she looked up the Columbia River she could see the morning sun in the East.

Her starting point placed her right outside of a pit-house built into an upper bank on the west side of the river, across the way from the sharpening stone she visited on her way to the simulation.

The village was large and lively as Sx̌ʷnitkʷ was an ancient fishing site where people lived year-round. The first time she visited the village she was shocked by the sheer number of people that inhabited the area. There were literally thousands of people gathered at the site. Even though her parents had taught her early on that there was strong archeological evidence that the Early Americas were richly populated, the generalized American narrative of an empty wilderness ripe for the taking was still hard to shake.

"Sleep in?" A handsome young man teased her as he jogged past on his way to the river. Her eyes followed his progress away

The Beta

from her as her mind tried to wrap around his comment. He had been teasing her. She knew it. But he was a computer program.

It took Kira a moment to adjust to the realism. The people in this simulation so far were all Non-Player Characters or NPC's controlled by the AI. While she often ran into real live players in other simulations, the Sinixt village was both remote and not as exciting as the popular historical re-creations the students could visit. No matter how many times she had toggled on the layer that indicated which characters were NPC and which characters were real people, she was always alone in Sx̌ʷnitkʷ. Sometimes she wished her cousin, who was also Lakes, could get access to *The Beta*, but this first round was only available in large urban areas and her cousin lived on the Rez.

It made it more unnerving that the NPC who had teased her was both cute and had a sense of humor. She would have to be careful to not develop a crush on a computer character.

Warming up to her new physical location she turned around and ducked back inside the pit-house. Kira was shocked by the sheer number of material goods found in the pit-house. Previously, she would have assumed all early people lived lives of relative simplicity, envied by those of a modern cluttered era. But here in this simulation her family members had multiple changes of clothes, a surplus of blankets, and a whole corner of the home dedicated to tools.

It was the clothing she was in awe of each time she returned. Moving to a corner of the room she rifled through several garments until she found the one she wanted.

Picking up a comb made of wood she pretended to fix her hair of which she could neither "see" nor "feel". That's when she realized she couldn't recall if she had long or short hair.

Curious, she jumped back and forth to see if she could use virtual gravity to whip her hair around into her field of vision. She was rewarded with the end of a thick braid flicking in and out of the corner of her eye. So she did have long hair!

Using her gloves she was able to find and grab this virtual braid and lay it over her shoulder so she could look at it. The bottom was tied with some type of leather and hide; and holy smokes, when she used her fingertips to tease the end of the hair tie it came apart easily and the braid fell apart in her hands. In real life she had thick Asian hair but the simulation used a softer brown with a slight wave. Kira was floored by how real it looked as the hairs separated and shimmered.

Kira momentarily forgot she was holding a comb. Because you couldn't feel an object in your hand something could be "stuck" in your palm without you remembering. She attempted to comb her hair and as she stretched the comb along her locks the hair parted cleanly between each comb tooth. Some programmer somewhere had coded the instructions that allowed her to actually brush virtual hair.

That gave Kira another idea. Abandoning the pit-house she bounded up the stairs before she ran into the blue chaperone wall that burst into view whenever she was close enough to the garage wall in real life. Boy, she wished her family garage was full of wrestling mats lined up on the wall. As it was she was a little unnerved to remember the metal shelving, stacked with chainsaws, chemicals, and other assorted dangerous objects that were stored along the cement garage walls right outside of her pre-prescribed VR boundary.

The VR play space at her house was only about five meters by seven meters in the garage, and the space she used at Microsoft was almost limitless comparatively. There she could run, jump, and cross almost fifty yards at a time before running into a chaperone wall. Here at home she had to keep reorienting and skipping ahead using hand controllers instead of her own feet. It really messed with the whole immersive feeling.

Drawn by curiosity, she made her way slowly through the busy village toward the river. On her right she passed a large group of women filleting salmon and flawlessly pulling long strips into a large drying rack. The salmon were enormous, way bigger than those her cousins pulled out of the modern Columbia River down at Chief Joseph Dam. There were old women and young women, pretty women and homely women, happy looking women and cranky looking women. Sometimes she would look into their eyes and wonder "Are you my great-great-grandmother?"

None of them actually were. She knew that for a fact, as no pictures of her great-great-grandmothers existed. But Kira hoped the faces molded for this simulation must be derived from real Native faces, and hopefully those of her tribe. If so, one of them was the closest she would ever get to seeing her ancestors.

A bee landed on her arm and she jumped a meter, past the chaperone wall, banging her head on a non-simulated shelf from the garage in real life. Ouch. She wondered what exactly she hit.

Sitting unceremoniously on her butt and staring through the web-like chaperone wall back into the simulation Kira could see the group of women had all paused in their chores and were staring at her. Her embarrassment propelled her to jump up and return to the VR area despite the swarms of bees and flies she now noticed around the salmon; finding her hands involuntarily brushing herself off and swatting at bees even though there was no logical reason to, they couldn't cause pain in VR.

As quickly as the women had paused to stare at her epic fall, they all resumed their working and chatting. Curious, she switched on her closed captioning so she could understand what they were saying in Salish.

"My auntie is going to go Huckleberry picking at Twin Lakes after the salmon. She swears they have the thickest patches south of the falls." one woman remarked as her knife expertly sliced through pink fish flesh, flicking flies just as easily.

"She does bring back the best berries," an older woman remarked as she attached fillets one at a time to a string much like a clothesline. "And not only does she have the best berries she also has the most handsome of sons." The women's wrinkled eyes twinkled as she threw her verbal bait out amongst the group of younger women and fish.

Several of the young women blushed and the middle-aged ones eyed the young-ones speculatively.

"That's him over near the river bank now?" pointed one mother with a questioning tone.

Kira's head swiveled along with the rest of the women and she could see from this distance that it was the same young man who teased her as she left her home only minutes ago. He stripped off his shirt and waded into the rocks along the western bank below the falls.

The Beta

Kira stared openly even though the other girls were sneaking in furtive glances. The boy turned in just the right angle so she could see his stomach and arm muscles neatly defined by the mid-morning sun. He was gorgeous standing there in profile looking across the river.

Like what you see do you? The words appeared in her vision suddenly, interrupting her unabashed stare.

Huh? Kira was confused. Closed captioning words only appeared directly under a speaker who was currently "talking" and floated directly underneath their body but she couldn't tell whose body these words were attached to. Turning around to look at the group of women the words were suddenly underneath the oldest woman in the bunch. Kira shook her head for a second and then chalked up the anomaly to a fluke. While the Google Earth History experience had been pretty seamless so far, there were more than a few glitches.

Kira was going to ignore the query but while all the other women were paying her no mind the older one was looking at her pointedly, so she felt obligated to respond.

"Very much," she said with a saucy grin.

The older woman raised her eyebrows but said nothing, however Kira swore she nodded in the young man's direction as if saying 'go on girl, go down there' while she continued to deftly hang the fish.

Still blushing, Kira reminded herself that all of these virtual people were sure to be computer generated NPCs. There was no reason to blush and no reason to be afraid. Maybe an 1800s version of herself wouldn't be so bold but the 2010s version was curious. Curious of that handsome computer-generated boy by the river and also curious about the whole idea that had initially propelled her out of the pit-house in the first place.

So she hardly noticed the women laughing at her as she made her way down to the river.

While Kira had been combing her hair in the pit-house it occurred to her that despite her extensive travels in Google Earth History simulations she had not yet tried to walk through any sizable bodies of water. Kira was dying to know if swimming was possible.

The Beta

Bold, but not bold enough to take off her clothes, Kira waded into the water behind the handsome young man and threw up a splash in his direction. The water droplets spread in a delightfully realistic arc and hit his back with water fight precision.

He turned around quicker than she expected, and it didn't take him long to respond to her with a smile and a splash of his own. What the heck was she doing flirting with a computer program; but just as strangely what was an NPC doing flirting with her? Who wrote this code? A little paranoid Kira flipped on her identification layer but sure enough he was surrounded in brown, which clearly indicated a coded non-player character.

But she wasn't here to flirt, Kira's real aim was to try her hand at VR swimming. Wading deeper into the river she bent her knees and dunked down until her head was fully submerged. The water was murkier than she expected and so realistic she felt immediate claustrophobia. Even though she technically didn't have to breathe in VR the reflex was automatic and she popped right up.

Little drops of water dripped across her VR lenses and she found her hand trying to get through her headset so she could rub the water out of her eyes. It only took a few seconds for the water to drip off before she could see clearly again.

Kira studied her clothes and arms to find them wet and soppy looking, as if she had jumped into REAL LIFE water.

She looked over at the handsome young man who was waist deep next to her in the water. Surprisingly, he asked "Wanna go for a swim?" The words he spoke she heard in Salish and saw in English.

"Um, OK," she responded without a second thought. If this NPC wanted to keep her company on her swimming explorations so be it.

He playfully dove in ahead of her so she had no choice but to follow suit. In real life she was such a wimp about getting into cold water past her waist. But here she dove right in and then glided forward in a swimming like fashion. If anyone was watching her back irl she was sure to look like a total dork.

There was obviously no floating sensation in her VR suit but the perspective bobbed a bit and her direction changed with the

The Beta

arcing movements of her hands. It seemed easiest to do a simple breaststroke while her legs stopped moving altogether.

She hadn't asked the NPC for his name, there was something awkward about putting a name to a computer face.

He slowed his pace and turned around to look at her, smiling with a wide grin; his teeth only slightly crooked but certainly not a modern bleached white. She wondered what a person from the 1800s would think about all the neon bright smiles in the 20th century.

Playing along she smiled back and started swimming past him in challenge. The river was huge but even if she made it to the other side she could always log-out of the re-creation and start over in the village.

She heard him call out urgently from behind. Was that worry she heard in his NPC voice? She turned around to see what he was saying.

"Wait!" She saw the text underneath him. "Don't go that far."

Ignoring his plea and his cuteness she increased her strokes a bit and enjoyed the view. Deep blue skies, tall thickly forested hills, and beyond the settlement not a car, house, or bridge in sight.

She didn't get to enjoy the view long before she realized he was right behind her and suddenly her avatar was turned around against her will. While she couldn't feel anything in real life it annoyed her that somehow this NPC could impinge on her freedom.

"Come on, turn back!" he shouted.

Then her annoyance disappeared as quickly as it started. Both of their bodies were twirling in a large, slow, but powerful whirlpool.

Because they were below the actual falls Kira had been seduced into thinking the slow-moving river was calm and serene; and now instead of a leisurely breaststroke she was throwing up her hands as quickly and powerfully as possible in an all-out crawl. Somehow the NPC was holding on to her with one hand and swimming with the other. It took all of her effort not to flop over sideways irl and kick.

Heart pounding, time went slowly as they made molasses like progress toward the edge of the whirlpool. Although the depth of

The Beta

the whirlpool's center was probably only a foot or so from her view it felt like she was about to fall into a black hole.

"Help me," she finally called out, mostly because her arm muscles were killing her. Why hadn't they tied her high school PE credit to Google Earth History? She would have to give Professor McKenzie and *The Beta* team that feedback the next Friday they met.

Tired, frustrated and embarrassed Kira paused for a minute, first glancing at the handsome boy's face, brown brow furrowed in intense concentration, and then in the other direction at the center of the whirlpool.

That simple pause was enough slack to reverse their progress. They were only a few twirls away from the center.

Feeling the irrational fear of drowning well up within her Kira hit her settings button and a wide berth of familiar text windows popped up, reassuring her conscious that this was all just make believe.

Unable to look at the face of the handsome young man Kira waited just long enough for her head to be sucked into the dark blackness of the river before pressing the exit button.

The strangest thought crossed her mind. Why in heaven's sake hadn't she asked for his name. He may be a long string of numbers but he was a long string of numbers who tried to save her life. That much she owed him. Knowing his name was the least she could do to honor his sacrifice.

Kira took off the headset and found herself gulping for air despite the copious amounts of oxygen obviously surrounding her. That was the strangest thing about VR, you really could trick your mind into thinking you were doing something like drowning in the Columbia River.

She stood still for a bit as her labored breathing normalized. On the far side of the garage she saw some egg cartons scattered on the floor, which must have fallen when she hit the shelf earlier.

Something was bothering her about the experience, but she couldn't quite put her finger on exactly what. Oh well, Kira didn't think she would be going back to the village right away after drowning, but a small illogical part of herself wanted to go back right away and ask that handsome piece of code his name, and maybe flirt a little. Some practice for REAL LIFE.

Asante

"Kira!" Her mom's voice sounded a little odd so Kira paused her studies and stripped off her VR equipment. By now she was quite proficient in getting out of her gear in record time.

"Coming!" she replied loudly through the propped open garage door.

She and her mom crashed into one another as Kira passed around the corner and they both laughed.

"What's up Mom?"

Her mom's voice and face turned questioning in response. "There is someone here to see you, a tall young man?"

Kira could hear the curiosity in her voice.

Kira was stumped. What tall young man would have driven all the way into the Redmond suburbs to visit her? She certainly hadn't invited anyone.

Kira's quizzical face must have satisfied her mom's suspicions that she wasn't conspiring with some young lover. Her mom motioned her toward the front hall while making her own way back to the kitchen to give her some privacy.

She opened the front door without peeking through the peephole or checking the security camera video and then stopped in her tracks, speechless.

"What are you doing here?" she asked, her voice triangulating somewhere between anger, disbelief, and desire.

"I. . . ," he practically whispered, looking beyond her shoulder as if unsure if they were alone. Then speaking a little more loudly. "Will you go for a walk with me?" Kevin used his head and shoulder to gesture to the sunlit road behind him.

Kira squinted against the bright light and did an interior mental shrug that was less emotionally stable that she would have

The Beta

expected. Might as well get this conversation over with and get some vitamin D at the same time.

"Mom!" She shouted louder than necessary.

"Yeah?" Came the reply from an appropriately close eavesdropping location.

"I'm going on a walk around the neighborhood!" Kira was out the door and down the steps before she could hear her mother's reply. She was determined not to be forced into making introductions between this ass and her family.

They walked down the long driveway not really looking at one another or talking. There was always this feeling that cameras and microphones were everywhere, even once they made it to the long single lane road lined with trees and bushes. It was early winter and leafless blackberry brambles provided a thick and prickly edge to the road.

He started to speak but she interrupted him bluntly, "Why are you here Kevin?" Never mind the fact that it was just weird that he knew where she lived, it's not like the location of her house was a secret but it was still crossing some invisible line of privacy for him to stop by uninvited. Although she supposed there would be no other way for him to communicate with her since she was no longer in school and had blocked his phone number. If he was texting her she would have no clue.

"I'm sorry," was all he said. But he stopped, looked straight into her eyes and grabbed her arms in his rather forcefully though without threat. A pleading stare accompanied his grip.

She melted and cried inside, fully unable to mask her feelings and fully unable to understand them herself either. He was a jerk, so why did she feel this way? He lied to her and would do it again and that was a self-evident truth.

"Why won't you answer my texts?" he asked, moving his head to force her wandering stare to meet his.

"You know why." She responded with the generalized comment and rounded her own stare back at him in offensive accusation. "You lied to me. The whole time you were with me you were still with her!"

Finally, out with the basics she shoved him and turned away. There was nothing he could say that would change those facts. She

The Beta

waited in bewilderment for whatever ridiculous excuse or lie he was sure to follow up with.

"It wasn't like that . . ." he started.

Extending her silence into infinity, she was determined not to help him here. He was one of those guys that always needed help.

"It's more complicated than you can imagine, she was blackmailing me." His voice broke in desperation.

Kira had not expected that answer. His claim didn't change anything and she wisely kept her silence.

Kevin seemed to be waiting for her response, but when nothing was forthcoming he shrugged, walked over to a large rock and sat down, then quietly he began. "You see, she had these pictures . . ." pausing again he looked at her and she didn't bite so he went on, ". . . and she said she would share them if I didn't hang out with her. And she kept threatening me no matter what I would do."

The silence settled between them and between the blackberry bushes. She could almost feel the thorns of their relationship. Like there was a microcosmic high-pressure system hanging over them they both stood heavy, neither saying anything or looking at one another.

Finally, he spoke up "I'm sorry. Will you please forgive me?"

None of her anger had abated, and her heart still held itself in a defensive, suspicious, unforgiving posture, but she felt obligated to say yes and so she did.

"Yes." But she would not yet look at him.

He surprised her by sneaking up behind and holding her in a gentle embrace. Kira knew it was wrong and she should wrench herself out of his arms but in all reality, she missed this. Would letting herself enjoy this one last time be only a minute transgression against her own self-worth?

And so she let herself go in his arms. Kira was too done with him to cry, those initial tears had dried up, but for just a moment she would pretend that he really had and really did love her.

If only it were the truth.

After a while he pulled back and looked down at her. His ready smile was more than suspicious and she wondered if he had any inkling about how she really felt inside. Did he actually think she would really forgive him so easily? Did he actually not see the deep distrust in her eyes?

"So how's school?" he pitched out a curveball to change the subject.

"Um," she responded honestly but with little detail. "It's actually pretty great, but we aren't supposed to talk about it much outside of class."

"Are you starting to go blind from never seeing the sun?" he joked.

"Well, the VR is actually pretty realistic, but yeah, you're right." Then she added even more honesty to the conversation. "In fact, one of the only reasons I agreed to go on this walk with you was to get my daily dose of vitamin D."

He laughed back as if she was telling a joke, but he was missing her signals by a lightyear. There was nothing funny about her reasons.

In preparation to deflect any more prying about *The Beta* she responded with her own question. "So how is Redmond High?"

"Well, you know, the same old." He pulled her in a little closer to a shaded crevice of a blackberry bush and Kira almost froze, she had no idea how she was going to respond if he tried to kiss her again.

"Mr. Allen is still giving those crazy chemistry quizzes." He started, but instead of looking into her eyes like he used to when he asked her to get the answers, he was looking behind her in the distance.

That tiny part of her that was vacillating between never seeing him again or melting back into his lies firmly strengthened her resolve. She didn't even have to wait long for him to dig himself into that trench.

"Do you think? . . . Would you mind? Getting me the next chemistry test info?" He asked, finally looking straight at her.

If someone would have gently pushed her over at that moment she would have fallen over like a straight log, her spine was so stiff with determination. Kira was almost thankful that he was holding her up to keep her from falling, but despite the rigidity of her back her strong arms pushed on his shoulders reflexively so that she could get the purchase to slap him across the face.

The Beta

She had never, ever, hit anyone in real life before. Although ironically, she had now killed a few people in VR.

He backed away, with eyes blazing in an anger that surely matched her own. An almost growl was on his face.

The hard parts of her body relaxed into a shaking mass but she responded clearly, "I never want to see you again. Stay away from me and never come back."

She turned and walked right back to her house with the creepy knowledge that he had to follow her at some point to get into the car he must have borrowed to stalk her all the way out to her house, but she vowed not to look and she didn't hear any footsteps.

Finally, thankfully, she made it back into her cool air-conditioned house and closed the door. Not hearing her mom, or anyone for that matter, she bounded up the steps into her room for privacy and brought up the house cameras on her phone.

His car was still there alright but there was no sign of him. For all she knew he was borrowing 'her' car for this visit—that cheating bastard. For a while she sat there watching the live feed of her peaceful driveway as her vital signs slowed to normal. Eventually she saw him walk across the driveway where he paused at his car and looked up at the house. Though she couldn't tell from such a fuzzy picture so far away, Kira swore he was saying something, but as she turned up the volume she could hear nothing but the familiar buzz of the microphone feedback.

Not obsessed enough to replay the video and sound, Kira was determined to forget everything, and the quickest way to forget this would be to do her schoolwork.

Kira laughed at such a thought. A few months ago she would never have dreamed that history homework would serve as an emotional panacea for a high school break up. Well, it wasn't a break up exactly but her heart was still sore.

Not quite ready to see her mother Kira chose her route to the garage carefully, proceeding slowly in her bare feet and successfully grabbing a drink from the fridge in the process. She didn't mind telling her mom everything but sometimes processing things on her own was a lot easier compared to talking about it right away.

VR equipment on and adjusted, Google Earth History opened, Kira knew that the type of therapeutic counseling she needed would have to be some topic that put her in another person's shoes. Hopefully, it would help put her own problems in perspective. It was just the type of advice her mother would give.

Sometimes, figuring out where to start in Google Earth History was the hardest part of each day. When the options were nearly limitless and her curiosity unbounded, Kira simply couldn't decide what to learn next. So, she pulled up her high school credit graphs to review the current credit percentages. By far the subject in which she had the least credit was U.S. History. She opened up the class and started to skim through the most basic assigned tasks on a timeline.

Today she was ready to tackle something hard, and it didn't take her long to find the experience that would most likely fit the bill. Skimming over the basic info she saw that although the lesson only took seven hours of 'seat time'—the required length from start to finish was four months! What in the world would need a four month wait time from start to finish?

The beginning was a five-minute introduction that focused on West-African geography and ancient history. Kira was impressed with the long list of mathematicians, scientists, and advanced civilizations that were described in such a short clip. Her early education always put such an emphasis on the European origins of society, and while she was intimately familiar with ancient Asia she never learned much about Africa. After satisfying the AI that she understood all the basics she entered the first simulation for her African-American U.S. History segment.

The title flickered above as her screen transitioned seamlessly. This section was called "The Asante Empire." Her starting location was dark, almost black. There were small blocks of blinding white sunlight coming in from two tiny windows that lined the top of the wall, so while she couldn't see anything she could tell it was a huge long room, yet the bright slats of light actually impaired her vision. Kira walked forward peering into the darkness when she suddenly heard voices speaking a language she couldn't understand. Tempted as she was to turn on the closed captioning and translation options, something told her to take her time and pay attention without relying on any exterior help. At least not yet.

The Beta

Her controls continued to indicate she was bumping into something and people kept talking in irritated tones. She really couldn't tell for sure in the dark with an unfamiliar language. Turning around so the lights from the window no longer blinded her sight she waited. A few seconds later her VR goggles slowly adjusted to the light just like her eyes would have in real life.

She sucked in her breath. A dim backlight began to rise in her vision outlining hundreds of people with still indistinguishable features. Now that she was standing still and the voices had stopped she could hear coughing, slow tiny movements, whispers, and somewhere far off a quiet song.

As minutes passed her VR vision adjusted even more and she knew exactly where she was. Kira looked down at her own body which was nearly naked, voluptuous, and beautiful. A myriad of bruises and scars told another story and then her gaze traveled to her hundred companions.

She walked around the crowded room wanting to explore from one end to another. Sometimes the people would part to allow her to pass and at times an NPC would refuse to budge. Once she literally had to push her way through—feeling awkward and rude.

At the corner of the room the crowd thinned and when she realized what she was looking at she quickly averted her eyes. There were several women squatting on one side and three men relieving themselves on the other. The corner was piled with excrement.

This was a stand-alone re-creation so Kira knew that all people in the room were simply NPCs but her heart was already broken. This was so wrong. She was bearing witness to one of humanity's darkest hours.

She was claustrophobic in real life and her next reaction was to trace along the perimeter for any sign of an opening, but after carefully combing the walls she suspected she was in was a true prison.

To confirm her hypothesis Kira made her way to the wall of tall windows to see if it was possible to look outside. As she passed once again through the crowd, she felt a strong pull to hug, kneel next to, and care for every person; simultaneously she was filled with a dark rage that wanted to rise up with the crowd and violently break free of the cage.

The windows were high up and difficult to access. Finally giving in to her crutches Kira enabled the translation software and all of a sudden could hear what was going on around her. She turned to the nearest big tall man and asked, "May I stand on your shoulders? So I can see out the window?"

Not expecting an NPC to be pre-programmed to respond to such a request Kira was surprised that the man offered his hands, creating a small platform to give her a boost. The AI behind this thing was phenomenal.

Awkwardly she lifted up one foot irl and in VR she was levitated three feet up which was just enough to grab on to the wire bars that crossed in an X across the small window. Once again, her VR sight took time to adjust to the bright light but her suspicions were confirmed without a doubt. She could see the white walls of a fort or castle of sorts, the crystalline blue of the ocean, hot sandy beaches and not much further out a large 16th or 17th century ship. This was probably the one that she and her fellow prisoners were bound to board before too long.

Kira couldn't take it anymore and she exited the simulation suddenly when her teacher rudely interrupted her and asked if she would like to take a pre-test on the African Slave trade. She didn't want to take a pre-test on the slave trade. What Kira wanted to do was cry. But one of the best ways to prevent tears was to distract oneself so she opened herself to the onslaught of the pre-test.

Kira was a pretty quick student and so her AI teacher didn't hesitate on asking the questions to her as fast as she responded. For one of the first times in her life Kira felt completely out of sorts, she wasn't getting ANY of the questions correct.

That's when it hit her. Kira was smart, Kira was well read, but she didn't know anything about the African Slave trade nor much about African-American culture for that matter. After experiencing what it was like in that dungeon Kira felt a deep sense of anguish and guilt. How could she have chosen to know so little? Why did she always ignore the stories about African-Americans on the news?

The Beta

Then her feelings took a whole different turn—there was this desperate need to erase the feeling of helplessness she felt while she was in the dungeon. Trapped, despised, trampled, and owned. But just as suddenly, Kira knew exactly where she needed to go. It didn't take her long to find the simulation she was looking for.

All of a sudden she was in a gorgeous black dress. She looked from side to side and as far down as her headset would allow her to see. Kira was in ok shape irl but the body she currently inhabited was beautiful, in fabulous shape, and much taller than she was used to. It made her giggle to think about trying out Abe Lincoln or Yao Ming one of these days.

Her avatar was already marching and this particular simulation didn't give her the freedom to move so she simply enjoyed the ride as in the background a narrator's voice began, "You are now experiencing the 50th Anniversary of the Selma to Montgomery Marches and will soon be crossing the historic Edmund Pettus Bridge."

The narrator kept talking but Kira's gaze and mind wandered. She was walking arm in arm in the first row of a huge crowd approaching the aforementioned bridge. To her left was an older man, his gaze steady and strong, while to her right was a beautiful young teenager whose carefree gaze shared only an inkling of the man opposite. But the joy of the moment was palpable to all in that front row, there was much to celebrate, much to mourn, and much, much more to do next.

Her dive into this particular simulation was having the exact effect she was looking for. Instead of that claustrophobic, smashed despair she felt earlier, instead there was this strength and solid pride that filled every pore of her being.

Kira allowed enough time for some healing to massage itself into her lymphatic system and then she made two vows to herself. First she would return to the Asante Kingdom simulation in due time and finish it till the end. The second vow was little more than an excuse, she hadn't heard a word the simulation narrator said. She promised herself she would return and really listen next time, and not only when she was in Google Earth History. But more importantly she would prioritize listening in real life.

The Beta

Though feeling better Kira felt as though she needed to make one more stop and the list of possibilities available to her did not let her down. Within minutes she made her choice.

This historical simulation started with the low thrum of a crowd that slowly increased and the world was divided into dark corners and bright spotlights, reminding Kira of her time on stage at a middle school play. She peered into the far reaches and shaded her eyes from the lights but all she could do was imagine the huge crowd that filled her ears.

Suddenly, in front of her were two lines of women in white costumes who began to walk forward down a long runway and within seconds a quiet narrator prompted her to follow.

At the end of the walkway the dancers stepped onto a stage with a shimmering surface and it took Kira a minute to realize they were all dropping into ankle deep water. Delighted, Kira didn't hesitate to follow them and looked down at her feet as she sloshed her way to the middle of the dancers, for now she knew that is exactly what they were. Of course she couldn't feel the cool water but nonetheless it took her breath away to see how realistic the water moved around her virtual avatar's feet. Testing the limits of the programming she gave a quick kick and the water responded accordingly with a huge splash that stretched four feet in front of her. This was brilliant.

Two more teaching screens popped up from the darkness, one of a figure dancing and one with text. The figure was holding a microphone and the text was suddenly highlighted as she could hear a quiet voice singing in her right ear.

Feeling both silly and powerful Kira began to sing quietly at first, and then without fear. After all she was alone in her garage. "Freedom! Freedom!"

A visual prompt guided her forward on the stage as the dancers kicked up water all around her. Then following the movement of the figure holding the microphone she was dancing and kicking water as she sang. Well, not exactly, as she couldn't quite dance and sing at the same time. A great joy welled up inside her as she finished off the chorus.

The Beta

There was a power coursing through her like she rarely felt and she sought to remember the feeling and send it back through the virtual years to prop up and support the spirit of the body she initially inhabited in that slave dungeon in the Asante Empire.

All of a sudden she heard laughing, real life laughing, so she ripped the headset off faster than she ever had before in embarrassed indignation.

Sure enough, there was her mother wearing a huge smile. Her laugh continued and so after a perfunctory glare Kira let herself join-in.

"What were you doing?" her mom asked curiously and perhaps even a bit jealous.

"I think I just got high school credit for karaoking Beyonce on stage! Seriously!" When Kira said it out loud it seemed shallow—but the feeling inside, the newfound expanse of understanding no matter how small—was precious, deep, and worthwhile.

She explained a bit more to her mom starting with the slave quarters in Cape Coast Castle and the feelings it invoked. Then how she chose to find modern role models that filled her with hope to counteract the pain of slavery. Her mom listened without saying a word.

"And now," Kira continued, sitting down on the garage stairs next to her mom and wrapping her arms around her knees, "I feel a little conflicted. I mean, dancing around on stage acting like Beyoncé was fun and enjoying myself like that felt like . . ." searching for the right words here was tough, "Well it also felt like the most insidious type of cultural appropriation I can think of."

Her mom was looking intently at the motor oil on the shelf across the room when she started speaking. "It's complicated sweetie. Did you enter the simulation with self-serving motives?" she asked.

Kira felt like a deer caught in bright lights. Did her mom have any clue that the whole reason she jumped into a difficult situation was to get her mind off that mean, mean boy? But she couldn't tell her mom that, so she only responded with the other legitimate self-serving reason, "I did want to get more of my U.S. History credit out of the way."

The Beta

And now she felt simply horrible, like she had betrayed every African-American woman in history by using their pain and pleasure to solve her own problems.

"Let me ask you this," her mom began, "Does Mrs. Cerillo begrudge your love of her homemade cooking even though you are not Hispanic?"

Kira paused and then responded hesitantly, "I don't think so."

"How do you feel when your friends want to learn Chinese or celebrate New Years with us?"

"Well, I laugh at their attempts to understand some things—they don't really get it—but I guess it is kind of nice they are interested, I suppose." Kira responded. "But they will never really understand."

"How do you feel when you are on the reservation?" her mom asked.

This question opened a whole other can of worms. Her mom was half Lakes and so she was only a quarter Lakes and while her mom was a registered tribal member her blood quantum was small enough that she was not allowed to be a legally registered member of the tribe. Like every other non-Indian she was required to be with her mom or grandparents to pick huckleberries. That always made her mad.

"I suppose that's why I like spending time at the Sx̌ʷnitkʷ simulation Mom, I actually get to be part of the tribe there." Yet on the flip side this made her think about what her real life half-blood and full-blood Indian relatives would think of her forays into an imaginary historical tribal life. Some wouldn't care, some would be pleased, and some would be pissed.

"You really didn't help me Mom." Kira said in an accusing tone, but accompanied by a sideways hug.

"I don't think that's what I meant to do." Her mom's arms tightened in response. "Life is like that, grey and messy. Most of the time there are no clear answers and none can weigh your heart except you."

"But," her mom continued, "there are those that will always love you. And you can depend on us while you are doing all that hard work in your soul."

Kira leaned her head on her mom's shoulder.

The Beta

"All your life you will be crafting your inner being, listening, changing, torn or self-assured. It doesn't change when you grow up." At this her mom smiled. "But adolescence has its own special charm my girl." With that her mom turned her shoulders to look into her eyes. "I am proud of you, you care deeply for others."

Kira let out her breath slowly; feeling conflicted, content, and utterly exhausted all at the same time. She needed to sleep.

Sarah Franklin-Bache

Boston 1767

Pick one, pick one, Kira mentally repeated to herself. Choosing a character was always a tough decision.

Most high school diplomas required one year of U.S. History in addition to another year of Government and Current World Affairs. Even the traditional World History requirement was focused on a U.S. centric view of the world. Therefore, despite her desire to dive into Native American and East Asian History, Kira knew she might as well try and complete most of her U.S. requirements first.

Spinning the globe and flying closer to the Eastern seaboard Kira slowly began to add layers to see her historical learning options. Visually, the East Coast looked busy enough irl with its large sprawling cities, and overlaying the historical timelines made for quite an icon rich screen.

She picked the "meld" option before asking the AI to take her back in time from 2020-1650 and set the total time for five minutes. Then she found her soft padded chair irl and sat down to relax as she watched the Earth below her slowly transform.

There were two main things she noticed as the East Coast began to slowly turn back in time. First the way suburban sprawl creeped back revealing thick green patches of land between the ever-shrinking urban areas. Second, as they approached the industrial revolution. Each winter thick swirls of smog threaded in

The Beta

and out of the most populated areas reminding her of the air quality maps that tracked August wildfire smoke across the Pacific Northwest. As the map neared the 1700s she pressed pause and noted the American Revolution.

Not exactly sure why, Kira typed in "Women of the Revolution" and she was presented with a menu of over thirty women with details of their particular simulations. Although most of the simulations in Google Earth were simplistic single player simulations where you were a passive watcher, the few interactive multiplayer simulated towns were so engaging you could end up spending way too much time on the same subject simply because you were enjoying yourself so much.

"Aha," Kira said under her breath. "That's it."

There was a multiplayer city simulation in Philadelphia spanning the years of the American Revolution and a historical figure that fit her desired criteria. She would become Benjamin Franklin's daughter.

Kira was already imagining what it would be like to flit around Philadelphia as the daughter of the famous and well-respected figure of Ben Franklin. To be honest, Kira was excited about waring the fancy ornate dresses worn by the ladies of wealth at that time in history.

Kira tapped 'accept' and began a required pre-assessment of the Revolutionary War and Sarah Franklin-Bache. The pre-assessment seemed to take longer than usual as she kept getting question after question incorrect and when the test zeroed in on her knowledge of Franklin she was rather surprised to hear that he spent most of Sarah's young life abroad in France from 1776 to 1785. She also learned that Franklin retired from the newspaper business at 42 to pursue inventing and other pastimes.

Her original assumption that she would be traipsing around in dresses as she watched her "father" print newspapers and stir the hearts of the revolution was all wrong. What exactly would she be doing in Philadelphia in 1779 without a father?

Kira was about to find out. This particular simulation was an open-ended multiplayer re-creation of Philadelphia. There were three different servers currently running separate versions and all three of them had the Sarah Franklin-Bache characters available

The Beta

for use. Feeling social, Kira picked the busiest simulation that had 96 out of 100 possible real life characters filled.

While normally Kira would check her list of game objectives and do a bit of background reading on her character, today she felt like doing a cold drop so she flicked her wrist and closed her eyes.

She paused for a bit and then opened them slowly. The room was light and airy with sunlight streaming through two paned windows chaperoning a large armoire. Unlit candles sticks and lamps festooned wall sconces and tables throughout—a decoration choice she still yearned to implement irl, never mind the fire danger.

She was lucky to be lounging on the couch irl, because her beginning position was lying prone in a bed surrounded by draperies.

Giving herself an illusionary morning stretch Kira pulled back the covers and stood up, eyeing the armoire covetously. She began to walk across the room when she saw something protruding out from her stomach and she wondered if the program had a visual glitch.

Holy crap. There wasn't any glitch. She was Sarah Franklin-Bache and she was ten freaking months pregnant.

Suddenly regretting her lack of preparation Kira stared down at her virtual pregnant stomach. This was not what she expected. What the heck was she supposed to do?

It only took two steps to position herself in front of a full-length mirror and see her entire figure filling out the reflective surface.

Flinching a bit Kira came face to face with a rather plump figure, plump *and* pregnant, who looked almost like Ben Franklin himself with little of the feminine wiles Kira was expecting.

I look ugly she thought and then suddenly blushed with embarrassment by thinking that the intelligent and talented daughter of Ben Franklin was ugly.

Regathering her fleeing wits about her Kira was once again struck by how Google Earth History surprised and expanded her view of how the world worked. I mean, she expected to learn new facts about people and places, but she didn't anticipate having to suddenly think about childbirth, war, and love in her history class.

The Beta

I mean, what did being pregnant mean to Sarah Franklin-Bache? Was she happy? Was it easy? Was it what she wanted? And more pressingly, here Kira paused and pretended to touch her virtual pregnancy, was she going to have to give birth in VR?

Shuddering with the memory of a middle school birthing video Kira took another deep breath. At least in VR she could take off her headset.

But Kira didn't have much time to think because she was suddenly distracted by a child's cry. Confused she looked around to try and figure out where the sound was coming from. Even in the VR headset she could tell the sound emanated from somewhere behind the only door in the room so she hurried across the room and opened the door.

Turning down a small hallway she was forced to choose between a staircase and two open doorways. Following her instincts she headed toward one door and peered inside.

Sure enough the source of the sound was staring her in the face. A ten-year-old boy was standing on a chair reaching on to a high shelf to grab a toy, a six-year-old boy was crying next to a broken dish and a two-year-old child dressed in white was playing happily amongst a pile of wooden blocks.

Holy cow, not only was she pregnant was she supposed to care for three children? They had got to be kidding.

She burst out laughing which ironically caused the NPC children to stop and stare at her for a moment before returning to their previous occupations. Well, she wasn't a bad babysitter irl so she would humor the simulation for a while. Hauling up the crying six-year-old in one hand and telling the ten-year-old to 'get down right this instance' quickly restored order to the room. Thankful for her virtual health, she picked up the other little one and ordered the two boys to follow her downstairs.

On the first floor she made her way to the kitchen and was greeted by a housekeeper. Handing the little one over, Kira said a prayer of thanks as she instructed the other two children to sit down and eat the meal the housekeeper had prepared. Now she could begin exploring Sarah's domicile.

She knew Sarah lived in Ben Franklin Court and as she walked outside she could see exactly why it was called a court. Surrounded

The Beta

on all sides by four-story brick city buildings, the interior court was a haven from city life complete with gardens and trees. An archway built into the brick allowed carriages access to the inner sanctuary.

It was a beautiful day and she felt completely at odds with the normalcy as she grappled with the surprise pregnancy of Sarah Franklin-Bache. Suddenly she laughed out loud realizing if high school boys were required to choose female avatars for a specific amount of time, some of them were sure to end up in her situation. It was funny and satisfying to think about.

Ready to work, Kira pulled up her list of assignments and actions. She didn't want to join other players right away because she didn't fully understand her character yet. One option piqued her interest. The description read. *Write a two page letter to your father Ben Franklin. Find artifacts and examples in the Franklin home to guide your correspondence.*

Kira/Sarah went back inside the house and observed the happy chaos of children eating a meal. Moving to the next room she found what she was looking for, a writing desk with paper, quills, ink and there it was—a small cache of letters from Ben Franklin addressed to her. Kira read through his most recent letters and then thought about what she observed in the house so far.

The door to the parlor opened and the children streamed through, the youngest child carrying a slice of apple pie. Kira accepted the two-year-old on her lap and tried her best to make conversation with the older two.

"Why doesn't grandpapa have teeth?" the little one asked. Kira didn't know what to make of the statement. Teeth? That's when she noticed the child looking at a picture of Ben Franklin on the wall. "If he had teeth he could talk with me."

Kira burst out laughing and continued to smile as she watched the small child take the plate of apple pie to Ben Franklin's picture and tempt him to come out of the frame to eat the dessert.

Smiling, Kira knew the exact story Sarah Franklin-Bache would be writing to Ben Franklin about in her next letter; teeth, talking, and apple pies. And if Kira was right the inclusion of that detail would net her a few extra points on her next writing assignment.

The Beta

Math

It was early winter in the Bay Area and the persistent fog kept James's spirits dampened almost as much as his math.

James did math old school. As the exalted child of Google parents, one of whom worked directly for Google Earth History, he not only got to join the Google Earth History Dev team but also had automatic access to *The Beta* without having to officially petition any school system or partnership. He, and probably a bunch of other Google progeny, didn't have to follow all the rules, attend weekly meetings or answer a bunch of surveys.

None of that got him out of math.

The Beta had multiple math options. You could attend online seminars going on almost continuously throughout the day on different topics, or you could access different pre-recorded videos kind of like Kahn Academy. You could do a problem with your 3D headset on or a do a problem on a tablet with a stylus in your own handwriting. James quickly figured out that one of the reasons *The Beta* was so keen on having students complete math in 3D on their tablet was that the age old problem of cheating had, for the most part, been eliminated. Most of the high school students he knew searched up most of their math homework answers without ever trying to work them first. You couldn't do that in *The Beta*.

When James used his headset to do math his irises were consistently being rescanned and the audio could easily record any ambient sounds. No one could access outside notes within VR—at least yet.

When he tried the stylus and tablet version of math, one requirement was that you had to take tests in front of your laptop enabled camera. At first James was able to hide notes on visible posters behind the camera but he must have looked up too often because out of the blue in the middle of a calculus exam a commanding voice boomed.

"Possible cheating detected. Exam terminated."

The Beta

And while no one ever contacted his parents, there was this small red mark on his math course indicating possible cheating. The system did manage to allow him to retake the exam, and he had obediently pulled down the posters.

Sick and tired of constantly connecting himself electronically, James was able to complete his math homework with a third option. He used an actual physical textbook. James was able to write each problem on real graph paper and then scan the homework in for correction and credit.

Still forced to take the tests online he willingly submitted to the assessments with his virtual headset, but his grades were suffering miserably as a result. That finally caught the attention of his parents who were beginning to monitor his Dev time versus his actual progress through *The Beta's* official high school courses.

Parents monitoring anything online was a worst case scenario, so James buckled down in all things school for about a week. Sitting there, funneling weeks' worth of math homework into his scanner, James realized it hadn't taken much time to catch up on English, Science, and World Language. In fact, there were so many science and world language courses tied to Google Earth History that his time spent in VR was satisfyingly efficient.

A computer that could automatically analyze his handwriting and grade his homework could also give him instant bad news. All the work on Chapter 75 was for naught. 66% dang.

He knew the first thing he would see when he suited up and slid on the VR headset would be that annoying teacher voice asking him if "he wanted to review problems from chapter 75?"

His answer to teacher would be a clear, "Heck no." —a calculated response that he learned to use with the software. If you swore repeatedly the teacher would object, eventually shut down, and notify parents. However frustrating that forced politeness was, the software would not actually lock you out of one subject just because you were sucking at another subject, so James could gleefully ignore the teacher and move on. Besides, chapter 75 sucked.

Feeling a little bad about having evil thoughts about scholastic software, James gave his pre-planned "heck no" response and then with a shoulder slump, chose to start up his U.S. History course.

The Beta

H he picked a prominent multiplayer simulation from the East Coast as it had something to do with the American Revolution, and joined the server. It was packed so his choice of characters was slim. He wanted to get things over with so he picked "Samuel Powell" and clicked start.

The multiplayer simulation would be available every afternoon between 1 p.m. and 2 p.m. for over two months and would include events from 1775-1783.

Honestly this was James's first multiplayer historical simulation and he wondered exactly what it would be like. He read the directions and parameters carefully. While technically he could indeed enter the simulation at any time of day to explore, high school credit would only accrue for those hours spent during the 1pm to 2pm Eastern time. That seemed kind of restrictive to him, but then he supposed it would be difficult to get all the players in character to have interactions if there was not some type of limit.

There were also a significant number of plot points his Samuel Powell had to accomplish within a specific time period—along with a fair number of restrictions that would not allow players to impishly change the historical timeline. Those found to break with the timeline were likely to be kicked out and replaced with an Non Player Character or NPC.

A little frustrated he hadn't been able to pick a main character, James contemplated dropping out and entering a newer simulation, but the more he read about Samuel Powell the more he became convinced this character had a little more freedom to explore than most. Not to mention a front row seat at some of the most important events of the American Revolution.

Strictly speaking Samuel, and his wife Elizabeth Willing Powell, were socialites who hosted parties for all the Revolutionary elite in Philadelphia. So besides being a businessman, merchant, and mayor, Samuel's main duties were to make friends at the City Tavern and host balls at his home on 244 South 3rd Street. Regular guests at his virtual home would include George Washington, Benjamin Franklin, and the Marquis de Lafayette.

James finished the background reading and looked at his watch, it was actually 1:15 pm Eastern time so he might as well drop-in.

The Beta

He found himself positioned in a small bedroom. Dark blues dominated the furniture and in front of him was a wash stand with a small mirror. He took a minute to look in the mirror. It was weird imagining himself as an old white dude, but granted, he looked younger than he expected. He had mousy blonde hair but at least he appeared to be wearing his own Samuel Powell hair instead of one of those powdered wigs.

James walked to the door near the fireplace and clicked to open it, but it didn't budge. He tried again and still nothing. Clicking everywhere he zoomed in on all the black hinges poking around for some kind of a lock but still nothing.

What the heck? He turned around and headed for a mirror image of that door on the opposite side of the room and it swung open easily, revealing two staircases, one long one on his left that led down to the first floor, while the other was a handful of stairs leading to a secondary landing. Walking up the long staircase was a lovely young woman with red fabric roses in her hair and green ribbons trailing down her back in what looked to be an uncomfortable dress.

"Why my dear husband, our guests have all been waiting on you." She reached out her hand warmly as she tugged him up the second set of stairs. "Wherever have you been?" She asked with an impish smile.

Forced to follow her up the stairs in the virtual world James was standing stock still irl trying to use his free right hand to bring up the NPC settings. Sure enough his dear "wife" Elizabeth was not an NPC but rather some other high school kid matched up with him in this simulated life.

Reorienting himself within the simulation he began to walk to match her step and the nausea at his peripheral subsided. They entered a decorated with exquisitely detailed woodwork, a plethora of candles, and heavy floor to ceiling curtains. The middle of the room was bare of furniture and several couples were dancing while more people were sitting on chairs that lined the wall. Currently it didn't look much different from a middle school dance to James.

He was pleasantly surprised to see George Washington in attendance and his "wife" led him over to the general almost right away.

The Beta

"Oh Mr. Washington, I found my recalcitrant husband dithering in the bedroom." She glanced slyly up at him before continuing, "Yet now he is here to help us finalize our political discourse." Then she winked at him.

Turning bright red underneath the VR mask, he was thankful that although some of his facial expressions were tracked the technology did not pass on a change of skin tone. James recovered his sense of dignity and reflexively "winked" back at his wife. Suddenly aware that the wink was sure to have been copied in VR, James couldn't help but feel that this situation was like a school group project—he was the one procrastinating and his wife was the group leader annoyed because she was doing all the work and he was slacking.

Floundering about for some response to fill the silence James said, "General Washington, we are pleased to have you tonight." Then he bowed stiffly.

George almost laughed in response, "I'm no general and have no desire or experience to command such a post."

George laughed way too much for James's liking and that is when he realized George must be laughing at him for not realizing George Washington was not yet a general.

Quickly he brought up his timeline and bullet point list of to-dos, and sure enough he only had one day left to "encourage" George Washington to accept the appointment of general that would be bestowed upon him by the Continental Congress on June 15th. Not being prepared by reading the simulation background information James realized he was going to have to wing it.

And what better way to wing it than to depend on his "dear wife" to hit the salient points. Yet she was currently only staring at him with a sweet smile pasted on her face.

He decided to lay it on thick himself. "My beautiful wife," he said raising her white gloved hand to his lips and planting a virtual kiss upon them. "Wouldn't you agree that George's experience in the . . ." it took a minute for the name to come to mind, "French and Native American war make him quite qualified?"

It took but seconds for Mrs. Powell and George Washington to burst out laughing.

The Beta

"Oh my," she paused with effect, "DEAR husband, You must mean the French and Indian war? Wherever did you come up with the term Native American?"

They continued to laugh at his expense and James's cheeks continued to burn unnoticed, but his straight face must have belied his discomfort.

Suddenly his wife turned quite serious looking and leaned in to George who turned an attentive ear to her. "The future of our fledgling union cannot be trusted to just anyone George and there is no other I would trust more than you." She paused and dropped her voice low, "You will never be alone George, there are many here in this room whom you can lean upon for help." She reached out and squeezed George's free hand, but then stepped back and linked her arm back into James's.

"Think upon it George." Then smiling at both of them she added, "When you have decided to say yes you can steal a dance with me." She pulled James against his virtual will out onto the dance floor and he found Samuel Powell's body somehow taking the lead in some complicated 18th century ballroom dance while his 20th century body was awkwardly following suit to try and prevent the nausea that tended to accompany any drastic difference in VR and REAL LIFE movement.

He had not yet been in a simulation where another person, in this case his so-called wife, could pull his virtual body against his will. While he made no attempt to stop her, he was still concerned that his avatar did not stay in one place like his real body. There must be something specifically coded to allow it and perhaps it had something to do with the ballroom dancing. After all there is no way his contemporary high school students would be able to replicate the highly skilled dancing he observed around him. And so James found himself ballroom dancing in circles glancing momentarily at images of George Washington, fleeting images of the chaperone wall that he skillfully avoided crossing, and then a face that made him stumble and stop. With great satisfaction, this time his avatar caused his 'wife's' avatar to pause and a frown crossed her face.

"That's Benjamin Franklin," he couldn't help but blurting out, "Isn't it?"

The Beta

"You really are new here aren't you?" she asked, temporarily shedding the pretense of her 18th century alter ego. Some kids were better at play-acting than others and it was obvious she was quite good.

"Yeah, I dropped right in without doing much background research," he admitted sheepishly. "Sorry . . . but it was live and I decided at the last minute to join up." Noticing the obvious irritation on her face he took a wild stab at why and brought her virtual hand up to his lips once more. "Madam, I do apologize for my momentary lapse of judgement. Would you like to continue our dance?"

"Yes," was her curt reply but he could tell it was the dancing she loved. Despite his lack of experience he did feel a natural instinct to lead rise within him and it didn't take long before he was firmly guiding her across the floor.

As they danced they talked a mix of American Revolutionary politics and quizzed one another on which AI assigned goals they could collaborate upon for mutual benefit. Somehow he found himself committing to attending the live version every Monday through Thursday with her at 1 p.m. Eastern which wasn't really a commitment he expected he could keep. But what could he do? She was that persuasive.

Thankfully it only took two dances to satisfy her desires and she excused herself to talk with their guests. Benjamin Franklin seemed to have disappeared and so a disappointed James took a seat on the sidelines to assess the situation.

He watched the crowd curiously. While the program must have inserted sophisticated 18th century dance skills into all their avatars, the live teenage players were less than consistent in their application of 18th century speech and norms. From time to time he would hear the weirdest bits of modern speech and at one point he saw some clown trying to mess with the dance code by bursting into some modern dance moves.

Being part of the Dev team gave him permissions that no other high school student had. He could actually see the names, faces, and profiles of the other players. Other participants could do no more than access a numerical code assigned to each person.

The Beta

It amused him to see who was playing who, so he overlaid a list of students with their chosen avatars, selecting their name, picture, age, school, geographic location, and academic status to browse. George Washington was being played by an African-American kid with big glasses from Los Angeles, Benjamin Franklin by a youngish looking white girl with a pointy nose from Oklahoma, his 'wife' by an incredibly homely looking girl—he didn't want to even privately think it—but in real life she was so overweight he was having a hard time reconciling it with the virtual avatar he was dancing with minutes ago. He felt horrible for thinking such a thing. James knew being overweight had nothing to do with the worthiness of the person inside.

It was then that he began feeling guilty for the way he was categorizing and judging everyone by their physical and geographical attributes. No wonder the Google Earth History kept the identities of the students private—protecting their personal data was only part of it—protecting the integrity of the historical simulation was important as well.

James was about to turn off the information layer when something caught his eye. At first, her picture was one of many small thumbnails, but then within seconds he brought it to the forefront and enlarged her image.

She was one of the most beautiful girls he had ever seen. Asian for sure, but probably mixed like him. He couldn't really even attempt to place her heritage. Thick long dark hair that actually glistened. The pictures were similar to the Apple photos that captured milliseconds of movement, or like the NFL player mugshots that ran on the corner of the screen with almost imperceptible natural movements. Her image kept cycling through a smile that began to tug at the corner of her mouth before reverting to her initial serious face, her black hair turned into a glint of red, blonde, and blue highlights that hinted at something more, and her eyes—a golden deep brown gazed somewhere off in the distance and then returned to stare deep into his soul.

He dove into her profile unabashedly, stalking this total stranger. She lived in Redmond, Washington and was part of *The Beta* in the Seattle area, two mere states away from him. He knew what he was doing was wrong, but he continued to comb through

The Beta

her data. Like most of *The Beta* students she immersed herself in all of her virtual classes and received high scores on most graded work. But who was she here? In 1776 Philadelphia?

James accessed the next screen which matched up her real-life profile with the character she played within the American Revolutionary simulation.

He burst out laughing when he saw who she was at the moment. Two completely dissimilar portraits hung in the air in front of him, both different in their eras and different in their physical characteristics. This beautiful young teenage girl was playing a portly woman with double chins and an almost masculine face. He didn't quite place why the character looked so manly to him until he noticed the name underneath. Her character was Sarah Franklin-Bache—and that is why she looked so familiar. It was obvious now from the eyes and the chin that this was a relative of Benjamin Franklin. It made him laugh out loud.

He was thrown off balance when his 'wife's' head popped through his private screens. Her three-dimensional body had coincidentally inserted itself directly between the two-dimensional portraits of the beautiful girl and Sarah Franklin-Bache.

"Sitting in the corner laughing to yourself?" His wife's eyes blazed furiously and she let out an audible 'humph' and crossed her arms. "We only have two more days to talk George Washington into accepting the position of General and you haven't done much to help. You better be more prepared tomorrow. Now get up and socialize!" She reached out, grabbed his hand, and his avatar was once again pulled into a standing position against his will.

In the standing position he was forced to be face to face with the beautiful girl. His nose almost touching her two-dimensional nose. Before closing his private layer he clicked back to see the one piece of personal information he needed the most. Her name was Kira.

He followed his wife's lead and began to move about the room making 18th century small talk. Sarah Franklin-Bache was not in the second story ball room so he moved along through the only unexplored door and found himself in the 'retiring room.'

The Beta

At first he was diverted by several long tables of mouth-watering appetizers laid out along the edges of the room, of enough variety and style to outshine any modern gathering. The fake but good-looking food also fooled his stomach into letting out a rather loud growl despite having eaten lunch irl mere hours ago.

Yet he wasn't distracted for long, for across the room he saw her. The feminine face of Ben Franklin, framed by an odd white kerchief hat, a pudgy body, and covered with a swarthy gown made of fine material. Despite the outward appearance he could almost see the image of Kira underneath.

James knew it was almost 1:45 irl and in fifteen minutes the characters would begin clearing out of the simulation once the credit accruing time period passed, so he had no time to lose.

She was talking to someone he didn't know but James jumped right in and pulled her hand up for a kiss. "Welcome to our home, I am Samuel Powell." James realized he almost called her Kira which would have been a dead giveaway that something was up.

Startled, the image of Sarah Franklin-Bache took a minute to recover but then replied, eyes looking amused, "Thank you Samuel, your wife Elizabeth is a delightful host."

Her comment inferred that his late start in the simulation cost him some social currency amongst this group. They may have been playing together for a week or two before his entry. He wondered if they knew he joined late or perhaps thought he never showed up for 'class.'

"May I get you something to drink?" he asked and swept his arm indicating the copious amount of choices.

She hesitated but then nodded her head. "White wine, please."

He nodded back in copied affirmation and headed toward a table full of drinks and glasses, suddenly realizing he wasn't really sure which alcohol was which. He was one of those few teenage holdouts who didn't drink irl, in fact his parents never drank in front of him either so he didn't know much about drinking.

But white wine shouldn't be too hard right? He knew what a wine bottle looked like and it didn't take long to decipher between the white and the red, but when it came to choosing a glass he was at a bit of a loss. There were skinny glasses, wide glasses, small glasses, and tall glasses to choose from. Hastily picking two

The Beta

medium sized ones, he poured the clear looking liquid into them and made his way back to Sarah/Kira.

James laughed a little at the audacity of a high school history simulation that included simulated drinking. There was documented evidence of alcohol playing a significant role in much of history so it made sense it was not completely omitted.

He handed over the drink and she began to take small sips as he began to make small talk. "How long have you been in the simulation so far?" he started off point blank with a real life question. It may be a bit rude to move out of character but he felt the need to connect with her on a personal level irl.

"Oh," she paused as if shaken out of one era and revived in another, "It's been a little over a week, how about you?"

"This is my first day actually, I wasn't planning on joining a simulation today it just sort of happened. I've been putting off U.S. History for a while actually." He lifted the simulated cup to his mouth and tipped it toward his real life mouth. It was weird to see an ounce of the drink disappear out of the cup yet to have nothing in his mouth. All of a sudden he was thirsty irl. "Where are you in *The Beta*?" he asked boldly.

"Um, well since they restrict us to thirty hours a week of VR time I am only at about four or four and a half months of credit." Then she looked at his face and realized what he meant, "Oh, you meant where my class is located, didn't you?"

He nodded.

She responded but immediately requested an equal data share, "From Seattle, where are you from?"

"San Francisco," he replied, not specifying his true location in Mountain View, figuring it was close enough to the truth. In fact he wasn't technically part of any cohort. "So what's it like being Ben Franklin's daughter?"

She laughed, "Much different than I expected." Here she paused and drained her glass. "Do you mind getting me another one?"

It was his turn to laugh but he obliged her at once. Two regular old high school students getting drunk during history class at two in the afternoon—virtually drunk that is.

The Beta

"I have always wanted to see Ben Franklin's Print Shop," he admitted to her when he returned with the refills. "Have you been able to explore it yet?" He was fishing for a compliment by mentioning the print shop. While James had not officially tackled much U.S. History through *The Beta*, one of his early assignments in dev mode had been to research the ink daubers used in Franklin's print shop. So technically if Sarah/Kira had been in the print shop she would have unwittingly seen the product of some of his early research. All of a sudden he felt the desire to tell her all about his Dev access, but he knew he couldn't.

"A little, Sarah Franklin-Bache does live in Ben's house and the print shop is in the same block. But did you know Ben Franklin basically retired in 1748 by selling 50% of the print shop to his partner David Hall? The agreement was that Franklin would leave to pursue other hobbies but still receive 50% of the profits for 18 years. That's when he went on to discover electricity and delve into politics." Sarah/Kira stopped rather suddenly, probably aware that her history rich monologue had swiftly changed the tone of their original one sentence back and forth conversation. But James found it kind of sexy—she was smart and beautiful.

"I didn't know that," he responded. Was that really all he could come up with? Think James, think. Now he was feeling even worse about not having any preparation whatsoever for this simulation. Well, he knew what subject he would be studying in-depth the next few weeks. At least his U.S. History would be over with faster than he had originally anticipated. "It's getting late, would you mind if I accompanied you back to the print shop? I could take you there in our house carriage." he offered, hoping they had a house carriage.

"Sure," she replied, "but instead let's walk. It's not far to Franklin Square and the city is quite beautiful." She smiled at him mischievously. "Did you say this was basically your first time in a MMO history simulation?"

He paused as technically this was the first time he was a player and not a developer. He had little clue about what she was trying to get at here, "Uh, yeah, actually it's sort of my first." He almost felt like he was revealing his virginity, especially when he saw her smile light up even more.

The Beta

"Then I must insist in getting us more refreshments before we head out." She was swift on her feet moving toward the table stuffed with food. "Some shrimp perhaps? And lemon cakes?"

Sarah returned with a plate loaded with food and another huge glass of white wine filled all the way to the top, "Here, drink this first then eat. I still need to wheedle George Washington one more time before two o'clock." Her double chins wobbled as she turned her head and winked. "I suppose you shall need to do the same before your 'wife' kills us both. Did you realize all those close to George Washington will lose 50 points if we don't adequately persuade him to accept the position of Army General?"

James watched her walk away and recognized a probable glitch in the simulation. Sarah Franklin was quite heavy but Kira moved her avatar through space with a lightning quickness that didn't match the bulk of the avatar. He would note that discrepancy and pass it along to the main Dev teams that focused on the plausible physics of the VR world to enhance the realism of all Google Earth History simulations. No one had thought through skinny high school kids piloting heavy avatars.

He obeyed and gulped down the white wine first, not really believing that in less than an hour he was already doing everything two eighteenth century sixteen-year-old girls told him to do. James always prided himself on a careful check of the inherent sexism that seemed to reside in most males, including himself, but at the moment he could honestly hypothesis that women had, and always would, find a way to get what they wanted. He finished the wine, stuffed half of the food in his mouth, and marched straight over to George Washington to give him advice.

"You better just do it George!" he started out without a touch of class or stab at appropriate language for the era.

George Washington raised his eyebrows in reply, "Do what Samuel?"

Confused, James continued with his brief monologue, "You're the man for the job George. No one else is more qualified." With a quick glance across the room at his 'wife,' James made eye contact with Sarah Bache and nodded to the mezzanine and their escape route.

The Beta

She caught his drift and made her way to his side and the two slipped out without a scene. The staircase was skinnier and higher than he expected, and he felt kind of wobbly as he made his way down behind Sarah. "Whoa, this staircase is crazy!" James exclaimed.

Sarah craned her neck and smiled at him but didn't slow her pace, going out the front door and out into the street. "Dear sir, may I take your arm?" She inquired sweetly while coming to a simultaneously sudden halt.

He was either really clumsy or losing control of his avatar because he found his body two feet past hers and it took effort to turn and look at her. When he did look directly at her his entire field of view was tilting back and forth at the edges making him feel slightly sick to his stomach.

"What are you doing?" he asked accusingly as her smile identified her as the likely culprit.

"You said you were new and what you are now experiencing is authentic 18th century drunkenness!" She then grabbed his arm and began leading him slowly down the street laughing with mirth.

"Not very pleasant is it?" she inquired.

"No, I wonder how I can turn it off," he muttered and then halted, realizing she couldn't know he probably did have the power to turn it off if he only knew the proper command.

But she took his comment in stride. "There is no way to turn it off, in fact the second day in the simulation many of us met up at the City Tavern and of course what do you think a bunch of high school students would do?"

"Well, drink," he replied, gripping her arm more tightly as his real life body tried to do an awkward walk against his will.

"Yes, of course we were drinking and we drank a lot. That is when we learned we couldn't turn it off and a few of them who were crazy enough to drink way too much 'blacked out' and were kicked out of the simulation for ten hours only to wake up in their beds later, except one who actually woke up in a ditch outside of town," Sarah laughed out loud and then continued, "The rest of us realized playing a simulation that was spinning like a top wasn't worth it so we logged out."

The Beta

"Well why the heck did you do this to ME?" he asked accusingly.

"I didn't force you to drink!" she laughed, "but someone had to initiate you to the group, and maybe this will help them forgive you for joining so late. Your wife, Miss Elizabeth there, is quite an aggressive player but she has also been covering your butt by doing work meant for two. You probably want to try and get on her good side."

"Well, thanks a lot," was once again the only clever thing he could think of saying, but then he paused and looked down at her remembering the real person under the avatar. "I owe you one."

"Don't worry, you only had three glasses of wine so the effects will wear off soon." she said. "The effects are fairly realistic are they not?"

"Um, sure . . ." he said.

"Wait a minute! You've never drank before have you?"

"Well, actually, since you asked, no, nope . . . never." This was the second time this night he felt like he was losing something akin to his virginity, VR drinking simulation virginity and knowledge of his lack of real life drinking virginity. "Although to be honest that is something I am really proud of. No one in my family drinks, and none of my friends either for that matter." Although to be truly honest he was so busy he really didn't have many current friends.

"Oh, cool." She replied, but then narrowed her eyes, "Are you Mormon?"

"No," but then feeling a little indignant he reprimanded her, "but if I was why would you care?" His recent study of world religious had brought forth in him a protectiveness of all people to worship as they choose.

"Sorry." Sarah/Kira didn't let go of his arm but awkwardly looked up at him without looking where they were going and added, "I suppose I was curious because most of the kids I know back home who don't drink are Mormon." Her face looked odd and he couldn't read the accompanying emotion. "Actually, I have a few best friends who are Mormon." She added as possible protective layer, although in this day and age it was generally recognized that having a 'friend' who was of a certain religion or race was not sufficient evidence against bias.

The Beta

James realized the conversation was tanking so he did his best to look around the city of Philadelphia. They were walking on an old sidewalk made of wood and the street below was composed of packed dirt. He idly wondered when they would be replaced with cobblestones. He was impressed with tall wooden stakes that lined the sidewalk to give a fashionable air to the line demarcating the dirty street from the more sensible sidewalk. They passed two horse drawn carriages and never being around horses often irl he now understood the sense of wildness they imparted on a nearby walker.

"That's Robert Bell's print shop over there," Kira pointed to the right. "You know, that's where Thomas Paine's 'Common Sense' was published, selling half a million copies in a little less than seven years."

"Really?" James replied, glad she was willing to start up the conversation again. "How close are we to Franklin's Print Shop?"

"Just another block or two. We go straight on 3rd street and then take a left." She gave him another one of those unnerving stares but asked rather sincerely, "How are you feeling?"

"Well, I think I've grown accustomed to virtual drunkenness but it's not very pleasant. I can't make out the words on that sign over there," he said pointing in the direction of what he thought she said was Bell's print shop. "But thank goodness the same effect is not applied to my in-game controls. Those at least are still normal."

"Well you learned your lesson," Kira's smile was infectious.

"I didn't have any lesson to learn in the first place!" he retorted knowing full well she didn't care what he thought on the subject. Trying to come up with some sort of revenge, and now accustomed to the rolling scenery around him, he dragged her arm and broke into a sprint of sorts down the sidewalk.

Only a few seconds later he heard a "Hey, you're dragging me!" and turned around to find that he was rather brutally pulling her along.

"Oh, sorry!" He stopped immediately and reached to offer her an arm up. "I've just never been in a simulation where you can physically yank someone and I was tired of being pulled around myself."

The Beta

"Yeah, the creators still have a lot to figure out," Kira replied as she was smoothing out her dress which luckily didn't receive too much damage from the wooden sidewalk. She wouldn't have been so lucky if she had been dragged on the street.

"Hey, that gives me an idea!" James hopped the few inches down to the dirt road and purposely kneeled down with one knee and dragged it along the road for a few feet. Sure enough his pants were covered in muck from the road and there was a line in the mud where he disturbed the soil, "That's so cool," he muttered mostly to himself. Perhaps he was offended by her comments about the developers and wanted to prove her otherwise, but part of it was a reminder of how each little detail added to the simulation—like dirt that acted like dirt on a road, or rain that fell naturally, pooled, and then evaporated—it gave him a sense of wonder every time he experienced a new feature for the first time in VR. It would only get better as developer after developer added more details. It was going to take a lot of coding. Sometimes he thought of coding like arranging the protons and electrons in an atom.

"What the hell are you doing?" Kira was staring skeptically at him from her perch on the sidewalk.

"Oh," he decided to reply honestly, "Well, I wanted to see if the dirt on the road would act like dirt." then he looked up at her as he rejoined the conversation. "But you are right," he acknowledged, "the developers have a lot to clean up and add."

They turned left on Market Street and were soon standing in front of Franklin Court. There was a sign for the Franklin Print Shop, above the sign several stories of windows, and right between it all a deep cave meant for allowing carriages into the court beyond the shops.

"Well," she asked, turning toward him with a question in her voice, "Would you like to see the print shop first like you mentioned earlier? Or perhaps you want to head through the carriage gate to see Ben Franklin's home?"

"The print shop," he replied. He followed her in feeling decidedly steadier on his feet. Either the effects of the virtual alcohol were wearing off or he was becoming accustomed to it—he wasn't sure and he didn't care.

The Beta

Although one of James's earliest development projects included the research that helped refine the details on the ink daubers used in Franklin's Shop, at the time he worked on the project the shop itself had not yet been fleshed out. He was intensely curious and excited to see the effects of his work in action, but he was rendered a bit speechless by his first impression.

The space itself was taller and loftier than he expected. Hanging from the ceiling were hundreds upon hundreds of papers running evenly along poles, giving the illusion of scales as if they were the underbelly of some gigantic paper beast. Yet his eyes were quickly drawn to the well-oiled machine of the printing presses on the ground.

The presses were in use and five NPC's worked steadily, one stopping to welcome Sarah in a friendly voice and then actually introducing himself to Samuel/James. They were then left to their own devices to peer and prod at the replica of Ben's famous print shop.

He didn't waste much time in making his way over to the printing machine and watched as a young man with blonde hair and a large leather apron closed a wooden template fitted with paper and then cranked the first half under the actual press. He then pulled a large lever across the machine and leaned back into it like he was on a TRX Machine.

After repeating the process for the second half, he pulled the final print off and used a long wooden paddle to hang it up with the rest of the drying papers on the ceiling. His partner swept in to fit a new sheet of paper and then turned to the wall where two of James's daubers hung neatly. After pressing them together to smooth out the ink the second printer proceeded to hammer down deftly on the lettering before moving out of the way so his partner could take over step two. James watched the process again from start to finish and counted under his breath. It took only fifteen seconds to print one page.

Unable to help himself James walked around the large machine and without a shred of concern for the NPC's jobs, picked up one of the daubers and looked closely. As far as he could tell his research was solid, as it appeared the designers applied every single one of his suggestions. He then picked up the other dauber and hit them together with a satisfying thick thud, then walked over to the press and used them to ink the typeform.

"You're a printer too Samuel?" Sarah/Kira asked from the opposite side, the NPCs looked confused at their displacement but they moved over to another part of the shop to give James and Sarah space. The AI was either purposely programed to have non-confrontational NPCs or that was a weakness of the system.

"Maybe, do you want to help me Sarah?" he asked, finally feeling in his element again.

It was odd but after having viewed Kira's real image for a few seconds, he could almost see her eyes and expression pour through the avatar of Sarah. Then suddenly he could only see Sarah Franklin-Bache.

"Sure, what's next?" she walked around to join him.

"Grab the top of that board, it's called the typman and frisket." he motioned in the direction of the board while he replaced the daubers on their wall hooks.

Sarah pulled the board over carefully and then looked back at him for further instructions.

"Now see that crank in front of you?" He walked behind Sarah and reached around to guide her hand to the crank and then helped her turn it two times, enough to move the first half of the board under the actual press.

Underneath it all back in Mountain View back in his basement, James was sweating like he was on a first date. He could almost feel her body in front of him. Acting ever so delicately like they were together in real life, he reached around and pointed to the large crank then guided her hands all the way back, pushing her form into his body as they both pulled on the gigantic lever that did the actual pressing. Taking secret delight in repeating the process James helped her to roll the crank twice, moving the typeset into position for the second half of the press, and then once again used the lever to move forward and back to complete the job.

"That should do it," he said as he moved around to the other side of the printer. "Now go ahead use the crank to pull it out and let's see how we did."

Sarah/Kira did as he instructed and together they opened the typman and pulled out the large sheet of paper with a perfectly printed piece of American Revolutionary propaganda. "Okay, one last step." James walked over and grabbed a paddle from one of the NPCs and then extended the paddle end toward Kira who was still looking closely at the print.

It was quite a while before she noticed him patiently waiting for her. "Oh," she said. He imagined the real Kira blushing. She carefully laid the large paper evenly over the paddle. Instead of doing it himself he walked over and placed the paddle in her hands and guided her by the waist over to where he saw an empty row on the ceiling.

"Carefully, gently," he playfully admonished her as they hung their printing up. James never knew printing could be so sexy.

It was then that Sarah/Kira noticed the way he had been guiding her avatar with her waist. Offended, but also feeling an attraction of her own, Kira backed away but opened up with conversation. "So how do you know so much about printing but were obviously unprepared for the simulation today?" she asked, half question and half accusation.

"Umm . . ." c'mon James he thought to himself, you've gotta be quicker than that. "I learned about Ben Franklin for History Day in sixth grade," he replied answering her question. "And to be honest, one of the reasons I wasn't ready for the simulation today is that I've never cared for U.S. History," he finished responding to the accusation.

She smiled at him, although he couldn't tell if it was a smile of understanding or an ironic tilt but since it followed with an invitation of touring Franklin House, James was encouraged.

They walked out of the Printshop and into the courtyard where a two-story brick house stood, centrally located amongst a lush garden. He followed Sarah/Kira down the path watching her walk deep in thought. Feeling bold and following his heart, James took a risk and opened a dev browser in his headset. Since she was walking ahead of him she couldn't see his hand motions as he broke the rules. If Sarah/Kira had looked behind her at precisely that moment she would have seen a large bouquet of white orchids appear out of thin air into 1780 New England.

James stumbled a moment as he grasped the bouquet out of the air and simultaneously closed his interior dev screen. At that same

The Beta

moment Sarah/Kira turned around and before he could decide what the wanted to do he whipped the bouquet behind his back, not quite ready to give it to her.

Sarah/Kira had a faraway look on her face, but before he could speak, she called out, "Coming Mom!" Focusing on his face, she shrugged her shoulders and said, "I gotta go! See you tomorrow!"

Her avatar paused for the briefest of seconds while it was being replaced with NPC code. James switched on the layer to confirm the change, but sure enough Kira had left the simulation to go back to Seattle while code now inhabited Sarah Franklin-Bache's body.

He watched with fascination as the NPC gave him a nod and a smile and then walked past him back the way they came to the print shop. Although one could only tell by checking the player layer to tell for sure, it was as if Sarah's body was now a ghost of its former self. Without Kira to guide and give life to the character, the space inhabited by Sarah's NPC was noticeably hollow. Code could never take the place of real people, no matter how advanced AI allowed these simulations to become. Simply knowing that there was a person or an advanced program behind those actions made all the difference.

He suddenly felt very foolish and very relieved Kira had not stuck around for the flowers. What was he thinking? The flowers were a dead giveaway. Kira would have been suspicious and he would have a lot of explaining to do. He was about to delete the orchids from the simulations existence when a middle ground came to mind.

Moving forward to the Franklin House, James let himself in the front door. He nodded to a housekeeper who was wrangling with a bunch of children at a dining table, then looked around for a glass of water and saw one on the table.

"Do you mind if I take this?" He asked the child sitting next to the glass.

"OK," the young boy replied before returning his gaze to the meal laid before him. Well that was a little weird. Most real children would have been vastly shy or incredibly curious if a stranger walked in and stole a glass of water.

The Beta

James took the full glass in one hand, orchids in the other, and took the steps to the second level two at a time. He found the bedroom shared by Sarah Franklin-Bache and her husband Richard Bache—simple but elegant by the standards of the time. James was not sure if Sarah/Kira even frequented the bedroom during her time in the simulation, but it was the only place he could think of where she might actually realize the flowers were meant for her.

He set the glass of water down on the bureau and then carefully arranged the orchid stems neatly inside, wondering idly if Kira would ever know they came from him. Then he exited the simulation leaving a befuddled NPC version of Samuel Powel wondering what he was doing in the bedroom of Miss Sarah Franklin-Bache.

Fluency

Still not over her fear of the drowning incident, Kira gave the Columbia River a wide berth. But the Sinixt village was her second home. For months now she had spent at least an hour every morning at the village honing her Salish. Even though it was now springtime irl, the Sinixt village was perpetually stuck in the fall when the salmon run was at its height.

This morning Kira was feeling particularly adept. Since she always logged in at about eleven in the morning, the Sinixt village was predictably swarming with noise, laughter, work and play. There was always more salmon to dry every single day. Kira arrived outside of her family pit-house where she had a wide view of the gathering.

"xast ɬkʷəkʷʕast. cki naspuʔús?," she greeted her VR NPC little brother as he whipped past her out of the pit-house and down the hill.

"Tiʔ knxast . nínwis ɬwikntsn !" he replied evasively and subtly increased his speed as he raced off to join his friends.

The Beta

"Haʔ anxm ink t ntytyix ?" she responded but her question was pointless because of his increasing distance and the fact that they were months into salmon season. Everyone was currently sick of eating fresh salmon. Although irl, she was dying for some salmon sashimi.

She was proud of her Salish, as every phrase she uttered was recorded, assessed and cataloged. The AI was even paying attention to how fast she was responding to a prompt, when she initiated a phrase, her pronunciation, tone and complexity. Currently she finished what would amount to one year of high school foreign language in less than three months and more importantly, when she visited her family in Grand Coulee this year she was going to be able to teach them. School had never been this relevant before.

"Sk̓ʷək̓ʷimlt caʔcaʔxúɫ!" Kira jumped a bit when she heard his voice and did her customary blush irl. Everyday she checked his NPC status but it never changed, he was her code crush. His nickname for her was as silly as he was. Young she may be but she wasn't really shy . . . was she?

"Kaʔkín kʷ sxʷúyaʔx ?" she asked flipping back her hair and smiling at him boldly, completely unencumbered by any traditional restrictions on flirting.

"Kn ksxʷúyaʔx kl saʔtítkʷ," he replied looking up the river.

Kira hesitated. In the past week they journeyed together across the village and nearby forests, but they had not yet ventured near the water again. The water which had sucked them under to a temporary virtual death though both reappeared the next day. While some simulations enforced virtual death's permanency this particular simulation did not.

Here she paused in her reply, surely racking up negative points that attributed her hesitancy to a lack of language knowledge, which was partially true as her brain vacillated between responding with Lut kn t ksxʷúyaʔx kl or kn ksxʷúyaʔx kl aʔ.

"Kn ksxʷúyaʔx kl aʔ saʔtítkʷ," was her final reply, but then she hesitated again and added, "Kn ksxʷúyaʔx kl stmtímaʔnaqs?" this last phrase roughly equivalent to 'I am going to see my mother's mother one' because she still didn't know if there was a way to say she was going to see her grandmother *first*.

He smiled at her and nodded, then replied, "kaʔkín kaʔ ckʷulm ?"

Kira listened and tried to figure out what he meant, where did her grandmother work? Well, she supposed that made sense but formulating her own response was tough too. "kl __ kaʔ ckʷulm. Ntytyix," she indicated with a hand motion in the general location of where women were processing, drying and curing the large batches of salmon caught each day.

His laughter was loud, infectious, kind and his reply was exactly what a language learning AI should respond with. He gently corrected her phrasing and prompted her to repeat the correction.

"Yes," she accidentally started in English before switching to Salish to repeat his correction.

"Nínwis łwikntsn saʔtítkʷ?" he asked as he turned to go.

"Ki," she replied with a wink. Since he was a piece of computer code programmed to represent 1800 life he couldn't understand a wink, right?

He laughed at her again and then winked back.

Startled, Kira smiled. Maybe that was the problem with people when they studied history, always assuming that those cultures and peoples separated by space and time were so different than themselves. For all she knew maybe associating winking with playful flirtation was a near universal phenomenon.

Kira hadn't been entirely accurate when she told him she was going to see her mother's mother, but she was going to see her adopted grandmother.

She made her way through the village smiling at people passing by and carefully observing everything around her. People were often gathered either working, playing or socializing. Kira supposed not much changes through time when you bring large groups of people together once a year, sometimes she felt like she was walking through a modern festival, the celebratory mood was infectious despite the serious work of gathering salmon.

Trade was rampant around her and much of her language acquisition happened when her VR parents requested she find or sell particular items. Kira would have to scour the village introducing herself to people, asking about items, learning about the objects history and worth, then hearing the feedback from her VR parents if her trade was lacking.

After months of exploring the summer encampment Kira learned that the pit-house she and her VR family lived in was actually a permanent dwelling here on the west side of the falls. Surrounding the smaller winter village were thousands of semi-permanent dwellings to house the people that visited each year. Tribes from as far as the Pacific coast to the west and the Great Plains to the east would visit the falls. Although people of all genders, ages and tribes mixed freely in areas surrounding Sx̌ʷnitkʷ there were two specific places where the women and men laid down invisible but clearly respected lines of demarcation. It was in the women-only space that Kira found herself feeling free and happy.

Feeling comfortable, feeling content, Kira made her way to an area ruled by the women. It was just off the side of the falls but separated from where the salmon fishing took place.

"xast sxlx̌ʕalt stmtíma?" Kira greeted an older woman sitting amongst a large gathering of women. It was easy to tell with a simple glance at their arrangement that the woman was not only the oldest, but also the most respected of the group. Kira often saw her give advice or directions that were quickly obeyed.

"xast sxlx̌ʕalt sn̓ʔímaʔt. haʔ tiʔ kʷ xast?" the women responded not waiting for a reply, her grandmother wasted no time in handing her a flayed salmon and sharpened stick. So accustomed to the routine and constant work, Kira deftly pierced the salmon by the tail and used her youthful VR legs to climb up a large drying shed to hang the salmon. Little sticks separated the fillets from the body and skin which would allow all parts of the salmon to dry as evenly as possible.

While her eyes picked up evidence of a warm breeze filtering through the shed, she didn't feel a thing on her skin. These were one of the times that VR unnerved her immensely, when visual cues contradicted the lack of warmth or wind on her real body back home, but the visual light and movement told her brain she should feel a wind.

The Beta

While the work of filleting and drying salmon was tedious and never ending, it was a task that gave her a sense of fulfillment and the group of women kept her talking almost incessantly providing for some of the deepest language learning.

The old woman's NPC character took a liking to her and early in the simulation asked Kira to attend her each day to help process the salmon. As near as she could figure, the AI must have decided that between a cute teenage boy and a revered grandmother, those two archetypes would provide the most compelling impetus to increase her language learning. Kira was a little freaked out imagining that a computer knew enough about human nature to make such a decision. It was akin to a teacher knowingly partnering you with your crush because they hoped it would motivate you to study harder.

Well, it was working with Kira. She even wondered if the AI considered her Asian heritage and reverence for older people in its calculations of which characters to send her way. Although she would never explicitly utter it out loud, the older woman drew more of her curiosity and respect than did the young piece of cute code. In fact she never referenced her grandmother as 'code' in her head like she did the young man, even though her grandmother was an NPC as well.

When Kira finished hanging all of the prepared salmon her grandmother motioned for her to sit down and help. She filleted so many fish in the simulation that Kira was pretty sure she could figure it out irl this summer. Her family caught more than enough to provide her with sufficient practice irl.

"Haʔ kʷ xašt ?" her grandmother asked conversationally.

"Tiʔ knnpillwáš," she replied, although she was never amused when she had to pull the guts out of the salmon. It was as icky in VR as it was irl.

"Haʔ Knnpillwáš sṅʔímaʔt ?"

"Knnpillwáš by the tiʔík," Kira pretended it wasn't a big deal to have so casually mentioned the young man but her grandmother didn't miss a beat.

"Swynu mtx ?" her grandmother asked pointedly.

The Beta

Kira didn't reply. Kira couldn't reply, but she did look shyly into her grandmother's eyes and smiled.

"Kaʔkín p sxʷúyaʔx?" her grandmother asked and this time Kira could tell a verbal answer was expected.

"Kʷu ksxʷúyaʔx kl čyxʷitkʷ" Kira replied, not quite knowing the name of that place but knowing there was some type of water falling there. Her translation was close enough.

"xsʕac̓ǝc." her grandmother's eyes twinkled with mischief, "Lut kʷu lm ," she ordered and grabbed the salmon roughly from Kira's virtual grasp, "xʷuyx ʔíčǝčknwi !"

Open mouthed, Kira's overall language scores took another dip as she failed to respond verbally, but that didn't stop her from hopping down from her seat and lightly running down the hill with a smile and a wave. Her virtual grandmother smiled, if Kira had taken more time to look back, she would have seen her grandmother's countenance change suddenly. First her grandmother made some strange hand motions, almost as if she was directing an orchestra. Gone was the smile and it was replaced with a serious look as her limbs returned to steady work.

But Kira didn't notice as her eyes were trained instead on the fishing along the falls. Squinting, she tried to see if her code crush was still busy working, but there was no sign of him so she decided to slowly make her way through the village.

It didn't take long for him to find her. He snuck up behind and easily matched her gait as they walked through the village and northwest along the Columbia.

Their hike was long, maybe three or four miles in both real life and VR. Because Kira was stuck in her garage at home she had to repetitively jump ahead each time she got too close to her chaperone wall. This was one of those times she wished dearly to be at the Microsoft campus where she could walk normally over 50 yards before having to recenter herself.

When they were about a quarter of a mile out of the village he became more talkative than ever, probably programed to push her language learning limits—and that he did. They stopped to inspect plants where he would teach her the names, uses, collection tips and preparations.

The Beta

Kira wanted more control of the conversation so she tried to quiz him with her limited ability asking about the animals, his family, and the lands beyond the falls. He was actually quite animated on all three topics, often puffing out his chest or walking in a particularly sexy way as he gave an answer.

That's when it hit Kira. She actually stopped in her tracks to think, staring at the hills across the river while shading her eyes with her hand without looking at him.

Was he courting her to teach her about marriage customs? That had to be it! Why else would an NPC be programmed to flirt like he was?

Now, fairly confident in understanding the code's intentions, Kira was able to relax even more and play along with this strange, strange language learning software.

She tried her best to create jokes with her limited vocabulary and let him hold up branches or help her down from any particularly high rock as they made their way through this beautiful country. The rocks here were pillow basalts that formed little hills alternating with hidden glens and copses offering many opportunities for him to help her across the terrain.

Kira let herself enjoy every moment as they made their way to where the Kettle River joined the Columbia. Irl Kira had driven over a bridge at this spot but she didn't remember much of what it looked like, so when they finally arrived at their destination she was by all accounts breathless by what she saw before her. Steep cliffs of beautiful rocks guarded the entrance to the Columbia from where the Kettle River flowed through.

Her awe was self-evident and he looked pleased by his choice of destination. He beckoned her to follow him down to the river's edge where he sat on a flat rock outcropping and pulled out a snack. He offered her food breaking off small bites for her one at a time, until finally sneaking a bite right into her mouth. This tantalizingly modern romantic gesture made her smile shyly at him, but didn't prevent him from doing it again.

He really was staring at her, teasing her, courting her. For a moment she exited the romantic trance to think about the programmers who actually typed in the code required for him to act as he was now, but then quickly reverted to enjoying the moment. Maybe modern developers could do a decent job of "reprogramming" actual teenage boys into being a little more romantic now and then.

After finishing the snack, he asked some odd questions, ending with a request to introduce her family to his grandparents.

It all made sense. His grandmother was going to ask her VR parents if they could marry. Well, other than the fact that she had never mentioned him to her VR parents . . . she supposed it would work out just fine. Why not get married in VR to an NPC? Would her next lesson be in Lake's child rearing practices?

Then without any warning he moved closer, put his hands along her head, and reached ever so slowly to kiss her. She reacted with a natural inclination and tipped her head accordingly and opened her lips . . .

. . . opened her lips to the stale air of her garage. With a long sigh she took off her headset without any attempt of closure and stared into the dimly lit space, thankful that none of her family witnessed that air kiss. It would rank up there with kissing a pillow.

Her VR headset was tilted up but if she would have been looking, her eyes would have seen the smiling face of her grandmother spying on them from the top of the cliff.

The Cliffs

The hill leading up to The Cliffs was steep and long. Riding a horse from his home in Philadelphia along the river that gave him meditative time to feel centered in this place.

The sky was a murky mix of blues like one of those times where the fog sits halfway to the clouds and the day is measured by minor increments of shading. Yet it was light enough his ride through the countryside brightened his spirits as he progressed along the river.

He knew Kira had logged into Google Earth History about twenty minutes ago and her first stop appeared to be a Native American simulation in Washington State. He wondered what she

The Beta

saw in that place. It was utterly void of other Google Earth History participants.

She seemed to make a habit of moving from Washington State to Philadelphia on a regular basis. Kira was usually in Washington State around 11 o'clock and showed up early to the American Revolution around 1:30 p.m. Once he figured out her pattern he 'accidently' showed up one day and got an NPC to invite him to The Cliffs on a regular basis. Since she wasn't yet avoiding him he was hopeful that this was an unspoken signal that she wanted to see him.

James continued his old school American Revolutionary trot up to the house, vacillating his gaze between the river gorge and his horse. His horse was a warm chestnut brown, and despite the doleful blues of the overcast sky, underneath it all the first hints of an early autumn were beginning to appear beneath the edges of the green forest.

The Cliffs consisted of a farm and modest Gregorian house with two floors, two chimneys, and five evenly spaced windows that around the front door. It was built by Joshua Fischer, a wealthy tradesman with an appreciation for Quaker values.

James—or Samuel Powell as dictated by his current avatar—was early and his knock on the door elicited no response. To pass the time he set up his hunting rifle and tried to shoot a few birds for sport but with no luck. While he didn't know if the difficulty of shooting a small flying object in real life was the same as in the simulation, either way he suspected it to be near impossible. At least with virtual hunting real lives were not harmed in the making of the simulation.

A chaise and four pulled up to the house. Esther Reed and Mrs. Sarah Fisher arrived and unlocked the house. James gave up on his unsuccessful bird killing to follow the ladies into the house.

The first time James stepped into The Cliffs he had been as shocked as anyone by the state of the rooms. The farm, used more as a summer home by the Fishers, had been temporarily transformed into a non-electrical sweatshop stacked with piles of cloth, thread and buttons. During his first visit James moved from pile to pile examining the exquisite stitching on the Revolutionary uniforms. The clothes of the 1700s were made with such care compared to the indifferent, but real, sweatshops of the 20th century.

"Good day Mrs. Fisher, Mrs. Reed," James greeted them, taking off his hat and nodding to the two ladies. Despite their NPC status they gave him nods of real affection—after all, even NPCs can learn to be friendly after days of repetition.

He jumped down some stairs to the basement where he helped the butler load up the two basement fireplaces with wood and started the fires. Although he was warm enough in his temperature-controlled basement back in Mountain View, this simulation did a fine job of requiring all avatars to eat and stay warm. So depending upon your combination of clothing, physical exertion and proximity to a heat source one would often be prompted to increase the comfort of one's avatar with heat, or food if hungry. While hunger didn't bother the well to do participants of this American Revolutionary simulation, seeking warm lodgings was a constant requirement. Thank goodness he wasn't required to pee.

She was there when he went back upstairs. Sarah Franklin-Bache was no longer pregnant during this time period, thank goodness. As an eventual mother of eight children, Kira's avatar had thus far appeared pregnant three times—the first time absolutely flooring James who had a hard-enough time reconciling Kira's real person with the female Franklin avatar.

"Hey Samuel," Sarah/Kira smiled at him.

"Hi Sarah," he replied. And for only a moment he juxtaposed his personal screen to view her real image floating next to Sarah. She had no clue what he looked like irl, and no clue that he knew exactly what she looked like since the beginning. The closer they got the worse he felt about it.

"How was your morning?" he asked conversationally as they both took their places next to the first floor hearth.

Her face changed with his innocent question but she was still quick to answer. "Well, uh, my last simulation was kind of weird," she started as if she wanted to talk, but then drew suddenly quiet. She was smiling and it made him intensely curious. "But it was also embarrassing!" Catching her breath she threw a pincushion his way causing him to duck and helping her to hide her face.

The Beta

"What do you mean?' he pushed for details as he tossed the pincushion back like a snowball.

"Oh never mind, I don't want to talk about it," Kira said shutting down the conversation and turning it back on him—deflection was her conversational style. "How was your morning?"

It was his turn to stumble, "Well, what I was doing was pretty embarrassing as well, so how 'bout those Seahawks?"

That got a look. James would do anything to have her look at him even if what she was seeing was a 18th century man.

"Ha!" was all she replied, but she grinned and threw the pincushion back at him, this time nailing him in the forehead.

"Owww!" he played back. VR was great like that. Food fights, snowball fights, any projectile could hit you without pain, although it took a while to suppress the natural instinct to dodge or flinch. At one point James was so used to not dodging obstacles in VR that he momentarily forgot to dodge them irl.

Tempted as he was to pick up the pile of American Revolutionary sleeves and toss it over Kira's head he refrained from doing so. If it was only a personal simulation that would be different, but these multiplayer functions required more restraint than he desired since it was a shared space. What one person did could affect the grades of the other participants.

"So . . ." Kira began with a mischievous yet serious tone to her voice, though she looked with 18th century demureness at the needle and thread in her lap, "What shall we do to appease Miss Powell this afternoon?"

"Oh, are you referring to my dearest wife?" he replied mockingly.

"The one and only!" another pincushion flew precariously close to his head.

Where was she finding all those pincushions? "I was thinking perhaps we could put some whiskey in her water pitcher?"

Sarah/Kira raised her eyebrows at that, but smiled and replied with her own idea. "Or, we could find a way to burn her wardrobe or steal her clothes during her bath?"

James looked up sharply, "Really? I wonder if she would be stuck in the bath or decide to run naked to the clothier?"

The Beta

At this image they both laughed although technically there was no nudity in their particular simulation. Both of their parents gave them permission to view R rated historical scenes and violence, but so far the creators had only approved childbirth, war, and gruesome visions of injustice and battlefield medicine. Innocent images of breasts and private parts were still blurred out by some prude developers, diminishing the possibility of following through with their previous plot.

Still, imagining his VR wife running through the streets of Philadelphia blurred out as she raced to find something to cover herself with made him almost choke with laughter. "Technically we would have to remove all the blankets as well as the carriage to fully prevent her from covering up before going out."

"Yeah, knowing your wife she is smart enough to use the curtains." Kira sighed. Mrs. Powell had proven to be a frustration to all simulation participants due to her bossy and overbearing nature. On the first night Sarah and Samuel met, their main group simulation goal was to convince George Washington to become general of the Continental Army. Technically, they missed their goal by 1 point and the grade of everyone involved was penalized. While it was difficult to pin the blame on any specific person, Mrs. Powell had confronted Sarah and James, convinced it was entirely their fault.

Despite their poor performance George Washington still agreed to be general but several key members received the equivalent of a B for their efforts and since that time Mrs. Powell had been a pain in all their butts. Secretly James was thankful for the turn of events for Mrs. Powell's actions only drove Kira and him closer together.

"Well whatever we decide," James reached for the real but non-accessible cell phone in his back pocket before reverting to the pocket watch in his waistcoat, "the rest of the crew is due to arrive at City Tavern in forty-five minutes, it should take us that time in a carriage or . . . ?" and this time he looked expectantly at Kira for a response.

"You want to take me for another ride?" she asked innocently enough but her smile was guilty.

The Beta

James almost choked but managed to remain steady. Memories of their last horse ride through the country were enough to make both of them tingle in anticipation. She must have liked it as much as he did. There was nothing as exhilarating as traveling in VR. Car, boat, plane, or in this case horse—transportation with no consequences lead to some thrilling experiences.

"I suppose we could wrangle a load of shirts on the way back again?" The only historical excuse he could come up with for visiting her at The Cliffs was his offer of transporting the finished shirts back to her home at Franklin Court, which was right on the way to City Tavern.

"Let's do it!" she replied with more enthusiasm than he expected.

He waited twenty minutes as more ladies entered the house and many more shirts were completed. Kira and James talked the entire time as they worked. It was days like these he liked most—where they had time alone and only surrounded by the quiet chattering of NPCs.

But all good things must come to an end and as the time drew near he gathered up the completed shirts into a bundle to transport. As Samuel/James added each shirt to the pile he reverently looked at the names stitched into the insides. Married or unmarried, the finishing seamstress of each garment carefully tailored her name in the linen to remind the soldiers that a woman from Philadelphia was thinking of them. He was persistently amazed by the small details of history he would never have learned if not for the VR simulation.

"Ready?" Kira asked. She was dressed and waiting by the door for him to lift the bundle and follow her outside.

The grey day had lightened considerably since his arrival and sunshine was peeking through clumps of clouds in god like interspersions. Kira was not shy of his horse so she grabbed the reins with familiarity, then nuzzled his nose as James tied the bundle to the horse's flanks. He was proud of his horse but he could never tell Kira the truth—that his horse was a carefully crafted animal of his own choosing from the dev menu.

The Beta

Gallantly he helped Kira into the saddle and then swung up behind her. Mounting a horse in VR was decidedly easier and more elegant than irl, and so was riding one.

The last time they rode together Kira had been a VR horse riding virgin and James the one with considerably more experience, thus reversing the roles they had played when Kira made him drink too much wine. During that first ride Kira held on for dear life as James pushed his stallion to gallop as fast as possible, hitting 25-30 miles per hour at times.

VR did cause James to take more risks than he ever would in real life, both with his own life and with others. The ride from The Cliffs to downtown Philadelphia skirted the river through tight trails edging the bluffs. There were times he was worried they would indeed fall over the edge and into the river.

Today James took a slightly slower pace, something you would call more of a canter than a gallop. Because of the immaculate weather the scenery was more breathtaking than he had ever glimpsed, vying even with real life.

"Horseback riding is awesome!" Kira volunteered out -oud, "You know I have never been on a real horse before."

"Really?" James asked, dumbfounded before realizing neither had he, unless you counted a pony ride at a birthday party. But he didn't come clean. He figured his experience in VR made up for part of what his real life lacked.

"No, no one in my family was really into horses so I've never been around them," Kira expounded.

James's hands were holding the reins tightly, and although Kira was technically over a thousand miles away his whole body tensed in a crouch and his forearms were gathered around her virtual waist protectively. His head leaned slightly over her left shoulder so he could see the path clearly and their virtual cheeks were so close they were brushed up side to side. Sometimes she would tilt her head up to look at him.

This American Revolution simulation allowed avatars to "die" twice before being kicked out for good. This reined in some of the more obnoxious high school tendencies to do ridiculous things in VR while still allowing for a little experimentation.

The Beta

"Have you ever been cut out of this simulation?" he asked Kira. Cut out was a gentler term he came up with for dying.

"Huh? Cut out?" she asked a little louder than normal since a simulated wind was part of the canter, "Oh, you mean dying, right?"

"Yeah."

"No, I'm not that crazy. Plus Professor McKenzie has pretty high standards. She frowns on us goofing off."

"Professor McKenzie, that's a crazy name."

"Yeah, she's a pretty cool professor though. Mostly because she works us hard." Kira gave him one of her glances, "I looked up her name and it is Sanskrit for 'friend of fire.'"

"What is it like working with a class?" he asked innocently enough before realizing how odd that sounded.

This time she turned her head and kept staring, trying to read his expression before replying, "It's ok, what's it like for you?"

"It's fine, I don't like working with others much," he replied. James hoped it sounded honest enough to cover up the fact that he didn't work with anyone much beyond his parents and a few other developers. Sometimes he wondered why his parents hadn't forced him to join a local school district, but he wasn't going to question his good luck too much.

"That's for sure." He thought he heard her whisper under her breath. He wasn't positive if he should take that as a compliment or diss. He pretended not to hear.

But in case it was a diss, he lifted his right leg and pressed into the horse's flank to increase speed. If she hadn't been cut out before now and they all got two free passes, he could be a little riskier on this ride.

He leaned forward, pushing her avatar ever so slightly with him as the horse began to run across the landscape. Since their last trip James went over his allotment of 'lives' so he could make this ride in record speed by practicing the tight curves. With his dev permissions he was able to give himself as many lives as he needed. He couldn't believe his luck that all that practice was about to pay off.

He kept up the pace for over seven minutes. From time to time he would hear Kira laugh or squeal as they made some particularly crazy turn. The ride came to an end much too soon and he found himself slowing the stallion down to a trot as they left the river valley and traversed east across the city streets.

"That was fun!" Kira said as soon as the horse slowed down.

"I was hoping you would enjoy it," James said into her ear, noticeably inches from his lips. Did she have any clue what it was like to be attracted to someone in VR? Could she tell what he was feeling? As if reading his mind she turned her head once again and their faces were inches apart. She looked into his eyes, smiled, and turned back again.

Women were so hard to read, both in VR and real life.

James sat up straighter as they both began to respond to NPC greetings, making their way slowly down Market Street.

When they arrived James guided the horse through the carriage underpass and into the magical place that was Franklin Court. He brought her all the way up to the house and jumped down so he could offer his hand. If there was one benefit to 18th century simulations it was that you could act like a gentleman under the guise of getting a good grade.

He followed her into the house with his bundle of shirts and piled them up in a corner with the earlier bundles.

"Hello there, my Benjamin, William, Eliza and little Louis!" Kira greeted her virtual children with real affection and was soon cradling the baby in her arms. Did women know how motherly instincts made them so appealing?

After handing the baby back to the nanny Kira turned his way. "Go on without me, Samuel." She smiled at him, "Besides, your dear wife might be a little put out if we were to arrive at City Tavern together. She doesn't know about us . . . yet," she teased. It had become a regular joke between the two of them that their VR spouses would become 'jealous' if they found out how much time they spent together.

James was disappointed and had a difficult time hiding it. This simulation only lasted three more weeks and he was afraid she wouldn't share her data with him and they would never see each other again.

She seemed to pick up on his reluctance to leave, "I'll be there soon, I promise. I have some quick assignments to catch up on

The Beta

before I go to City Tavern." She blew him a friendly kiss and then turned back to talk to the nanny.

Feeling like time was slipping through his fingers, James pulled up his internal dev screen and pulled out those same Dendrobium orchids out of thin air. This time he formed them into the shape of a flower crown. After tenderly putting them on her head he slipped out of the house without being noticed.

Stalker

James couldn't believe he had stooped this low. Cyber crush stalking, mobile phone crush stalking, and high school hallway stalking were all normal enough for his generation; not really anything to be embarrassed about and totally expected at some point in any kids' life. But this was totally different. Because of his status as a developer/employee he had access to some pretty specific private data. He felt terrible about what he had done and at the same time grateful for the trespass.

He was hovering above the Sinixt dev point in Google Earth History, unsure he should really go through with his plan. This place was obviously important to Kira and he wanted to know why, but he felt uneasy about the trespass.

It was late at night in Mountainview and his parents were upstairs somewhere. It was not unusual for his dad to come down and watch him work. James supposed that his biggest worry was that there would be no way for him to know if his dad was watching, and not a very credible explanation to explain his sudden switch in interests. So far, his only pre-prepared alibi was that he recently became curious about Native American history. His dad might buy into it. Maybe.

After entering he realized the dev unit itself was unique. While most units went with the original design that looked much like a break room or onsite work trailer, James found himself standing outside a rock-lined fire. He instinctively stepped back so as not to get burned and then looked around at the walls of the dwelling.

The Beta

The job board was crafted of natural tan and brown colors, and although it somewhat resembled a modern bulletin board, the jobs were scrawled in handwriting on pieces of dried skins. James couldn't even read the writing as it wasn't in English. Looking over his shoulder he wondered who was taking the time to make this place so difficult to decipher. He threw up an internal screen and applied the translator to see if it would work within the developer space. He had never found the need to do so before as all dev unit workspaces originated in English as far as he knew.

He let out a breath—without realizing he had been holding one in—as English began to overlay the language he couldn't understand. He began reading and combing through the work logs for more information on this place.

Strangely enough, only one person, was working on this particular dev unit and it was a woman by the name of Karen. He didn't waste time looking up her bio, he could do that at a less revealing location later on—but he could conjecture she was a descendant of the Sinixt people. She must be recreating an entire history single-handedly. He noted her login times that always started early morning Pacific time and ended in the afternoon, so she must be an early riser. Hopefully she wouldn't login while he was snooping around. As long as James didn't touch any of the work orders he wasn't aware of any way she would know he was here.

But since this was a one-woman show James wasn't going to learn much from the work logs. Instead he would need to pry a bit further into the multiplayer simulation data. The interface data was more restricted, and with good reason because minors accessed them for high school credit through Google Earth History. Only those developers associated with a school program, and had passed the same screening applied to school personnel—such as background checks and fingerprinting—were allowed to look through the details.

And that was where James's status was so damn valuable. Because he was a minor, concurrently a developer, and technically, at least on paper, associated with the local school district, he must have been accidentally classified as an educator. Reguarless he

The Beta

didn't care which glitch gave him the access he now coveted and abused.

There was only one multiplayer simulation running at this location. It was a stark contrast to the Early American Revolution Simulation in Philadelphia which boasted seventeen separate but identical simulations of about 95-100 real life players each. Not only was there only one simulation in Sx̌ʷnitkʷ, there was only one real life player—Kira.

So Kira was a regular in a simulation that consisted of only herself and a bunch of NPCs. Intensely curious, James turned to the one detailed, albeit time consuming, data set from which he could learn the most about Kira—the actual multiplayer movie logs. He picked a random one from a few days back and then entered the simulation.

He found himself floating above a large Native American village, the wide languid Columbia from the modern era was replaced with a comparatively thin and fast running river that rushed over the falls with tremendous force. Floating above the scene like this gave him a God-like feeling as he watched the NPCs weave in and out on their daily rounds. The player layer gave all the NPCs a grey tinge, but James could see one red dot indicating a developer participant near the edge of the crowd.

Zooming in to take a closer look, James found himself face to face with the same woman from the dev unit. He smiled at the audacity of this woman actually entering her modern likeness into a historical simulation. Well, he supposed, assuming she was really a tribal member, there was no better image to thread into history. James had never thought of putting oneself into the past like that. He thought it was pretty clever.

James followed her around for a bit and watched the woman perform her matriarchal duties throughout the community. While the replay couldn't show him her own private dev screens, he could, simply by following her hand motions, tell when she was interacting with the developer prompts while still actively participating in the simulation. It was actually a pretty brilliant idea. Since there were currently no real life players, Karen could both experience her simulation and edit it through her dev menus at the same time.

The Beta

Since he couldn't spend hours watching the replay while he waited for Kira to show up on the scene, he returned to the sky and began to fast forward and scanned the crowd for any sign of blue which indicated a real player. He remembered from her personal logs that she often visited this simulation in the late morning so he slowed it down to around 10 a.m.

Sure enough, a blue blip showed up around 10:45 and he was quick to intercept. Watching a simulation replay was a bit like exploring a three-dimensional movie, you could rewind, pause, fast forward, and fly to any angle in the scene. In fact James was surprised there were not more VR movies like that yet. He could only imagine the Hollywood hits that were soon to arrive on the scene, even though James couldn't figure out how editors would be able to capture the video in the first place. Starting with code to world build would probably be much easier than filming from multiple perspectives at the same time. Maybe the landscape would be coded and the people filmed, then melded together. That's pretty much what they were doing with CG these days anyway, if only on a smaller scale.

His distracted nature was immediately reversed as Kira's Sinixt avatar came into view. While she looked nothing like her real life self this avatar was similarly beautiful and a far cry from his only interactions with her as Sarah Franklin-Bache. He followed her through the village where she met up with the old woman.

He set the translator again and once the English was coming through he listened closely to their conversation. It was fairly normal considering the simulation—talk of fish, huckleberries, and then other avatars. He was pretty impressed with how both of them played their parts flawlessly. Not paying close enough attention, he almost missed her as she handed off a salmon to the old women and went skipping away. He pulled himself forward to follow her with a twist and a pull of his arm. He was lucky to have so much experience with development, as the controls used to move through 3D space like this took time to master.

He anchored his ghost to her avatar and was able to follow right behind her without doing anything. It was kind of nice to simply float behind Kira, taking turns glancing down at her neck

The Beta

and then at the expertly crafted simulation around him. Old woman Karen had done one bang-up job.

Suddenly a handsome young male avatar snuck up behind Kira and began walking amiably beside her, locked in conversation. Both Kira and the young man were smiling at one another. James was shocked to find himself jealous of this grey tinged NPC avatar, but he had no choice but to continue floating along and watch them together.

They continued across the village and along a path to the northwest of the river. Now James understood at least partially why Kira was so interested in this simulation. He observed them glancing at one another, the young man offering his hand and even picking flowers casually then placing them in her hair. Kira must know the avatar was an NPC but from her looks she was obviously enjoying every moment. James was both embarrassed for her and jealous at the same time.

Their long walk finally ended at a secluded spot. James had fast forwarded much of the walk after he got tired of their flirting but he couldn't leave Kira yet. Unfastening his ghost from Kira, he gave the 'couple' some space as they made their way down to the water. James wasn't sure how he was supposed to compete with code—it was hard enough irl and he certainly couldn't complete with that NPC's tan abs.

From far above he was a bit shocked when he saw the NPC reach out to cradle Kira's avatar and move in for a kiss. He wasn't sure he was aware of any other programed kissing within the simulations and so he watched with mixed emotions. He felt a bit relieved as he saw Kira's avatar flicker and then turn from blue to grey. Kira hadn't finished the kiss but instead retreated into real life. This gave James a little hope that she wasn't really in love with this NPC.

"Hummph!" a human sound startled him from just a few feet away. The old woman Karen was peering at the couple from a perch not far off from his own.

He walked over boldly and spoke out loud into his own headset in Mountainview. "Well I hope you are satisfied with all that you've created!" he stated with open hostility and reserved admiration.

The Beta

The old woman Karen didn't hear him. She was only a replay after all.

Annie

"Listen Annie, this is important because once we go in the garage and I turn on the system, every word I say is recorded."

Annie nodded and moved to go in but Kira held her hand on the door for a moment longer to make sure the seriousness of the situation sunk in properly.

Annie was careful but Kira didn't want to risk her place in *The Beta* just so her friend could try and find a way to cheat the software. Besides Kira didn't understand why Annie was so interested. It might be years before the programs were widespread enough to provide a substantial pool of paying cheaters. But Annie was her best friend and Kira knew this was part punishment for helping earlier this year.

Kira's parents had placed an old sofa on one side of the garage so the family could watch when they wanted and Annie made a beeline for it when they entered the garage.

Kira explained some of the basics as she put on her suit and gloves. "Only two pieces of equipment actually require biometrics for login. The headset scans my retinas and these gloves run my fingerprints." Kira hoped Annie caught on to her subliminal message. You couldn't have one person put on the headset but another answer test questions using the controller gloves.

"Other than that, the devices do gather plenty of data including audio, my physical movements, facial expressions, and lastly my heart rate and blood pressure." Annie did look a little surprised as Kira completed her list.

"Most of our parents put up quite a fuss about the data collection during our orientation, but with every single type of collection there was a solid reason the VR would not work without it. The only compromise was that the personal data would be deleted after one month."

The Beta

"Yeah . . . data is never deleted," Annie responded with raised eyebrows.

"I know."

"So does this mean no one else can use your equipment? I mean, I can't even try it?" Annie asked.

"Yup, at this point. One parent per beta student is allowed so my dad's retinas can be scanned from the headset and he has his own pair of gloves."

"Lucky father."

Kira smiled. In the beginning she and her dad often competed for use of the equipment until his work picked up and he didn't have much free time anymore.

"There are at least three cameras I know about as well. One on the television and two on the outside of the headset. I am not sure if those things on the lighthouses are cameras or just sensors." Kira pointed to the corners of the room where multiple black boxes sent signals back and forth tracking her every move.

"What do you want to see today?" Kira asked, looking at Annie pointedly before she put on her headset.

"Hmmm . . . what about your favorite subject, physics?"

"You mean the one and only subject I have been neglecting?" Kira groaned loudly but acquiesced to Annie's request.

After completing the start-up sequence Kira took some time to show Annie around the High School Credit Machine software. "Think of it a little like a high school counselor," she explained. "Different companies are writing the software. Houghton Mifflin Harcourt wrote my Pre-Calculus course and Google wrote my history course but all of their data feeds into the same Credit Machine where it can be applied across traditional high school requirements."

Kira flipped to a wide view of her stats and all of the credit she earned thus far. "Google formed partnerships with other software companies which is why I can get World Language credit and English credit as I complete work in Google Earth History.

Kira clicked on her physics course which started with a very brief overview of the most recent lesson. It was a good example of VR schoolwork to show her friend.

The Beta

"I left off on a speed and velocity problem," Kira said as she made sure she was looking at the entirety of the problem set so Annie could see the same on the TV. "So I have two objects with no friction on a global x axis and I have to add a force adaptor, run the simulation, and figure out the answer based on the data from the analyzer." Kira figured she sounded pretty smart even though this problem was still plaguing her.

"Check this out Annie! I could rewatch these tutorials or get a hint from this 'teacher' over here, but if I access either of those options the software will add more problems, which means it may literally add an hour of coursework. So sometimes figuring the first problem out on your own is the easiest path even though it takes some heavy thinking."

"Can you just pull up YouTube?"

"Yep," and to demonstrate Kira pulled up an internal screen which was already linked to relevant tutorials across a variety of websites. She clicked on the first and it started to run. "But accessing any help online is also recorded and logged, so check this out," Kira then opened the outline of her physics course to show Annie. "If you look at this additional problem set just added you can see it will take at least another ten minutes to complete. Of course during a test you can't pull up internal screens."

"Dang, this thing is pretty tight."

"Yeah, but I love it. I hope you get to do it next year. Do you want to see Google Earth History now?" Kira crossed her fingers and hoped Annie would say yes. She didn't think it would be possible to concentrate on that physics problem with Annie in the room.

"Sure."

The switch into Google Earth History took mere seconds to load and Kira decided to show Annie the Asante Empire Simulation. True to her own word, Kira returned to the original simulation and was now three months and two hundred years into a path that took her down through generations of slaves.

Yet her avatar was a slave no more.

The Beta

It was night with the moon only a sliver of silver and Kira was surrounded by gravestones. Imagining what Annie must be seeing on the TV, Kira tried to look more systematically at her surroundings. The words 'Mt. Pleasant Cemetery' faded into oblivion to her right and then Kira did a slow 360 to take in the view.

Hearing a horse in the distance, Kira's instincts kicked in and she crouched low, moving across the room on all fours, keeping a gravestone between her and the road. This was not easy because the slabs all stood perpendicular to the ground and provided only minimal coverage. She was moving ever so closer to the trees and further away from the road.

The horse continued on its way, seeming to take forever to pass far enough along the road. By the time she couldn't hear it anymore she found her friend. Still crouched down, Kira was smiling into a well-known face and that face was smiling back at her.

"Dude!" she could hear Annie's exclamation from her corner of the garage. "That's Harriet Tubman, isn't it?"

"Shhhh!" Kira made a swiping motion in the general direction of Annie. Some simulations you could pause and some you couldn't without starting over. She needed to hear the details Harriet gave her.

"The baggage has arrived and two of them are wee ones." Harriet motioned down the row, where Kira could see shapes in the sliver of moonlight.

"But, yes," Kira tried to say to Annie under her breath. "It's Harriet." The simulated Harriet smiled at her and said nothing, waiting for Kira's response.

"Good, I have Nana's famous pack," Kira replied, patting a homespun bag on her hip. She pulled out two cloth dolls and some cakes ready for the occasion.

"They can make it to Bethlehem tonight. That's only two more miles without a drinking gourd." Kira glanced up and saw the sky was indeed clouding over, almost covering the moon.

"How was your trip tonight?" Kira asked.

"Quiet, but the harder routes lay to the north. You will join me there next week?"

The Beta

"Yes . . ." Kira paused, she still needed to study more geography and background knowledge before tackling a harder route. Something told her the simulation may not always be so easy or successful.

Her friend smiled, "God told me you will be safe tonight."

Kira looked at her companion and felt safe in her presence. "Go now . . ."

She obeyed and crept quietly over to those who were waiting nearby. Kira distributed the dolls and cakes, then hoisted the smallest child on her back. Two miles to the safe house in Bethlehem would pass quickly with the simulation's increased speed, but it was up to Kira to take the right route and know the proper knock for gaining admittance to the safe house.

Their trail wound straight through a thick forest to the northwest. There were at least two major farms to cross in their path. The first farm was a large house with six or seven small outbuildings. Only one small light emanated from a second story room and the rest were deep in darkness.

"Kira!" yelled someone and she jumped a foot, nearly knocking the small child off of her back.

"I think . . . something must be wrong with my brother!"

There was a pause while Kira was simultaneously responding and struggling to stay centered in her simulation. "Annie, don't scare me like that, this is serious!"

At that exact moment a large shepherd dog came round the corner of an outbuilding growling viciously and causing Kira's heart rate to skyrocket. She had to move fast. She reached into her pack and pulled out some dried meat to throw at the dog and then started to hand some to her companions when her hand was struck back by an invisible force.

"What?" Kira was confused but then reality sunk in as her headset was stripped off and Annie looked at her frantically. Kira had never *ever* seen Annie that way.

In her headset Kira could hear barking and yelling as her charges were being cornered by the dog. Her heart dropped as she imagined the small child being chased, or far worse—caught and returned to slavery.

The Beta

"What are you doing?" she yelled back at Annie, even though she was fully aware that whatever was happening in her simulation couldn't be as important as real life. Sometimes it was hard to feel the difference.

"I . . . I shouldn't tell you everything but will you come with me to find my brother?"

"Well, sure, of course. Let me turn this off."

Kira took off her gear and shut down the computer as fast as she could. Annie ran straight out of the garage and into her car with Kira hot on her tail. Although Annie was smart enough to go slowly down the driveway, as soon as they hit the main road her driving was as wild as her emotions. Kira was beginning to regret tagging along.

She let Annie concentrate on driving and didn't ask any questions. They flew most of the way into town before the westside Washington State traffic hit them, where they were one of a zillion cars stuck on a tiny artery covered in thick green vegetation with no offshoots, no sideroads, and no alternate routes.

Now that they were going twenty-five miles an hour Kira asked, "Where are we going?"

"Oh," Annie glanced over at her, making Kira uncomfortable as she stopped looking at the road. "The high school." She pulled her phone out of her purse and tossed it over to Kira. "Will you check to see if he's texted me again?"

Kira looked down but there were no updates. "Nothing yet. What was Lanh doing there on a Saturday?"

"Taking the SAT."

"Huh?" Kira was confused, "His scores were amazing, why would he be retaking them?" And that's when it hit her and she stopped asking questions. They sat in silence the rest of the way to the school.

Annie pulled into the parking lot, which was fairly full for a Saturday, when both of them spotted the police cars at the same time. They were parked right out near the front doors of the high school.

"Oh well," was all Annie said, although the occasion called for a stronger term. "I hope that isn't him."

The Beta

She parked at the first space she could find and then took a deep breath, "Kira, you don't have to come with me . . ."

"No," Kira admonished her friend, "I doubt the police are here for him. They don't arrest kids for cheating, I mean, if it has to do with something like that." Kira then realized Lahn and Annie turned eighteen not two weeks earlier. Neither of them were legally 'kids' anymore.

"Should you give him a text to ask where he is?" Kira suggested as she passed her friend's phone back over.

"Um, no, let's just head over and see what's going on first."

The long walk across the parking lot was painful with anticipation. There were two officers and three squad cars but hardly any bystanders. As far as Kira could tell that was a good sign.

Feeling bold and wanting to get reassurance, Kira spoke up as they were about to pass the two officers on their way inside the building, "Is everything ok?" she inquired of the officers. In this day and age of school shootings her curiosity wouldn't be out of place.

"Everything's fine. You can go inside."

Kira started forward but Annie grabbed her hand. Coming out of the building were two more officers and two people wearing FBI jackets. Lanh was handcuffed in between all four of them. He was far enough away he missed seeing them but Annie didn't skip a beat. She tugged on Kira's arm and they returned to their car, trying not to draw any attention.

Once in the car Annie started hyperventilating. "Kira, I really can't tell you anything else, but I have to go home now. I don't have time to drive you back home and you shouldn't go with me." Annie looked apologetic, resolute, and stressed out.

"Oh, OK . . ." how was Kira going to explain this to her parents? How was she going to get home? Yet Kira realized these were small problems compared to whatever Annie was facing at the moment.

"It's going to be all right Annie," she said, not believing it one bit. Kira reached across the seat and gave her a quick hug then hopped out of the car so Annie could get going.

The Beta

Kira didn't know what to do with herself as she watched Annie drive off. In the distance she saw all but one of the police cars head out, sirens quiet. What the heck would cause the FBI to arrest a kid taking the SAT? Seriously?

The Kiss

James had one week left to convince Kira/Sarah to give him her phone number, or email address, or anything. Of course, he hadn't the guts to ask her outright and that failing alone should have disqualified him from deserving her attention.

And once again he was probably going to do something stupid. After watching that NPC try and kiss her in the Sx̱ʷnitkʷ simulation replay last week he had spent many more nights staking it out. Now he was ready to make his move.

It was 10:45 a.m. which was about fifteen minutes before the time Kira religiously entered the Sx̱ʷnitkʷ simulation each weekday morning except Fridays. This time instead of entering the simulation from in dev mode, he logged into Google Earth History under his student name and picked out the character he had been studying closely.

He found himself standing outside of a pit-house and one glance down at his abs almost distracted him from his goal. Darn he looked good. Yet now was when he needed to open his internal dev menu so he could cloak his character to look like an NPC. Even though he entered as a student and was identified as such, it was possible with his developer privileges to hide that from the other players.

He learned the trick by watching the older woman in replay mode. Most developers didn't care about actually playing their simulation alongside high school students, either because they didn't have the security clearance to do so or because it was much more effective to either watch replays, dink around dev-only groups, or practice in empty simulations.

But the old woman was creating a simulation by herself and thus far had only one high school student participating. It was likely that the woman was either a teacher or someone really interested in teaching young people, so she had both the proper clearance and was highly motivated to see what her simulation was like from the inside out at the same time she was creating it.

After watching enough replays James figured out that the old woman hid her status from Kira. This whole time Kira thought she was all alone with only NPC players and had no clue that the old woman was a real-life person.

James was also able to discern that both Kira and the old woman had developed a strong teacher-student relationship. They truly acted like grandmother and granddaughter.

And so, like the old woman, James used his privileges to hide his real status behind an NPC tag. If Kira looked, all she would see is the same old code that kept flirting with her day in and day out.

The one risk he was taking was that the old woman would take the time to look at her player layer and see that he joined up today. Hopefully he could hang out with Kira without being seen by the old woman and everything could go as planned.

James wasted no time and walked immediately in the direction of Kira's family home on the west side of the village. He knew exactly where she lived and when he arrived he walked around a bit trying to figure out where would be the best place to wait.

Suddenly she materialized out of thin air in front of him, startling him by arriving five minutes before he expected. Their eyes met and the air sizzled—at least for James—and then he felt terrible for his deception.

"Way spu?sx?itx," Kira said.

Shoot, he had totally forgotten to enable the translator. With a quick flick of his right wrist to turn it on and a glance to the upper right he was able to confirm it was on. He only missed one phrase.

"Way spu?sx?itx," Kira repeated.

"What?" James said aloud, both to Kira and his translation software. Looking to the right of his internal screen he could see it was enabled, so why wasn't it working and what did Kira say to him?

Kira's face changed immediately, the calm smile from a moment ago was replaced with a cautious frown. James watched the familiar movements as he saw her wrist flick in what must have

The Beta

been a check of the player layer. She was suspicious alright and with good reason. James made the fatal mistake of speaking English as an NPC that only spoke Salish. He was screwed.

Not sure what to do, James turned around and ran into the closest structure he could find and exited the simulation.

Kira was weirded out. Her code crush, the one that taught her Salish, the one she was going to virtually marry soon, the one she checked daily to verify he was really a Non-Player Character piece of code said "what" to her in English and then ran away.

Yet her player layer clearly identified him as an NPC. Maybe there was some glitch in the system, maybe she hadn't really heard the word what. The Salish for hello sounded something similar to the English word whiiiite with a long drawn out I in the middle.

But then he ran away into the pit-house next door on the day he was supposed to be coming to meet her parents. Maybe he was getting virtual cold feet. Before following him she ducked back into her own abode to confirm her virtual parents were accounted for, and then headed out to track down her soon-to-be-husband. She hadn't expected virtual relationships to be as complicated as real ones.

As Kira approached the pit-house he walked out and they were standing nose to nose. She repeated her earlier statement cautiously, "Way spuʔsxʔítx?" the questioning tone at the end was inquiring on several fronts.

"Way spuʔsxʔítx," he wasn't smiling as usual, but his expression was comforting and properly serious to accompany the following request to meet her parents.

Kira checked her player layer one more time. It was the same color, the same meaning, the same embarrassing truth. She was about to virtually marry a string of code.

On their way back to the house her adopted grandmother showed up out of the blue and guided both of the young people through the cultural processes of marriage. Her grandmother represented the young man as he had no family in the area and her virtual parents accepted his proposals after quizzing her thoroughly.

The Beta

While Kira doubted traditional marriages moved as quickly as this one, she found herself feeling ever so contented as she absorbed all of the language, nuance, and cultural meaning of the celebration. She couldn't have never have had this depth of understanding taking hundreds of classes.

She had always wanted to marry a tribal member, but the odds of living so far off the reservation limited her chances. This might be as close as she would ever come to feeling like she was part of her tribe. Even if only a small one-fourth part of her belonged.

Idly, like any teenage girl, Kira wondered if kissing was part of the celebration. She listened to the elders give advice and was proud that she could understand almost all of what they said in Salish, a feast was shared amongst all, and sure enough in a quiet moment after the celebration they were alone for a moment, outside under the stars, when from behind his back he held up to her something delicate and white. She looked closer . . .

After ditching the simulation James didn't know what to do. He took off his headset, wiped off the sweat, drank water nervously, and then paced up and down the room, still dressed in his VR equipment. It was quiet in the house as his parents were on an out of town work trip. He was all alone and they wouldn't be walking in on him to see what he was about to do.

Well, if VR couldn't give you the courage to ask a girl out what good was a virtual world worth? He was going to march back to that simulation and tell Kira everything. Tell her the truth and give her his phone number. Why hadn't he thought of that before?

He logged back in as a student but this time he didn't cover his tracks. All it would take was a quick look and Kira would be able to see he was a real person.

This time when he entered he found himself surrounded by people in a pit-house with Kira sitting right next to him. They were both dressed in elaborate clothes and multiples dishes were spread out in celebration.

"ckin i? spʔustsəlx ?" said one of the older men in the room.

Then he saw the old woman and froze. Thankfully, she was listening intently to the man as well and not looking his way. Now he was trapped in what appeared to be a marriage ceremony with

The Beta

no chance to talk to Kira without the old woman overhearing. He laughed inside at himself. Things could be worse, he was marrying the love of his life even if she didn't know it.

The old woman then spoke to the group, "čpuʔsqílxʷ" and that was when James realized her speech was not accompanied by any subtitles. Why was the translator working sometimes and not others?

James tested one hypothesis by turning his head whispering to himself "you're in trouble." Sure enough, he could hear his voice in English. He was pretty sure he knew what was going on. If one of the main goals of this simulation was to teach language learning it was quite possible that the translation software may be disabled at times for real players, thus requiring them to practice as much language as possible with one another.

And if Kira, himself, and the old woman were the only real players that meant he was about to be discovered.

By some sheer luck the rest of the ceremony did not require him to talk aloud. He listened attentively to the speakers, ate of any dish passed his way and smiled with real sincerity at Kira whenever he was allowed to sneak a glance.

Then they were ushered outside by the family and instructed to wait there. While they had a few quiet moments alone under the stars James flicked open his dev menu and did what he had done so many times before. He pulled out a trailing bouquet of white Dendrobium orchids, but this time he miniaturized them so that they looked like tiny stars in the moonlight. From behind his back he brought them forth and clasped her hands in his as he presented his gift to her heart. She would only have to look a little closer to see who he really was . . . to connect the Dendrobiums to him.

Kira looked closer and saw the most beautiful bouquet of flowers. They were so tiny and delicate and they reminded her of the flowers from the ckʷəkʷiɬp bush.

She looked up and into his eyes with curiosity and questions. There was something familiar about these flowers . . .

James looked back into her eyes, hoping the flowers were enough. It was the only way he knew how to communicate. If an

The Beta

NPC had the guts to kiss Kira why couldn't he? He leaned in slowly, his face nearing hers, he thought he felt a bee stinging his neck but that wouldn't stop him from kissing Kira . . .

Kira looked into his eyes and threw all her trust in the universe. No matter who or what he was at this very moment she felt loved. He leaned in to kiss her and she moved nearer, closing her eyes . . . she wouldn't take off her headset this time.

Out of the corner of his eye James saw the old woman with a cross look on her face. Then everything turned black. He only had time to wonder, how did she get the power to nix people from her simulation?

The Beta

Part Three
Waves

"Stim aʔ ckistxʷ ??" shouted her grandmother. Kira's eyes flew open. Her new husband stood in front of her frozen in time. The kiss never completed.

Kira looked at the frozen NPC in front of her and wondered what was happening. She had never seen an NPC freeze before. In her other multiplayer simulations sometimes real players glitched as they moved in an out of their characters, but nothing like this. He was still as a statue.

"Tətwit kast." her grandmother said.

"Səxkinx?" Kira asked in Salish but followed in English. "He's just an NPC." She had a sinking suspicion that the NPC she thought was her grandmother was more than met the eye.

"He was an NPC until five minutes ago." her grandmother said in English. Kira then watched in fascination as her grandmother made all sorts of hand motions indicating she was working furiously on her internal controls. Her grandmother was definitely not an NPC. What the heck was going on here?

Kira walked around the frozen statue feeling cold all over.

"Something is very wrong—this only happens when the equipment measures a major medical event." her grandmother informed her. "I have to go." The shape of her grandmother flickered and was replaced with an NPC.

Kira was left all alone under the stars with his frozen avatar, clutching a bouquet of miniature stars, wondering what her grandmother meant by major medical event, and questioning everything she knew about her virtual world.

The old woman's name was Karen. Everything happened in a matter of seconds and she was quick on her feet, even though her feet technically didn't move much past her VR space.

The Beta

Karen wasn't used to real students accessing the simulation with the exception of her one loyal student named Kira. Even so she always checked the player layer before entering the simulation in case some random student suddenly became interested in Native American history and decided to join.

His character had froze out of the blue and was surrounded in a wide red light, probably only apparent to teachers and the AI. The fuzzy red light began to pulsate around him. While her training had been perfunctory on such matters she did remember that a red light meant medical emergency—a medical emergency irl.

She pulled up the player layer again and Karen was now able to see the icon that included some personal information including his name, photo, and student ID. She copy pasted the numbers as quickly as possible. His disembodied and serious expression hovered over her in the air.

🌑

He never really was in an unconscious state but twelve hours would disappear from his memory. All he could remember thinking over and over was 'how the heck did the old woman do that?' He wondered how she had the ability to actually kick a developer out, even though he wasn't thinking straight because technically he was logged-in as a student. He also wondered why she would've kicked him out, because her simulation was public anyone could join. He couldn't imagine that she was so protective or jealous of him leaning in to kiss Kira.

These jumbled thoughts floated through his head as his eyes repetitively looked into the dark lenses of his headset. Even though it was pitch black he could still clearly see the curved glass.

When his short-term memory finally kicked in, the moment intersected with his ability to try and move, which for some reason hadn't even occurred to him earlier. First he tried to reach up and take his headset off so he could see something, but he felt like he was in one of those dreams where you find yourself completely immobilized. He couldn't move an inch trying to wake himself up from the panic that was welling within. Next he tried to kick out with his legs, which usually worked when he was waking up from a bad dream, but this time all he could do was wiggle his thighs back-and-forth an inch.

That's when he heard the music. A female voice, some song off the radio, it seemed to repeat over and over like his earlier thoughts. He actually knew this song, it was by Joni Mitchell and talked about plants being replaced by rocks. The repetitive lyrics divided each of his attempts to move. He first discovered he could circle his ankles and toes, which also brought the realization he was not asleep. Next, he found his fingers could do the same even though his wrists and forearms couldn't move a millimeter. And last but not least he attempted to move his head, which, if it hadn't been pounding with pain he may have been able to raise it up quite a bit. As it was he could only lift it an inch before giving in to exhaustion. Then it became hard to breathe and he lost all memory of what happened next.

🌍

She knew what to do and her first action was to hit the help button within her Google Earth History dev menu. First, the help menu asked her to do a simple search with pre-prepared written topics, forums and videos to answer her questions. Karen wasn't going to depend on a forum for her to report a medical emergency.

Assuming the development search was connected to Google Search, she typed in the obviously redundant search terms of 'Google Earth History Developer phone number contact.' Luckily, this brought her straight to a 1-800 number so at least she didn't have to continue driving through presets.

That's when she noticed that her own vitals were starting to spike a bit; blood pressure and heart rate were up and there was a knot in her stomach from a combination of not eating and worry. As the 1-800 number rang she found her chair in real life, which happened to be a very comfortable recliner, and sat down. She took some very deliberate deep breaths and reached to her side irl life to grab a water bottle. Karen supposed she could've taken off of her headset to make the phone call on her cell phone, yet she had become so accustomed to VR that she felt she could connect with emergency services and help whoever that young boy was much faster from within her headset. The 1-800 ended up being as frustrating as her initial search and didn't offer an option to connect her with a real life person. She laughed at herself at the internal use of the term real life as she used it to compare customer service options.

Karen realized she shouldn't be worrying so much. Technically, the AI would notice the major medical event, whatever it might be, and either contact emergency services, teachers, or parents where the student was physically located. It was likely the student was actually in a school or home with help nearby. So technically, she shouldn't have to stress about the situation at all.

Yet since this was a new and untested system, and since the event happened in her simulation she did worry. Whoever that kid was he happened to choose and inhabit one of her favorite characters. Why that a strange kid would choose that day, that character, and that moment to join the simulation was beyond her but there must be some divine reason for such an event.

When she couldn't get the 1-800 number to connect with a real person she knew the steps that needed to be taken, and quickly, in case the AI wasn't doing its job, dialed her local 911 number and she was immediately connected with emergency services.

"I would like to report a medical emergency."

"Yes ma'am, please confirm your location."

"I'm in Inchelium, WA but the medical emergency is somewhere else, I don't actually know where."

There was a pause on the line.

"I need help connecting with emergency technicians at Google in California because they can figure out where and what is happening . . ."

Uncharacteristically the 911 operator interrupted her, "You're calling to report on an emergency but you don't know where it's taking place?"

"I was in a virtual reality simulation when a student, some minor child somewhere all of a sudden stopped working and the program indicated that there was a medical emergency. I want to

The Beta

make sure he's OK. I'm not sure if the computer is notifying emergency services or someone to help." Karen knew she was making no sense at all but she thought maybe one emergency system could talk to another right?

"So, let me get this straight, you want us to call Google in California?"

"Yes, specifically Google Earth History. Well, that's the company I was working with and when I called the 1-800 number to report the emergency I couldn't get through."

"Let me get some extra help on the line here to see what we can do, but can I clarify again that there is no emergency actually happening at your current physical location?"

"Correct, but I want to repeat that according to my computer there is a major medical situation with a minor."

"Let me put you on hold so I can connect with my supervisor. We'll be right back to help."

Karen tapped her fingers on the real life table with one hand and set the call visual to her upper-right corner, cursing quietly under her breath. What was she missing?

She went back to the beginning like she always did and entered another Google search using additional keywords including 'medical emergency' along with 'Google Earth History'. Eventually she found what she thought she was looking for in an instruction manual for parents of *The Beta*.

The first step instructed parents to first call 911. Then it told parents to contact their school district once the medical emergency concluded, and at the very end there was another 1-800 number that was used to report incidents of this nature directly to Google Earth History.

Karen opened a second voice call box and quickly dialed the number. As usual the call was directed to a pre-recorded voice instructing the caller to dial 911 in a medical emergency and then asking for details about location and school district. Karen tapped on '0' in the middle of the message and was rewarded with a real voice.

"Google Earth History, this is Jaleesa speaking. How can I help you?"

The Beta

Karen explained the whole situation and then asked, "Jaleesa, I need to know what has happened to this boy, he froze up right in the middle of the simulation I created and I feel responsible. There must be someone on a development team that can get back to me. At the very least to make sure there was nothing I could have programed differently? I have the student number associated with his account." Karen copy and pasted the info into the accompanying text chat box.

There was a pause on the other end of the phone, "Honestly, we have never received a call like this. But I assure you after I look into the details and make sure that boy is alright we will have someone get back to you, I promise."

They mutually hung up, the rep in a hurry to investigate and Karen in frustration.

Karen sat there quietly for a moment turning inward, completely oblivious of the real world she could feel and the virtual world that encompassed her visual space. She might have sat there for quite some time if the gentle beeping of her first voice call box hadn't prodded her back out.

"Hello," she said, thankful her local 911 rep hadn't forgotten her.

"We've made contact with the Mountain View Police Department and we think the best bet is for you to file a report over the phone. Can I connect you now?"

"Sure . . ." Karen responded slowly and then added, "While you were on the other line I did find a number at Google Earth History and talked with a rep, but I should probably report the details to the Mountain View Police."

Jaleesa connected her with the police.

Unsure if anything she was doing was going to help the boy, Karen repeated her story once again but her mind was already somewhere else.

James was cold. His last coherent memory was of his body laying prostrate, but now he was sitting up. Sort of sitting up, maybe propped up on a soft chair with a blanket. He could tell his headset was still tightly strapped to his head and that was bothering

The Beta

him. Whatever had happened to him, why would his headset still be on? It simply made no sense.

Testing his ability to move, he once again discovered the only motion allowed was a slight wiggling of his fingers, toes, and head. He wasn't exactly sure what to do next. There was still some music in the background but it was another song he couldn't recognize. He supposed he could scoot around and try to fall out of his sitting position, but it was comfortable enough he didn't want to exchange it for a place on the floor. Frustrated, he groaned, hoping to provoke some type of change in status.

The result was almost immediate. He could hear whispering far off, scuffling, positioning and then a familiar metallic sound. It sounded like the metallic clicking of a gun and was followed by a small circle of cold at his throat that lacked any humor.

James was scared stiff. Now that he could think and remember what was happening he felt a deep fear. He was about to die.

"Hold still," said a female voice. "You will obey every command we give you and obey immediately." Said another female voice in his other ear, this voice deeper.

What were the chances of being kidnapped by two women? What the heck were they going to do to him? Unaccustomed to this type of fear, or kidnapping for that matter, brought out strange thoughts. One minute he was about to virtually kiss the real girl he was in love with, and the next minute he was blind, tied up, and being ordered around by two women.

The first woman continued her threats as she pushed the cold barrel into his neck. "We brought you here for a purpose, for a reason. Until that purpose is fulfilled you will do everything we ask without question, without pause, and without thought."

He almost jumped when that second voice continued, "When we are done we will do something with you . . ." the pause here was deliberate and full, "but that will depend on if you give us any trouble."

Kira stood there for a long time. His frozen avatar in front of her, mobile and odd looking. The small bouquet of starlets still

The Beta

clutched in her hand as the whole village continued on around her with its busy NPC life, completely ignoring her plight.

She didn't know what else to do so she waited. Waited so that she could look at him, torn between wanting to punch him in the face for lying to her for taking advantage of her, and deceiving her. Whoever he was and whatever he did, she knew it was wrong. The lack of information was killing her.

Kira felt completely betrayed and dumbfounded. Two people— her grandmother and the boy—were so firmly implanted in her mind as NPCs that she had felt safe to act like herself around them. Thinking that they were just computer code gave her so much freedom and security. Knowing now that not only one, but maybe both of them, had tricked her and may have actually been real people this entire time—made her so angry that she wasn't sure what to do.

She had so many questions. How long were they real? How did they get the status to look like an NPC even when that wasn't true? Was it even legal? Kira was pretty sure that if she talked to Professor McKenzie she would get a clear answer—that posing as code was not allowed, but she wasn't ready to go to her professor yet.

Even though the feeling of betrayal was mutual for both grandmother and the boy, the thoughts themselves were unique, separate, and distinct. Kira's feelings about her pseudo-grandmother were all of a sudden amplified. If all these months it had been a real woman acting as her grandmother the relationship became all of a suddenly more precious. Though she did admit it would also make a difference if the woman was native, only time would possibly answer that question.

However, her reactions to the boy were not the same. She felt instead a deep distrust and disgust. How could someone pretend to be code and then try and take advantage of her by kissing her? Even though her final emotions would depend upon his true identity. . . he was in deep trouble either way.

The fear in her grandmother's eyes and quick exit from the system was strange. She was so curious about the whole situation that she continued to circle around his frozen statue. After seven

The Beta

minutes he suddenly disappeared without a trace, leaving her in comfortable and familiar surroundings but feeling utterly unstable.

Her grandmother hadn't returned yet and she wasn't sure what to do next. She looked at the list of simulation characters but both of their names were still listed as NPCs like they always were. There had never been a single real character in this simulation besides herself, so there was no way for her to contact them or message them like in other simulations. In the American Revolution simulation, she was able to directly message any real life participant. With no way to make contact Kira started to think logically of how she could leave a message for her grandmother in the simulation, assuming the woman was real and would return at some point. It was worth a shot.

First Kira ran to the group of women who were processing fish and started up a conversation.

"I need to leave a message for grandmother," she said.

"Yes, yes, what do you want to tell her? one of the motherly NPCs responded.

"Please let her know I will return at 3 o'clock."

The NPCs agreed to pass on her message. Now, whether they would actually do so was an entirely different question that couldn't be answered right now. As a backup plan Kira began to think about writing and pictures. There were several different ways she could go about leaving a visual message that may not be automatically erased by the simulation.

But looking down at the flowers clutched in her hand she realized they were the other important clue to solving her mystery. They were so tiny and delicate, obviously something that did not exist in this world or real life. But looking closely she was almost positive they were the exact same flowers that mysteriously appeared in the American Revolution simulation. The problem was that there was no way she could take these flowers from the Sx̱ʷnitkʷ simulation to the American Revolution simulation to compare the two. However, she could take a snapshot picture. So with a quick double click of her index fingers she took a few close-ups snapshots of the blossoms and filed them away on her desktop to look at later. Not wanting to lose the flowers she ran back to her pit-house and scavenged for a container of water and gently put

The Beta

the delicate blooms inside. She was not entirely sure the simulation would require cut flowers to be in water but she didn't want to take the chance. Kira then found an out of the way cubby hole in the house hoping that her VR brother wouldn't knock them over while she was gone.

Leaving a written message to her grandmother seemed more time consuming then she imagined. But she decided, if she was waiting for her grandmother to come back, it wouldn't hurt to spend another 20 or 30 minutes trying to find a way to connect.

Kira ran back to the exact spot the boy froze. She paced around a bit thinking and looking at the available objects around her. If she were closer to the river she might take the time to gather stones for a message, but in the end Kira grabbed a stick and began to slowly carve out a message in the dirt. At first, she began writing in English "Meet here at 5:00" but then had a sudden and decisive change of heart. Kira erased her English and the Salish began to flow . . .

Kira moved to the American Revolution Simulation. It was still twenty minutes before the rush of regular students would arrive and it gave her time to investigate. Even though she was sure they were gone Kira checked her room—Sarah Franklin-Bache's room—and confirmed that the flowers left on her bureau months before had disappeare. Whether it was a rhythm of the VR or her virtual maid cleaning up, they were not there to inspect anymore.

Kira already had a suspect, so her next step was to activate the player layer and zoom up into an aerial view of Boston. There were currently only two other real life players and neither of them was the one she was looking for.

It was a long shot, but she did have the vague memory of tossing a crown of mysterious white flowers off of her head at the City Tavern only yesterday. So even though it had been a week irl and mostly likely a month of VR time that had passed between now and then, Kira left her premises and headed down Chestnut street to Second where the City Tavern waited.

Kira doubted that 18th century women frequented the tavern, but whoever designed the simulation did nothing to prevent a woman's ability to enter and socialize within the Tavern. Since her

The Beta

early days in the simulation the City Tavern was a gathering place, from their first experiments with virtual drunkenness to an easy and fast way to pass their assignments with ease, the City Tavern was the social center of this simulation. Kira wondered idly what the City Tavern was really like in modern times. She made a note to self to search it up when she had time and even more boldly promised herself she would visit irl someday.

But now her time was limited and her objective was clear. She needed to find the flowers. Kira nodded to the barkeep and noted the inhabitants, all were NPC's lingering over meals or drinks. She let herself become immersed in her memory and she thought back to where she was sitting that night with a glass of red wine untouched in front of her.

"Are you starting some new trend in flower crowns?" Elizabeth Powell had asked. Elizabeth was always annoying or correcting everyone.

"Whatever do you mean by that?" Kira replied quickly. She had become accustomed to Elizabeth's pointless jabs, as had the rest of them.

But when Kira noticed a few looks in the direction of her head she paid attention to the original comment. Flower crown? Reaching up with her controllers she tried to toss or dislodge whatever was on top of her hair, and down fell a beautiful crown of delicate white flowers. They were gorgeous, but with all the laughter around her Kira remembered flinging them across the room nearly landing on Alexander Hamilton's head where they then disappeared somewhere on the floor and were forgotten by all.

Kira checked the bar floor, went through the kitchens and then out the back door into an alley to pick through a refuse pile that was half compost and half garbage. Thank goodness the current iteration of VR was not making use of olfactory technology that would force her to smell this mess.

Frustrated, she pulled up the picture of the flowers from her desktop and placed them in front of her in her personal view, then crossing her arms and tapping her fingers against her elbows she studied them with an anxious energy.

The Beta

Then it hit her like a ton of bricks. Replays! As a student she had access to view any past portion of the simulation like a recorded movie. In fact Professor McKenzie had guided the class through a few replays to help the cohort process the historic simulations. Kira should have thought of this first! Sliding the flower picture to the left Kira pulled up the replay archive and scrolled through until she found the day of the flower crown.

Luckily the scroll kept a view of her avatar in the center view so she was able to float above Sarah Franklin-Bache and watch as she rewound through the day, starting at the flower crown incident in the City Tavern. She watched Sarah walk backwards down Chestnut Street, backwards into Franklin Square, and backwards into the Franklin home, flower crown still firmly attached.

She watched herself say goodbye to the children and nanny, and then Samuel Powell walked in. Kira remembered the horse ride they shared that day as they returned to town from The Cliffs. She was staring at Samuel, everything was in fast rewind and when she glanced at her character and again and noticed the flower crown was gone. This was it, Kira had a sinking feeling that she knew exactly where the flowers originated.

Pausing the simulation she reset the controls to play forward at regular speed and set her view from the ceiling, floating like a ghost above the play. The sound was now engaged and she could hear herself tell Samuel she would meet him later at City Tavern instead of walking together and then turned her back on him to greet her VR children.

This time Kira could see his face. It was crestfallen for a moment, then indecisive, and then determined. She watched him do something with his internal controls and then the flower crown appeared out of thin air.

No way! How in the world would he get the power to make something out of thin air? The controls in these historical simulations were very specific and the characters forced to use only the objects on hand to give realism to any scenario. She watched him gently place the flower crown on her head and then swiftly depart.

It was one of those times, one of those moments where you think someone is your best friend and then they turn into so much more. Or they had turned into much more weeks ago but you never realized it.

Kira prayed fervently that Samuel was really a young teenage guy who was at least moderately, physically appealing. Because though he didn't know it yet, she knew he had won her heart and soul. Falling in love in VR was a pain.

Positive now that whoever inhabited Samuel's avatar was also the same culprit who took over the code from the Sx̌ʷnitkʷ simulation, Kira rewound and paused so she could look at Samuel's expression as he put the flowers on her head.

After a few replays that swirled her emotions into twisted pools, Kira re-entered the live simulation and checked for him but he was nowhere to be found. She pulled up her private messaging and began to write him a note when the world went white.

❂

James felt as though he was stuck in the black without any way to communicate. Sitting in a captive and blindfolded state was bad enough, but having his headset—the one tool that gave him freedom to roam and manipulate the virtual world—become a way for his kidnappers to plunge him in darkness was infuriating. His fear was slowly, slowly, turning into anger.

His attackers became quiet after their first speech and he remained quiet as well, though he could hear shuffling around the room. As his consciousness coalesced he began to itch. First his nose twitched, then he could smell all sorts of new smells that almost made him nauseous. Then he felt his pants which had obviously been wet but were now damply dry and smelled like pee. When the realization that he must have been knocked out for a long time hit him—combined with a whiff of what must be his own urine—James felt his whole body begin to itch from the dirt and grime that surely covered him from head to toe. Then he heard the sound of duct tape unwinding nearby which made him lean as far away as his constricted body allowed.

"Hold still," said a captor on one side while he could feel the other woman climb up and sit above but next to him on the soft stuff propping him up. That one started to hold his upper body still

The Beta

while the other must have been holding the tape. When he felt the first sticky section touch his cheek he flipped out and his body began a limited attempt to flop around in protest.

"Hold still," hissed the one with a slightly higher pitched voice.

Were they seriously going to tape his headset on? What the heck was going on? The headset, the one device that brought him unlimited freedom and power, was about to become his permanent prison. Duct tape was synonymous with permanency.

He wasn't wrong. It took a while but his headset was sometimes gingerly, sometimes roughly, but permanently, attached to his head.

🌍

Kira's headset was pulled off roughly and the invasion of unexpected light and sound caused her to yelp in protest.

"Kira!" her mom's voice held an unusual combination of fear and anger. It took a minute for her to see her mom's expression, which also betrayed confusion.

"What the heck mom, you scared me!" Kira snapped back.

"The FBI and a police officer are in the living room asking to talk to you. What's this about?"

"The FBI?" Kira swallowed nervously quickly going pale. Heer mom saw the look in her eyes. Kira couldn't lie and couldn't hide anything. Especially from her mom.

"Kira?"

Time slowed down and Kira felt a little like she was floating above herself. "I'm not sure mom."

"Kira?" this time her name was drawn out with accusation and concern.

"I . . ." Kira was searching for a way to tell the truth without detail. "I think it might have something to do with Annie and her brother."

"You have to tell the truth, Kira, whatever it is . . ." but her mom must have sensed there was no reason to force Kira to tell her now with the FBI in the house.

They made their way inside and Kira did her best to compose her features, but when the police officer in the room was the same one Kira and Annie spoke to outside of the school on Saturday, Kira almost lost her footing. She sat down on the couch, ensconced protectively between her mom and dad.

The FBI agents were fairly straightforward. They introduced themselves and began to ask simple questions starting with, "How many times did you take the SAT?" Even though the answer was easy Kira found herself slouching with her arms crossed and it took a while for her to answer.

"Once," then looking up at her dad—daresay he almost looked amused—added the basic details, "It was last November and I got a 1470." Out of the corner of her eyes she could see her dad smirking at her impertinence. At least he didn't seem all worried like her mom. But then he was the lawyer.

They continued to ask vague, broad questions about the test and finally hit one sore spot when they asked, "Have you ever talked about one of the SAT test questions with anyone?"

She turned a bit red but inside she was already feeling more confident. She looked at her dad for permission to speak but started anyway, as she knew what his response would be, "I did spend a whole evening complaining to my dad about the Geometry questions and probably did give a detailed explanation of one particularly vexing problem, but I may not have even had those details memorized really . . . " her dad looked composed but embarrassed, "But I mean it's legal to complain to your parents about math right?" Kira looked at the adults around her, knowing that the letter of the law says you can't discuss the SAT. Yet how could that really apply to one's parents?

Her dad smiled sheepishly, "I can confirm my daughter complained in detail the evening after she took the test and I vaguely remember a conversation that focused on congruent angles, but we never spoke of it again and I couldn't remember the particulars now."

The FBI agents gave them both stern looks but continued with a new line of questioning. Where was Kira last Saturday? What had she done with Annie that day? How did she know Annie?

Kira continued to give them frank and immediate answers. If Annie's brother was involved in something concerning the SAT and cheating, Kira didn't have anything to do with it, but did

The Beta

Annie? She could tell her parents were relieved the line of questioning was focused on Annie.

"Have you ever cheated on any test?" While it was a broad question would have many students hesitant to answer it was one Kira honestly replied to with an indigent air. "Never."

"Is there anything else you want to tell us?" they finally asked in closing.

Kira let out a deep breath and replied confidently, "No," there was nothing more she wanted to tell them about anything, especially her role in spreading the cheat sheets.

The men left. Her parents gave her funny looks that evening but they too seemed relieved the FBI didn't have any other questions for her. Kira spent the evening in Google Earth History looking for a sign of her grandmother or Samuel Powel, but after hours of switching between the two simulations she gave up.

Annie wouldn't answer any texts, and she found herself alone in her bedroom curled up on her bed. Kira was hungry, thirsty, sweaty, dirty, uncomfortable, exhausted and unable to sleep.

🌎

James was now warm, showered, hydrated, and there were several slices of pizza settling in his stomach.

All of this had happened with his VR headset firmly taped to his head. The two women were sure to have seen him naked as they forced him to shower at gunpoint before changing into clean clothes. A button-down shirt and zippered hoodie avoided the need to loop anything over his neck. Then after the luxury of eating and drinking with his own two hands they tied him up again. He was surprisingly rested for his condition. Sitting squished between his throne of pillows or what he assumed were pillows, James tried to relax for a moment, letting the cortisol flooding his body slow to a trickle.

He almost fell asleep when suddenly a white light forced his eyelids open. This was not something he was expecting. They had turned on his virtual reality headset even though both his arms and legs were still tied up tight.

The Beta

He heard the click again, that jolting click, and felt the cool metal of what he could only guess was a firearm nuzzled against his neck. All momentary feelings of peace immediately disappeared and his senses were once again on high alert. He thought they were using his headset as some kind of sarcastic or fancy way of keeping him in the dark, but now he was both morbidly curious and frightened out of his wits as he regained visual access to his former world.

He realized his freedom might be acquired from simply asking his computer to dial 911. But with the smooth metal on his neck he wasn't inclined to make such a sudden outburst.

"As you can see we are connecting you with your virtual reality software. And if you were thinking of asking for help let me allow you to think again." It was then that the coldness pressed closer into his neck, giving a clear description of its owner's intentions. There was something in her voice that made James understand that whatever the reasons, these particular women were dead serious about their intent.

For a fleeting moment he wondered if it would be better to have been captured by two men, but then he remembered his shower, the pizza, the water and the clean pants from the last two hours. They were currently a convincing argument in the case of female kidnappers.

"What we are requiring of you is relatively simple and shouldn't take long to complete, but you will obey every order we give you every minute, every moment. Immediately."

The other woman yanked him up into a standing position and he almost stumbled over. He was forced to stand there for what seemed like an eternity when he saw a cursor begin to control the desktop view that suddenly appeared on his private desktop. There was no doubt that they had hooked up his computer and were now controlling it with a monitor he couldn't see. They really would be able to track every movement of what he did in VR. He couldn't see the world outside so they must have covered the headset's external cameras.

It appeared they were running through the VR set-up when he saw his controllers materialize about two feet in front of him. They briefly touched the floor to calibrate and then circled the room in a tight space. This was going to be a big adjustment for him, at home he was used to a 30 ft. x 15 ft. area which allowed him the freedom of movement to walk nearly twelve feet in each direction. But here it looked as though he was restricted to a 6 ft. x 6 ft. box with some odd intrusions and extrusions. He could tell one of the rectangular sections was probably the tiny itty-bitty bathroom used for his earlier shower.

Once the set-up was complete he heard the snip of scissors that shaved right through his leg and arm bands, leaving him for the first time in who knows long free to move. There was a second where he almost gained the courage to lash out against his confinement, but a weakness in his muscles and an intelligent bit of decision-making prevented such action.

"If you step out of line or accidentally do something we have not asked you to do, you will be back where you started. In the dark and all alone. You are easily replaceable."

If he was so easily replaceable why did they take the trouble to kidnap him in the first place? There was something, some reason, and probably something to do with his parents that would cause him, a teenage boy, to be valuable enough for their time. He just had to figure out what.

For a moment all the people he loved—his parents, his family, and Kira—flashed before him, tearing at his heart. Then all was forgotten as the voices began to speak and the two controllers were placed in his hands.

They both spoke at once, "Open Google Earth History Simulation."

James obeyed, and even though his heart was dying to return to the Sx̌ʷnitkʷ simulation to try and figure out what happened with Kira—to apologize to her—it was only a minor twitch of his left leg that would've betrayed such an inclination. Instead, he sat there quietly floating head to head and toe to toe with the Earth. His two women captors were surely doing the same as he couldn't hear any sound. It was reverently quiet.

After a few minutes he couldn't tell which one of the women spoke. "Navigate to the North Pole."

The Beta

"Huh? Seriously?" James replied out loud. There was a little bit of disbelief and confusion in his response. Were they really trying to go where he thought they were going?

Everything around him was in hyperdrive as the gun was once again pressed against his neck, energy filled the air and hands tightened on his arms. "You will always do as we say immediately with no questions."

"Go there now!" The second voice growled.

Once again obeying, James pulled up the North Pole slowly, but not too slowly, and zoomed in on the red and white pole sticking out of the Arctic Ice. James, looking for trivia and Easter Eggs over the past year had learned a lot about the North Pole. One of the most interesting tidbits was that the North Pole location in Google Earth History actually closely followed the magnetic North Pole irl. He rested in front of the large mythical icon and waited for his instructions.

The deep voice ordered, "Enter the North Pole."

James obeyed, he had tried to enter the North Pole many times before with no success. After he clicked on the North Pole icon it expanded to give him several choices.

And sure enough, the location he could not enter was exactly the one they asked for, "Enter Santa's Workshop."

James clicked on the image of a Christmas Village.

The icon grew immensely as he was suddenly sitting in a foggy winter scene outside of a brick and iron gate. His avatar's identity key automatically tried the gate's lock. In a moment the AI's voice would deny his entry like it always had before. Nobody was allowed into Santa's Workshop, not even his parents.

But he was wrong. His key turned smoothly and the gate swung open. James sucked in his breath and everything changed. He was about to enter Santa's Workshop. Maybe getting kidnapped wasn't such a bad deal if you could live out one of your real-life fantasies.

Before him was a path that wound through alpine trees. Snow was softly falling and the frost on the trees made them look like they were dripping emeralds. It was as quiet as you would expect a winter forest to be, but there were distinct footprints in the snow in front of him. James wondered if they were real.

The Beta

"Follow the path," the woman holding the gun said. He could tell it was her by her breath on his neck.

He only walked a short way when a faint glow emanated from ahead and the trees and shrubbery thinned. Here he found a most charming winter village scene. Hundreds of little buildings complete with Christmas decorations, snow, icicles, warm yellow windows with little panes of old-fashioned glass, mailboxes, and chimneys topped with smoke. Far off in the distance he could see a few moving figures, but nothing close.

"Keep moving forward," she instructed him.

James moved slowly because he thought that was what they wanted and partly because he was in awe. He couldn't believe he was really walking through Santa's Workshop, or Santa's Village, or whatever you wanted to call this place.

A sign hung down above the door of the first building. It had no words but instead there was a carved, gilded picture of a globe. He approached the large, foggy window and used his controller to wipe the condensation from the glass to see inside. He looked down at his avatar to find he was dressed in warm winter clothes and his controller hand wrapped in leather gloves with fur trim. He also swore he was faintly glowing himself, like a ghost.

James looked inside, peering through the small pane to give the women a good view of what he was seeing. It looked like a little toy shop that specialized in making globes. Big globes, little globes, and pictures of globes on the wall. All of the globes were animated as if by magic, with their poles spinning slowly. James thought he saw different continental shapes but he couldn't tell for sure.

"Good, now go to the next building," she instructed. The woman closest to him, the one with the gun, was giving him all the instructions.

The building was similar in all aspects to the first except for the sign and the contents. This time the sign was of a glowing volcano, and inside it looked like a bunch of fourth grade science projects on fire. There were little miniature replicas of different volcanoes on every table—tall, loud, erupting volcanoes and small, short, slowly bubbling cauldrons.

The third building had a sign that pictured a rock collection. This time when James peeked through the window he saw a figure

The Beta

inside. The person was dressed in warm winter wear much like himself, yet they were not wearing any gloves and he could see them hunched over what might have been a large rock sample. There was an ever-so-faint glow or sparkle that surrounded the figure, but James didn't get a better look because of a quiet hiss in his ear.

"Get out of there!" the woman with the gun instructed. James quickly agreed. Who knows what would happen when someone discovered he was in this restricted place? Although wait, wouldn't that maybe help save him?

Unsure where to place his bets, James walked past the fourth small house and around the back before whispering, "Where do you want me to go?"

The two women did some whispering of their own before the higher pitched one responded. "Can you bring up an aerial map of Santa's Workshop?

Huddled in the darkness behind one of the cottages he used the Google Earth History command to bring up a map but nothing happened. He tried twice more before admitting defeat. "No luck," then he had an idea, "Do you want me to see if there is a player layer?"

"Go ahead."

He used his left trigger to access the menu but instead of the menu a small red book appeared. It floated neatly there in the air in front of him, only three feet away. From this distance he couldn't read the gold lettering on the front.

Without prompting, he walked closer and held the book still so he could read the title. Although he was sure his kidnappers could see everything on an external screen, he whispered the words out loud anyway. "*A Christmas Carol*, by Charles Dickens."

"What the hell?" he heard one of them remark.

"Why would a player layer be replaced by that?"

They were echoing his own sentiments exactly but also giving him clues to their identity. He was intensely curious about what they were up to and fairly positive he knew where they came from, or at least who they worked for.

"What next?" he asked, itching to do something other than stare at the falling snow.

The Beta

"Keep going."

From his initial views he thought the village was shaped almost like a football with five to eight streets that started on one end and followed a semi-circle to the other. In the middle was a hill with a more elaborate building on the top, but it was hard to see details from so far away. Since he was already on the "west" side of the village he continued along the outer road, inspecting each house in the same methodical manner.

There was a theme of sorts on this road. Most of the signs had something to do with the Earth's landforms. He passed cottages with signs representing mountains, cliffs, plateaus, plains, coasts, islands, rivers, and finally he arrived at one that had a picture of a large wave on the sign. Through the window he saw miniature globes and maps, all covered in three-dimensional water. The water swirled and glistened, so life-like he thought he could reach out and touch it.

"Go inside!" the command surprised him, as he hadn't been instructed to enter any of the other buildings.

James opened the door and cautiously took one step inside. There were no apparent traps or alarms but the room held faint sounds of waves crashing against the surf.

The interior was like a cross between a space ship's bridge and a toy store. High-tech graphics of the world's oceans plastered the wall with both close up and distant views. On tables underneath each wall screen were miniature three-dimensional objects that moved like little animated toys. They reminded him of the way 2D pictures moved in the Harry Potter Movies, or the whimsical scene where they explore Weasleys' Wizards Wheezes joke shop. He fully understood why this place was called Santa's Workshop, it was as magical as his childhood memories of the real Santa Claus.

He walked past several displays and eventually stopped at one to look closer. The title on the wall read "Global Coupled Ocean-Atmosphere Model of Thermal Expansion Only" with a large toggle to the left running from $2xCO_2$ to $4xCO_2$. On instinct, James reached up and slowly moved the toggle that was set to the lowest setting up to the highest. He let out a low gasp as he watched at the little three-dimensional model of the East Coast below him. As the toggle moved up the little ocean began to rise in

The Beta

concert with a time stamp in the upper right-hand corner. It didn't take him long to figure out he was changing the projection of future sea rise as it related to CO_2 in the atmosphere.

"Put that back!" ordered the voice in his ear.

Hey obeyed and continued on his circuit of the room which revealed more screens, models, and data. One screen contained information from the National Climate Assessment, another by a man named Jim Hansen and another by the Intergovernmental Panel on Climate Change. Some of the models came with toggles he could switch and adjust. He bet those changes would be reflected in the three dimensional 'toys' laying in front of each.

He made it about two-thirds of the way around the room when he saw the door to the cottage begin to open. He also heard a gasp from one of his kidnappers and then his headset suddenly went black. They pulled the plug.

"That's enough for now." He could hear a bit of strain in her voice. Didn't she know they were going to find him soon enough? For the exact same reason they needed him and his biometrics to access Google Earth History, they were going to get caught. It was only a matter of time.

Mark and his wife were strolling through The Venetian hand in hand. They were here for work, but with most of the stressful jobs behind them they were looking forward to two more days to explore booths and mingle with other attendees. He heard an odd sound coming from his phone.

"What's that?" he mused out loud to his wife. They were both techie enough to have their phones completely silenced, nothing short of a presidential alert should be able to make it through the silence mode. Curious, Mark pulled out his phone to look. A red alert icon grabbed his attention, and immediately suspecting a hack, he pulled his wife over to the side of the grand hall. It was not an icon he was familiar with, but once opened he realized it was a parental medical alert from his son's virtual reality headset.

The Beta

"Well, that's odd?" he said out loud as a question, not really alarmed yet. With new tech all sorts of weird things could happen and Google Earth History was certainly new tech.

"What's up, babe?" his wife looked over his shoulder.

"Well, it says James's VR headset registered a medical event."

"What does that mean?" His wife's voice betrayed a slight hint of concern, though neither of them were prone to overreact without more data.

"Well, I think it's just a security precaution built into the VR equipment to notify supervising parties if it registers anything out of the ordinary. Heart rate, blood pressure etc." He turned toward his wife with a sudden realization. "Actually, I heard a rumor somewhere that the medical alert could be triggered by, uh, how should I say this . . ." he paused and looked around, "boyhood urges?"

"Are you serious!" she laughed out loud. Growing up in a family of girls, Eve wasn't as familiar as Mark was with teenage boys, but she understood what he meant. "Do you think he has a girlfriend?"

Mark shrugged, generally unsure of what his son was up to these days.

Speaking of girls, Eve looked around at the crowd passing by, utterly devoid of women. Grandmothers, girls, children, or any type of female form was not a common sight at CES. There were a few brave career women like herself but not enough to change the culture yet. CES was working hard to make that change, but the shift was neither easy nor fast. "I suppose this is why I've never wanted him to come to this event yet. I don't want him idolize a culture that hasn't found its way to honoring women yet. They'll get there someday."

"Oh, come on, it's not like the men here are purposely excluding women."

"No, but until women are really walking these halls in large numbers they won't have the influence on future technology that we need."

"We digress . . ."

"I'm already calling him."

214

The Beta

This argument was ongoing, one in which they didn't really have different goals, but they did have vastly different views of the current reality.

"No answer, will you try?"

"Yup"

"His phone says he's still at the house, I'll check the cameras next."

"He wouldn't answer me either."

They spent the next ten minutes trying to connect with their son and pouring over the house cameras, but everything looked normal.

"Would the VR medical alert give you more info or repeat if anything is really wrong?" she asked her husband.

"I'm not entirely sure, I think it is more of an experimental safeguard than anything else and I don't see any more data in the app. No second alert. I say if he doesn't get back to us by this evening we'll call a neighbor to go and check on him, ok?"

"Well, I suppose maybe you're right babe, maybe our sweet son was just getting a little extra exercise." She smiled sweetly

Mark put his phone in his pocket as they continued to walk hand in hand.

🌍

His hands hurt. James was left tied up and in the dark for another indeterminate amount of time, but now that he was fully aware and remembering his surroundings he knew where they were keeping him. Well, maybe not where, but how?

At first the constant music, lots of girly hippie stuff, drove him insane. Then as he was sitting, squished in his pillow throne, he could feel a jolt and he figured it out. The women were holding him in some kind of large vehicle and they were moving locations. That also accounted for the small VR space and the close proximity of the toilet and shower.

It also meant the chances of his parents finding and rescuing him would be a bit more complicated. He wondered when they would figure out he was gone. Hadn't they seen anything on the house cameras? It seemed like they had a zillion of them, or at least

The Beta

enough to dash any dreams of having a house party while his parents were out of town. Or preventing a kidnapping, for that matter. Had his parent's noticed his absence yet? Where in the world was he?

"Annie, where are you?" Kira muttered to herself. It was a Thursday morning and she felt so disconnected from everything. At least she had the whole day to figure things out before she was required to go into campus on Friday. Her parents were both at work and she had the house to herself.

A small part of her was tempted to drive to Annie's and figure out what was going on, but it would take at least a couple hours to drive there and back in Seattle traffic. Maybe she would drop by tonight if she still hadn't heard from her friend.

While her anxiety kept her up late into the night, it hadn't affected her ability to sleep in, so by the time she woke up it was almost eleven. She was still tired, still hungry, and still didn't have any answers.

Kira was leaving the bathroom when she paused to look at her image in the mirror. She examined all the details; the flyaway hairs, dirt in her pores, extra hairs under her untidy eyebrows, and the mild tightness that comes with lack of sleep and worry. Sometimes she wondered if volunteering for *The Beta* was a good decision. While in general she didn't regret anything—the software made her education so much more meaningful and worthwhile—there was still a trade off. A trade off of days, a trade off of space, a trade off of experience. This summer she was going to completely unplug, go to the Rez to visit her cousins and be her 100% real life self for weeks at a time.

But not yet.

She went to the kitchen and forced down a large glass of water, a bowl of cereal, and a banana. Then she used the bathroom one more time before heading into the garage. Her experience thus far had taught her to be prepared before putting on the headset. Thirst, hunger, and bathroom breaks were the three main things that interrupted the full immersion of VR. She would be totally

The Beta

engrossed in a task when all of a sudden she needed to pee, and it would ruin the whole effect.

Just like in her dreams, Kira would sometimes forget VR wasn't real life and she would go in search of a toilet before she realized where she was. In her dreams she would wake up suddenly, in VR she would take off her headset, thankful she hadn't peed all over the floor thinking the virtual toilet was real.

Nervous and excited, Kira pulled on her headset, bodysuit, thin gloves and controllers. She didn't need every piece of equipment but wearing as much as possible gave her the deepest sense of immersion. She felt truly present when her equipment was complete.

She said a quiet prayer over the day, over her family and over herself. Then she turned on the equipment and started Google Earth History. Every time the program loaded and she found herself floating in space next to the Earth, the moment automatically became a prayer for her planet. It was almost as if everyone in the world who used Google Earth History could now have the same feeling as those first astronauts who gazed down from the heavens.

Kira used voice activation to load her options and was soon zooming in over North America. The Puget Sound was on her left, the Columbia River straight below, and then within moments she was sitting outside of the Sx̌ʷnitkʷ Simulation.

One deep breath and she dived right in.

She was at her family's pit-house. This wouldn't be her pit-house anymore if technically she was now married to the cute piece of code turned Samuel Powell? Would he be here today? The code or the real life boy?

Impatient and wasting no time, Kira pulled up her aerial map and player layer so she could look for him and her grandmother. Both characters were immediately located and currently listed as NPCs—as they had always been. She sighed, why would they have tricked her that way and were they still doing it?

He was located closer than her grandmother, so Kira followed a common path through the village to the area where he should be. It didn't take long for her to come upon him. He was crouched with several men next to a fire.

The Beta

He stood up, smiled with that handsome expression and walked toward her in earnest, "Haʔ ṱiʔ kʷ xast ?" he asked her in Salish.

Her anger exploded in English, "You lied to me! Who are you?" She began to pace around him, as if somehow getting a good look at him from a different angle would reveal the truth.

"Sxílwiʔ," he replied, with what could have been authentic confusion.

Kira realized she had no plan beyond outright confrontation to try and figure out if he was a real life person or a computer generated piece of evolving code, so she tried anything that came into her head.

"Did you give me those white flowers yesterday?"

"scaʔákʷ ?" he still looked perplexed.

She picked up a rock and threw it at him. He looked hurt and rubbed his arm.

"Who are you?"

"Sxílwiʔ," his eyes flashed a little in annoyance. It was enough to make her even more suspicious and she moved closer to look deep in his eyes. If that Samuel Powell was hiding behind those eyes again Kira would punch him in the face. She should have checked the American Revolution simulation before coming here.

"Are you an NPC?" While the player layer was supposed to give her clarity on who was real and who wasn't, she had never thought of asking outright.

"Ki," he said.

Then she realized her mistake. Kira didn't even know if a real NPC should respond with a yes or should ask in return 'What is an NPC?' She was not aware of any protocol surrounding the response. So now either he was a real NPC answering as programmed or he was really Samuel Powel pretending to be him.

"Arrrrgh!" she screamed in an uncharacteristic lack of control and then threw a totally inexperienced punch with her right fist which he blocked. Her VR equipment couldn't provide the resistance to feel a block and her hand irl passed through his body. There was some latency in the simulation that made it look as though her fist was stopped in his palm and eventually her real life body reunited with her VR one. Interesting coding choice, she mused internally. Most simulations let your VR body glide through objects without resistance but this one penalized your VR form.

She played with it for awhile, air boxing all of her anger out on her lying virtual husband. Kira didn't really know how to fight but it felt good to pretend like she did.

"Kira!" her grandmother's voice used her real life name. Startled, Kira stopped in her tracks and slowly turned around.

"Stmtíma?," Kira reverted to Salish. Even though she had every right to be angry, Kira felt a little foolish and embarrassed to have been caught slugging it out on her husband.

"Kira, I am sorry I hid my true identity from you."

Kira could only stare. After so many months of obediently listening to her grandmother it was hard for her to hear the same voice speak English. Who was this woman?

"My name is Karen." She extended her hands out openly as if creating a safe nest for her words, "I have been working with several other tribal members to create the simulation with some degree of accuracy and honesty." She paused to look around. "Although I am the only one who goes in VR and does the actual coding."

"It's . . . it's beautiful," Kira responded cautiously, but inside joy welled up as she realized the woman in front of her was actually related to her. Even if Kira was only part Native American she still shared some DNA with her virtual grandmother.

"You were the first student to visit the simulation, you know." Her grandmother smiled, "Actually the only student to visit until that boy yesterday."

"Do you know him?" Kira asked too quickly. "Was he really real? How did he? How did you hide your NPC status?"

"That is still bothering me granddaughter." Her grandmother had unconsciously slipped back into Salish, but that concern in her voice was evident. She quickly reverted to English with as little thought. "Did you know him?"

The whole story came out. Slowly at first, but then Kira began to speak more quickly and allowed all of her hopes and fears to somehow creep out. She draped them plain as day on her person. Her husband, who must be an NPC at the moment, gave up on his

The Beta

attentions and joined the men at the fire. She and her grandmother ended up sitting side by side on an empty log.

Kira didn't know how much time passed, but everything suddenly felt right with the world. She wondered if her real life Lakes grandmother knew this woman? She was about to ask when her grandmother spoke again. "I found out who that boy is." she said.

"What?" Kira was diverted by the unexpected news.

"Well, you were as shocked as I was to find him in this simulation." Her grandmother's eyes drifted across the grass to the new husband. "It was strange because his permissions tag him as being both a student and a developer. From his real life picture he looks quite young." her grandmother looked at her slyly out of the corner of her eye, probably to judge her reaction to that tidbit.

"And?" was all Kira said.

"I called 911 and Google Earth History to report the event. They said they might get back to me, but there were no promises. Have you seen him back in the American Revolution simulation?"

"No, at least not yesterday. I haven't tried today, yet." Kira looked at the lines on her virtual palms. "I left him a message there."

Her grandmother stood up and looked down at her. "Let's go find him . . ."

"Babe, I still haven't heard back from James." Eve was looking down out of their hotel window along the Las Vegas strip, "I'm going to call Jack and see if he can check on him."

"Make sure to unlock the side door for him!" her husband yelled from the shower.

James's mom made the call with her earbud and sat on the hotel bed. Minutes later Mark came out of the bathroom and looked at his wife sitting upright on the edge of the mattress.

"What did Jack say?" he asked, as he lay on the bed and wrapped his form around his wife in a gentle embrace.

"He said he wasn't home right now but would be back in an hour or two."

The Beta

"That works." He laid there for a minute trying to think of a way to get her to stop worrying. "I'm hungry, let's go downstairs and get something to eat. Let's stop worrying until Jack has a chance to check things out. Maybe he smuggled a girl past the cameras and into the house. They'll be sitting on the couch and that's how Jack will find them."

🌐

"Go find him?" Kira asked, not really understanding what her grandmother had in mind.

"Yes, let's find him. He entered this simulation without our permission and under false pretenses on one hand. But you say this Samuel Powell was a pretty nice guy right?" She looked down at Kira for a response.

Kira bit her lip and nodded.

"So, either way, good guy or not, we need to figure out who he is and what he is up to."

She stood up, even though standing up wasn't actually required and asked her grandmother one more question. "Do you know his name, I mean his real name?"

"Oh, yeah, I had to search a bit more than I expected but I figured it out. His name is James."

"James?" Kira let the name sink in. She wasn't positive but she thought it was an Asian name. That was interesting. "OK, what do you mean *we* will look for him? How can *we*?"

Her grandmother smiled with a slight smirk of her eyebrow, "I am a developer and an educator, which means I have access to both edit Google Earth History and interact with the students in their simulations."

"Oh, that means you can follow me anywhere?"

"Yes"

"O.K. where to first?"

"Where do you think, my child? I only need a few more details from you."

The Beta

Mark had a full belly and his wife ate enough that he didn't feel the need to pester her to eat more. He was thankful when he heard Eve answer her phone.

"So, you're in the house now . . . is James there?"

There was a pause as his wife listened to Jack, but her frown lines didn't budge in relief so Mark stopped relaxing and sat up to give her his full attention. He still wasn't worried, but he didn't want her to worry either.

"Do you mind using video while you look around?" Eve asked, pulling out her phone.

Jeesh, thought Mark. His wife knew no bounds when asking friends for favors. But he didn't say anything and the couple wordlessly moved closer together on the restaurant booth so they could both see the video streaming.

Jack had lived in their neighborhood since he was a boy and now he was an old man, a favorite of everyone up and down the road. He was a good guy with a long, white mustache.

"It's nice to see you Jack," said Eve peering past Jack's shoulder into their empty house. Jack was standing in their kitchen and nothing looked amiss besides a few stray dishes next to the sink.

"Good to see you guys." Jack nodded his head at Mark and then turned his camera around to give the couple a more sweeping view.

"You said you already checked upstairs?" Eve asked.

"Yep, everything looks pretty normal."

"Did you go downstairs yet?" asked Mark. It was likely James was deep in VR and hadn't heard Jack enter the house. He didn't want his son to be startled but he might deserve the fright for not checking in with his mother more often.

"Not yet, heading that way."

The camera bounced down the stairs unevenly and then smoothed out a bit as their view rested on the VR room. Normally devoid of furniture anyway, it took them both a minute to notice.

"No James down here," Jack responded nonchalantly. Jack was a frequent visitor to their home but he hadn't spent much time in the VR room.

The Beta

"Jack," —Eve's voice was deeper than normal— "can you slowly pan the room?"

"Pan?" he hesitated for a moment, his hearing interfering with the meaning, but then appeared to have caught on. "Oh, sure, here you go."

The screen of their phone slowly wrapped from one end to the other and Mark mentally ticked off each missing item. No lighthouses, computer, black screen, empty armoire, and wires that were usually bunched around a charging station were conspicuously missing.

"I think I found something," said Jack, who was still unaware that what he was looking at was out of the ordinary.

"I think I found his phone."

🌑

The RV stopped about an hour later and James marked the moment with the song refrain that they were playing over and over about some monkey who had gone to heaven. Some weird song he had never heard before which oddly made him think of *The Monkey King*.

James heard more scuffling and whispering through the soundtrack. Sometimes he could make out what they were saying. He remained silent, pretending to be asleep in the hope that he would hear something they didn't want him to. Perhaps it was working as they slowly began to talk in higher tones.

"Why did you buy that?" the deep voice asked.

"I don't know! Why the hell would they put the book there if it didn't mean something?"

"Don't read too much into it, one of the Elves must have some childhood fascination with Christmas—that's all."

"Well, it's short. I am going to check it out anyway . . . in case."

"In case what? We had a plan. Stick to it!"

This was followed by a silence and James had a hard time regulating his breath. He could almost see them staring at one

The Beta

another, waiting for the other to back down and give in, a silent test of wills.

Suddenly the deep voice was inches from him, whispering in his ear. "Time to wake up handsome . . ."

James jerked up, fully awake now. His heightened senses could feel how close she was and the use of the word handsome was messing with him. Was she teasing him? Did she really think he was handsome? How old was she anyway?

He found himself slightly aroused by the compliment. Kind of like how he heard captives can fall in love with their captors. But even though their voices were enticingly female, it was all a mirage. Because of the headset permanently strapped on his head he had no idea what they looked like.

And deep down inside, all he could think about was Kira. She was real. He knew what she looked like, he knew her—her mannerisms, her voice, her likes and her dislikes. Then it hit him like a brick and a deep foreboding sense of accountability set in. He didn't really know Kira—he spied on her, joked with her, talked with her, and gave her anonymous presents, but irl they had never actually met. In fact, during those last minutes in VR when they were about to kiss he had cloaked himself in the shroud of an NPC so there was no way she would know that was him. She would never care for him the way he cared for her.

He was all alone.

Suddenly everything changed and became darker. Kira didn't know him, his parents hadn't even noticed he was gone, and a headset was duct taped on his head. James crawled deeper into his internal abyss.

The ropes that held everything together were loosening on his wrists as he lost his mind.

"Let's get to work." The deep-voiced one said while massaging his upper arms, then wrists, then hands. He could feel the fabric as she slipped a VR glove on his left hand. The last time he was connected the controllers were the only way he could interface with VR, but they must have nabbed his gloves. In combination with the controllers they would give him an ever-increasing

The Beta

accuracy over his virtual world. What did they have in mind for him today?

"Um, can I use the bathroom first?" he asked awkwardly. The VR glove on his right hand stopped suddenly, and then reversed.

"Yeah, he should probably eat something too," the far away one said. They often talked about him as though he wasn't there. Now he knew what it felt like to be ignored.

He was guided over to the toilet where he endured the embarrassment of knowing they were probably watching the whole thing. He couldn't see the toilet and only a brief touch with his hand to lift the seat up gave him any clues about where to aim. Feeling spiteful, James purposely aimed poorly, imagining at some point they were going to have to clean it all up.

"Hey, watch it!" the close one reprimanded him.

"Sorry," he muttered—not sorry at all. He went back and forth between calling them the 'close one and the far one' because so far they hadn't slipped and spoken their names out loud. In fact, they never spoke his name out loud either. Did they even know his name? Why did they pick him?

After the luxury of washing his hands he was plunked back down on his pillow throne and a paper plate with pizza was placed in his lap. He could smell the cheese.

He took a bite. "Cheese pizza again?" he complained, "Do you think I could get some, you know, fruits or veggies?" There was silence. James realized that whenever he caused that silence he was striking a nerve.

"Eat," was the one-word response that eventually came, along with a plastic bottle of water. They were in a hurry because after the pizza he was zipped up and jacked up into as much of his VR gear as he could possibly wear.

"Where are we going today?" he asked.

At that moment the white loading screen activated within his headset and the deep one came close. "Back to Santa's Workshop, baby." She was almost purring with anticipation.

James wondered if his biometrics would work on the lock again but surprisingly everything went smoothly and he was back on the short path leading to the village entrance in no time.

The Beta

He was instructed to take the road to the right. There was no sun shining on this winter village, but instead bright light behind a thick layer of high fog provided permanent day time weather.

He did the same as before, stopping at each house to inspect the sign and then peer inside the window. The first ten houses displayed signs with ancient life forms on the outside. James wished he remembered more about evolutionary taxonomy because he was fairly certain each house corresponded to a time period of evolution on Earth.

He wasn't surprised then when one of the signs was a hand painted cluster of dinosaurs. His ten-year old self checked the window as normal, but as soon as he verified there was no one inside he entered the building without his captors' permission.

"What are you doing? Get out of there!" the deep one barked.

"No, c'mon man, it's dinosaurs!" He turned his masked head in her direction to plead. "Just one little look?"

He jumped across the room and peered closely at one of the models. There were tiny dinosaurs running around an ancient landscape. If he leaned in close enough he could hear minute sounds emanating from the creatures as they wandered. Looking up above he learned that these models were based on the fossils and studies of the Late Jurassic Morrison Formation. He clicked on one study and as he did so the small model dinosaur rose slightly above the table model so he could see her in even greater detail. Additional studies and information popped up on screens all around for his viewing pleasure.

"That's enough," the deep one brought out the big gun again, or should he say the real gun. James was getting desensitized to the metal barrel on his skin. Captivity would do that to you.

🌍

VR equipment gone, phone left behind. Mark knew his son well and nothing was adding up. "Jack, could you check the rest of the basement? All of the VR equipment is missing. If you can't find anything I'm going to call the police." Eve's hand tightened on his wrist.

"Yeah, sure." They could hear Jack's breathing increase substantially and Mark all of a sudden felt bad about asking the old man to be in this situation.

He wracked his brain but he hadn't noticed anything out of the ordinary with James in the last few months, and he couldn't think of any reason James would move the expensive equipment. Eve pulled his phone out of his pocket while he continued to monitor Jack's inspection of the house. He watched Eve bring up their home cameras and start scrolling back in time to look for clues.

Jack's voice piped up "Nothing here Mark. I'll walk around the house to see if I notice anything."

"Thanks, Jack."

He whispered to his wife, "Do you see anything?"

"No, the last motion alert was last evening. It shows James returning to the house with take-out. Nothing out of the ordinary."

They sat in silence.

"Wait, you said the last movement alert was last night?" Mark traded phones with his wife and he stared scrolling himself. "Why isn't Jack registering? He entered the house twenty minutes ago and he's walking around the northside right now."

They carefully watched both screens, and sure enough, their security cameras were not matching what was happening in real life. Their system had some lag, but that lag was measured in seconds.

"Somehow our security system has been compromised." Mark whispered to Eve not wanting to scare Jack.

"Hey Jack, I think we're going to report this to the police and send them over to check things out. Do you mind asking around the neighborhood to see if anyone has seen anything?"

"Of course, Mark. Whatever I can do." Jack's voice was gruff. "I made a full round and nothing." Jack was using his phone to show as much of the landscape as possible. "I'll keep my phone close."

Eve spoke up, "Jack, stay on the phone till you're back on the road. We want to make sure you're safe."

"I'm fine Eve." Jack replied, but he stayed on the phone as asked.

The Beta

Mark and Eve didn't talk. She dropped three twenties on the table and they headed back to their hotel room. The Mountain View Police line was ringing.

🌎

Kira sat on Sarah Franklin-Bache's bed with her housekeeper beside her. All of her children surrounded them. Two were playing with a top in the corner of the room, one was jumping on the bed behind her, and the housekeeper was holding the youngest up high for examination.

"Even virtual babies," her grandmother paused to reflect, "are almost as cute as real-life babies." She cooed and played with the infant on her lap and looked closely at every detail. "We don't have many pictures of Indian babies to feed into our AI and I still haven't tried to gather images of modern Indian babies, so the kids in Sx̌ʷnitkʷ are based off the images I borrowed from other tribes." The two kids in the corner started arguing over the toy at the exact same time the one on the bed began whining for some milk which caused the infant to screw up her face in consternation, ready to cry out.

"They make them so life like!" her housekeeper/grandmother exclaimed.

"Thank you for coming here with me grandmother." Kira said simply. She was curious about her grandmother's frank appraisal of the American Revolution simulation.

"You know granddaughter, over 1,200 developers have worked together on this particular American Revolution simulation. It's like making a gigantic three-dimensional movie that runs for a whole month." Her grandmother soothed both the infant and the child on the bed while Kira settled the fight between the two oldest. "I could learn a lot by visiting other simulations more often, they show me the potential for my work."

"Your work is amazing grandmother."

"I am practically alone in the coding," she took the compliment with grace, "but the tribe is putting a lot of money behind the research, so there is lots of support and information. I need more people who can code."

The Beta

"Really?"

"Yes, if I can get even five tribal members who could code with me we could do so much more. There are three people I know who are taking the courses they need right now."

"Is that something I could do?" Kira asked, forgetting her grandmother didn't really know much about her.

"Perhaps."

"Where do you do your work?" Kira asked out of curiosity.

"Ohhh," her grandmother's eyes sparkled. "Out in the mountains near a lake. The tribe owns a resort and there was an old abandoned house behind the store. It has a big room that was all fixed up for the VR and lots of little rooms for research."

Kira sucked in her breath. She was fairly certain she knew exactly where her grandmother was referring, "Does that mean . . ."

The baby started crying loudly before Kira could get in her question.

"We need to get to work," her grandmother replied putting the baby in the cradle next to the bed before turning to the kids with a stern voice, "You three behave until we return, take care of the baby." She then walked out of the room and motioned Kira to follow her.

Kira hesitated. Even though the children in the room behind her were only virtual constructs, in Sarah Franklin-Bache's real life no one would have left those four young kids unattended. But her grandmother was right, between the crying and her grandmother's fascination they would never get to work if they stayed here.

Kira pulled up her player layer and her grandmother was still listed as an NPC. If any of the other students in the American Revolution simulation were to walk up to them now they would see her listed as such.

They walked out into Franklin Court, the weather was properly foggy but the garden was beautiful. They far enough away they could no longer hear the baby crying out the window.

"Ok, share what you know and let's try to learn about this boy." Her grandmother instructed. "Did he message you back?"

"No, and he isn't here right now either." Kira pulled up her internal menus and started to piece together the bits of information into tiny packages. The dates and times she spent with Samuel Powel, the time stamps and geo locations of the moments Samuel gave her flowers.

Her grandmother, dressed in 17th century clothing—it was so weird not seeing her in Native American garb—was also doing something with her internal screens. Kira wondered if the real world would soon be like this with mixed reality glasses. It was bad enough right now when half the people in public places had their heads cranked down into their phones. At least with mixed reality people's necks wouldn't get stuck looking down even if you couldn't tell who was really looking at who.

The two went on that way in silence for a bit when her grandmother spoke up. "I've found you, so now I am going to try and message your student profile. I can't actually connect with you from this NPC but since I have educational developer access I can still message you from my main profile."

Kira waited patiently for the message to arrive and then neatly attached all of the pertinent info in a reply.

Suddenly her grandmother's face grew cross. "Stay here Kira, I'll be back."

The housekeeper froze for a minute, and then deep below the code Kira could tell her grandmother was gone and the true NPC was back.

Her housekeeper looked around for a moment, almost confused. "Where are the children mistress?"

Irritated Kira gave a sharp reply, hiding none of her feelings. "They are waiting for you upstairs, go tend to them!"

Kira was tired of people freezing on her, tired of being left alone, and tired of waiting.

🌎

Mark was waiting on the phone with the police and Eve was on the phone with corporate headquarters. They were alternating between sitting on the hotel bed and a chair next to the single desk in their room. There was lots of waiting, questions, and angst.

The Beta

"No sign of a break-in?" Mark asked the officers who were inspecting the house.

Eve was on her computer talking with a manager who was able to access the software that controlled their home camera security system.

"Eve, the images you are seeing have been looped in from last week."

James's mom stood stock still. "What do you mean? How could that be?"

"It'll take me a few minutes but I'll be able to return them to live streaming."

"I don't care, the police are there now. What happened to the footage from today? Where is my child? How did this happen?" Eve knew the rapid fire of questions was useless, —the manager on the phone wouldn't be able to fix this right away—but it made her feel better.

"I don't know, Eve, but I'm working on it. I'll get my whole team to work on it."

"I know. Thank you. Let me know as soon as you find out anything."

Eve hung up and made airline reservations to get them back home. Mark was going back and forth with the police and looking over his wife's shoulder at the available flights.

An update on his phone blinked. "Thank you, Detective Reigns. Can I call you right back? I may have something on the other line. Thank you."

Eve looked up, "What is it?"

"A message from the Google Earth History Division." Mark tapped on the phone number hoping it was a direct line. He put it on speaker.

"Hello this is Jaleesa, Google Earth History Division." The young voice on the line answered professionally.

"Hi Jaleesa, this is Mark Chiu from DeepMind, I'm returning your message."

"Oh wow, nice to meet you, sir." the girl seemed a bit blown away. Mark was high enough up in the company to have some notoriety. "Yeah, we monitor the student accounts in Google Earth History being used for *The Beta* and a student account attached to

The Beta

your name registered a medical event earlier today and then went offline. However, I have good news, the user is up and online again and all stats look good. Normal heartbeat, blood pressure etc."

"What? Really?" Mark and Eve looked at one another.

"Yup, I can see the stats here in real time. Pulse 85, blood pressure 120/79."

"Well, thank you Jaleesa. Ask your manager to message me next week. We need to reflect on the whole process with medical alerts, it gave us quite a scare. We appreciate your help." Mark was already pulling on a jacket to head downstairs. Wherever his son was he was about to get the biggest talking to in his life for scaring them like this, even if the admonishment was delivered in VR. What was James thinking moving the VR equipment? Probably showing off for friends somewhere. Mark was livid, that was company equipment.

"One more thing, sir." Mark didn't even hear Jaleesa, but Eve did.

"Yes, Jaleesa," Eve spoke up loudly to garner Mark's attention.

"We got another call from an educator-developer who was concerned with your son. She said she was in the simulation when his medical alert went off and was worried about him."

Mark looked impatient. "Call her back, Jaleesa, assure her that everything is fine."

"Will do sir." Jaleesa responded.

"Wait," Eve interrupted." Can you give us the educator's contact info?"

"Mark?"

"I'm going down to the pavilion Eve. Whatever James is up to he's in big trouble, big trouble with me."

"The flight leaves in three hours?" Eve sighed, but her worry warped from fear for her son's life to the general hopelessness a mother feels when her child makes bad adolescent decisions. "Should we keep it? I can do the packing."

"Keep the flight."

"Do you want me to call Detective Reigns?"

"Not until I figure out exactly what the hell is going on."

🌐

The Beta

After the disobedience with the dinosaurs James followed directions again like a good little boy. Looking at signs and looking in windows. If only he was here of his own accord. Even his father who had access to more secrets than James could imagine, was not allowed into Santa's Workshop.

About fifteen houses later James found himself looking at a hand painted wooden sign that reminded him of that ride at Disneyland called 'It's a Small World.' There was a circle of painted dolls holding hands, different clothes and skin tones represented a diverse culture of people.

He rubbed the foggy window to get a closer look, pondering the wet spot on his mitten that continued to grow authentically with the number of windows wiped.

Inside the cottage were little toy dolls and it was devoid of any glowing real people.

"Go inside," the deep voice ordered.

James walked inside boldly, no longer really caring if he was caught, almost wishing he was. This was getting old and he was ready to be rescued.

They asked him to walk around the room, inspecting different dolls and their information panels. He looked with curiosity at the Asian dolls as he passed them. There seemed to be dolls representing different time periods and geographic regions. Almost as if someone had taken a map of all the recent evolutionary knowledge and created a timeline of dolls to represent that information.

"Stop there," deep voice instructed.

James was now standing in front of a small African-American doll. There were two of them actually, a man and a woman. Both were about twelve inches tall and were making small, almost imperceptible movements. All of the dolls in the cottage were dressed in plain underclothes almost mimicking modern swimsuits so you could see all of their features and smooth skin.

"Bring up the info panel."

James pulled up the information behind the dolls and all at once a huge plethora of screens erupted on his internal view. Starting at the left he focused his VR view on each one. He had no clue what they wanted to learn, and they often chided him for going too fast, too slow, or needed to look again at some passage or control before moving along to the next. He could imagine the far away one scrunched up next to some screen reading everything he saw.

Then he heard her voice from across the room. "We start here. Do you see the lever on the upper right-hand corner of the screen?" she asked.

"Yes," James replied, and he put his VR glove next to the lever to demonstrate his understanding.

"Pull down on the lever until the number beside it reads 67."

James slowly began pulling.

"No let's go to 64."

As he pulled on the lever the size of the right ears on each doll began to decrease in size. What the heck were these women up to?

"Now go to panel seven and increase that dial to 89%."

James did as asked and he saw the noses on each doll grow in size. It was like he was being directed to change his avatar in a role-playing game.

He was asked to make several more changes, most of them were aimed at making the faces and bodies of the dolls less symmetrical, and the last instructions had him furrowing eyebrows and increasing frowns. The little dolls in front of him, looking into the distance and unaware of his presence, became angry little ugly creatures.

It was then that it hit him. He knew exactly what they were doing.

He was not going to be a part of this. Soon they were going to have him super slanting the Asian eyes.

"You racist bastards!" he said out loud.

Then, not really knowing why he chose her instead of 911, James shouted out as quickly as he could, "Teacher, American Revolution Simulation, Send Message to Sarah Franklin-Bache that says 'Help! I've been kidnapped.'"

He closed his eyes but he didn't have to. The far one pulled the plug, the close one tackled him to the ground roughly, yelling and threatening him. Within minutes he was tied up again and this

The Beta

time he was left unceremoniously on the ground. The RV was moving and the music was up full blast again.

As he prayed Kira got the message, and could make sense it, James heard another set of lyrics repeat over and over again. Something to do with a woman named Greta and her gun.

Well, one thing was for certain. His captive had a gun. James didn't have to call her the deep one or the close one in his head anymore. Her name would now be Greta to him.

Mark headed downstairs, through the Venetian and into the Expo Hall. The Google Earth History pavilion was crowded as usual. There were six stations set up, four for the CES participants and two with employee only demos that required biometric access. He flashed his company credentials, and then when he received pushback he very quietly and honestly explained the situation.

Bewildered but convinced, the tech running the show bumped off the current employee and Mark strapped on the headset and controllers. They were not a perfect fit but they would do in a pinch.

After scanning his irises Mark accessed his developer view and then searched for his son's developer code. Immediately James's location in Google Earth History was acquired and a small blue pin appeared. Mark clicked and headed directly to the pin. With ever increasing speed he found himself flying over ice on the north side of the planet. Closer and closer until his avatar stopped dead in its tracks.

The pin was pointing toward the North Pole. Opening the dev menu Mark saw the pin move more specifically toward one particular icon.

Santa's Workshop.

James was inside Santa's Workshop, a place that only a limited number of people worldwide could access. Mark, as high up as he was in Deep Mind, didn't have access to Santa's Workshop. The

The Beta

Google Earth History Division kept that under wraps even as they gave the general developers free license.

"What are you doing in there son?" Mark said under his breath.

Suddenly, the blue pin disappeared. James must have logged off.

Mark opened his messaging system and sent James a simply worded note.

Go home now. You are in big trouble.

He slipped off the headset and handed it back to the employee who was looking quizzically back at him.

"Thanks," was all Mark said before he stepped off the showroom platform.

Santa's Workshop. Mark knew exactly who to call.

🌐

Kira waited twenty minutes in the American Revolution simulation before becoming exasperated with her grandmother. Then she realized she didn't have to wait around for her. Since Karen messaged her through her general student/teacher controls, it was much like how Professor McKenzie could reach her if necessary. Kira would be able to message her grandmother back and forth at will. It wouldn't take the extra step of entering the simulation.

Kira had separate mail boxes for each separate simulation and a main mailbox for school. For example, her classmates at *The Beta* in Seattle could message her anytime, but those students she met in American Revolution could only message her in the American Revolution simulation unless they willingly exchanged contact info. The extra layer was intended to prevent harassment in case you didn't want to connect with those you simulated with.

Kira sent her grandmother a quick message asking her to respond when she returned, checked one more time to see if

The Beta

James/Samuel Powell was around, and then moved back into the open space floating above Earth.

What experience would center her, what simulation would bring her strength? Well, if she couldn't help herself at least she could help Harriet Tubman free slaves. Once again Kira wondered if using African-American simulations as therapy was the worst kind of cultural appropriation. A sudden but self-imposed burden settled on her soul. Hopefully she would someday be able to make it up to those she wronged.

There were hints that this next task would be more difficult than the last but Kira was up for the challenge. She melted down into the 19th century Eastern Seaboard and opened up as task titled "Poplar Neck, Christmas Eve 1854."

It only took her a few minutes to read through the player prep information and she was surprised to find her part was to play the role of Ben Ross, Harriet's father. Kira looked down the list of actions her character Ben Ross would need to complete in order to finish the simulation successfully. It was an odd list: meet with Harriet and his sons, lead them to the Leverton's safe house, avoid looking at his sons, not tell his wife Rita, and successfully respond to inquisitors. Not look at his sons? How was he supposed to lead his sons to freedom but not look at them?

Kira was almost ready to pause the simulation and do some research before making her first attempt, but like refusing to use a video game walk through, the ability to complete a simulation successfully without much outside help was always more satisfying.

She found herself sitting down to a Christmas dinner across the table from a sad looking woman who must be Rita Ross, Harriet Tubman's mother. The somber expression was understandable, her three sons slated to go on the auction block the following morning but Rita had originally hoped they would be visiting for Christmas dinner. Instead, she and Ben were eating the meal alone, and Ben couldn't tell her the truth.

Outside in the corn crib, right within view of the dinner table, Harriet and her three brothers were peeking through a slat watching their parents eat. It was all Ben could do to not tell his wife Rita how close her children were to them at this moment.

The Beta

The meal finished, Ben/Kira hugged his wife wordlessly and went to stand on the porch in the dark as evening had long since faded into night. Everything about the sky was ominous. Yet Kira still didn't understand how he was supposed to not "see" his boys as he helped them on their way. He approached the corn crib without looking too closely and as he heard a gate swing open he was grateful to find it was Harriet who stepped out first.

She was silent, the whole world was quiet, even the crickets. Ben could barely make it out but Harriet was offering him something so he reached out and took the item out of her hand. It was floppy like a fish and because Kira couldn't 'feel' it with her VR gloves it took her longer than normal to realize she was looking at a piece of cloth. That's when it all made sense in Kira's head.

She reached up and use the cloth to wrap around her/his head trying her best to tie a knot. It was pretty ridiculous on many levels. Because Kira couldn't feel the cloth through her VR gloves there was really no way to tie a knot, but she tried it anyway and was rewarded with a firmly secured blindfold. It was also insane that irl Kira put on a VR headset that blocked out all real-world light, which was replaced with a virtual world, which now was completely dark.

All Kira was left with was a jerk on her glove that must be Harriet's hand and the whisperings of Ben's boys as they made their way to a safe house. Kira realized he could see out of the bottom of the blindfold and not far into their journey Harriet took it off, motioning that his boys were making their way in the woods parallel with the road. Kira realized that all this trouble was so that Ben Ross would be able to answer honestly when the slave owners came to question him later. "Have you seen your sons?" they would ask, and then Kira/Ben would be able to honestly reply, "No". Kira admired Ben's logic as she wasn't much of a liar herself, even when it was for a righteous cause.

There were a few different intervals of blindfoldedness and periods of time walking side by side with his daughter Harriet. Standing in the shoes of Harriet Tubman's father forced Kira to think about Harriet in a different light. As she stared down at Harriet Tubman, Kira imagined a father's love for his brave daughter—how as a father he knew and cared for her since she was

The Beta

an infant. In this small way Kira's love and admiration for Harriet grew as well.

They approached the back of a house which he/she assumed was the Leverton's, the end of the road for his journey. Unbeknownst to Ben and Rita, Harriet would eventually return to free her parents and they would spend many future Christmas dinner together in Canada.

He could hear his sons pass by, leaving the woods and entering the house. The real Ben Ross would be imagining that this was the last time he may ever hear his sons' footsteps.

Once the brothers were safe from his view, Harriet pulled the blindfold off Ben and looked up at her father. This would be one of the many times she would say goodbye.

Yet when Kira looked down at Harriet she couldn't help gasp loudly, totally out of place with their need for quiet secrecy during the escape.

This wasn't Harriet Tubman in front of her. Kira knew Harriet's face well from the simulation. This person displayed an ugly scowl overlaid upon a jutting chin and uneven features. Kira jumped back several paces and the stranger followed, reaching out and whispering something she couldn't hear.

Shaking, her thoughts were interrupted by a gentle ping. Kira had enabled the sounds on her message notifications, and with a quick glance she was able to tell it was her grandmother asking her to return to where they left off in the American Revolution simulation. Thankful for a reason to leave Kira didn't even try to save her progress.

It only took a matter of minutes to logout and login to the Amerian Revolution Simulation, but the whole while Kira felt deep down in her bones that something was wrong. Something was obviously wrong with Harriet Tubman, she looked so different than when they last met.

Those feelings made Kira feel self-conscious. For years white people had described African-American, Native Americans, and Asians as 'different looking' and ascribing them negative features like angry, mean or haughty. Was this some type of deep and insidious racism rising in her? Self-reflection could be so difficult.

The Beta

When she joined her grandmother in the American Revolution Simulation she loaded right in front of the Franklin house inside the courtyard.

But she didn't get any more time to think because her grandmother was staring at her, also cranky looking and cross. "Why didn't you wait for me?"

"I'm sorry." Kira replied.

She sniffed in irritation, "I have good news. The representative from Google Earth History called me back and James's parents confirmed he is ok."

"Oh! Good." Kira was looking over her grandmother's shoulder at a man working in the garden bed, tending some flowers.

"Since he is ok, I think I should stop snooping around here and get back to Sx̌ʷnitkʷ."

"Oh, ok . . . um," Kira wasn't even paying attention to her grandmother. She was walking closer to the gardener to get a better look at his features. His name was King and he was a personal servant of Ben Franklin's.

"Kira!"

She looked into King's face. It was an angry, mean, ugly face. This was not the face of the King she knew.

ding

She needed to turn off the message notifications. She hated being interrupted.

But the little envelope distracted her from King's face when she realized it was from Samuel Powel.

"He sent me a message grandma!" Kira exclaimed. Her grandmother turned toward her, listening.

Kira read it aloud. "It says, '*Help, I've been kidnapped.*'"

It didn't sink in for either of them as it wasn't what they were expecting. "Grandma? Why would he say that?"

"I don't know. I'm sure the authorities at Google Earth History know the truth. After all, the representative said she talked to his parents."

The Beta

"Grandma? Can you find him? Like find him anywhere in the world?"

"Well, I hadn't thought of that but I think so. Give me a minute."

Kira turned away from King but something was still bothering her about how he looked and how Harriet looked. As she waited for her grandmother's response she typed a quick message back to James/Samuel Powell. *Where are you? Are you ok? How can I help? Meet me where we sew buttons.*

"He isn't currently logged in." her grandmother replied.

"A second ago he was here, he must have been in order to send me that message."

Her grandmother was looking thoughtfully up at the large tree in the middle of Franklin Court. "Can you forward that message? I'm going to call the rep back to let her know what you found," she said while turning to look directly at Kira. "I am sure he is fine and I'll double check for you." She put her arms protectively on Kira's shoulders. "You look tired granddaughter, even through all these virtual layers I can see what you feel."

Kira nodded in agreement. She was suddenly curious to know who was taller irl, her grandmother or her. If they were irl who would be looking up to who?

"Why don't you take a break. Go outside wherever you are and look at trees. Where are you from again?"

"Redmond, right outside of Seattle."

"Oh yes, you aren't that far from me technically, aye?"

"No, not that far," and *I'm related to you* Kira thought. But it wasn't the right time to share that. Not yet.

"Will you be back at Sx̌ʷnitkʷ tomorrow?"

"Oh," a shadow crossed Kira's face, "On Fridays I have to go to the Microsoft campus with my cohort, so I won't have time to visit Sx̌ʷnitkʷ till later in the evening."

Her grandmother paused thoughtfully, "Will you meet me later in the evening then, so at least I can give you word of James?"

"Yes, grandma, what time?"

"Let's say seven."

The Beta

Kira had her own favor to ask, and while it was a bit impertinent she doubted her grandmother would be mad. "Grandma, how will I know it is you?"

"Oh, my child. I am so sorry." she smiled down at Kira, "From now on I will make sure to login as myself. In fact the next time I meet you in Sx̌ʷnitkʷ you will see the real me."

"What do you mean grandmother?"

"Oh, you'll see. Tomorrow then."

"Wait!" but her grandmother froze suddenly and her NPC housekeeper returned.

🌐

Mark entered the hotel room still on the phone to find Eve with several nearly full suitcases on the bed. She looked at Mark as he entered but she could tell from his expression that she would learn more from listening to his conversation then interrupting with a question.

"I don't know how he got in and I certainly don't know why, Doug. That's why I'm calling you." Mark sounded frustrated. "Honestly, I don't know where he is. He must have taken all the equipment."

Eve decided to interrupt. "What about the cameras?" she whispered in his ear.

"And Doug, we checked in with the Nest Division and someone with internal access switched out our house cameras with old footage. Is that something James could have done from home?"

Mark's face got darker. "Eve, who did you speak to at Nest?"

"Hannah,"

"Her name was Hannah," Mark relayed the information. It was quiet again while Mark listened.

"Our neighbor and the police saw no sign of forced entry. Doug, I can't go there yet, even though suspecting my own son isn't making much sense at this time either."

Eve finished adding the last items to her purse so she sat down to squeeze Mark's hand.

The Beta

"Thanks, Doug. The detective's name was Reigns. Feel free to call him if you need to. Text me in the air if anything happens while we're flying. Can you meet me at the office when we land?"

Mark hung up and looked at his wife. "James was in Santa's Workshop. He logged out but I left him a message. James must have done something stupid. He's going to be in so much trouble, and so are we. I don't know how he possibly could have gained access. Santa's Workshop is the most tightly controlled project at Google."

The flight from Las Vegas to San Francisco was only a couple of hours. Eve stared at the dark trees below.

🌎

Kira did as her grandmother requested. She took off her headset and walked outside their home. The sky was cloudy but the trees were still a vibrant green. Thick, wet, sweet-smelling trees. She stayed outside, walking through the woods of their half-acre parcel. It wasn't huge but the light rainforest made it seem secluded.

She saw her mom drive up the driveway with her little sister and her dad arrived shortly after. Dinner was Thai food take out, the paper boxes spread out all over the table—Kira was feeling a little better after all the excitement of the last few days.

They were all still eating when the doorbell rang. She and her parents exchanged triangulated glances that asked *who is that and who is going to get the doorbell* at the same time.

"I'll get it," Kira offered, feeling energetic and thankful. She opened the front door which was hidden from the dining room.

It was the principal from her old high school.

Oh crap thought Kira. She knew who the principal was but had never talked to him, never had a reason to.

"Kira?" he asked, almost as a question even though it was obvious he knew who she was. "Are your parents home?"

Her dad was already right behind her.

"I'm Kira's dad, can I help you?"

"I'm Mr. Cavanaugh. There have been some issues with cheating at the school and I would like to talk to you and Kira."

The Beta

"C'mon in, let me get my wife."

Kira's dad led them into the living room, opened the dining room door and beckoned to his wife. Her little sister was preoccupied with a tv show and wouldn't require any supervision.

Kira walked slowly to the couch, back to the same place the FBI questioned her earlier.

Mr. Cavanagh didn't waste any time explaining himself and her recent experience with the FBI made them less suspicious of his request to ask questions. "Do you spend time with a student named Kevin?"

Now Kira was the deer staring into a Jeep's fog lights. "Uh, yeah."

"So I was having a chat with Kevin yesterday and he told me that you used to help him buy cheat sheets, answers for his chemistry tests."

Kira's heart stopped. That bastard. "I . . ."

Her parents were looking at her curiously now, and it was not a good type of curiosity.

"Kira," her dad said. He didn't need to say much.

Obvious tears came just to the surface. Making a last ditch calculated call, figuring Lahn was screwed already, she confessed simply. Maybe Lahn was taking the fall and Annie could get off. Lahn would do anything for his twin.

"Yes, I . . . thought Kevin liked me and he pressured me into getting him answers . . . " she let that hang there for a moment, hoping there was some measure of sympathy that would stop the conversation there.

"And who did you get the cheat sheets from?"

The tears began their trickle and Kira's headache was immediate.

"From Lahn," she said, hoping it was the right decision.

Principal Cavanagh left without much sense of closure. He explained that the student handbook wasn't really clear when it came to their new collaboration with *The Beta*. There would be some type of consequence but he would need to consult with the other administrators and professionals to see what would be appropriate. At this point, he was happy with her cooperation.

The Beta

Her parents however, were not happy in any way, shape or form. After a half-hour of crying and yelling, her parents grounded her indefinitely and took away all access to electronics. No computer, no phone, no use of family electronics and worst of all she saw her dad boxing up her VR equipment.

"But what about school tomorrow?" she pointed out logically.

Her parents exchanged glances. "You can attend Professor McKenzie's class tomorrow. But you return home immediately to continue your grounding."

Ok, Kira was ok with that. Her parents hadn't turned completely unreasonable. She ran up to her room and sat on her bed looking out her window. Like her grandmother said, it was time to look at the trees. The gentle wafting of leaves calmed her down. Losing her electronics wasn't the worst thing in the world after all.

If only her parents knew. There was so much they didn't. You know nothing Mom and Dad.

His parents must know nothing of his disappearance. He wasn't exactly sure how long since he was abducted from his house. 24 hours? 36? 48? James kicked himself for not paying attention to the time and date on his computer when they put him in VR the last two times. It was sitting right there in front of him the whole time and he hadn't the sense to pay attention.

It may be the smallest detail that ended up saving his life. He needed to start paying attention to the small details.

The only detail he seemed to be able to concentrate on was the annoying music. Something about traffic jams and beach sand were the current lyrics stuck in his head. He wasn't sure how many songs were on their playlist but it was definitely on repeat.

The current song finished and was replaced with something quieter. Suddenly James realized he could hear their conversation.

"We knew this was going to happen pretty quickly and we have a plan. We're fine."

"I know, but it was nice not to have to worry."

"Do you think they'll try to cut access?"

The Beta

"Not if they want him back they won't. We made that clear already and he'll do it again in person."

"We're almost there."

"One last time, one hour and we're out."

🌐

Mark and Eve didn't talk much on the plane as it chased the sunset into the west. They were frequent fliers and nothing about the trip felt out of place other than the deep, gnawing lack of knowledge about their son's whereabouts.

Either he was in really big trouble (with them) or he was in *really* big trouble. Waiting through something as normal as the flight into San Francisco was excruciating.

Mark's phone lit up and he was on it. The text read, *he's up to no good. I am waiting at the office*

What the heck, Mark thought to himself. James was a good kid. What in the world could have caused him to do something crazy like this? Mark didn't even begin to think about the consequences to his own career. They didn't matter to him at this point, but his son did.

🌐

This time when they connected the VR the cold metal muzzle stayed near his neck, and Greta was holding on to his arm so tightly he thought he was going to lose circulation. They meant business.

"What do you want me to do?" he asked before the application loaded.

"Open your messages."

This order surprised him. He couldn't erase the message he sent to Kira/Sarah Franklin-Bache. What did they think would happen? Eventually, even if it took a few days for his parents to return from CES and discover his absence, his developer access would be turned off. He still didn't know how the heck they got him into Santa's Workshop. Once that access was gone he wouldn't be a valuable captive.

The Beta

There were three new messages. That surprised him. He started at the bottom and worked his way up and Greta didn't object. The first message shocked him because it was from his father.

"It's my dad," he told them out loud as he opened the message. "He says I need to go home now and I'm in big trouble."

The impact of that assumption hit them all at the same time. James's parents didn't yet know he had been kidnapped.

"Open the second."

The second was from Kira and he held his breath as he read her message. She wasn't mad, she probably didn't know he was the one who tried to kiss her at Sx̌ʷnitkʷ, and he needed to get to The Cliffs. The last part of her message said *meet me where we sew buttons* and that was at The Cliffs in the American Revolution. How the hell was he going to get to The Cliffs? He wasn't exactly sure which of those internal statements about how Kira felt were true, but he was suddenly filled with hope and testosterone.

"What is Sarah Franklin-Bache to you?" asked the far one.

He realized they didn't see her real name on the current screen and he was relieved. "She's a friend, we've been hanging out in the simulation."

"Hmmph," said Greta.

James wasn't sure what to make of that remark.

"OK, now open the third one," This one was from a name he didn't recognize. It read . . .

Quit messing around kid. Come on home and stop worrying your parents. If you get back soon we'll find a way to forgive and forget. - Doug

He couldn't tell who Doug was from the current screen, but it was obvious to him and his captors that everyone thought he ran away. Everyone thought he was goofing off. Then it struck him. Everyone probably thought he was a racist if they saw that last foray into Santa's Workshop.

The elation from seeing Kira's response disappeared and a nice thick knot formed in his stomach.

The Beta

They were making their way through the airport to the car. Mark was hurrying despite dreading their destination, and Eve was struggling to catch up.

She stopped to take a call and had to raise her voice to get Mark to notice.

"What?" she repeated into the phone. "Thanks for letting me know." Eve motioned for Mark to join her. "We're heading into the office. I hate to ask this of you, but is there any way you can stay late and meet us? We are connecting with Doug at the GE History Division in about 45 minutes."

Eve hung up and looked up at Mark, "We need to call Detective Reigns."

The credentials they carried sailed them through several checkpoints to a highly modern Mainframe.

They found Doug on the north end of the Mainframe. The Mainframe was a play on words yet quite literal. Huge beams were used to raise the provide the supports for such a large VR room. Up to 30 developers could work seamlessly within the space at one time. Tracking covered the entire space and a Developer could run almost the length of a football field without having to reset their location. There was nothing like it in the entire world.

The Mainframe was open day and night, and while Mark couldn't expect complete privacy he was thankful to see that everyone was so preoccupied with their work they probably wouldn't notice them. Looking around at the back screens he could tell at least half of the developers in this room were working on projects based in Santa's Workshop.

Doug strapped in and Mark could see him walking through some gates into a snowy forest on a screen nearby.

A youngish girl walked up to them as they approached. "You must be Mark and Eve?"

They nodded in acknowledgement. "You must be Jaleesa?"

"Yeah, I already told Doug what I knew. He has a few people working on the leads," she pointed to the two stations next to them, "and you said a detective from Mountain View was coming in too?"

The Beta

Mark was thankful for the rapid pace of the response. He should have known someone messing around with Santa's Workshop would get immediate attention. They would need more help before this was over.

Eve walked over to Jaleesa. "Show me the message."

"I think you can view it best here," Jaleesa walked Eve over three stations. The room was covered in a variety of wall mounted screens and sit-down pods where collaborators could view what developers were doing in real time. While developers immersed in VR could roam the room freely, many of them stuck close by their initial stations if they were working with the help of a team. Eve could tell the woman in front of them was the one whose motion matched the screen. Her long brown hair was tied up in a braid to fit neatly under the head set.

On the screen Eve could see a Native American tribe involved in some ceremony, probably a wedding, as the scene focused on two young people in the center of the group.

"Your son sent the message to a kid from Seattle, probably a friend or someone he met through a simulation. Barbara is reviewing their interactions right now to try and figure out what their relationship is all about."

Eve was startled, "I thought James would have contacted Mark." She looked puzzled as the image of a young Native man froze and the girl looked with confusion at her interrupted kiss.

"Found it!" said the woman named Barb. She marked the moment and then pulled off her headset, "Doug, I found the moment his signal was first interrupted. I'm going to get Chase on the IPs."

Barbara whipped her hair around and wiped the sweat off her brow. It was then she caught Eve's eye. She looked back and forth from Eve to where Doug still had his headset on.

"What did you find?" Eve asked. "I'm James's mom and I'd like to know."

Jaleesa jumped in before Barbara could reply, "We've been in contact with an educator from Washington State, a woman named Karen. She phoned in to Google Earth History and expressed concern over a medical alert she witnessed on a student in her simulation." Both Jaleesa and Barbara pointed at the screen where

The Beta

the young man was frozen, his mouth slightly open as the kiss he was expecting never came.

Eve blushed for her son, "is that him?"

They nodded in unison as well and Barbara continued. "I just found the exact visual moment of when the medical alert was initiated." She used the touch screen in front of her to rewind and then let the scene play while she pointed out specifics. "That older woman there is the avatar used by the educator who was checking on the medical alert, and that avatar there is the one used by a girl named Kira. James contacted her via message with the text . . . " it took a moment for Barbara to pull up another side screen with a screenshot of the message.

help! I've been kidnapped.

"But it's even more complicated than that. The message was sent to Kira's avatar in another simulation, an American Revolution simulation. I haven't reviewed their interactions in that one yet but I know he was part of the same simulation."

"How did the girl contact us?" Eve asked.

"It was the educator Karen again. I think Kira told her and she reconnected with Jaleesa."

"Eve!" Mark yelled.

She ran across the twenty feet of empty space between them and Mark pointed at a screen where Doug was running through the streets of a winter village.

"So that's Santa's Workshop?" Eve asked. She looked over to where the real-life Doug was jogging across the floor. The sensors informed him if he got too close to other developers but the space was so big they didn't often impinge on one another's presence.

"James's back online. He doesn't have the capabilities to track in Santa's Workshop."

"Where was that?" she asked her husband.

Mark's brows furrowed as he pulled up and expanded a side screen on the nearest monitor. There she saw a figure dressed in warm gear manipulating screens in front of two small dolls.

"What is all that?" Eve asked, obviously confused. Santa's Workshop didn't make much sense to her at the moment. If James had been kidnapped, what did the kidnappers want?

The Beta

"He's logged in three times since his signal left the house and we have a team trying to track down the location. The last time he was inside, his avatar began manipulating these two figures. They are the blueprints, the basis for western and central African figures in Google Earth History. He manipulated the models to make them less symmetrical." Mark stopped there and sucked in a deep breath.

Less symmetrical? Eve didn't make the connection at first but then it slammed down hard, "Do you think he's been kidnapped by racists? But even if they could change history, change perceptions of a whole people, the changes will never stick. What could they ever hope to accomplish?"

That's when they saw him. The avatars in Santa's Workshop were drawn from developer's real-life images and the image of their son in Virtual Reality startled both of them.

"Now let's get to work. Go to Santa's Workshop, head to the same place we left last time." Greta's instructions were clear and rough. "They might figure out you are here but they don't know everything yet."

It sucked to be in such a small space. James had to keep manually jumping ten feet ahead and that always made him a little nauseous after a while. At least back home he could stretch his legs by walking the length of the room. Like many places in Google Earth History, Santa's Workshop restricted how fast you could travel from place to place and teleporting long distances was not allowed.

They weren't as paranoid about running into other people as they were before and James brushed past two developers on his way to the cottage. Neither looked at him with more than a passing interest.

The cottage was empty and all the little dolls were moving ever so slightly like before.

"Start with the figures on the right. Same first step, move the lever to 64%"

The Beta

"Summer? We want 64 percent right? Did we decide that was the final figure?"

There was a silence. It took James a moment to understand the significance of the moment as he was concentrating on the lever. Greta, or whoever she was, called her partner by her real name. The other one's name was Summer.

He ignored it, hoping they would too, and asked. "What next?"

Greta replied, "Go to panel seven and increase that dial to 89 percent"

He was then instructed to go to every set of dolls in the room and repeat the exact same instructions. The dolls became lopsided, mismatched, ugly, and bulbous. Sometimes they instructed him to make the ears bigger and sometimes the nose, but always the forehead and brows were pulled into wider and angrier protrusions.

James was now genuinely confused after completing three-fourths of the room. When he first edited the African dolls, he was positive his captives were working with racist intent. Now he wondered if misanthropy was at the heart of their evil plan. Since he was changing both female and male dolls equally, sexism was not likely the root cause.

So intent on his work and thoughts, James was caught up short by a tall man standing next to him.

"James?" asked the man.

Greta pressed the cold muzzle against his neck. "Who is that?"

"I don't know," James stuttered, "Who are you?"

"My name is Doug," the man paused. "What are you doing here?"

"Working," whispered Greta.

"Working," repeated James.

"How did you get in here?" asked the man.

Greta was only breathing hard, not giving him instructions, so he followed her lead and kept on breathing.

"I repeat, how did you get in here?" The gig was up, his captors had to understand.

"I work here," whispered Greta. "I work here," repeated James, at first using a whisper but then after realizing what he was doing he spoke up clearly.

The Beta

"No, you don't, where the heck are you, James? Your parents are worried sick!"

"I . . ."

Greta finally spoke up, "Tell them the truth now, James. You've been taken hostage, you don't know where you are, and they will need to keep your Workshop access if they want you back alive."

James wished they would just tell Doug themselves. Greta could put her mouth to the microphone and say everything, "Why don't you tell them?" he asked Greta even though Doug was sure to hear.

"Tell them what?" Doug asked.

"Tell him NOW!" Greta said in her whisper hiss.

"I've been taken hostage, I don't know where I am, and you will need to keep my workshop access if you want me back alive."

Doug stared at James and began to ask more questions as fast as he could but James couldn't concentrate enough to understand them. Greta was pushing, and pointing, and pulling him back irl.

"Tell him one more thing, James . . . tell him if they change any of the work you've done . . . we'll make changes to you. You may go back to them alive but you won't come back whole."

🌍

Mark and Eve were watching the screen in real time. They were huddled over a pair of headphones that gave them audio, one ear tucked into each side.

They looked at one another after James uttered the last sentence and then his avatar disappeared into thin air. There were no NPCs in Santa's Workshop.

Doug ran over to them looking as white as a ghost. "I'll get my team tracking the location of that last login, Mark. We'll have to pull more people in."

Mark nodded.

An employee walked up behind the group and asked, "A Detective Reigns is at the gate asking for Mark or Eve? Does he have the clearance to come in?"

Doug and Mark answered at the same time. "Let 'em in!"

The Beta

"Let me in, let me in," she whispered to herself as she rang the doorbell at Annie's house. There were no funny faces this time. No future presidential bids for Kira.

Eventually Mrs. Zhao answered the door. She looked ten years older than the last time Kira saw her.

"Is Annie there, Mrs. Zhao? I've been texting her for days and she never answers." Kira asked, hoping for an invitation inside.

"Annie won't be talking to anyone for quite some time Kira. You know why, don't you Kira?" Mrs. Zhao looked both pained and suspicious.

"I don't . . ." Kira fudged. She simply didn't know how much trouble Annie was in specifically.

"We're sending Annie to live with some relatives. I'll tell her you stopped by, but I'm sorry Kira, you can't talk to her." Mrs. Zhao closed the door slowly.

Kira looked up at the window to Annie's room but the curtains were drawn tight.

Kira hopped back into her parents' Jeep and yawned. It was 7:15 in the morning. Professor McKenzie would be expecting her at the Microsoft Campus at 8:00, and that was the only reason her parents allowed her to take the Jeep into town. Kira wondered what Professor McKenzie did if someone didn't show up for class. So far no one in her cohort had missed a single Friday, *The Beta* was too exciting to skip.

If James/Samuel was really in trouble, if someone had truly kidnapped him—Kira couldn't stand by and do nothing. And knowing her parents were as strict as the Zhao family, she couldn't possibly hope to be back in VR at her home for weeks at least. Her parents were so disappointed when she confessed to helping Kevin cheat.

Part of her wanted to drive to the high school and confront Kevin, kick his ass, and scream at his girlfriend. But he didn't matter that much to her anymore, much like the Sx̲ʷnitkʷ code meant nothing. The attention he paid her had just felt so good.

The Beta

James, now he was real. They may have never met irl but he was a living, breathing human being she cared deeply about.

That morning her mom relented and let her bring her phone for the drive into town. Parents were always suckers for safety when it came to driving with cell phones. Kira opened the settings and turned all tracking and location services off.

Stopping at a convenience store she filled up the gas tank and purchased a good old-fashioned map. That stop was followed by a Starbucks drive through, a double-tall black and white mocha, and a warm croissant. Sitting in the parking lot she drew a light pencil line heading east across the Cascades.

She sent a quick text
hey cuz, what are you doing after school?
Without waiting for a reply, Kira headed east on I-90.

🌐

James was trussed up again like a turkey and stuffed into his pillow throne. After an hour or so of sitting, and both women pulled him up. They untied his legs but left his arms tightly bound.

"We're going to go on a little walk," Greta ordered.

It didn't take him long to figure out they were leaving the RV. They guided him down five big steps and he could tell when his feet hit dirt. It was actual dirt, not pavement.

The world was eerily quiet but the wind on his neck a welcome disturbance. James wondered if it was night or day.

They scuffled him across dirt or sand and he tripped on a few plants or logs or something. Next they were walking across a surface that was hard but slightly unsteady, still not pavement.

Not quite figuring it out he had to step up, step down, duck his head, and then a few steps later he was back again on a pillow throne. Greta then tied up his legs again and he sighed as his head tipped to the right and James let his body finally rest.

His parents *must* know he was missing by now. Whoever Doug was he *must* be a Google employee. James was positively, absolutely sure that they *must* come after him.

Then they started the soundtrack again. He could hear it faintly. This time it was something about time and how it ticks out.

The Beta

They *must* know how annoying that soundtrack was getting. And yeah, time was ticking out.

🌏

Kira almost hit a truck, caused another car to swerve, and was honked at no less than two times. She wasn't a bad driver but she was inexperienced. The cars were going so fast and the curves on the pass were tight. Sometimes there was no room on the shoulder and a large truck would be inches from her side mirror. Her parents may not get the pleasure of killing her personally.

At the top of the mountain pass Kira pulled over and stopped to rethink everything. Should she really be stealing her parents' car? Would she even make it over? Would her cousin drive to Inchelium with her? Was her grandma really there? Her entire plan hinged on her grandmother being at the big old house behind the Rainbow Beach Resort store. If Kira couldn't find her grandmother, all this would be for nothing.

Kira considered going in to school today and asking Professor McKenzie for help. In fact, the thought almost caused her to turn around and head back down the pass. But her grandmother was family and something deep inside her was telling her to keep going.

So Kira kept moving east as the green pine trees thinned into sagebrush.

🌏

"Mark, Jen asked that we move our base of operations into the Bridge." Doug looked pointedly at Mark, "You and Eve need to take care of yourselves and we will take care of you. We got this. Jen will be here in the morning to help."

Mark sighed internally. This was going all the way to the top. He supposed, instead of being embarrassed he should count his lucky stars that the best resources in the world were mobilizing to get his son back.

Doug and Mark went back years, but it was only recently that their work in DeepMind and the creation of Google Earth History

The Beta

brought them back together. Mark turned to Eve. "We'll get him back, Eve."

Eve nodded, eyes red. "I'm going to go back to the house with Detective Reigns to go through the house and check in with Jack." She looked up at Mark, fierce with strength. Her strength allowed Mark to momentarily let down his guard. They were a good match.

"I guess we have our suitcases in the car, but I'll bring some fresh clothes. Do you want anything else from the house?" Eve asked.

"No,"

Eve kissed him and turned to go.

Mark spoke up, "Wait . . . if he left any notes in the VR room, anything, no matter how seemingly inconsequential. Maybe . . ."

"I will."

Kira drove all day, gaining confidence on the freeway as the lanes flattened and straightened out. The second half of her trip consisted of rocky, desert-like sagebrush lands. The really scary part of the trip was a narrow bridge that crossed the Columbia River at Vantage. Signs warning of winds challenged truck and car alike as the lanes narrowed across the water. It reminded her of why her mom's knuckles always turned white when she drove over the floating bridge. She breathed a sigh of relief once she had crossed over the bridge.

This was a trip Kira made with her father almost every summer, so the roads were familiar to her, but this was the first time she was alone behind the wheel. Now that the stressful driving was past, she began to enjoy the freedom of the open road. It seemed that her parents still hadn't tried to track or call her.

It wasn't long before she found herself at Grand Coulee Dam. Her grandparents, aunts, uncles and cousins all lived in this small town. She would have to find a way to remain inconspicuous while waiting for Nina to get out of school.

Taking a quick left, she took a back road on the west side of town and up to Crown Point on the cliffs above Grand Coulee.

The Beta

From here she had an expansive view of the dam, the river, and small towns hugging the shore. It was this type of view that gave her an appreciation for the world, and it was the same view she so often was privileged to see in Google Earth History. While nothing could replace this real life experience, Google Earth History had taken her to times and places she would have never visited. And all with a first-hand bird's eye view.

And there she sat for an hour. Listening, thinking, drinking it all in—real life was pretty freaking cool.

Yet 2:30 p.m. inched closer and she was itching to be on her way. At 2:15 p.m. Kira hopped back in the Jeep and headed down to Lake Roosevelt High School. Her grandparents lived only a few houses down from the school and avoiding them made her feel a deep sense of guilt. She wanted to stop in to get a hug and a cookie; not doing so felt like sacrilege.

But she needed her cousin, and the only way to pull this off was to nab her on the way out of class.

Nina texted her back and they agreed to meet in the parking lot. If Kira's parents didn't get suspicious they may not notice her absence until around four or five that evening. That gave her enough time to convince Nina to go with her.

The spring air was warmer than usual and the sun was flooding the air around her, so Kira jumped on the hood of the Jeep and allowed the warm metal of the hood to soak into her backside. There was something about these moments, the days or hours between running away and getting caught, that felt so adult like. She would enjoy them while she could.

"Kira!!!!!" screamed a familiar voice. Nina was at the front of the crowd of students streaming out of the high school and into the weekend.

Unbridled joy propelled the cousins into a binary orbit of hugs and squeals. They were cousins. —although they didn't look like cousins. Kira looked straight up Chinese and Nina had the light-haired brunette that was always inching toward her mother's white blonde. No one would suspect their shared Polish, German, Irish, and Native American ancestry.

Kira let it all out in a rush, every detail of what happened, what she felt, and what she wanted to do. Nina listened like the perfect listener and cousin that she was. When Kira was done with her story she looked at Nina and waited for a response.

Nina smiled slowly. "Let's do it! But we have to go ask my mom." She looked down at her phone to check the time. "She'll be at Logan's basketball game in thirty minutes. We can stop by, explain why you're here, and ask permission to head to the lake."

"What about your dad?"

"He's not home until late . . . and if your parents don't figure it out until this evening I doubt he'll be after us until tomorrow." Nina's father traveled the whole Rez on a regular basis. They couldn't hide from him for long.

"Why don't you just ask your mom? We don't have to tell her I'm here, do we?" Kira pleaded.

"The only person in the world she MIGHT let me go with is you. And she's so into watching Logan's games that if we ask her at the right moment she probably won't be suspicious. She thinks you're an angel, you know!"

Kira just stared ahead, unsure of who was right.

"Trust me Kira, follow my lead."

Kira trusted.

Nina was right. Within an hour they secured her mom's permission, swung by her house for clothes and snacks, and were headed east once again; this time through pine forests and bumpy forest roads. If anyone was looking they would have seen the Jeep headlights moving back and forth through the pines, and then they were gone.

They were going. He was gone. Everything was gone. Nobody gave a damn.

The pointless lyrics were becoming gospel to James. Every song they played droned on until it held some hidden meaning for his predicament. He was gone, going, everything was gone, he was gone, and nobody gave a damn.

The Beta

To top it all off he was sick. Only minutes ago James had thrown up all over the place. Out of self-preservation he tried to aim for the floor directly in front of him instead of his clean fluffy pillow tower, but he challenged anyone to throw up with a virtual reality headset forcibly duct taped to their head. *You try it,* he dared the cosmos.

He only puked once but the nausea didn't abate. He wondered if he had the stomach flu, food poisoning, or maybe living in a headset for days at time was taking its toll. Everything in his world was rocking.

He could hear their frantic whispers as they cleaned his puke off the floor. He was messing with their carefully laid plans. Good.

James tipped his head to the left this time and tried to fall asleep despite the elevator music playing in the background. More lyrics punctuated his vertigo. They were more sympathetic. He should have mercy on himself. Things certainly weren't what they used to be.

And lastly, when would he see the blue sky again?

The Bay Area didn't have many days of pure, blue sky but this had been one of them. Now the sun had set and Mark was looking out into a pitch-black night.

The Bridge was large, spacious, and exclusive. Used for emergencies, used for privacy, it had everything the company would need in case of a worldwide catastrophe, including a great view protected by blackout windows, anti-drone devices and any number of security protections.

There were fourteen people working together so far, the crew that Mark and Doug scraped together due to the late hour of the request.

"I have coordinates for the first two logins, Mark."

Mark moved across the room and looked at one of Doug's screens.

"The first was Gilroy Garlic RV Park and the second Sommerville Almond Tree RV Park." Doug pointed to the screen.

The Beta

"Garlic and Almonds huh?"

"RV Parks"

"They haven't crossed state lines so far?"

"You sound disappointed?"

"Kidnappers have to cross state lines in order to get the FBI involved, right?"

"Jen already authorized cooperation with the FBI. There's some connection, threatening telecommunications or such."

Mark looked at his friend, "I couldn't make it through this without you, Doug."

"We're family, Mark, even if we aren't related by blood."

He was hesitant to drink the water and the most recent lyrics warned him it might be tainted with blood.

"You feeling better?"

"Do you think I might have food poisoning?" James asked them.

"Take a sip of water, hon." There was actually sympathy in Summer's voice. Usually it was Greta who got this close to him. But for some reason this time it was Summer. He still didn't know Greta's real name.

"What if the water is making me sick?"

"Don't be silly, it's bottled water. You're going to be feeling better in no time." He could feel her stroking his hair above the headset. Why was she all of a sudden being kind to him?

He felt a little better.

She fed him sips of water and patted his mouth dry. "Would you like some crackers? Or Seven-up? Those always make me feel better when my stomach is out of whack."

"Yes, please." He might as well try a little solid food. "Can I go to the bathroom?"

"Ummm . . . not right now, soon though."

This made James wonder, was the other woman gone? So far he wasn't aware that they ever split up. He could always hear both of their voices.

The Beta

After a few minutes of being fed bits of crackers and Seven-Up James decided to speak up.

"Why?" was all he started with a nice open-ended question.

There was silence.

"I mean, I know why you took me, I have developer access. But how the heck did you get me into Santa's Workshop? Even my dad can't get into Santa's Workshop."

Still silence. The crackers stopped making their way into his mouth. He was annoyed and he really needed to pee. "Why are you doing this?"

More silence. And then it broke suddenly when Summer asked him a question. "Tell me about Sarah Franklin-Bache?"

"Huh?"

"The person who sent you that message, 'Meet me at The Cliffs'. What did that mean?

"It's just a girl."

There was more silence on both of their parts.

"Just a girl, I've heard that phrase before. She's special to you, isn't she?"

That was the funny part about the darkness. Whether it was hiding behind illusions in VR or having a perpetual blindfold—when one couldn't 'see' with their eyes they could hear so much more. How did Summer know?

"She's a friend," James replied. At least that much was honest. He wasn't sure how good of a friend she was.

"Do you have a girlfriend? In real life?"

"No."

"Do you like that girl, Sarah Franklin-Bache?"

"No," but both he and Summer could hear the blatant lie in his tone. He decided to come clean.

"I was about to kiss her when you knocked me out."

"Oh . . . so that's what you were up to? I thought I saw that on your screen when we walked in but I was so preoccupied. Well . . ." He could almost see her tilting her head in contemplation. "Help us finish what we set out to do and you can go back home and try to kiss her again."

She placed another cracker on his mouth. He coughed it up, half-laughing and half-spitting. "Fine, if you won't tell me why you

The Beta

nabbed me, will you at least tell me which one of you picked out the songs on that horrific playlist of yours?"

This time Summer laughed at him and slapped him on the shoulder. "Maybe you should listen a little closer, smarty pants."

"Any luck tracking the location of the third login?" Mark's headset was on and he was reviewing his son's last twenty-four hours in VR before the kidnapping. That was the problem. Even though he was lucky enough to have access to all of James's past actions the sheer mountain of data was nearly impossible to dig through.

"Nothing yet." Doug looked out the window into a deep darkness.

Kira and Nina arrived at the lake at the same time the sun set over the mountains, plunging them into darkness. It was cold up here but the air was fresh.

They drove past the old building and Kira looked eagerly out the window. There were no signs of life in the interior, but a newly installed motion light turned on as they passed the building. It was all Kira could do not to jump out and pound on the door.

They arrived at the family cabin and parked. Nina pulled out her keys and let them in the front door and they unceremoniously dropped armloads of stuff on the kitchen table.

"Will you go with me? I need to check it out!"

"Yes, yes, hold your horses. I need to pee first."

They both used the bathroom and then headed outside. It was dark now but the resort lights illuminated their path to the house behind the store.

"When were you up here last?" Kira asked her cousin.

"About two months ago, but I didn't pay any attention to that old house."

The Beta

They quieted down and crept up close. There were no signs officially restricting entry to the property, but because it lay dormant for all those years it had garnered an official spookiness.

The motion light suddenly turned on, blinding them and revealing their approach in the process.

"Dude, there are cameras everywhere now." Nina pointed to the corners of the building where dark round sentinels now kept guard.

They walked to the front door and knocked even though there were no lights on inside.

Kira used her hands to shield her eyes and looked through the window. She could barely make out the shadows of what appeared to be lighthouses hanging from the ceiling, and if that purple light didn't belong to a gaming machine powered by a state-of-the-art graphics card . . .

"This is it, Nina! I was right!" Kira sucked in a thankful breath.

"Well, we can't just go in tonight. You said the grandmother was an early riser, right?"

"I think so."

"Then we get up early tomorrow."

They turned from the house and walked back through dark silence.

🌍

James didn't need to walk through the dark. He couldn't have known that dense clouds of fog were blocking the starlight.

His world was already dark enough.

"Are you feeling good enough to get back to work?" Summer was asking, although he could hear Greta's breathing as she waited for his response.

"The sooner we start, the sooner we finish, and the sooner I get home right?" he asked.

The Beta

Greta let her breath out, "Yep, you got the right idea."

"If you get dizzy or nauseous again let us know and we can take a break." Summer added.

"I'm ready," he said. And he really did feel ready.

"Mark, he's back on!"

Mark yanked off his headset and joined the small crowd watching over Doug. Another employee with access to Santa's Workshop was suiting up nearby. Mark only wished he could get into the simulation and wreak havoc on James's captors. Yet since his son's kidnappers didn't have any avatars, Mark would have no one to rail against.

But he did want to talk to James. A moment with his son was all he wanted.

"Let's set up on both sides of the entrance so we can follow him."

"Got it! What if he already beat us in?"

"Plan B—you take the north road and I'll take the south."

"You already missed him!" A girl who was monitoring screens shouted out. "He entered Santa's Workshop one minute ago.

There was some scrambling around on Doug's part as he jumped as fast as he could across the landscape and into the village, hoping to catch sight of James.

Five minutes later Mark heard the golden words, "I got him!"

At first Doug stayed back a bit, watching. James entered a cottage with a swirling planet on the sign. It was the Earth with exaggerated layers of the atmosphere.

Doug followed James inside.

"So, we need you to do something a little different before each of these adjustments from now on," explained Greta. "Do you see the time signature on the side of each screen? Click that one."

The Beta

James clicked and a simple calendar expanded, extending into nothingness on the edges.

"You see the month of April?" she asked.

James began to do as he was told when he heard Summer interrupt, "What about Christmas?"

"Our original plan was April, I don't want to change it."

"But the book, think about it. Visited by three ghosts—past, present, and future—all culminating in a redemptive morning. A complete 360 in actions and deeds. Isn't that what we want?"

James couldn't believe he was hearing this conversation. He still didn't know what it meant but he knew it held the key to their intentions.

"I think we should stick to our original plan." Greta insisted.

"Fine."

"Now, sweetie." Greta gave him a date and he highlighted it accordingly. "Next, set it to repeat annually, start at noon, and set the duration of the loop for 30 minutes."

James did each of those commands, and in the glare of the virtual screen he saw Doug behind him.

A message appeared on the screen in front of James.

Trigger access required to make date specific changes. Tagged for future permissions.

"We have a problem." Greta said out loud. But it wasn't for James's benefit.

🌍

"Can we get a live location on this login?" Mark asked the room.

"Not fast enough, but we just received the last one."

Eager to see his son's most recent physical location on the map, Mark looked over their shoulders as Maps zoomed in on an RV park in Southern California. Chula Vista RV Resort.

"Doug, they keep heading south. The third RV park in a row." Mark studied the map, "I wonder if they are going to try the border or head east to Arizona?"

The Beta

Greta and Summer worked him hard. Tweaking the air, switching up the water, choosing odd data sets with drastic outliers as the parameter for their changes. Yet every time he set the dates the same cryptic message appeared.

Trigger access required to make date specific changes. Tagged for future permissions.

Summer offered him some microwaved mac and cheese but he asked for crackers. He still felt sick to his stomach, but at least he hadn't thrown up again.

As he tried to find a comfortable angle for his head on the pillows he could suddenly feel it. He knew why he felt sick all the time. He knew where he was, sort of.

Oh crap, his parents were never going to find him.

Morning broke over the lake and Kira was up early, she didn't even need an alarm clock. Maybe she didn't even sleep at all. Nina was still knocked-out and she didn't wait for her cousin.

Slipping on sweat pants and a warm hoodie, Kira left a note and walked over to the abandoned house that wasn't abandoned.

There was a car parked in the driveway and Kira's heart leapt. It probably belonged to one of the resort employees, but maybe? Maybe it was her grandmother? There was enough morning sun that the security light didn't trigger when she closed in on the porch.

Kira didn't even try to knock, she simply put her face to the window and looked through the glare of the sunrise on the glass.

Inside was her grandmother.

The Beta

"xast sxlx̌ʕalt stmtíma?" Kira whispered through the window as if practicing for real life. She watched the woman inside who moved her hands as if conducting an orchestra.

A low growl emanated from beyond the porch to her left. Caught off guard, Kira backed up slowly as a huge animal cornered her against the wall.

The polar bear in front of James may have been tiny but that made it no less intimidating. "You want me to do what, exactly?" he asked Greta and Summer. He was back in Santa's Workshop in a cottage that specialized in arctic animals. There was a map of polar bear habitats and migration patterns spread out before him. The tiny polar bear was rooting around in the snow for something, then it pulled its head up and reared to full height.

"We need you to talk to your shadow Doug over there for us."

He looked over his shoulder to where 'Doug' was standing patiently, always following his every move. It was unnerving, even if he knew that Doug was a friend of his father who was helping to find a way to free him from the clutches of his kidnappers.

"What exactly do you mean?" he asked, trying to keep the conversation internal until he knew exactly what they wanted. Doug could hear everything he said but Doug couldn't hear Summer and Greta. At least he thought that was the case. Maybe every VR set had some kind of ultrasonic acoustics that picked up the smallest ambient sounds. He wasn't sure.

"We need a way to trigger all the changes we are making across all concurrent simulations for the specified date and time period. The coding doesn't currently exist so we need your friend Doug to find someone to do it for us. We need a trigger."

"Huh?"

"You understood me, don't ask questions, just do it!" Greta ordered, and then James felt a small bite on his earlobe that hurt.

"Owwww! Cut it out." he protested. Greta hadn't used the gun barrel recently, but she exchanged that threat tactic for a variety of bites, pinches, and slaps. James wasn't really sure what to make of

The Beta

the change but either way he felt abused. These girls were messing with him.

If only it was Kira biting his earlobe.

"Fine!" he turned to Doug. Doug was Asian like James, and he was dressed in something reminiscent of a parka. He almost looked like a Native Alaskan here in Santa's Workshop. "Doug, the women who-"

"Ouch!" Greta must have stepped on his bare toes with stilettos. The pain was unbearable and he couldn't help but jump up and down, dropping one controller so he could grab his foot in his hand, howling and rubbing to try and dull the pain.

"You told him we were women!" Greta hissed. Her hisses were deep and penetrating. Not snakelike, but angry.

"Sorry, I . . . they probably already know who you are."

"James are you ok?" Doug asked.

James riveted his head away from Greta's voice to face Doug's visual image. "Yeah, I'm fine." he glared in what he guessed was Greta's general direction.

"They . . ." he emphasized despite the now obvious revelation of gender, ". . . need a favor."

Doug looked at him carefully and responded slowly, "Go on, James, we're listening."

He knew it! His parents must be able to hear him! Even though Doug could be referring to any manner of amassed Google employees, deep down James knew his parents were there, hearing his every word.

"They need someone to code a trigger so that all the changes they make can be activated across all simulations for the same designated date and time duration." James was impressed with himself. He was pretty sure that was a more explicit and detailed way of explaining what 'they' wanted.

Doug didn't make any reply at first. He simply stood stock still for a minute or two. James did the same and held his breath the whole time.

"I think we can do that for them." Doug started out slowly, each word spoken with purpose. "But we will need one thing in return."

The Beta

"What's that?" James asked eagerly, feeling an opportunity arise.

Greta and Summer must have felt the threat, because Greta stabilized his arms with hers, as though daring him to move, as though he could run away off through the North Pole and back home.

There was another long pause, "Your dad wants to talk to you, he needs to know you are safe and sound. He can meet you in a simulation. You choose."

"Bullshit!" it was Summer that burst out with that uncharacteristic swear word. "They can give your dad access to anything they want!"

Doug smiled as if he heard Summer out loud, "That's the deal. Meet your dad tomorrow at 5 p.m. Pacific and we will hand over the code they need. Where do you want to meet him?"

James answered immediately so Greta and Summer wouldn't be able to get a word in edgewise. "The Cliffs, in the American Revolution."

"Done," and with that last word Doug disappeared.

Greta pinched him, pinched him hard, "Don't make deals for us."

"But it worked. They're going to meet us aren't they? I made your deal didn't I?" he blurted out quickly to cover the nervousness in his voice.

"They will do it because they want you back!" Summer scolded.

There was a long silence.

"But what's done is done." Greta acknowledged.

James, his guard finally down, sat down on the floor and started rubbing his bruised foot. "Can I get some ice here?" he asked. With all the harassment and coddling, these women were starting to make him understand what it could be like to have older sisters.

He could tell they were dissatisfied with the situation, having to wait on fate to get what they wanted, and that made him feel better all around.

The Beta

Summer complied with his request for ice and dinner was microwaved ramen noodles. He wasn't used to the new surroundings that made his stomach so queasy.

Settling into his pillow tower for the night he wiggled his sore toes and realized he hadn't worn proper shoes or socks in days. His feet were tired and cold. And as always, those darn lyrics fit perfectly, something about shoes and burning bridges.

🌍

Kira could have sworn the animal in front of her was a direwolf. She backed away from him slowly until he had chased her all the way off the porch. Thankfully there was the sound of a pick-up truck bouncing over the slow speed bumps to divert his attention and this distracted him long enough. She got the nerve to dash down the street in front of the store. It was early enough in the morning that other than the pick-up truck there wasn't a single soul in sight. It didn't take her long to run back inside the family cabin and jump on Nina's bed.

"Nina, you have to wake up! I went to the house and I found her! My grandmother is there now but I tried to knock on the door and a huge direwolf chased me away!"

Nina looked up at her, blinking, and her response was, "huh?" and then her eyes closed and she flopped back on the bed.

Kira repeated everything but slower and in more detail. And then before Nina could make another ridiculous response Kira jumped up and said, "I'll make you hot chocolate!"

Giving Nina a few moments to get up, Kira went to the kitchen and mixed some chocolate syrup and milk on the stove top the old-fashioned way. There were no marshmallows or whipped cream to be found, but the two warm mugs clinking in her hands helped steady her nerves.

Kara didn't even look at her phone because she didn't want to see any indication that her parents were worried.

And that's when it hit her. Even though Kira thought she covered all the bases when she planned this trip, she only now realized her parents had tracking software on the car. Crap! They must absolutely know where she was or at least had a pretty good clue.

Thankful that the cabin didn't have a landline, and that cell phone coverage was practically nonexistent unless you walked out on the dock at the right time of day, she continued on her way to the back bedrooms.

"Nina," she said hesitantly, "I just realized my parents have tracking software on the Jeep, there's no way they don't know that I'm here. We've got to get going. We need to go talk to my grandma now before they can stop me."

"Your grandmother?"

Nina thought about that for a minute, "I've gotten into such a habit of thinking about her as my virtual grandmother it's almost like she's become my adopted one."

"Really?"

"I know it's so weird . . ." she felt like she was betraying her real grandmothers so she tried to explain, "I can't wait till you get to try VR with me. I wish these modern headsets didn't need biometrics, otherwise you could try it right now." Kira paused, her train of thought returning to the idea of getting caught. "I'm surprised they didn't send your dad over already?"

"Yeah, well I should probably check the docks and give them a call by nine. So you're right, if you want to get this done it had better be now."

"What about the direwolf?"

"Huh? Oh yeah," Nina smiled a wicked smile void of any anxiety. "I know what dogs like . . ." she opened the fridge and pulled out a six-pack of hot dogs.

"Seriously?"

"Seriously."

Kira felt at home here. As they made their way back to the abandoned house the sun streamed through the pine trees sending shards of light across the dusty road. It was a quiet corner of the world.

She hung back as they got closer and watched Nina approach the dog, admitting to herself that although the mutt was huge it wasn't exactly a direwolf.

The dog didn't take the food from Nina's hand but it didn't bark either, at least until Nina made it close enough to ring the

The Beta

doorbell. Everything on the old house was updated with state-of-the-art equipment including a video doorbell. Old wood mixed with new electronics.

"May I help you?" came a voice through the device next to the door. The dog was still growling, making it hard for Kira to hear.

But she took a chance and spoke up while walking closer to Nina and the dog, "Stmtíma??,"

"Stmtíma??" Kira repeated herself, this time more loudly.

"Sṅʔímaʔt?"

●

Jen's forehead was scrunched in a frown, due to a combination of her brain working away at the problem and her concern. Doug was only beginning to de-suit when he began to issue a long list of expletives, "Those guys are messing with our base code. What the hell do they think they're doing? It's going to take months to set everything right."

When Doug approached she raised her eyebrows at his language but was quick to inquire, "Who would you like pulled off of their current projects to get this done? We have twenty-two hours."

Doug had the best working knowledge of who they would need to complete the code the kidnappers requested. As Doug listed names to the activation team, Jen grabbed her glass water bottle and moved to the center of the Bridge where she could look over the entire room.

This was actually their first use of the Bridge for a true emergency. While the big picture idea was to provide a space to use in the case of a worldwide situation, such as a nuclear war or other catastrophe, someone hitting them this close to home—by targeting the child of a Google employee—was reason enough to use the Bridge. Everyone in this room was thinking about how Mark and Eve must be feeling, how they would feel if it was their child.

Jen made her way across the room to Mark and Eve. She was honest and to the point. "I don't think we can meet their coding demands by tomorrow but we'll try. And you'll be ready to meet

James in the evening?" The question was surely a moot point, but Jen didn't want to assume anything.

Mark only nodded.

"Do you know where the Cliffs are in the American Revolution?"

"We found it." Doug called from across the room. "It's a historic house outside of old Philly."

"Something is bothering me . . ." Jen started out hoping one of them might subconsciously know a solution and put the words in her mouth. So often, people were the key to solving their own problems, they only needed a sounding board to reflect their thoughts. This certainly wasn't a problem of their own making, but since the kidnappers targeted their son in particular they all needed to figure out what that reason was.

"He sent us one clue," Mark began, obviously proud of his son. "Now we know there is more than one kidnapper and that they are women."

"Has anyone figured out how our Nest cameras were compromised?" Eve asked.

"And the access to Santa's Workshop?" Mark looked pointedly toward her. They wouldn't grant him access even when his son's life was in danger, but no one could figure out exactly how his son was granted access. "How did that happen?"

But Jen ignored their questions as her forehead wrinkled characteristically again. It always did that right before a sudden breakthrough. "I think I know where to look now!"

🌍

At the sound of Salish the dog suddenly quieted in front of Kira. She knew this dog! Why hadn't she recognized it before?

"You're not a scary dog, you're ntytyix from the simulation!" she cried. The more she spoke Salish the more the dog calmed down and even began to sit quietly.

Nina felt a bit jealous, both because of her Salish skills and because the dog was responding to Kira instead of to her.

"Looks like you are going to be teaching me this summer instead of the other way around, cuz."

The Beta

At that moment the door opened and before her stood her grandmother. It was really her grandmother from the simulation, the same eyes, the same hair, only her 20th century clothes were different.

"Stmtíma??"

"Sn̓ʔímaʔt ?"

The tone in their voices conveyed everything; their surprise, their apologies, their happiness, and their commitment. Real life was like that, a simple glance could tell you everything, unlike in VR.

It was at this moment that Kira realized the finite limitations of VR compared to real life. The last few months VR had dazzled her with its potential, depth, and breadth. Yet after all that time VR could never provide the authenticity of the actual moment. That space that separates what comes before and what comes next, the nowness. That moment of singularity was irreplaceable, and only available in reality.

"Come inside," Karen beckoned to them, easily accepting them both through the door. The dog followed as well and made himself at home on a dog bed snuggled against the wall.

"How?" asked her grandmother.

"I . . ." Kira wasn't exactly sure how to begin and in the excitement her Salish was failing her, at the exact moment she wanted it most. "I meant to say something earlier."

Kira looked to Nina for support before continuing and Nina looked back steadily. Even though the emotion on Nina's face didn't change, Kira could tell she was sending her strength through a simple look. "I grew up visiting here every summer, so when you mentioned a lake, and a store, and a cabin I couldn't imagine any other place on the Rez that would fit that description. And I knew you were on the Colville Rez . . ." Kira stopped, realizing that she hadn't actually know that. Her grandmother could have been Spokane, or Kalispel, or from any number of Pacific Northwest tribal areas. Possibly, but not probably.

Her grandmother still looked thoughtful and so she continued. "Nina is my cousin. My grandmother is full Lakes even though we're only a quarter." Here she paused to really look into her grandmother's eyes. "So if you are Lakes then we are actually related, at least a little."

Her grandmother looked them both over—one girl who looked very Asian and one who could be taken as a light-haired white girl from any part of America—and laughed. "Yes, my granddaughter, I suppose we are."

This was new to all three of them, but at the same time second nature to all. You didn't always choose your family, and more often or not you didn't care, family was family after all. Blood or no blood, little blood or a lot of blood. There was always more than one way to bind yourself to those you loved.

"You're here?" Was all her grandmother said, sticking to English for her cousin's benefit. There was an overt questioning tone to her voice.

"I want to help James."

"I know that . . . but why are you *here*?"

"Oh," Kira's face turned red. "I got into a little trouble and my parents took away my VR. I didn't know where else to go." Her eyes were pleading now as she could sense her grandmother's hesitancy. "We have to help him, and soon!"

"Your parents don't know you're here?"

She and Nina looked at one another, "Well . . . sort of. Probably not yet."

Nina spoke up, "I'm going to give them a call in about an hour when the cell service hits the dock."

Grandmother turned her attention directly on Nina, "You'll tell them exactly where you two are and why?"

"Yes," they said in unison.

"You can access a phone line through VR," Karen offered.

Nina and Kira looked at one another but it was Kira who spoke first, "It might be best if Nina called, not me."

'Hmmm," she replied with guarded emotion. "I suppose that will have to do. Now granddaughter, I have something you may find helpful." Her grandmother headed into the kitchen area.

So focused on how her grandmother would respond to her plight, Kira hadn't taken the time to become familiar with their surroundings. It was only now that she looked closely. The large old living room they were standing in was retrofitted into a

The Beta

fantastic modern room. On one side was a floor to ceiling curved screen, much like the displays Kira used on the Microsoft campus, and on it was a scene portraying a real time image of the Sx̌ʷnitkʷ simulation.

Kira walked up to the screen and it was of such a height that she almost felt like she was back in VR with the curved screen stretched about both sides. Similar to standing in one of those multi-mirrors in a dressing room where you could see every angle.

Nina was staring curiously over her shoulder. On either side of the screen were big, comfy recliners. Next to one recliner was a basket of yarn and the other a beading box. On the east side of the room were several computer stations along with bookcases full of papers and texts. Pictures, articles, and notes were scattered across several bulletin boards.

As she took this all in her grandmother opened a cupboard and by the time Kira turned around she was surprised to find Karen holding out a gift.

In her hands she had a headset that matched the one her grandmother had been using. It took a few seconds but then Kira immediately understood. She could use this set alongside of her grandmother! As long as the school or *The Beta* hadn't been instructed to restrict her access she should be able to get back into VR!

The elder and the young one strapped on matching headsets while Nina sat in a recliner to watch. The direwolf made himself at home on Nina's feet.

On the Bridge, Doug was now sitting down at a main terminal with Jen, Mark, and Eve behind him.

"So far, we've started to comb through the last six months of coding from these three employees to see which one of them gave James access to Santa's Workshop. Two of them are being questioned right now and this third one, Autumn Emch, left on a trip to Alaska and we have yet to get in touch with her." He wiped his brow out of habit even though he wasn't sweating. "So either they coded the access in months ago, which would have taken

The Beta

quite a bit of pre-planning, or there is some weakness in our system."

"Our protocol is pretty tight, Doug." Jen reminded him needlessly. They all knew the copious designs that were used to keep the integrity of Google Earth History's core coding under wraps. Only a small contingent of coders were allowed to enter the North Pole.

"Has our internal investigation brought up any suspicion of the first two?" Jen asked Doug.

"No red flags as of yet." He smiled. "They are both acting pretty offended that we are reviewing their work."

Jen nodded. "That's to be expected. Since Autumn is the only employee unavailable let's shift some additional resources over to combing through her records, also hit her personal files, communications, and any other legally procurable data."

🌎

"I'll show you where he is," her grandmother began, "he's active right now."

Kira's heart pounded. Her grandmother already knew where he was! She was floating above the Earth when she realized she wouldn't be able to see her grandmother standing in her own Google Earth History preview, yet it would be easy to ask for directions since her grandmother was standing only feet from her irl. They had split the original play area down the middle of the living room, so even though their spaces would be smaller than normal at least they wouldn't' be bumping into one another. Kira wouldn't want to knock over her grandma!

"Go to the North Pole," her grandmother instructed.

Now this was curious, Kira thought. What would he be doing up at the North Pole? Kira had never visited the Arctic in all of her days using Google Earth. She typed the request in the search bar and flew directly to the location. Clicking on the icon, a variety of options sprouted up.

"Which option do I pick, grandmother? It says North Pole, Arctic Expedition 1, Magnetic North Pole History, and Santa's

The Beta

Workshop." Here she paused and laughed out loud, "They have a Santa's Workshop?"

"That's where he is."

Kira clicked to enter Santa's Workshop.

Jen was at the main station and Doug was back in Santa's Workshop while Eve and Mark were keeping their steady vigil.

Jen turned to Mark and Eve with a serious look on her face. "I don't think we're going to have the code ready by the deadline." Her look continued to convey her sympathy to James's parents. "But we will do everything in our power to make it happen."

Mark only nodded but Eve looked livid.

The Bridge was so much quieter than the Mainframe. Several hours went by and everyone in the room could hear the tapping of keyboards, Doug's shuffling, and the clicks of controllers and tracking pads.

Jen's phone rang and she answered it. Even though she was facing away from Eve, something in her body language tipped Eve off. Eve was up and next to Jen before the smile hit her face. It was good news.

"We know who they are!" Jen almost shouted. But she didn't need to shout for everyone to hear.

"Nine months back Autumn Emch created a time specific access account for James that was activated on the night of his kidnapping." She took a deep breath in, "She, and another long time employee in the Maps Division, Summer Larson, have close ties and both scheduled vacations taking them out of contact since the night of the kidnapping. We don't know if more people are involved, but we can be fairly certain these two are."

Doug was listening but his face didn't relay the same elation. "I just got bad news. The last tracked point of contact was in Mexico. They've taken James out of the country."

Silence settled across the room.

The Beta

"I know the Mexican officials will help us, but James just got a whole lot harder to track."

Mark spoke up, "We obviously have good pictures of the suspects, right?"

"Yep."

"Can you send me a set of images and other pertinent info?"

"No problem."

"Mark, what are you thinking?"

"I know who to call who can help us find them in Mexico."

Nina left Kira in the house and walked down the dock to call their parents as promised. It was a chilly spring morning so she pulled her hoodie over her head as she approached the cool wind that topped the lake. When she sat at the end of the dock the sun warmed wood toasted her butt nicely.

She pulled out her phone and was pleased to see the cell tower bars pop up as expected. She was about to call when a little dragonfly landed on the corner of her phone. It held perfectly still, allowing her to see every minute detail; the thin wings, iridescent colors and multifaceted eyes. A vague memory from biology class crossed her mind, something like each eye having 30,000 parts or something like that. Either way, Nina knew the dragonfly could see much more than she could.

Her perfect view was interrupted when the dragonfly flew away. She looked up and was stunned to see an entire swarm of dragonflies encircling her head. Hundreds of brilliant little insects were watching her every move.

They inspected her closely and then flew off. It was as if creation was sizing her up but she didn't mind the lack of privacy, she knew the dragonflies were on her side.

The phone was ringing and she heard her mom's voice. "Hello?"

Access Denied

The Beta

"Why?" Kira asked out loud, not sure where her grandmother was at the moment.

"Have you ever heard of Santa's Workshop?"

"No . . . what is it?"

"Santa's Workshop is kind of like the Big Bang of Google Earth History. It's the blueprint for the Earth, it controls change through time, and all creatures big and small. All of the base coding for our world is controlled there."

"Akin to God and creation?"

"Exactly, to create our Sx̌ʷnitkʷ simulation, or any simulation for that matter, all of the presets are originally from The North Pole. The graphics, the sky, the land, the way things move, the creatures, all that data comes from one place."

"Why can't we go into Santa's Workshop?"

"Only a few select engineers have that access. Imagine the trouble you could cause if you were able to get your hands on the base code."

🌐

The clock struck four-thirty.

"Can I go in?" he asked Summer and Greta. "It's going to take me a good fifteen minutes to ride to The Cliffs."

"Seriously? You can't go straight there?"

"Nope, because I'm a student, the simulation will drop me down in Philadelphia and I have to ride a horse real time to The Cliffs. The last time I was there I was in student mode, if I switch to dev mode it will take us about the same amount of time to choose and get cleared on a new project." While that wasn't exactly true, it would probably only take him about five minutes to enter in dev mode, he learned enough about Summer and Greta recently to realize neither of them worked in the coding or development process so they didn't actually have a good understanding of how the basics of Google Earth History worked.

He could almost hear their indecision but their reply was still swift. "Go ahead, but remember, your main goal is to prove to your dad that we haven't irreversibly harmed you."

The Beta

He let out a sigh of relief to be going somewhere other than Santa's Workshop. While he missed real life the most, he also missed the freedom of going anywhere in Google Earth History whenever he wanted.

James spun the globe out to the Eastern Seaboard of the United States and zoomed in with a practiced ease directly to the American Revolution Simulation. He was plunked down in the bedroom of his avatar Samuel Powell and immediately headed out the door and down the stairs.

Taking the last stairs two at a time he scanned the street and found exactly what he wanted, two men on horseback ambling along at a slow pace. James grabbed the bridle of the nearest horse and pulled the rider off with a hard yank.

James thought stealing a horse would be more difficult and he was as surprised as the rider at how easily the man fell off the horse. He jumped up in the saddle and leaned forward. James was a remarkably good VR rider and it wasn't long before he left the two men in the dust heading west along the river.

"He's really riding a horse?" Summer observed aloud with a hint of appreciation in her voice.

James realized that he probably looked ridiculous with his legs slightly bowed irl, but he was proud of his horsemanship.

The rest of the ride was quiet, but as he approached the house up high on the cliff he was aware of Summer and Greta waiting anxiously by his side.

There was no sign of life outside the house and the day was a dismal grey. Part of James worried that his dad wouldn't be able to meet him for some reason, that his carefully laid plan might not work out.

He brought the horse around to a hitching post in front of the house and jumped down, his boots hitting soft sand. James tied up the horse and walked a few feet forward.

"There's no one here?" Summer asked, prompting him to turn full circle to give her a complete view of the location. They were wary that this would be a trap.

"He'll come," James said calmly. He knew his father. Surveying the scene, James realized that the best spot for his plan to work out was actually right where he was standing in the dirt

The Beta

next to the hitching post. It was that day walking through Philadelphia with Kira that gave him the idea, the way the dirt responded so realistically when he dragged his knee across the mud.

"Aren't you going to go inside?" Summer asked.

"Nah, we can just wait, they wouldn't be inside." He tried to sound nonchalant about staying put and hoped they wouldn't force him away from this spot. He only had one chance.

🌍

Kira was taking a break on one of the recliners, watching her grandmother sift through what little information they were finding on James.

Her grandmother stood stock still and Kira could see her pointing irl to something she saw in VR. The screen in front of Kira was so big the alert popped up in a huge font. James was in a different part of Google Earth History! In fact, he was in the American Revolution. This was the first time his avatar left Santa's Workshop.

Kira jumped up and threw on her gear. She and her grandmother didn't even have to talk as they both entered the American Simulation, her grandmother in an omni-present and invisible dev mode and her as Sarah Franklin-Bache.

Kira's starting point was always the house at Franklin Court. As soon as she popped into existence she received a message from her grandmother including a screenshot map with James's location. He was on the river road only a short way from The Cliffs, and the little arrow representing his trajectory was slowly moving closer to the house overlooking the river.

Everything was a blur as she raced down to the courtyard and called for Othello to bring the carriage around. King was driving the carriage as it came around and Kira wasted no time jumping in and calling out their destination. If only James had taught her how to ride a horse as fast as he did in VR, but she shouldn't and she figured this way would be the most reliable way to get to The Cliffs.

The Beta

Another message from her grandmother popped up in the periphery. *I will go on ahead. Be cautious.*

Kira was suddenly frustrated that her grandmother was able to whisk ahead to The Cliffs immediately while Kira needed to wait within the constraints of the student simulation.

She waited impatiently for a few minutes and took the time to compose herself as she stared down at the Schuylkill River. It was then she realized she had no clue which tribe originally called this river home. She also subconsciously compared it to her own precious Columbia.

Kira took a breath, pressed pause, and pulled her headset up. On the large screen she could see The Cliffs from above and it only took a minute to pinpoint a lone figure standing next to a horse tied to the hitching post.

"Can you get closer to him, grandmother?"

Her grandmother didn't answer but the large screen slowly zoomed in and she saw the familiar avatar of Samuel Powell.

"That's him, alright. Were you able to cross check on your dev side?"

"Yes, it's James."

"I'm going back in, grandmother, but I can hear you, so let me know what happens." Kira was still staring at James/Samuel, who was standing fairly still but looking side to side as if monitoring the landscape for signs of life. His left boot heel was twisting back and forth, leaving a hole of dark sand contrasting with the light.

"It doesn't look like he's going anywhere." her grandmother observed.

Kira took that as the hint to pull down her headset and resume her simulation. She estimated they would arrive at The Cliffs in about twelve minutes. If only James would wait.

☽

Mark was sweating more than normal and that made his VR gear itchy and uncomfortable. "You say he's in student mode, Doug?"

"Yep, not sure why he didn't just drop in via dev mode, it would have made his entry a lot faster. We've tracked him from

The Beta

Philadelphia and he should just now be arriving at The Cliffs via horseback."

"Any more luck on his location?"

"The Mexican authorities are scouring every RV park in range but nothing yet. The last two trace backs came up empty. They are managing to stay one step ahead of us every time. Their last ping was at a place called Puerto Los Cabos on the tip of the Baja Peninsula. They can't really go anywhere in an RV but north."

Mark was in dev mode and his avatar was currently invisible. It was only moments later he saw his son in the avatar of Samuel Powell approach the house on a dark stallion. There was something oddly satisfying, watching his son adapt so easily to avatars from different times and places.

James/Samuel dismounted and hitched the horse, but instead of making his way to the house he walked a few feet and then stopped.

"Why is he stopping right there, Doug?" Mark asked.

"Not sure . . . let's give him a minute."

The minute stretched forever but Mark zoomed in close and tried to stare into Samuel's eyes. Somewhere behind that blonde hair and blue-eyed face was his son's dark eyes and jet-black hair. He could feel it, and technically James's VR suit headset was replicating not only the direction of his real life gaze but also many of his facial expressions. James/Samuel looked anxious and tense. He could only imagine what his son had been through these last few days.

We're going to get you home. Mark promised his son silently.

"He doesn't appear to be budging from that spot so I'm going to drop in from behind the house." Mark moved his invisible being to the back of the house and triggered his real life body to appear. He chose to use a replica of his actual body in real life when meeting with his son and son's captors. Even if he couldn't see his child's real body, he hoped showing his own would bring James some comfort.

Mark walked out slowly from behind the house and approached his son with measured steps. Even from far away Mark could see his James's head snap into attention when he noticed his

The Beta

father approaching, but James didn't make any move to come closer and Mark thought that was odd.

🌐

James felt strange standing there waiting for his dad, but then his dad appeared walking toward him from behind the dad. It really was his dad, decked out in 20th century clothing and in his real life skin. It was also odd knowing that this whole scene was being played out to a larger audience. Summer and Greta would have a screen open with his point of view and Google Earth History was sure to have multiple employees screen casting the whole thing. It might look like two lone figures next to a house on a cliff, but in reality there was a huge audience.

His dad was quiet for the whole walk over, stoic looking and serious. Yet he was the first to open his mouth, "James?" he asked in affirmation, though none was needed.

"It's me, dad." James shrugged, all sense of pretense and had his Samuel avatar hug his father. He may not get another chance to do so irl and he wasn't going to waste his chance in VR. "Tell Mom I'm fine and I love her." James couldn't help but look up in the air and give the whole sky a smile, hoping that one of those directions would be a perspective she could immediately pick up on.

"She knows, son." Mark was staying close and gripping James's shoulders. "She wanted me to say she loves you and to get home soon."

James needed the conversation to take a more serious and distracting tone in order to pull off his plan. Now that his dad was here at the hitching post he needed an excuse to walk around a bit without drawing Summer and Greta's attention.

"The code!" Summer poked him in the ribs. "Ask about the code!"

"Do you have the code?"

"First we get to talk more, then we talk code."

"They don't have it!" Summer hissed to Greta. "They're only doing this to keep us busy so they can finalize a trace or get some clue. We should leave."

"But we need the code. We don't have the skills needed to make this work," Greta responded while tapping on his arm in a thoughtless fashion, making James anxious. "Tell your father you have five minutes starting now!"

"My captors say we have five minutes Dad, then they need the code."

His father looked stressed, James prayed they actually had the finished code. He was fairly positive Summer and Greta would be willing to keep him forever to get what they wanted.

"Are you healthy, James? Have they been feeding you well?"

James almost laughed. Of all the possible questions his dad asked him he choose to ask about food? Was there any way he could form a response that would include a clue to help his parents find him? "I'm good Dad. They've been treating me fine. In fact, they have kept me fed on a teenage boy's dream, carbs via microwave. Mac and Cheese, pizza, ramen noodles, you name the microwave meal, I've eaten it." James managed to move his feet a bit as he made large hand motions imitating him eating out of bowls and pizza boxes.

His dad managed to crack a smile. "When you get home we'll eat salad and sushi. Are you sleeping well?"

That was another odd question but James answered as honestly as he could, "I get plenty of sleep and I have lots of pillows." At least he thought all that soft stuff keeping him upright at night were pillows.

Another poke in the ribs. "Time's almost up. Boy, are you more talkative than normal."

James reached out to slap Summer's hand away almost playfully, which allowed him even more movement, "It's my dad, what do you expect?"

He turned to his dad again, his plan almost complete. "Tell Mom I'll be home soon, at least before summer I expect."

"You idiot!" Summer punched his arm hard. Harder than she ever had before.

Oh crap, she must have caught on to what he was doing. It took all of his self-control not to look at the ground.

"You told them my name is Summer!" she shrieked in his ear.

The Beta

He was screwed and he knew it. "Dad, do you have the code?" he pleaded as he stepped one last time to the side, gesturing wildly for no apparent reason, he had to keep everyone's focus up high. His dad must wonder what the heck was going on.

"Not yet."

James's heart stopped.

"It's not very clean code but so far it's tested out alright. Three more hours and we can deliver it to your inbox."

He let out a breath of relief.

"Can we wait three more hours?" He asked to the air, he asked his captors, he asked to the audience listening.

"They must know all of this will be dismantled if anything happens to you, James? That's our one condition."

James remembered the date they kept having him set and he saw the date on his interior monitor, he knew that the team had watched him repetitively set that date in Santa's Workshop so his dad must know it as well. It was only 24 hours before the trigger was set to go off. Would his captors be content by then?

"Tell him it's a deal. Deliver the code in three hours. You will be returned to your family shortly."

That was not the answer he was expecting. Did they mean shortly like after the trigger in 24 hours? Or shortly like next month. Despite the lack of specificity, he repeated their demands to his father.

His father's face was set in stone, but he nodded in affirmation. James could tell it was with great reluctance.

There was a low rumble coming from the road and James and his dad looked up to see a horse drawn carriage crest the cliff trails. Hanging out of the window was a woman waving her hands wildly in their direction.

James's heart stopped again for the second time today. It was Sarah Franklin-Bache. It was Kira. Coming for him.

Summer pulled the plug and everything went black.

Kira leaped from the carriage with tears beginning to roll down her cheek. In her headset they pooled and made her vision blurry.

The Beta

Mark looked at the image of a female Ben Franklin stepping out of the carriage and had the sudden and ludicrous thought that the AI for this simulation must have misrepresented Ben Franklin's gender. Then the shock of having his son disappear set in, and the thought of not seeing James again crossed his mind. As his gaze was drawn to the female Franklin, he could see a tear roll down her cheek. He wondered if she was crying in real life.

It all clicked. She was that girl.

"Snʔimaʔt?"
"Ki, Stmtíma??"
"Look at the ground."

Kira hastily shook out her headset and with a sacrilegious swipe dried the lenses with an edge of her tank top. They were clean enough to do the job. Peering back into the simulation she looked at the ground.

In the spot where Samuel/James was standing moments ago was a messy but clearly distinguishable five letter word.

She used Sarah's hand to point at the ground and spoke one word only to the strange man in 20th century garb, hoping he was friend, not foe. "Look . . ."

Mark, still bewildered, looked down. Scraped into the ground was a clear set of letters, he put them together in his head. O-C-E-A-N. James had left a clue. It was his son after all. He was proud.

🌎

"Do you believe them?" Summer asked Greta.

James listened intently but didn't say a word. His feelings were flopping around like a fish on a dock. He was thrilled that Kira was coming for him, angry that Summer pulled the plug before he could talk to her, and thankful for both events at the same time. Kira may have been the distraction he needed to pull off his plan.

"We don't have any choice but to believe him."
"Should we stay put or move on?"
"If we have three hours we might as well move on."

The Beta

"James, get some sleep." Greta instructed.

Quietly, and triumphantly, James used his hands to guide his way over to his pillow tower and made himself comfy. He could feel the rocking of the boat as Summer and Greta navigated their way on the ocean.

Greta and Summer hadn't noticed a thing. But hopefully his father had.

O-C-E-A-N

Mark stared at the words and then looked up at the woman in front of him.

"Who are you?" he asked point blank.

Startled, a look of suspicion came over Sarah/Kira's face. "Who are you?" She demanded with a commanding emphasis that worked with her avatar's stern gaze.

Kira's grandmother materialized next to Sarah and she immediately addressed the two. "You must be James's father?" She didn't wait for a reply. "This is Kira and I am Karen. We knew James was in trouble and we want to help. She's a student from Washington State and I am an Educational Developer from the east side of Washington State."

Kira realized her grandmother must be using her dev access to see through the avatar in front of her. Was it James's father? How could James's father be here? But more important to her she asked. "Is he alright?"

It was Mark's turn to look mildly startled. "Not yet . . . but this may have been the clue we needed. Thank you for pointing it out."

"He sent me a message saying he was kidnapped." Kira spoke up.

"Yes . . ." Mark was still looking at the ground but he lifted his head enough to make eye contact with Kira. "Thank you for passing on that information earlier." Now he was connecting the dots.

"What do you think ocean means?" She asked, completely honest and lacking patience. Out of the corner of her eye she could

The Beta

see her grandmother looking on with mild humor and James's dad continued to respond with kindness.

"Not sure yet." Mark responded. "Do you have a clear image, Doug?" Now Mark's head was tilted up as if he was speaking to some invisible person.

"I have to go." Mark offered his hand to Kira. It took her a minute to realize he wanted a hand shake. She gripped his hands and he looked into her eyes, "Thank you." Then he did the same to her grandmother.

"But we want to help!" Kira blurted out.

"I . . ." Mark's head tilted again, but this time as if he was listening.

Kira's grandmother finally spoke up. "We know he's been in Santa's Workshop."

"Yes, that's true." Mark paused again. All these weird pauses. "If we need help we will contact you."

"Wait!" Kira said, but it was too late. Mark was gone.

Kira pulled off her moisture laden headset and saw her grandmother do the same. The trees outside the large window calmed her nerves, despite the transition from VR to real life always being a bit disjointed.

"Oh, grandmother," was all Kira said.

Mark took off his headset and the bridge was humming. They were getting closer, they all knew it.

They knew who the kidnappers were and they knew what they wanted, a nearly-completed bit of tricky code. But more importantly, Mark was fairly sure they could find them. As soon as Summer or Autumn stepped out into public they were sure to get a call. He looked over at his wife to see if there was any word on that front, but a brief look at her expression let him know the answer was negative.

That's when it clicked.

The Beta

"Doug! Can you bring up a map of the last confirmed traces?" Mark shouted to Doug across the room. The whole room continued to work but every ear was now tuned into their conversation.

Doug repositioned the map they were using to track James's position from a side screen to the front screen. Now the words and details were so large it only took a few seconds for Mark to confirm his theory.

"That's what James meant by ocean!" Mark said, satisfying no one's curiosity. "We've been looking for an RV but they must be on a boat now. Ever since their last location in the U.S. they have been at an RV park attached to a marina."

"Which means instead of being cornered on the Baja Peninsula their next destination could be anywhere," Jen added. It was almost as if all of their gazes locked at the same moment, eyes drawn together in a diamond vector.

For some reason, seeing his dad in VR made everything right in the world for James. As soon as he hit the pillow tower he fell into a deep sleep despite the permanent crick in his neck from the headset. Someday Summer would have to let him take it off. He could only imagine the crusty sores that had developed along his neckline over time.

He heard a slam that woke him from his sleep. The rocking of the boat was minimal now and he wasn't quite sure what that meant, other than it was a lot easier to move around in VR when the floor held still under his feet. No wonder he was seasick those first few days.

"It's been three hours. Use the bathroom then let's get logged in, James." Summer ordered.

James got ready and logged in. Holding this breath, hoping that the message would be waiting as promised, hoping that the code would be legit.

There was one message in his inbox. He zoomed in and read the subject line to himself.

Greetings Summer and Autumn

The Beta

James froze. If that meant what he thought it meant.

"Oh crap," came the confirmation. "They know who we are Autumn!"

"Damn, damn, damn!" Autumn replied.

"I thought your name was Greta," James offered up to keep them off balance. It didn't work for longer than a millisecond.

"Open the code, James."

He opened the email and attached at the top, labeled for easy reference, was the code they needed. Until they ran the code they wouldn't know if it truly worked or not.

"You'll be needing that in Santa's Workshop, let's get going."

🌍

"I feel so helpless, grandmother. What should I do?" Kira asked.

"Until James's father reaches out I don't think there is much we can do. But follow your heart."

Kira prepared herself for a long vigil, petted ntytyix's head, and secured her headset. This time she pulled a recliner into the VR area so she could sit and wait comfortably. Usually she entered Google Earth History standing tall, but this time she was relaxing on a throne.

Kira closed her eyes and reached out with her soul, searching for her friend, James. When she opened her eyes she directed the avatar to the North Pole and opened the sub menu that showed the entrance to Santa's Workshop. She would wait here. Even if James's avatar only passed through, at least she would get a glimpse of him. That was when she realized even though she knew his real name, Kira had yet to see an image of his real life face.

🌍

James worked another six hours straight. When he asked for food they let him sip on a protein shake and said he couldn't have real food until he was done.

The Beta

The more he tweaked, changed, added, and reviewed, the more James began to understand what they were doing. If he was right, he finally understood their motives. It was a much different picture than those first moments when he thought they were white supremacists.

"That's enough for now, James. Autumn, let's roll out."

James returned to his regular position. He wasn't sleepy so as he sat stuffed between the pillows with his arms tied up, the realization hit him. When he could tell the boat was moving again and at least one of them must be back in the cabin, he spoke up. "Summer? Autumn?"

"Yeah," Summer replied.

"If the police already know who you are, what's the point of keeping my headset on?"

There was silence.

"My neck is getting raw with all this duct tape."

There was still no response, but after about ten minutes of shuffling one of the women walked over to him and began peeling the edges of the duct tape away from his neck. Some spots were sweaty and already falling off where small holes allowed in bits of air, but others were stuck tight.

"Go ahead and pull hard, I can handle it." he advised them. "Pretend it's one big band aid."

Still, he grit his teeth, but a few minutes later the VR headset lifted and slowly unveiled his eyes and skin to thick fresh air.

He blinked slowly in little snippets to protect his eyes. All being equal he was a little afraid of seeing his captors face to face even though he wasn't really scared of them. He knew that people who were kidnapped often formed a bond with their kidnappers.

Although they were very different, different heights and different coloring, they were both considerably beautiful. Considerably beautiful for being so old. Well, at least a heck of a lot older than him, maybe in their 40s or something. But he didn't spend too much time thinking about their looks because now he understood who they really were underneath.

"I know what you're doing." It was a statement of fact.

Summer and Autumn looked at each other, then looked at him, but they remained tight-lipped.

The Beta

"I . . ." he didn't know how to say it, because he agreed with what they were doing and he felt horrible about tricking them at The Cliffs. "When I was at The Cliffs I wrote the word ocean in the sand." There was no visible response evident on their faces at first, but as the implication of this statement set in, obvious new worry lines set in. James didn't know how to respond other than saying, "I'm sorry."

"Well, it was bound to happen anyway," said Greta/Autumn, more to Summer than to him.

"We don't have much time left," Summer replied. All of a sudden, now that he could see them as well as hear them, James could feel the sadness and the tiredness in their voices.

"I think I can finish it for you," he offered, surprising even himself.

Now they both gave him their full attention.

"Finish it for us?" Summer repeated him.

"I can finish it for you, and you can get a head start and try to lose them before they find you."

There was silence for a while, and then Greta/Autumn gave him a little smile, "You know, Summer, I think he means it and I think he can do it."

"We did have that one escape plan, even if we never meant to use it."

In their usual fashion Summer and Autumn let the silence sink in, but now that James could see their expressions it was almost as if he could read their unspoken language. He could tell they would agree to his idea.

"Next port?" Summer asked Autumn.

"We're only about an hour away."

This time Summer turned to him with her arms crossed. "You promise to finish what we started."

He hesitated for a moment, checking his own internal moral compass first and quickly combing through the possible consequences.

"Yeah, nobody ever has to know I kept on going. With the headset taped to my head I'll just tell them I thought you were still in the boat." His freed vision finally gave him confirmation of the

The Beta

fact that he was on a boat. Then he froze . . . "You wouldn't be leaving me out at sea, would you? That wouldn't work?"

"No silly, we'd tie you up at the next marina."

Autumn pointed to a large screen in front of her, which they must have used to monitor his online presence this entire time. "This is a list of what we have left. Maybe four or five more hours of tasks and it should be done. Then the code goes off at noon."

That's when James realized it was early morning, before sunrise. Even with access to an internal clock, keeping a headset on all the time messed up his sense of time.

"Thank you," said Summer.

"Don't thank me yet, I have two requests, actually two demands . . . " James started.

Both of their eyes narrowed in his direction. He shrank and stuttered but didn't back down. "Why did you disfigure all of humanity? At first I thought you were white-supremacists or something."

"Seriously?" Summer breathed out in exasperation.

"I get it, Summer." Autumn seemed to understand where James was coming from. "We had him alter the African-American models first."

Summer looked horrified. "Oh, dear. That's why you called for help, isn't it?"

"Yup, so why did you guys do that? It doesn't make any sense." James pressed them for an answer.

"Well, we wanted people to really understand the greed, the self-centeredness, the ugly side of humanity that has brought us to this precipice." Summer spoke.

Then Autumn added, "So we thought that if people viewed our simulation and at the same time saw a disfigured humanity . . . they might really begin to understand how we are responsible for what is happening."

"Huh…" James didn't totally understand why it was necessary, but the answer made a little more sense.

"You had one other demand?" Autumn said impatiently.

"You have to add a song to the playlist."

"What song?"

The Beta

Now James was worried they were going to deny his request, "Shake It Off," he paused. Didn't they know who sang that song? "By you know . . . T Swift."

But it was worse, Summer and Autumn broke out laughing. Summer was the first to respond. "Ok, ok we will add your song."

"It doesn't really fit with our theme," complained Autumn.

"That way you can shake them off when they come looking for you." he offered in explanation.

The next port was only an hour away. By that time James ate his fill of real microwaved food, stashed a bunch of snacks within ready reach of one corner of the room, and inspected the infamous pillow tower which was really a whole lot of cushions mixed with bedding. It had been a soft place to lay his headset in at night. That's when he realized, if everything went as planned he would never have to sleep here again.

"Well, are you ready?" Summer asked. She had a fresh roll of duct tape in her hand.

"I think so . . ." James put the sweaty headset on and held still as Summer wrapped him back up.

"You remember what to do?" Autumn asked, clearly still nervous that he wouldn't finish the job.

"Yeah, I got it."

"I hope they don't find him before the code goes off. They could just scrap everything we worked so hard for."

"Yeah, well I also hope they don't find us."

And without another goodbye or another thank you, James heard the door shut firmly and a familiar voice begin to sing.

He hoped Taylor could help them shake 'em off.

James got to work. This time with a vengeance.

🌍

Kira was in some sort of trance, looking at the stars twinkling over the Earth in the background while keeping an eye on an icon

The Beta

that looked like a little hearth decorated for Christmas. The Santa's Workshop icon.

Then she saw him. She saw James. He had dark hair, sort of grown out like he hadn't had a haircut for a while and dark eyes much like hers. This must be his real life image. The idea that she now knew what he looked like almost evened the playing field he had taken advantage of earlier. She already forgave him and wanted the chance to know who he was irl.

She started to call out but he disappeared almost immediately.

🌍

Autumn was right and the task list she left took almost five hours to complete. There was an hour and a half left until the code dropped and he could watch their work in action. James planned to drop back in Google Earth History and watch it all go down. As long as his parents didn't find him before then and spoil it all.

With some time to kill James looked curiously at that strange house on a hill right in the middle of Santa's Workshop. None of Summer and Autumn's tasks took him to that odd building and he never got around to asking anyone what it was.

Doug and a handful of employees were shadowing him. It had been hard at first when he saw them to keep up the ruse. There were a few times Doug tried to engage him in conversation and he had to "pretend" Summer and Autumn were threatening to hurt him. Finally Doug gave up and they all sat like silent shadows.

So when James, technically free to do what he wanted, began to walk toward the middle of the village at a fast pace it took Doug and his shadows a bit to catch up.

In his earlier visits to the winter village James rarely came close to the house, and from far away it looked a bit like a miniature tower, not too gaudy as to contrast with the surrounding village, but definitely with an air of warm grandeur.

Now that he was getting close something strange was happening. For a few footsteps he saw an old gothic church, and then in the next few steps his vision was replaced with ancient Egyptian architecture, then something East Asian, and then an old stone church. He tried moving left and right but the image kept

The Beta

switching. This building at the center wasn't a single building, it was an amalgamation or conglomeration of history's iconic places of worship.

Intrigued, James kept on moving despite the random fluctuations. At least the location of the hill stayed the same.

🌐

"Kira!" it was her grandmother's voice, but different. She could hear some serious emotion with undertones of worry and anger. "Please come to Sx̌ʷnitkʷ."

Kira didn't ask any questions and it took only a short while to arrive at the simulation at Sx̌ʷnitkʷ. She dropped in as herself and quickly realized with her student login she still couldn't see her grandmother's avatar on the big map.

"Grandmother, where are you?" Kira asked out loud irl.

"At the center." was the cryptic reply.

Kira pulled up the map and tried to figure it out on her own. There were several informal gathering centers in the large settlement, but from an aerial view there was one that appeared to fit the bill so she began to run swiftly in that direction.

She was running so fast—technically standing still irl—but jumping as far ahead as each click would allow her to go, that she didn't really pay attention to her surroundings. To fight the nausea such a tactic entailed she kept her eyes closed for the most part, only opening them enough to make sure she was traveling in the right direction.

The gathering space was oblong shaped and packed with people so Kira positioned herself right in the middle then swiveled her head slowly as she looked for grandmother.

Kira scanned the first face, then the second, by the third her whole body tensed. These were not her people. The man in front of her had a bulbous nose and his expression was pulled back in a ferocious sneer as he talked with a group of men. These were not her people, they were angry imposters.

Frantic now, she called out irl for help, almost ready to pull off her headset, "Grandmother! What is wrong with everyone? Where are you?"

The Beta

James reached the base of the hill and paused. He looked behind him to his left and right only to see his small hoard of followers had finally caught up.

"What would they need here?" Doug asked out loud to the air, fishing for a response from James.

Startled, James did respond with a gruff lie, "Can't talk now."

The interaction propelled him into forward movement and as he climbed the hill to the building entrance James was startled to see some familiar places pop up. Kashi Vishwanath, the Blue Mosque, Notre Dame, Naritasan Shinshoji, Basilica of our Lady of Guadalupe, Mahabodhi Temple, the Cave of Hira, Po Lin Monastery, Mt. Arafat, Rachel's Tomb, Sagrada Família, Makkah, Mount Sinai, and the Pagoda Forest.

He took one last step and was genuinely surprised to find himself in front of a fictitious sci-fi location, one that he recognized. It was the hollowed out remains of a gigantic tree with three tall prongs. James was on the threshold of an opening that served as the door to the interior of the tree. He walked in reverently, and with a brief glance behind he casually noticed that everyone else remained outside except for Doug, who was only inches behind.

In the movies the interior of this science fiction temple was plain—but in this version the walls of the dead tree were composed of hundreds of tiny holes dug from the interior. Each small alcove contained a miniature scene. He peered at one set to eye level and saw a small turtle swimming in water. Upon the turtle's back was dirt, trees, and plants—an entire world in miniature. On the island were three figures, they were so tiny it was hard to make it out but it looked like twin boys holding the hands of their mother.

Suddenly an ethereal figure appeared before him and his jaw dropped unceremoniously. It was Obi-Wan Kenobi, straight out of *Return of the Jedi*. What the heck was a science fiction figure doing in Google Earth History? A place known for its meticulous attention to reproducing realistic details of the real world.

"Welcome James," Obi-Wan offered in greeting with calmly clasped hands and a slight smile.

The Beta

James really didn't have anything to say, he couldn't even formulate a question that wouldn't seem ridiculous.

Turning to Doug, Obi-Wan offered a modern wave, "Hey Doug, good to see you man."

"Good to see you, too."

"What is this place?" James ventured to ask, having thought of nothing else, and truly not understanding the purpose of a multifaceted place of worship.

"Do you have some time to look around?" Obi-Wan asked.

James hesitated. Would Doug and the others become suspicious if he said yes? Checking the internal clock, he noted that there were fifty-five minutes until the clock struck twelve. Taking a deep breath, he turned to Obi-Wan and nodded.

Obi-Wan motioned for him to explore and so James did. The first alcove he inspected was almost immediately recognizable. A large boat floated on the ocean, stuffed to the brim with small animals. Two of each animal.

In the next alcove a little beaver swam around a vast ocean and pulled up mud which turned into land. A miniature man and woman appeared and the man hit the woman with a fish, and then the woman began to have so many children the island quickly filled up.

The third scene he looked at started not with water but was divided into four levels, the bottom dark, above it blue, above that yellow and the final top level white. The action began in the lower layer with a small island and a few creatures. James's eyes followed the progress as a small handful of figures made their way up to the next world, then the next, and finally the top world.

James looked up to see Obi-Wan and Doug exchanging glances. He was catching on and they knew it. "Myths."

Obi-Wan nodded, "These halls hold creation tales from around the world, as well as stories that form the basis of religious thought."

It was almost too much to take in at one time. The center of Google Earth History, the center of Santa's Workshop, was devoted to places and stories that didn't exist.

"I was working on a project called The Cave of Hira and there was a scene where the Angel Gabriel visited Mohammad, and the

The Beta

dev team had to choose between two different versions of the story. But why is this whole place . . ." James motioned around his head, ". . . devoted to the make-believe? Especially when Google Earth History is so focused on replicating the real past? Almost all of my work has been about finding the truth and sticking to the facts as we recreate history."

Obi-Wan smiled. "You are right, when we first started this project we realized that sticking to the facts as much as possible was going to be the key that gave this world authenticity, that made it worthy of visiting. Whoever writes the history books not only chooses the narrative we read but impacts what happens in the future for years to come."

Doug finally chimed in with a serious look on his face. "In a worst-case scenario, we worried about what could happen if someone inserted a completely revisionist history. For example, if someone were to erase or mitigate the Holocaust?"

"But myths?" James once again prompted. He understood what was in the room but not the why.

"The stories each culture tells—about creation, spirituality, understanding the world—essentially provide the starting point for understanding what ancient peoples believed and the choices they made. Here at this place of universal worship the Google Earth History team gives ancient stories the preservation they deserve. Our spiritual roots are truly as important as our physical origins."

"James, why are Summer and Autumn revising Google Earth History?" It was Doug asking the tough questions this time.

"I can't talk anymore!" James had no problem looking scared, he was afraid Doug would figure it out. More importantly, James was surprised Doug hadn't figured it out on his own yet. But none of that mattered. The whole world would understand in less than thirty-five minutes.

James knew he may never return to Santa's Workshop or this strange church on the hill. He gave the room one last longing look, then he ghosted.

"Mark! He's gone." Doug stated the obvious.

The Beta

Eve spoke almost simultaneously with her phone stuck to her ear. "Guys, we have a match on Autumn and Summer. We have an address!"

🌐

Her grandmother appeared at her elbow, but upon closer inspection she could see the crossed eyes, protruding lips, and uncharacteristic expression. Kira stepped back in fear of the twisted version of her dear grandmother.

"What's happening?" Kira almost choked in confusion as the words came out.

"Someone has hurt our people, even you granddaughter. Look around, it has affected us all like some leprous disease."

As Kira inspected the crowd her heart stopped and her hands clenched. Why would anyone do this? That was when Kira remembered King and Harriet Tubman.

"Grandmother, I don't think this only happened to our people. In the American Revolution simulation I noticed that the last two characters I saw also had changed."

Kira grabbed her grandmother's hand in VR and that was when she felt the comforting flesh and blood hand of her grandmother reach out irl.

🌐

James wanted a front row seat to what might be the most important show of his life. He picked the hill in VR that was right above his real life house and floated his avatar high above the landscape so he had a clear view. He flipped his clock to analog and watched as the second hand clicked nearer.

The Beta

Part Four
The Clock Struck Twelve

The clock struck twelve. Yet neither Kira nor her grandmother were paying attention to the time. Still horrified by the changes to the people of the simulation, they didn't notice the smoke until one of the NPCs pointed up the hill.

Kira looked up to see the entire hillside dotted with flames. Fires were growing rapidly along the slope. Doing a slow 360 she could see that the fires were not contained to one side of the river. Then the winds began to pick up and the smoke billowed above the river, obscuring the sun.

Even though it wasn't possible in VR, Kira could have sworn she smelled smoke. The eerie thing was that in the real world she knew the hill to the west had burned last year and she remembered days of thick smoke blanketing Washington State last August. It was simply too real. Who was destroying the simulation?

§

Lucia stood next to the little two-story Brown's Hotel. It was a simple structure really, with the entry way protruding out from the front, plain, rectangular windows and a roof facade that made her think of the old west. As the first hotel built in Miami Beach, Lucia had been shocked to learn it still stood irl.

A brief historical recreation accompanied the hotel and Lucia had learned about the original owners and early avocado plantations. She looked in the upper right-hand corner where the ever-present date and time were displayed. Some students toggled the date off but Lucia always wanted to know 'when' she was in Google Earth History. She adjusted the date so it would slowly fast-forward until it hit modern times. As the years flew by buildings rose and fell all around her but they also grew significantly taller

The Beta

each decade. Eventually a large Hilton hotel blocked the view of the Atlantic from Brown's Hotel.

Irritated she could no longer see the ocean, Lucia walked around the large hotel until she was standing on beach sand listening to the hypnotic sound of the waves. Here she stood, shielding the sun with her hand and relaxing as virtual water lapped over her virtual feet.

Lucia lived in Midland, Texas and had never been to the ocean irl.

The clock struck twelve.

Lucia was staring at the blue sky, looking just past the floating date of 2020 when it changed suddenly to 2021. Winds slowly picked up and a storm whipped through the beach and she saw the date tick to 2021, then 2022.

Startled because she hadn't moved the date manually, Lucia spoke up to her AI teacher. "Teacher, stop date."

Her AI responded automatically. "Unable to stop date."

"What?" Lucia said. She had never been in a simulation, recreation, or other experience that would control the date. Lucia was looking around Google Earth History at her own leisure and should be the only one able to adjust the date. Was her AI messing with her?

"Teacher, stop changing the date!" She used a more commanding tone of voice and manually reached out to pause the advancing years. 2023 had already passed and now it said 2024.

There were a few experiences that projected future scenario's but Lucia had only heard of them. This was the first time the date ever advanced past her current year, 2020.

Weirded out, but also intensely curious now, Lucia gave up trying to control the date and simply watched the spectacle unravel before her eyes.

Two years passed in Google Earth History for every minute irl. Massive hurricanes passed over the beach, temporarily obscuring her view before returning to blue sky. As the intensity and number of storms increased Lucia could see the surf slowly inch up her legs. First to her knees and by 2055 the water was lapping along her

The Beta

lower stomach—that part of your body that was always so resistant to entering the water when you were entering a swimming pool inch by inch. She could feel her abs involuntarily contract as if anticipating the cold water.

Nervous, Lucia lifted her VR headset for a moment and peeked into real life to make sure it was still there. Reassured, she closed her eyes and looked back at Miami Beach, 2065.

She turned her head in all directions. Looking back at Ocean Drive, Lucia could see water creeping up the steps, nearing some lower windows and glass store fronts.

The hurricanes didn't stop and neither did the water.

Lucia was surprised at how calm she was despite the events surrounding her, despite the fact she didn't know what was controlling Google Earth History.

The water now encircled her neck, and she resisted the urge to take off her headset. The date read 2085. Lucia had been born in 2005 so she would be eighty years old by that time.

The water completely engulfed her head as the date settled and stopped at 2100. A fish swam by and Lucia could see trees, benches, sidewalks, and the sides of buildings glimmering beneath the crystalline ocean water. In its own way it looked idyllic.

But Lucia knew 2100 wouldn't look this pretty, especially to people living in Miami at that time.

§

王秀英 was a high school senior and she knew exactly what she wanted to do with her life. She sat in a tall tower overlooking the Jiyang District agricultural lands. First, she pulled up a list of flight and measurement programs she coded over the past month and chose the ones she needed. Hitting another button, 王秀英 felt extremely powerful as five scientific drones flew in five different directions into fields surrounding the tower.

The Beta

Her teacher from 济阳县第一中学 worked with a local college professor and Google Earth History to help create a fully automated agricultural simulation.

Focused like an airplane pilot, 王秀英 kept a close eye on the maps and instrumentation in her workspace. She knew the panels and fields so well even a minor change in reading could alert her before the AI could pick up on any abnormalities.

She was startled out of her intellectual reverie by a knock at the door. Peering outside she saw her NPC sidekick outside so she opened the door, gave a friendly wave, and accepted the small Shaixi watermelon with reverence. There was a sticker on the watermelon that said "Grade AA" and 王秀英 couldn't even begin to describe the pride that welled within her. China would soon be home to some of the most high-quality organic produce in the world and she planned on being an instrumental part of the process. She ran her thumb over the sticker to smooth it down before taking a giant knife and slicing a thin slice out of the watermelon, then she prepared the VR organic matter for intake into a spectrometer.

王秀英 always frowned over the results, even when they were pleasing, as her brain calculated the next adjustment for her simulation. The entire simulated growing season was sped up to go from seed to watermelon within three hours, and every day she faithfully completed one season, no matter how tired she was.

The clock struck twelve.

王秀英 was about to log off when something on the panel caught her eye. The simulation speed was out of whack. It wasn't just advancing months at a time it was flying through the years!

She couldn't help but react as if the simulation was real life. Frantic, she tried to keep pace with the temperature, humidity, irrigation, planting, and harvesting functions but it was no use. The increasing temperature and humidity crept up relentlessly and her harvest NPC knocked on the door over and over. A pit began to form in her stomach as she raced over to answer the door.

The Beta

An exhausted NPC leaned on the doorframe, his skin clammy yet dry. In his hands and around his feet were hundreds of shriveled and dried watermelons. Looking behind him in the fields she saw acres of parched ground, shimmering in the heat.

§

It was 1851 and a modern-day teenager from Minnesota claimed the skin of one Robert McClure. Robert stood proudly upon the deck of the *Investigator* in the Canadian Arctic, the walrus head figurehead and 10 horsepower locomotive engine demonstrating clear support for such an important mission in pursuit of the Northwest Passage.

Robert's sideburns were covered in mini-icicles and the facial hair gave the teenager underneath great confidence. There was nothing like playing the part of a great sea captain. While the student knew the *Investigator* mission to sail through the Northwest Passage was doomed from the outset, most of this simulation was actually like a treasure hunt. It was the custom of these sailing expeditions to leave rock cairns along the route and most of his job was to find or build these small structures, kind of like modern day geocaching.

He knew the *Investigator* was approaching impenetrable sea ice and the end of its journey, but he held his avatar's head high and the ship made slow progress through the icy waters.

The clock struck twelve.

He thought he saw something odd so shielding his eyes to the bright sun, teenage boy/Robert McClure peered ahead. The ice blocking the *Investigator* was literally melting before his eyes creating a clear path through the water. Teenage Robert watched as the Northwest Passage opened up where it never existed. He gave a low whistle and wondered what the heck was going on.

All of his joyful anticipation in finding the Northwest passage melted away as he saw two polar bears struggle to maintain their

The Beta

balance on a slippery iceberg. The bears lost their footing and slipped beneath the icy waters. Teenage Robert almost felt like jumping in after them.

§

It was 8:30 p.m. and Pope Francis was walking with thoughts of sleep beckoning him forward. He didn't immediately say anything when a man joined him, matching his gait effortlessly.

"Fernando?" he asked, both in greeting and in question.

"Santo Padre, ci proverai adesso?"

Frenando had been asking the Pope the same question for weeks. Yet something was different this time. The weariness that was so normal this time of night suddenly dissipated and a lightness filled Pope Francis. This was the sign he had been waiting for. The time was right. "Si, sono pronto, Fernando."

Fernando hooked him up in minutes. The Pope decided to sit in a chair to begin. He suspected the experience might make him feel dizzy. Why had God brought him here now, he wondered?

"Dove vuoi andare?"

At exactly that moment a model of the Earth appeared before the Holy Father. He sucked in his breath, awestruck. This is what Fernando had described but it floored him to see it this way. So close and intimate.

Here Pope Francis hesitated. He loved all of creation. To choose one place seemed impossible. But then the answer became clear. It was a place he had never visited, but several Popes before him had made the trip. "Il luogo in cui Gesù fu battezzato."

Fernando didn't say anything but the world around Pope Francis began to change. He was flying rapidly toward the Holy Land. As he did so he recognized so much. There was Jerusalem, the Sea of Galilee, and his final destination on the Jordan River.

The Pope fumbled for a bit with the controls. He had never done this before and it wasn't exactly intuitive, but Fernando patiently walked him through until he found himself floating directly above the Jordan River. To the west, on the Israeli side,

The Beta

was a location called Qsar Al-Yahud and on the eastern bank in Jordan a place called Al-Maghtas. These divides of people and places made the Pope's heart hurt. If only they could see the view from above. The view of an astronaut. The view from heaven. God's view.

Pope Francis was suddenly floating straight down into the river even though he didn't think he was touching any of the controls. "Fernando, fermare!" He panicked a bit as the muddy water rushed toward him but he then reminded himself that none of this was real and his blood pressure began to slow.

Peaceful now, he assured Fernando that he was ok but asked him not to play with the controls. Fernando denied interfering.

He almost felt as though he was being baptized as his virtual body dipped below the water's edge. He thought of Jesus. He thought of the meaning of baptism. A peace settled over the Pope.

The clock struck twelve (Pacific Daylight Time)

At first the Pope didn't notice anything, yet his thoughts were drawn to all of the people who lived up and down the Jordan River. He thought of the water, of drinking, of bathing, of baptizing.

The water level dropped. Slowly at first but then with increasing speed. Within five minutes the Pope's avatar was floating in dry air and below him the River Jordan was reduced to a trickling steam.

The VR controls once again began moving his avatar. Pope Francis was going to have to get after Fernando for interfering or teasing him

His virtual feet touched the virtual stream, but it was only a minute more before all the water dried up.

The waters which had baptized Jesus Christ no longer existed.

§

The Beta

Emily was a nephologist, a person who studies clouds, and Google Earth VR provided her with everything she ever needed to understand how clouds work.

The clock struck twelve.

"What the?" Emily said under her breath. This was new, but she took it in stride. As the years began to swiftly move and the ppm increased the simulated clouds began to swirl.

Emily's head kept ticking in the shape of a triangle from the year, to the ppms and then the Earth.

It was quiet for several minutes with only the imperceptible sound of her neck clicking from corner to corner.

Then it was all punctuated by a sharp intake of breath. As a nephologist, she could see it clearly now, signs that the uninitiated would easily miss. The cloud layers were beginning to thin out near the equator, pushing storms and masses closer and closer to the poles, and Emily knew what that meant.

She picked a location at mid-latitude and zoomed in closer to examine the cloud layers. Tilting the earth enough so she could tell the difference between the Troposphere and the Stratosphere, she was able to confirm her suspicions. The low-level clouds that block heat from reaching the Earth's surface were quickly dissipating as warming extended to the Troposphere, and were being replaced with clouds higher up in the Stratosphere that were more well known for trapping heat.

"Oh crap," she whispered.

§

Luke carefully scooped up the soil to take back to the lab. All around him he was surrounded by picturesque farm fields. Soft, gentle, even rolling hills deposited by an Ice Age flood millions of years ago created a bread basket called the Palouse. As far as his eyes could see fields of swaying golden wheat filled every corner.

The Beta

The wheat contained exactly the right amount of moisture to nearly guarantee one of the best harvests ever seen in VR.

Weeks on the job took him through several decades of soil testing and yield analysis so that he could make the same measurements and predictions irl. This was his fifth VR soil collection and he was getting pretty good at the process. He headed back to his pickup.

The clock struck twelve.

All of a sudden, the wind picked up. High winds were not uncommon on the Palouse, and the coding for this wind didn't affect his VR avatar or his real life body. However it sure as heck was messing with the fields around him. Within a short period of time the wheat fell flat in many mismatched directions, making it look like an endless herd of deer slept there overnight. This type of flattened wheat could never be harvested. Yet the wind didn't stop and the VR sun continued to beat down.

Soon shafts of wheat were breaking off and spinning into clouds of golden thread. After the winds were gone the dust picked up and Luke found himself in the middle of a sandstorm.

It was fascinating to be in the middle of something such as a sandstorm and be able to look with wide open eyes. Yet the view was bland, like a blurred, brown picture from an old school TV.

Eventually the wind began to die down and Luke looked at the hills around him. The near idyllic scene he had been standing in only minutes before was now scarred scabland. It was like some giant hand had taken a shovel to the top of every hill, scraping away the precious ancient loess.

In all the commotion Luke hadn't noticed he dropped the precious soil sample. It was lost along with his hope for the future.

§

The Beta

Matías moved carefully off of the ski lift chair and with a practiced ease glided across the mountain top at the Chacaltaya Ski Resort.

His view of the Andes was more than breathtaking as he was at a ski resort built on top of a glacier. The weather in Google Earth History was clear today so he could see far down the mountain. His eyes followed the curve of a river valley and rested on a full reservoir behind a large hydroelectric dam.

Matías was ignoring his studies in Google Earth History. He already squeezed all the possible high school credit of this mountain of all subjects, but the thrill of skiing down the glacier slope never got tiring. Before Google Earth History Matías had never touched snow irl, but now he was bound and determined to someday go to a real ski slope.

Until then . . . Matías pushed off and began his downward decent.

The clock struck twelve.

Matías was an excellent VR skier, and so when the snow under him began to clump erratically, causing his skis to catch or slide at odd intervals he wasn't sure what to make of it. Within seconds small rivulets of melted water began to coalesce into larger streams all around him. His VR ski hit a VR rock that came out of nowhere. More rocks started to appear and Matías wondered briefly if Google Earth History had some glitch in its weather patterns and the AI was causing rocks to fall instead of snow. He glided to the top of a snow hill, planning to stop to evaluate the situation—but when he stopped the 6 ft. mound of snow literally disappeared and both skies were on wet, bare ground.

The glacier melted away in the span of ten minutes during his assent, and now he could clearly see the repercussions of the fast melting. He watched in awe as the ungodly amount of water inundated the reservoir and sloppily sloshed over the sides. He stayed to watch as the accelerated time frame then drained every last drop. Matías was left on a rocky hillside, his skis of no use even in VR. The reservoir below was dry and barren and he swore he

The Beta

could hear the sound of the hydroelectric generators whirling to a quiet halt. His world ground to a halt.

§

Ibrahim studied everything closely in Google Earth History, he was cautious and picky to a desirable fault. Many of the scholars working to create Middle Eastern history were not from the Middle East and that worried not only him but his parents. And so, Ibrahim studied.

He studied the images, carefully combed through wording, and triple checked historical sources. When he thought something was out of whack he would leave detailed feedback for the Google Earth History development team. If there was one thing Google Maps and Google Earth History were well known for, it was the ability to gather, disseminate, and act upon feedback in ways that made a difference.

Ibrahim also prayed in VR. There were a few days when all of his prayers were said in a virtual space, although he was always sure to align with the real life directions.

One thing he could do in VR that other people couldn't do irl was make a virtual trip to Makkah and the Kaaba any day he wanted.

Today he was closer to the Kaaba than he probably ever would be in real life. Ibrahim was actually floating high above the crowd closely inspecting the black and gold writing of embroidered silk that covered large parts of the Kaaba.

The clock struck twelve.

Ibrahim knew it was hot in Makkah, especially during the summer months. Personally he couldn't feel any heat in VR. Yet, for some odd reason the sun seemed suddenly brighter and as he floated down closer to the pilgrims he became concerned. Something wasn't right. The NPCs looks like they were moving in slow motion, their eyes squinting, their lips dry and cracking.

The Beta

Ibrahim never had felt heat in VR, but suddenly he started to sweat. Pulling up a VR weather thermometer, Ibrahim read a temperature of 52 degrees Celsius and climbing.

He put out a hand against the Kaaba as if to somehow steady his floating figure, as if to reach out for moral support. Yet when he pulled his hand away the silk tapestry came with it, stuck to his hand like a sticky black and gold tar. Silk doesn't really burn, but the VR heat was causing it to melt and stick. Ibrahim put another hand on the tapestry as if somehow, he could cool it down and prevent the sacred words from disappearing. He was suddenly very scared as he tried desperately to put the melting silk back together.

§

There were hundreds of students using Google Earth History in São Paulo. Some students were inside exploring museums while others were taking a virtual tour of a park or in a re-creation of the Old Republic period.

The clock struck twelve.

At first it was like a fog as grey brown clouds began to dominate the sky and no one really noticed the change. But as the virtual air thickened students began to look up with apprehension. The sun was now a deep red orb only faintly visible through the cloud cover. Almost every pair of eyes were now trained on a sun that couldn't burn their retinas but could burn their souls.

Then all became darkness.

§

Afton was a military brat. She wasn't entirely sure where that name came from and she certainly wasn't a brat, but the nickname accurately described her childhood moving from base to

The Beta

base around the world. Most of her father's deployments were overseas and only once in her sixteen years had they stayed briefly at Ft. Lewis in Washington State.

Still overseas, Afton longed to go to the home she had never seen in Salt Lake City. While there had been ample opportunities for traveling back to her father's home town in Salt Lake City after her mother died, making the excursions to see family in the states didn't make it to the top of their list.

So, when Afton was allowed to join *The Beta* with a small cadre at her international school it felt like she hit the jackpot. She would visit her father's childhood home, his parents' farm, and all the family haunts surrounding Salt Lake City.

Afton also became a regular visitor to Temple Square. She would position herself to the east of the Reflection Pool so she could look at the Salt Lake City Temple in all its glory. A reflective twin of the building stretched itself along the perfectly still water to her feet.

She was here again today imagining herself getting to visit Temple Square in real life. Next year she would apply for BYU and prayed it all worked out.

The clock struck twelve.

The sun was often bright in Salt Lake City but something suddenly changed. Afton wasn't paying attention to the date in the upper right-hand corner as she had set it to a transparent grey so it wouldn't interfere with her view in Google Earth History, but the slow ticking of the years irritated her subconscious.

She often prayed in front of the temple. Sometimes with closed eyes and sometime in wide-eyed reflection. But something was bothering her.

There is no temperature in VR and Afton didn't have any equipment that might transfer a faint feeling of heat or cold, so she didn't notice the subtle changes at first. But ever so slowly the Reflecting Pool was evaporating before her eyes.

Afton watched in wonder as the reflection of the temple began to shorten and contract. The spires and foundation were the first to go, followed by the moon stones, the big dipper, and clasped

The Beta

hands. As the water in the Reflecting Pool shrunk, only the very middle of the Salt Lake Temple could still be seen. The last thing Afton saw was the All Seeing Eye looking directly at her, and then it was gone.

"Please watch over us." Afton whispered.

§

張小龍 wasn't in VR and the time was 3:00 a.m. It was a ridiculous time to be leaving work but at least it was quiet. The Tencent Binhai Mansion loomed above him as he exited the building. He still marveled at the architecture. A building that could connect people, a building that could connect the world. A building that reduces carbon emissions by 40% if you just want to think environmentally.

That's when 張小龍 started to cough. The air outside the building wasn't filtered. He checked his air pollution app and saw the PM2.5 readings were at 244. He was proud of what his country had done to improve pollution levels, but sometimes it wasn't enough.

But that's when the idea came to him. It was time to move on from WeChat. It was time to do something new.

張小龍 kept walking, 張小龍 kept coughing, but things were about to change.

§

James knew what was going on in Google Earth History around the world that day from 12:00 - 12:30 p.m. After all, he had single handedly pulled every switch, turned every dial, and clicked every button. He could only imagine the shock on people's faces as they saw twisted looking NPC versions of humanity in concert with the effects of rapid climate change. He understood a little more why Summer and Autumn had decided to disfigure

The Beta

humanity during their show. So that when people looked at themselves in the mirror they could better recognize how their actions represented a moral choice. And he completely understood why they sped up the visual impacts of possible climate change.

James was calm but grim as he watched the water creep up the shore near his childhood home of Palo Alto. From high altitude he observed the water first spiral into the streets of 1 Hacker Way and almost immediately the Googleplex began to flood.

James wasn't scared anymore but he was determined, and he was forever thankful that this Google Earth History was only a beta project and not the real thing. At least he hoped that is all it would be.

The Beta

Epilogue

James was home and within a few days before he found himself sitting with some of the most powerful people on the planet at The Bridge. In his hands he held a little red book.

Doug was performing some last-minute adjustments in Google Earth before taking off his headset and joining the informal group surrounding James. "Everything's back to normal. NPCs have all been returned to their original presets and the climate changes reversed, but recorded in a separate location for analysis."

Mark looked at his son. "I want to introduce you to someone. This is De Kai, he is a professor, musician, linguist, and a member of our AI Ethics council."

De Kai had long flowing hair and merry eyes.

"Nice to meet you James," De Kai's smile matched his eyes. "When we heard you insisted on requesting the copy of *A Christmas Carol* from the crime scene I knew I needed to meet you. I didn't actually place the VR copy in Santa's Workshop, but I knew the woman who did."

James nodded in acknowledgement as he fingered the red binding. "I think I know why Summer and Autumn bought a copy."

The low hum of chatter in the room was brought to a standstill and James had to clear his throat to gain his confidence. "I know what they did was wrong . . ." He paused here thankful that no one ever figured out his small role at the end of his kidnapping. "But I think we all now understand why they did what they did."

He waited again to see if De Kai wanted to say anything about the woman who placed the book in Santa's Workshop but De Kai didn't speak up. James doubted they could be connected—it would be too crazy of a consequence—but he was pretty sure he knew what Autumn and Summer wanted. "Autumn and Summer picked Earth Day for the clock to strike twelve. But before they escaped I overheard them arguing. One of them was thinking of changing the date to Christmas Eve."

The Beta

He slowly let that thought sink in, but he could also tell there were a few in the crowd who couldn't quite make the connection between an old Christmas Tale and Earth Day so he went ahead and detailed his own theory. "You see, Scrooge visits the past, present, and future but the next day there is a chance for redemption. Summer and Autumn thought of the possibility that every Christmas Eve Google Earth History could do exactly that, take its participants to the past, present, and future—clearly outlining what will happen if nothing is done to mitigate climate change."

His parents looked proud and that gave him the strength to continue forcefully.

"What they did made an impact, just look at the response from the small percentage of people who were in Google Earth History that day? *The Beta* is going to soon reach a larger audience, allowing millions of people to experience what we did in VR. There is something about watching Palo Alto sink under the ocean that is so much more real in VR than reading about it in an article."

James was tired. That was all he would say for now. He didn't know if these people would listen to him. He didn't know if they would salvage Summer and Autumn's plans with his idea. He couldn't care right now. But he did care about, and had a crystal clear understanding of his life's purpose.

"There is a video call for James ready on Bay 1." Jaleesa's voice penetrated the room.

James looked up, startled. Why would he be getting a call in public? And from whom? He glanced at his mother and noticed a mysterious smile.

"Would you like to use my headset?" Doug offered.

James shook his head emphatically. "No!"

Doug laughed, "Sorry kid, I should have realized."

"Not for a long, long time. Go ahead and put it through." James walked ten feet over to Bay 1, fully aware of his audience. Was this going to be like Mark Zuckerberg or something? Maybe Sundar Pichai?

Nope.

The Beta

It was Kira.

And now she could see him. She was standing there as beautiful as he imagined with her own chaperone behind her.

His dad explained, "We thought you would like to meet some of the people instrumental in helping save you. This is Karen and Kira."

Suddenly worried, James put on his most formal behavioral attire, "Nice to meet you in person. Thank you for everything you did to help me."

Mark and Eve were now standing behind James, introducing themselves and providing their own thanks. Eve spoke up, "We would love to fly the two of you down here and meet you in person."

Karen and Kira exchanged a glance and it was Karen that spoke up. "We wanted to extend the same invitation to you. In particular, Kira has willingly banned herself from VR for a month, we were guessing James might do the same. We have a great lake up here, acres of forest, and it's pretty near impossible to get service in most areas."

James's response was automatic, "I'd like that."

Kira smiled.

James's parents enveloped him in a loving embrace.

The Beta

Real Names = Real Tech Companies

I was unsure if I should use the real names of technology companies in the book. Should I replace them with false but recognizable pseudonyms? Should I fret over which companies would sue me for libel because I predicted Amazon would solve the health care crisis instead of Apple? Would Alphabet send an army of lawyers down on me because Google Earth History is a really darn good idea?

Please don't sue me. ;)

In the end I believe that using the real names of technology companies was the most honest and authentic way to share thoughts, impressions, hopes, and dreams of our current world. In the end, each of these companies will change our society for the better or worse. Currently there is great discourse in the public square debating the advantages and disadvantages of Big Tech. I hope this book this fuels better conversations both inside and outside of technology companies.

Besides, the opinions contained within this text only shine a light on the view from my small corner of the world and in no way represent reality. After all, the Consumer Electronics Show runs early January and James is kidnapped in mid-April. So my timeline proves this is all just fiction.

My intention in writing this book is to nudge all technology companies to work together to make a bigger investment in education and include female perspectives. Get to work. If our state and federal governments won't invest in education maybe another sector will.

The Beta

The Present

Everyone has always told me I have a good nose—one that picks up the slightest whiff of a possible fire, misapplied pesticides, or the offensive use of some household cleaner.

I can still smell 1985 with precision. The grass, the sky, the occasional jet crossing, horizons and sun sets. All those sights and smells are focused on my seven-year-old world in Eastern Washington at the time, and they are crystal clear. (~350ppm)

I now smell 2019 with my own seven-year-old in tow. The sunrises and sunsets are still gorgeous, the horizon still something to behold, plants continue to grow all about my childhood home, albeit different ones from 35 years ago. But 2019 smells different. And although the change is slight I KNOW without a doubt that subtle change is a warning. I smell smoke. (~410ppm)

Sometimes I actually do smell smoke. In Eastern Washington local news stations have recently added a new "season" to our region called Fire Season including detailed maps of air quality use each newscast side by side with our weather forecast maps. We have three different air purifiers in our home. I once thought that images of smoke masks on children would be confined to polluted cities in Asia. Now my seven-year-old knows how to put on an N-95 mask to go outside when the air quality reaches "hazardous for all people" but we still need to go to the grocery store. When it gets that bad each August the sun disappears for weeks at a time under a fog-like smoky haze and the garden plants preparing for fall harvest take pause . . . unsure what to do without their hot August sun.

Like I said, I smell smoke. If you have childhood memories think back, do you remember what it smelled like? Then take a step outside your home tonight and tell me what you smell.

The Beta

Colville-Okanogan Salish Language Translations
These are approximate and to the best of my current knowledge and may be updated.

Salish	Translation
Sx̌ʷnitkʷ	Kettle Falls
"xast łkʷəkʷʕast cki naspuʔús ?"	Good morning how are you?
"tiʔ knxast nínwis łwikntsn !"	I'm fine see you later.
haʔ anxmínk t ntytyix ?	Do you want salmon?
"skʷəkʷimlt caʔcaʔxúł!"	Nickname = Young, Shy
kaʔkín kʷ sxʷúyaʔx	Where are you going?
kn ksxʷúyaʔx kl saʔtítkʷ or Piyʕáʔ	I am going (river). Kelly Hill
lut kn t ksxʷúyaʔx kl or kn ksxʷúyaʔx kl a?	I am not going I am going
kn ksxʷúyaʔx kl stmtímaʔnaqs?	I am going Grandma's mom side Number 1
kaʔkín kaʔ ck̓ʷulm ?	Where do they work
kl __ kaʔ ck̓ʷulm. Ntytyix	Yes, work salmon
nínwis łwikntsn saʔtítkʷ?	See you later river

Salish	Translation
xast sxlx̌ʕalt stmtímaʔ?	Good morning grandmother (Mother's Side)
xast sxlx̌ʕalt sn̓ʔímaʔt. haʔ tiʔ kʷ xast	Good morning grandchild Are you well/how are you?
swynu mtx	handsome
kaʔkín p sxʷúyaʔx	Where are you folks going
kʷu ksxʷúyaʔx kl čyxʷitkʷ	We are going to the water fall
xsʕacəc	beautiful
lut kʷu lm	No Work
xʷuyx ʔíčəčknwi	Go Play (more than one person)
way spuʔsxʔítx	First spouse/first love
ckin iʔ spʔustsəlx	How is my first love
čpuʔsqílxʷ	Married into the people
ətwit kast (correct to tətwit	Boy bad
səxkinx	What happened
Sn̓ʔímaʔt	Grandchild

The Beta

| Ntytyix | Salmon |

Made in the USA
Columbia, SC
11 February 2021